P9-CFP-667

FAMILY OF LIES

Also by Mary Monroe

The God Series
God Don't Like Ugly
God Still Don't Like Ugly
God Don't Play
God Ain't Blind
God Ain't Through Yet
God Don't Make No Mistakes

Mama Ruby Series
Mama Ruby
The Upper Room
Lost Daughters

Gonna Lay Down My Burdens
Red Light Wives
In Sheep's Clothing
Deliver Me From Evil
She Had It Coming
The Company We Keep
Family of Lies

"Nightmare in Paradise" in *Borrow Trouble*

Published by Kensington Publishing Corp.

FAMILY OF LIES

MARY MONROE

KENSINGTON BOOKS
http://www.kensingtonbooks.com

DAFINA BOOKS are published by

Kensington Publishing Corp.
119 West 40th Street
New York, NY 10018

All Kensington titles, imprints, and distributed lines are available at special quantity discounts for bulk purchases for sales promotion, premiums, fund-raising, educational, or institutional use.

Special book excerpts or customized printings can also be created to fit specific needs. For details, write or phone the office of the Kensington Special Sales Manager: Attn. Special Sales Department. Kensington Publishing Corp., 119 West 40th Street, New York, NY 10018. Phone: 1-800-221-2647.

Library of Congress Card Catalogue Number: 2013920826

ISBN-13: 978-0-7582-7474-8
ISBN-10: 0-7582-7474-2
First Kensington Hardcover Edition: June 2014

eISBN-13: 978-0-7582-9471-5
eISBN-10: 0-7582-9471-9
First Kensington Electronic Edition: June 2014

10 9 8 7 6 5 4 3 2 1

Printed in the United States of America

This book is dedicated to Sheila Sims, Louise Cooks, and Felice Sanchez.

ACKNOWLEDGMENTS

I am truly grateful for the support I continue to receive from booksellers, book clubs, radio stations, libraries, and my media escorts.

Thanks and lots of hugs to the folks in the sales department at Kensington Publishing; the rest of my Kensington family (especially my editor, Selena James); my awesome literary agent, Andrew Stuart; and most of all, my incredible fans.

Lauretta Pierce, thank you for maintaining my Web site and for spending hours at a time on the telephone chatting with me!

Please continue to share your comments, thoughts, and suggestions by e-mailing me at Authorauthor5409@aol.com or visiting my Web site, MaryMonroe.org. You can also communicate with me on Facebook and Twitter.

All the best,

Mary Monroe
June 2014

PROLOGUE

VERA

San Francisco, 1984

"THANKS FOR INVITING ME TO BREAKFAST AGAIN, VERA. I THOUGHT we had already finalized the arrangements for Kenneth's surprise birthday party."

"I didn't ask you to meet me to discuss my husband's party. And you can forget about being a guest. If you come within an inch of my property, I will have you arrested for trespassing."

The look on my husband's mistress's face was priceless. I had never seen such a confused and stunned expression before in my life. Her lips quivered for about five seconds before she was able to speak again. "Huh? Wh-what did I do?" was all she could manage.

"You can stop your little innocent act right now! I know you've been sleeping with my husband!"

"Oh. Um . . . how did you find out? I didn't tell nobody."

"How I found out is not important. What's important is that I know *everything* about you now." I had to pause and hold my breath for a few seconds to keep the stomach acid from rising in my throat, spewing out of my mouth, and soiling my eight-hundred-dollar silk blouse. "I can even tell you the names of the hotels you laid up in with my husband and the dates of every single reservation—including the ones you canceled," I hissed. I had hired one of the best private investigators in the city, so I had an extensive report on my husband's latest affair. "I even know what you ordered from room service."

Lois blinked a few times. For a woman brazen enough to get involved with her much older married boss, she came across as a real wimp to me. "I hope you enjoyed having somebody spy on me," she whimpered.

"Pfftt! I've had diarrhea that I enjoyed more than having somebody spy on you," I snarled.

Her hands were shaking and there was fear in her eyes. It was a true delight to watch her squirm like a worm on a fishhook. "I guess if you know everything about me, you know I'm pregnant with your husband's baby too! He doesn't even know yet!" She narrowed her eyes and looked at me with contempt.

"Yes, I know about that baby! You need a baby like you need another butthole! You are a low-down, lowlife, two-faced slut, and I hope that if you ever get married, another slut fucks your husband and has his baby so you can see what it feels like!"

"In the first place, your husband came on to me, not the other way around! Here you are all up in my face when it's him you need to be jacking! You got some damn nerve, lady!"

I gasped and shook my head in disbelief. I couldn't believe that Lois was just as angry as I was! You would have thought that *she* was the victim in this tragic mess. I gritted my teeth to keep from spitting in her face. "You ought to be ashamed of yourself, girl," I said, speaking a little more calmly now. "I heard you grew up in the church and was raised by a good woman. How girls raised like you end up being so trifling is a mystery to me. How many other married men have you fooled around with? Are you going to abort this baby like you did the other two when you were in high school?"

"Who told *you* I had those abortions? I only told my closest friends about that!"

"Why should a tramp like you even care who told me? Like I said, I know everything I need to know about you. Whose husband are you going to fuck next?"

"Who I sleep with next is none of your business, Vera!"

"Well, as long as it's not my husband, I don't really give a shit. Now, there are a few things you need to know. First, Kenneth will never divorce me to marry an ignorant, nose-ring-wearing, dollar-store-shopping tramp like you—his secretary, for God's sake!" I delivered one of my most disgusted looks across the table at my husband's latest and most threatening girl-toy. All of his other gold-digging bitches had taken all they could from him and promptly moved on. A few had been only one-night stands.

Despite the fact that my husband had spent thousands of dollars on his whores, I had not let that bother me too much. At the end of the day, I was still the Queen Bee and the *only* woman with the keys to the castle and access to his massive fortune.

I was a lot of things, but I was no fool. There was way too much money at stake for me to make a fuss about my husband dipping his silver spoon into a bowl of grits. His trysts were what I called assembly-line sex. I believed that most men were natural-born dogs. Therefore, when it came to sex, they would hump a fire hydrant. Besides, I hated having sex with Kenneth these days. It had become downright gruesome. Just the thought of him flopping up and down on top of me with his three layers of blubber and foul sweat turned my stomach. Apparently his vile body didn't bother his other women, but then the right amount of money could make just about anything tolerable.

I had never confronted Kenneth about his affairs and I never complained about him leaving me home alone so much. Because no matter which one of the fancy hotels he took his women to, he always came home to me.

But I was really worried about Lois. For one thing, he'd been with her a lot longer than any of the others. At nineteen, she was the youngest and the prettiest. And the nail in the coffin was the fact that she was carrying his baby! For the first time, I was worried that I would lose the best meal ticket I ever had. I was not about to let it go without a fight. And when it came to doing battle, I didn't fight by the rules. I did whatever I had to do to win.

"You can call me what you want. But the thing is, I'm having Kenneth's baby. I'm sure he'll leave you and marry me when I tell him he's finally going to be a daddy. He told me that he's been wanting a child for years and if I—"

"Shut up!" I had to cut the bitch off. So far, everything that had spewed out of her mouth made me feel nauseous. "Don't you think I know that, too, little girl? But . . ." I paused, leaned back in my chair, and patted the side of my head. Then I continued with the smuggest look on my face that I could manage. "At least the child I'm carrying will have his name."

Lois couldn't have looked more dazed if I had thrown a glass of blood in her face. "What . . . you're pregnant too? I didn't know that!"

"Of course you didn't know that. But you know it now. I'm two months along. You and I will probably give birth around the same time." The way Lois's face looked now, I thought it was going to melt. I enjoyed watching her reaction during the few moments of silence that followed. She looked like she wanted to cry.

"You're two months along? Kenneth told me he hasn't touched you in *six* months," she mumbled.

I froze and glared at Lois in outraged disbelief. The huge knot forming in my stomach felt like a cannonball. Kenneth and I had just made love a few hours ago! I couldn't believe that he would tell this slut such a bald-faced lie! "Sister, that brother lied to you. Married men who cheat on their wives do a lot of that, you know. By him telling you he hasn't fucked me in six months, he thought it would make you feel more special. Well, I've got news for you—he told his last three whores before you the same thing."

"The last three? He told me I was the only one . . . the only one he'd cheated with."

I threw my head back and guffawed like a hyena and clapped my hands. "And you believed him? Girl, if you knew he was lying to me when he was shacked up somewhere with you, what made you think he wasn't lying to you? You're dumber than you look!"

"I'm not as dumb as you think! You're the one that's dumb if you think Kenneth is still in love with you! He told me he's only staying married to you because he feels sorry for you."

My chest suddenly felt constricted, as if somebody had wrapped me in a straitjacket that was two sizes too small. It was one thing for Kenneth to tell his bitch that he had not made love to me in six months, if he really did tell her that. But it was another thing for him to tell her he no longer loved me and "feels sorry" for me. Well, I didn't believe he'd told her that. If he had, he'd lied to her about that too. One thing I was certain about was that Kenneth still loved me. I was the kind of trophy that successful black men like him—who didn't want to marry outside of the race—fought over. I was fair-skinned with keen features, slim, and intelligent. And just to sweeten the pot, I had become a blonde a few years ago.

"I'm sure he won't feel that way when I give birth to his child," I sneered. I could be just as big a liar as anybody else. And I was good at it. It was a skill that I had been honing since grade school.

"Are you sure you're pregnant?" There was a suspicious look on Lois's face. "I mean, a woman your age . . . uh, maybe it's something else."

This time I thought my face was going to melt. I gasped so hard I almost passed out. "A woman my age? What the hell— Girl, I'm only *thirty-four years old*!" I hollered. I was no longer just angry. Now I was worried too. I had spent more money on cosmetic surgery to maintain my youth than any woman I knew and here this bitch was sitting here insinuating that I was *old*. If that was true, I needed to find me some much more competent surgeons. "What the hell 'something else' could it be?"

"Maybe it's just a tumor," she answered with a sniff so aggressive it probably cleared her sinuses out for good.

"Well, you are wrong. I've been to the doctor. I'm two months along!" I said again as I rubbed my belly. I had paid a visit to my doctor but not to see if I was pregnant. Each time I found out Kenneth was involved in another affair, I got an AIDS test. Once when he was involved with a stripper I made him wear condoms when we had sex. He had balked about it, but when I told him I had a chronic yeast infection that could cause him erection problems, he stopped complaining.

Lois dropped her head and stared at the table as if she wanted to crawl under it. "I . . . I wonder why Kenneth didn't tell me you were pregnant," she crowed, looking back up.

"Kenneth doesn't know yet. I am going to surprise him with the news at his surprise birthday party next week. And let me make one thing perfectly clear: I will *never* give him a divorce so he can marry you. Besides, a prominent man like him is not going to leave his elegant, cultured, *slim* pregnant wife for a *plump* back-street ghetto floozy like you! You will strut your chunkified butt out of my husband's life! And I will see to it! If I wasn't such a lady and neither of us was pregnant, I'd pimp-slap the shit out of you right now!"

I sucked in some air, which was quite stale I noticed. I looked around the restaurant, not because I was afraid one of my friends would see me; none of them would be found dead in a low-end establishment like Denny's. I hadn't been in one since I was a broke-ass teenager still living in the hood back in Houston more than fifteen years ago. It had been my choice to meet my husband's whore in this dump because this was where she belonged, along with other members of the lowlife population. I snorted and looked around the room in disgust. A black teenage female at the table across from us wore a weave that looked like a well-used mop. She had *three* whiny, snotty-nosed toddlers in tow and was pregnant again. They were eating grits off the same plate, using the same spoon. Every other patron in the place looked as bad off as the pregnant teenage mother. A toothless, middle-aged white man occupied another nearby table, gnawing on a piece of bacon with his gums. I shook my head and returned my attention to Lois. It was easy to see why Kenneth had been attracted to her. She was young, beautiful, and stupid. It was a damn shame to see so much dollar-store makeup on her caramel-colored, heart-shaped face. She had outlined her full lips with a dark brown eyebrow pencil and then slapped on enough bronze lipstick for three people. She looked like a goddamn clown. It hurt my eyes to look at the outrageously long weave hanging off her head like a horse's tail. It was hard to believe that there was a baby growing in her voluptuous young body. I hated the ground she walked on. And I hated Kenneth for cheating on me with her. And I was going to make him pay for it until the day he died.

"Okay, Vera. I'm busted." There was a sorry expression on Lois's face, but I knew that the only thing she was sorry about was getting busted. "Where do we go from here?" she squeaked.

"I'm going to cut to the chase because I have a very busy schedule today." I glared at Lois so hard she shuddered.

"Cut to the chase, then, so I can get up out of here. I have a busy schedule too," she threw back at me, folding her arms. I was surprised she had not touched the scrambled eggs and grits she'd ordered, especially since I was paying for it.

"I can make things very comfortable for you and your baby," I told her. "And I can assure you that my deal is a lot sweeter than one you'd get from Kenneth if you tell him about the baby."

"You mean you didn't want me to meet you just so you could get in my face for me sleeping with your husband?"

"I know you don't think I'd waste my time coming into a place like Denny's on a Saturday morning just to get in your face. Like I just said, I can make it possible for you to live like a queen."

"Why? How could you be so mad at me and then turn around and tell me you can make it possible for me to live like a queen? That don't make no sense to me." The suspicious look had returned to Lois's face.

"Marriage is hard enough without complications like you. I want you to stay away from my husband for good. I don't want him to *ever* know about the baby you're carrying."

"I work for your husband, Vera."

I shook my head. "Not anymore. I want you to resign from your job immediately."

"Lady, I need my job! You can't—What if I don't quit? What are you going to do about it?"

"If you turn down my offer and return to work on Monday, I'm going to storm that damn store and beat the dog shit out of you in front of Kenneth and all your coworkers. Us both being pregnant won't stop me! How long do you think you'd have that job then?!"

"You wouldn't do something like that!"

"Try me, bitch," I said in a smooth voice. "From what I've heard, you won't be missed." According to the report I'd received from my investigator, this heifer spent more time sitting at her desk reading tabloids and filing her nails while the other clerical employees did most of the work she was getting paid to do! Ow! This shit was really hurting me. Kenneth was going to pay through the ass for this one!

Lois unfolded her arms and gave me an incredulous look. "But I can't just leave my job without giving notice. I don't want to leave Kenneth in a lurch."

I gave her a hot look. "You let me worry about Kenneth," I told her. "I'm sure the employment agency can send somebody to replace you right away. There are a lot of folks out of work these days." I would make damn sure of one thing: The next secretary that agency sent to work for my husband's electronic equipment and supplies main store was going to be either a man or a fifty-year-old frump with a face like a baboon and a hump on her back. I should have known better than to allow my husband to hire a young pretty woman to be his secretary. Especially since I already knew how weak he was when it came to pretty women. But he'd felt sorry for Lois. He had told me how she had started crying halfway through the interview. As a matter of fact, by the time Kenneth had finished telling me how she had dropped out of high school in her junior year so she could get a job and help her mother pay the bills, I was almost in tears myself that day! According to her, her father had owned a janitorial service. He'd had an affair with his secretary and got her pregnant. He'd sold his business, divorced Lois's mother, and left town with the mistress. Now here was his daughter doing the same thing to me that her father's mistress had done to her mother. Well this case was going to have a totally different outcome. I was going to make sure of that.

"How is your mother, Mrs. Lilly Mae Cooper, these days?" I asked, looking at Lois out of the corner of my eye. "I know everything there is to know about her too."

"My mama is doing just fine," Lois snapped. "Why? She ain't got nothing to do with this."

I shrugged. "I just thought I'd ask. Is she still waiting tables in that chicken shack where two people got shot last month?"

"Yeah, she is," she muttered, looking at the floor.

"Does she still belong to that sanctified church on Third Street?"

She nodded. "Yeah. So do I. So what?"

"Your mother is a big shot in that church and the pastor's wife's best friend. I'm sure the congregation won't look at her the same way when they hear her daughter's caught up in a scandal with a married businessman. Especially after your daddy left you and her and took off with his secretary. It must have been hard on her raising you by herself. Her having such limited skills, if she loses that chicken shack job, a woman her age will have a hell of a time finding something else."

"Don't you worry about me and my mama. I'll get on welfare if I have to."

I rolled my eyes. She would come up with something like that. Why young black women were still falling back on the welfare system in this day and age was beyond me. My mother, my three sisters, and almost every other one of my female relatives had fallen into that same trap. Before I was even old enough to have babies, I vowed that I would not become a welfare queen. As a matter of fact, after three abortions, I vowed that I would never have any kids anyway. To this day, nobody knew that I had my tubes tied right after my third and last abortion fifteen years ago when I was nineteen.

"Have you told your mother you're pregnant?"

Lois gave me a sharp look. Her eyeballs looked like they wanted to pop out of the sockets. "I didn't want her to know until I knew what Kenneth was going to do," she bleated, sounding like she had a sob trapped in her throat.

"Well, now that you know what Kenneth is going to do, or *not* going to do I should say, you can tell her. But this is what you're going to tell her." I looked around again and leaned my head closer to hers. "You tell her that somebody slipped something into your drink at a party that knocked you out and when you woke up, you were naked. Do some serious whooping and hollering when you tell her, and make sure you tell her you already asked the Lord to forgive you."

Lois stared at me in slack-jawed amazement. "Woman, what is all this gibberish coming out of your mouth? Nobody would say some off-the-wall shit like that—especially me. Are you crazy?"

"No, I'm not crazy. But you'd be crazy to pass up the offer I'm prepared to make. Now, do you want to hear what it is or not?"

"Go ahead," Lois said with her lips trembling.

Shaking my finger in her face, I told her, "You tell your mother that somebody, uh, took advantage of you while you were passed out."

She gave me a helpless look as I glanced at my watch. "Go on. I'm listening."

"I will pay you twice your salary for this month just to give you some cushion. Then, from next month until your child turns eighteen, I will support you. I am not sure of the amount yet, but it will be more than adequate. My attorney will send you a cashier's check on the first of every month until you have your baby. After you have your baby, I will double the amount. I will cover all of your medical expenses, as well as your baby's after it's born. If you get another job or get married or if I die unexpectedly before the child turns eighteen, the payments will continue. If you ever tell anybody about this arrangement, even your mother, it's over. I won't give you another plugged nickel." I paused and sucked in some more of the stale air—which seemed to get worse by the minute. "I'll drag your name through the mud so hard nobody else in this city will hire you. San Francisco is one of the most expensive cities in the world to live in. If you have to get by with only a welfare check, you won't be happy. You and that baby will always have to live with your mother in that one-bedroom apartment in that crime-infested neighborhood. I'm sure she won't like that. And once she passes, you'll be on shit creek in a sinking boat. Girl, you'd be a damn fool if you turn down what I'm offering you."

"What all do you want me to do?"

"After you resign, you are to have no contact whatsoever with my husband. If you see him on the street, whether he's alone or with me or someone else, you will not acknowledge him. Is that clear?"

"Now you look, Vera. I don't know what you think I am—"

"No, you look." I shook my finger in her face again. "I do know *what* you are. You are a scheming little whore who fucked my husband and didn't have enough sense to protect yourself."

"Kenneth didn't protect himself either. Don't you put all the blame on me!"

"Like I said, you let me worry about Kenneth. I know him a whole lot better than you. And for the record, you're not the first woman he's cheated with."

"You already told me that. So?"

"So, don't you think he's told them the same lies he's told you? We've been married for eleven years and he's had numerous affairs. And he's still with me. Does that sound like a man you can expect to have a future with? Out of the thousands of women who get involved with married men every year, only a few end up with the husband."

"Well, this year I just might be one of those few women!" Lois hissed. "Kenneth is in love with me." Her words stung my ears like a bee.

"Balls! Get real, Lois! Kenneth loves me too! And I'm his wife! He tells me all the time that I'm a wife and a half, so compared to you, that makes me *three* times the woman you are!"

For a man as educated as Kenneth was, he did some of the dumbest shit a man could ever do. I glanced at my watch *again* and started tapping my fingers on top of the table. I wanted this bitch to know just how impatient I was. I prayed that Johnny Watson, my twenty-two-year-old trainer and my current lover, wouldn't get impatient himself and leave before I got to his apartment across town near Coit Tower. I really needed to see him. Not only was he a very thorough and expensive personal trainer, but he was also a very thorough and expensive lover and I pampered him like he was a prince. He worked hard for his money and so did I. It had taken me too long to land a rich husband and I wanted to keep him. And Kenneth was the best kind of rich husband; he was twenty years older than me and had a bad heart and a few other health issues. He could drop dead any minute and that was what I'd been counting on since the day I married him. There had been a few close calls, but each time he had recovered. But the way things had been going lately, I knew that it was just a matter of time before I'd be a very wealthy young widow.

I was not about to let some little ghetto bitch ruin my life!

"Do we have a deal or not?" I asked, still tapping my fingers impatiently on the tabletop.

Lois took her time responding to my final question, but I already knew what her answer was going to be. "Yes, ma'am. We have a deal."

CHAPTER 1

VERA

Sixteen years later

I COULDN'T BELIEVE HOW MANY YEARS HAD PASSED SINCE I'D MET WITH Lois Cooper that Saturday morning in a Denny's. I can still see her face in my mind and how frightened she looked by the end of our meeting.

We had both kept our end of the bargain. I made sure she got paid on time every month. And just to prove that I had a heart, each year I gave her a ten percent "cost of living" increase. Just like she was getting paid to do a job. As far as I was concerned, her staying the hell out of my husband's life and not letting him know about that baby was her job and I was her employer. She never returned to work for my husband after our meeting. And since she had not communicated with him, he had no idea why she had up and quit, leaving him in a lurch. I will never forget how baffled he had looked that evening when he came home all those years ago. Not a day goes by that I don't replay that conversation in my head.

"Uh, one of the secretaries called up personnel this morning and told them she was not coming back to work," Kenneth announced. He had come home later than usual this particular day. But I was used to that. He had been spending up to twelve hours a day at the store, several times a week for years. I wondered how much of that time was spent with other women. Even though he had a great team of loyal and competent employees who could run the place without him, his office at his main store had become his second home. He even kept a couple of suits, fresh underwear, and some toiletries in the closet behind his desk.

"Which secretary was it?" I'd asked dumbly. "That white girl with the red cornrows, I hope."

"No, it was not Amber. She's a single mom who is taking care of two toddlers and her disabled older brother. She's not going anywhere anytime soon. And she loves her job." Kenneth hesitated for a few seconds. There was a strange look on his face when he continued. "It was Lois in the main office."

"Hmmm. Isn't she the one you hired because her mother needed help paying her bills? She just up and quit? No explanation?"

Kenneth scratched the side of his face and shook his head. "No explanation whatsoever. I had a feeling something like this might happen."

"Why do you say that?"

"The girl was not that sophisticated and she couldn't get along with too many folks, especially the women. Every time I looked up, somebody was in my office with complaints about her doing or saying one offensive thing or another. She was always late for work and she made a lot of personal telephone calls. None of my immediate staff liked her."

You liked her enough to screw her, I wanted to point out.

I didn't want to remind Kenneth that he had fired his previous secretary because she had always come to work late—if she showed up at all—and she argued with him and everybody else. He had put up with Lois's behavior and probably would have continued to do so if I hadn't stepped in. So in a way, by me getting rid of her, I had also done him a favor—in more ways than one. Had he known she was pregnant with his baby, we would be having a totally different conversation.

"I feel sorry for the girl. The poor little thing. She's had a hard life and I really wanted to help her."

"You sure did help her." I couldn't help myself. Those words just slipped out of my mouth on their own.

"I'm sorry?" Kenneth sucked on his teeth for a few moments and gave me a curious look.

"You did help her. You gave her a job," I said quickly. "Honey, you've helped a lot of people over the years. Everybody loves you for giving so much back to the community. But you're not the Wizard of Oz or a witch doctor, sweetie. You can't solve everybody's problems. Lois is a grown woman and she's going to do what she wants to do. I think it was pretty tacky for her to quit without giving proper notice, though. Some people are so inconsiderate! Tsk, tsk, tsk. I don't know what this world is coming to."

"Yeah. I won't argue with you about that. She resigned over the phone and that's about as tacky as a person can be—especially in this case. She told the bookkeeper to mail her last paycheck to a post office box," Kenneth croaked.

"And she's such a pretty young thing," I allowed. "But she's also as ghetto as oxtail stew and fried chicken on the same plate. You know how those girls like her are. Most of them have one man coming in the front door and one going out the back door at the same time. I'm sure she attracted a lot of admirers, so maybe she met somebody . . ."

"Maybe she did meet somebody," Kenneth grunted. "Oh well. I hope everything is all right with her regardless of why she quit." A sad look appeared on his face and he shook his head, blinking hard as if to hold back a tear or two. Apparently he had loved that heifer, and her mysterious disappearance had really upset him. But I had no sympathy for her or him. "I'll miss her," he admitted, his voice cracking.

"I'm sure you will miss her," I said, too low for him to hear. And then I gave him a hug. "Now come to bed so I can give you something that'll take your mind off your troubles."

We had made love that night and I forgot all about Lois Cooper and her baby.

* * *

Now, sixteen years later, my marriage was stronger than ever. Not only was I looking forward to the new millennium coming up in a few days, but I was also looking forward to the day Lois's child turned eighteen. I had no idea what the child's name was or if it was a girl or a boy. But none of that mattered to me anyway. All I cared about was that in three more years I'd be off the hook.

And that child would no longer be part of my life!

I was in such a good mood I practically raped Kenneth that night.

CHAPTER 2

KENNETH

I HAD EVERYTHING A MAN COULD WANT. I OWNED LOMAX ELECTRONICS, which consisted of five of the most successful electronic equipment and supplies stores in the state of California. I owned a vacation cabin in the wine country; a spacious condo in downtown Frisco; and a beautiful mansion with a full-service bar in the living room, eight bedrooms, six bathrooms, and a six-car garage.

I had a beautiful wife, a loyal and dependable staff, lots of friends, and a prestigious position in my community. But that still was not enough. I loved pretty young women. I was a dirty old man and I would probably be one until I was a dead old man.

Of all the dozens of affairs I'd had since my marriage to Vera, Lois Cooper was the only one who had really meant something to me. She was the one I still thought about from time to time.

I was convinced that Vera didn't know I was a serial cheater because she had never given me a reason to think otherwise. One night during my affair with Lois, I had called out Lois's name while I was making love to Vera. And since she didn't respond to that, I didn't know what to think. Either I was married to a damn fool who didn't care what I did or said, or she was deaf and hadn't heard my slipup.

I had done it again a few minutes ago, called out another woman's name while I was making love to Vera. She had not responded to it this time either so I played it off. "Oh, baby, that was so good," I told her, rubbing the side of her hip. Being a businessman in what had become a hostile environment, I had to do a lot of damage control, so I was good at it. "If God made a better woman, he kept her for himself." I rolled over onto my back, which was aching like I had fallen off a horse. The rest of my body parts were giving me some discomfort as well. Vera was already on her back. I reached over and squeezed one of her recently surgically enhanced breasts, a prize that had cost me over seven thousand dollars this time. I was huffing and puffing and wheezing as if I'd just been injured.

"Now don't you get too excited and overexert yourself. You're seventy years old now and you can't be humping like a bull the way you used to," Vera scolded.

"A lot of men my age can no longer hump period," I quipped.

"I don't care about other men. You know what Dr. Cortez told you about too much strenuous activity after that heart attack last May. And don't forget to take your pills tonight."

Despite Vera's exasperation with me, there was a smile on her face. How a woman could smile after her husband had called her by another woman's name during a moment of intimacy was a mystery to me. I promised myself to be more careful in the future, but that was a promise I had originally made to myself years ago and I was still committing the same offense! Being a man was hard. There were so many ways for us to fuck up, and that's why it was important for a man like me to have such a patient and understanding woman like my Vera. Oh, she was vain and extravagant, among other things. But I ignored her flaws because she was a prize I would always treasure.

"Pffffft!" I squeezed her tittie even harder and laughed. "If I have to die before my time, I can't think of a better way to go."

"Well, I don't want to be a young widow. And you know how much I hate funerals and black clothing," she complained.

I gave her a loving look. "Vera, not only are you the most beautiful and considerate woman in the world, but you are also the most honest and I appreciate that. I always know where I stand with you." I sounded like a broken record because these were the things I told her on a regular basis. "You're the best thing that's ever happened to me." She had a fragile ego, so she needed to be stroked often.

"I know that," she replied dryly. This was the way she usually responded to my worn-out compliments. Her statement would have sounded arrogant to most people. But to me it was amusing and endearing because my wife was one of a kind. Despite her few minor insecurities, Vera still had a lot of confidence in herself. She was not being arrogant, just honest. To me, honesty was an important virtue, especially in a woman. That was one of the reasons I had married her.

"Baby, if you're still with me when I die, I will die with a smile on my face," I whooped.

"I love you, Kenneth," she whispered as she rubbed the side of my face. "And believe me, I'm not going anywhere."

Without saying another word, I dived under the covers, grabbed her thighs, and spread them open, and then I licked her crotch like a child licking a lollipop for ten minutes nonstop. "Want some more?" I panted, hoping she'd say no. But I had to ask anyway. No matter how hard it was for me to perform in the bedroom these days, I wanted my woman to think that I was still at the top of my game.

"I'm fine. But please take a break," Vera told me in a raspy voice.

"Why? Baby, I'm just getting warmed up!"

"Didn't I just remind you of what Dr. Cortez said?"

"Fuck Dr. Cortez!" I hollered. "I'd like to see him resist a pussy this good!"

"Well, you need to stop because you're wearing me out," she accused.

Thank you, I said to myself. Vera gently pulled on my arm, but it was too difficult for a petite woman like her to lift my hefty two-hundred-eighty-five-pound frame. Somehow I managed to sit up on my own.

I was happy to see that Vera was still smiling. I was smiling too. I was so glad she had turned down my offer to continue our romp. My heart was still racing, my dick was numb, and my back was so stiff I felt like I'd been rinsed, starched, and hung out to dry. I may not have even been able to complete another session anyway.

I hadn't eaten dinner, so when Vera insisted on getting up and going downstairs to get me a plate of the roast that Delia, our cook, had prepared, I didn't protest. She rolled out of bed and was back in her gown and out of the room within five minutes. That was the last thing I remembered. When I opened my eyes again, it was the next morning.

"You went out like a light last night," Vera told me. She folded the morning newspaper and set it on the nightstand next to her monogrammed coffee cup. "I went downstairs to fix you a plate and ten minutes later when I got back up here, you were dead to the world. I'm telling you, you need to slow down," she added, gently lying down next to me.

I felt like hell from head to toe. "I will slow down," I said, rubbing my chest. What I really meant was that I would take a break from all that young pussy I was getting on the side. I had recently ended a monthlong relationship with a sweet young thing who lived in Oakland. That affair had almost cost me my life. Too Sweet (she refused to tell me her real name), an exotic dancer in a gentlemen's club that I'd gone to with some clients, had pulled a gun on me when I refused to give her money to bail her eighteen-year-old brother out of jail for carjacking some young woman with her two toddlers in tow. I ended up giving Too Sweet the money, but I knew then that I had to change my ways or choose my women more carefully.

In the meantime, Vera was going to have to be enough woman for me for a while, maybe for the rest of my life. I was tired of all the sneaking around, the lying, and the drama that went with cheating. Not to mention all the money cheating had cost me over the years.

Now my goal was to make sure my wife remained happy and that I remained somewhat faithful. "Honey, why don't we check into the Mark Hopkins for the weekend? Let's celebrate the new millennium in a quiet suite with just us and a bottle of champagne. People are going to be acting crazy at most parties and the clubs and I don't want to get caught up in all that madness." I stroked Vera's face.

"I've got a better idea. Why don't we spend the whole weekend in Clear Lake," she chirped, rising. She stood by her side of the bed with her hands on her hips. "They have a few new wineries that we can visit. You can do some fishing and I can shop in some of those cute little boutiques."

"You want to go to our cabin in Clear Lake? Uh, I don't want to go back up there so soon," I said quickly.

"Huh? What do you mean by 'so soon,' sugar? We haven't been up there in six months!"

I hated getting old. In addition to my most important body parts breaking down, my memory wasn't what it used to be. I had forgotten that *I* had recently been to our cabin in the wine country, but not with Vera. I had spent a couple of nights there just last week with that dancer from Oakland—that's where she'd pulled the gun on me. I had told Vera that I was attending a two-day sales meeting in Silicon Valley.

"Huh? Oh! That's right." I sat bolt upright in bed and blinked hard. "I forgot. I really must be getting old, huh?"

Vera gave me a blank look and shrugged. She strutted over to the full-length mirror on the wall facing the bed and started vigorously brushing her long hair, which was platinum blond. That made her look even more exotic and sexy than the black hair she'd had when I met her. "Well, do you want to go to the cabin or not?" she asked, talking with her back to me.

"Sure. Let's do that," I said, swinging my legs to the side of the bed with a groan. Almost every morning before I got up and about, I either passed a gallon of gas or something on my body ached. I experienced both this time. I was glad that Vera was too far away from the bed to smell or hear me. I was surprised that I was still able to get around without the aid of cane, a walker, or a wheelchair. I wondered if all older men with young wives felt and thought the way I did.

"Baby, I want you to know that I love you," I said. "I might not be as exciting as I used to be under the sheets, but I'll always do my best because I don't ever want to lose you."

Vera looked surprised. She gasped and walked back to the bed and sat down next to me, still brushing her hair.

"How many times do I have to tell you that I'm not going anywhere?" she said in mock anger, rubbing my tightening chest. "You're stuck with me. And in case you haven't noticed, the years are creeping up on me too. I'm probably not as frisky under the sheets as I used to be either," she chuckled, glancing at her watch.

One of the few things I didn't like about my wife was her annoying habit of looking at her watch more frequently than most people. In just the past five minutes, she had checked the time twice. I knew she didn't like to be scolded or questioned about things as trivial as that, so whenever she felt the need to check the time in my presence, I never asked her why. But this time I couldn't help myself. "Is there somewhere you need to go this morning, Vera?"

She stopped brushing her hair and gave me a puzzled look. "Why do you ask?"

"Because you can't seem to keep your eyes off your watch."

"Well, if we're going up to the cabin, I'd like to keep track of the time. I'll need to pick up a few things before we leave. I'd like to visit that little place on Clement Street that sells those edible crotchless panties you like to feed on so much," she replied. She winked and slid her tongue across her lips.

"Oh shit," I managed. "Make sure you get a few pairs of the cherry-flavored ones."

"I will." She winked again and kissed me on the forehead. "I'll be back in a few hours. Don't forget to pack your pills."

CHAPTER 3

VERA

After I had driven to that adult toy store on Clement Street and purchased the edible panties Kenneth loved so much, I headed downtown. I couldn't concentrate on any more shopping, so I ducked into the first bar I saw and ordered a martini. I quickly downed the martini and left the bar with my cell phone in my hand. If I was going to be holed up alone with Kenneth for a whole weekend, suffering through his frequent gas attacks and belly-aching, I was going to need something to keep me from losing my mind. Just being away from him for a few hours now was one way to avoid that. But I had another way that was even more effective: some rough, raw sex with a real man.

I needed a session with Tony Anderson, my mechanic and newest lover. He kept my BMW and my body tuned up.

When Tony didn't answer his phone, I dialed up Lincoln Harbor's number. Lincoln was my current trainer and he was an adequate backup for a good fuck when I couldn't get in touch with Tony. When Lincoln didn't answer, I gave up. I was frantic. I had always been able to reach at least one of my lovers. Good sex had become like a drug to me over the years. As I stood there glaring at the telephone in my hand as if it were the reason one of my lovers didn't answer on his end, I experienced withdrawal symptoms. My head began to throb and my hands began to shake. It looked like I was going to do a whole lot of drinking this weekend. That was the only way I was going to get through it with Kenneth.

Sex with Kenneth had become a chore I despised. For one thing, he had problems performing. It had been months since he had climaxed—at least with me. Last night had been a joke and I had almost laughed out loud as he pumped into me, flopping around like a fish out of water. But I didn't feel like laughing when he slipped up and called out another bitch's name *again* while he was still inside me!

I had kept myself from going off on Kenneth because I'd focused on something more pleasant than him lying on top of me. Like the day we met and how important that random encounter turned out to be.

The first time I laid eyes on him, during a software conference in Houston more than twenty-eight years ago, I decided I was going to marry him. And I didn't care what I had to do to make that happen. I was twenty-two at the time, struggling to make it from one day to the next, and I hated being poor.

My father, a janitor in a fast-food restaurant, died before I was even old enough to walk. Every man who came into my mother's life after him was broke and/or physically and verbally abusive. But that didn't stop her from having three more daughters, each with a different man, each one just as broke and unambitious as the next. I vowed that I would never marry a broke man or a man who abused his woman. My younger sisters, all attracted to the same kind of men that my mother liked, came home one after the other pregnant.

The last year that I lived at home, two of my sisters were pregnant at the same time. So was I for that matter, but I knew what to do about the situation. I'd get rid of it and move on.

"I'm moving out. I just got hired as a cashier at Jupiter's department store," I told my mother as I packed my clothes that night. It was the Friday after Christmas. I had turned nineteen a week earlier. "I'll be staying with Cynthia Spivey until I find my own place." I had always wanted to be a teacher, but I knew that the only way I'd ever be able to attend college would be in my dreams. We didn't have the money to pay for that and my grades had not been good enough for me to land a scholarship. I had accepted the fact that with only a high school education, I wasn't going to have a lot of job opportunities. But I was determined to live the good life. And that was the main reason why I had to find me a wealthy husband.

"I'm proud of you, baby," my mother said with tears in her eyes. "I'm glad you ain't as weak or as unlucky as me and your sisters when it comes to men. They'll end up like me, alone and on welfare with a bunch of kids, and a useless man that's going to keep them down. But find you a man anyhow. God didn't mean for you to be alone. A piece of a man is better than no man." My mother had been saying stupid shit like that about men as far back as I could remember. I had never commented on her opinions because I had not wanted to burst her bubble about men. My stepfather at the time shined shoes on his good days in a downtown hotel lobby. And he beat my mother, and us, on his bad days. To me, having "a piece of a man" was unacceptable, and now that I was about to move out, it was time for me to let my mother know how I felt.

"I will not stay with a trifling, violent man. The first time he hits me will be his last. And the only thing a broke man can do for me is tell me where I can find the men with the money," I declared.

My mother's mouth dropped open and she looked at me as if I had just lost my mind. "Vera Lou! I can't believe you'd say something like that. How do you expect to find a husband with such a negative attitude? Men ain't perfect, and we women ain't neither. We all got flaws and we just have to learn to live with them flaws. I hope you don't teach your unrealistic beliefs to your children!"

"And that's another thing—I'd rather get a whupping than raise a child. I know how hard it is and how crazy they might turn out, and that's not something I ever want to go through. If I do accidentally get pregnant, I'm getting an abortion lickety-split!" My mother looked like she was going to faint, so I didn't have the nerve to tell her the whole truth. I had already made arrangements with a med student I'd met at a party the week before to abort the baby in my belly that had been fathered by a stock boy who worked at a feed store.

"Vera, I'm going to pray for you day and night!" my mother wailed. Despite my outburst, she wrapped her arms around me and hugged me. "I just hope you find happiness with somebody."

"Don't you worry about me, Mama. I will find the right man for me."

I didn't like the way that my roommate, Cynthia, was always up in my business. That was bad enough. But there were other things that I didn't like about her. She was a slob who would leave her nasty underwear on the bathroom floor and she was always late with her share of the rent. She was always depressed about one thing or another and couldn't stand the fact that I was so optimistic and upbeat. Her family situation had been a lot like mine, but she had never complained about it. It saddened me to know that, like my mother and sisters, she was also willing to settle for so little. She cleaned rooms in a cheap motel and was involved with an unemployed cabdriver who lived in somebody's garage.

"I don't know what makes you think some rich man is going to want to be with you, Vera. You don't have any more to offer than I do," Cynthia told me the night I packed to move out of our shabby apartment.

"Except for money, I have the same things to offer a rich man that a rich woman has. If he's a good man, it won't matter to him that I'm poor." I had so much confidence in my ability to get what I wanted I didn't even get upset with Cynthia.

As soon as I got situated in a furnished studio apartment above a Chinese-owned fish market, I began to search for my prey like a well-armed hunter. I read business magazines and the society pages in the newspaper. That's how I found out where the rich black men hung out in Houston. And I wasn't choosey. As long as the man had very deep pockets and was generous, his looks didn't matter. I preferred older men. They were easier to manipulate than younger men. Another important factor was that a girl my age was more likely to outlive an elderly husband.

A geezer who was in poor health and had no children or other close relatives was a bonus.

CHAPTER 4

VERA

I HAD KISSED A LOT OF FROGS ALONG THE WAY. IT HAD BEEN FUN BEcause I loved men and I loved sex. A few times I had even fallen in love—but usually with men who had less than me and small dicks. Well, there was no chance in hell that I was going to settle for *that.* I learned from my mistakes. It didn't take long for me to decide that good money was a lot more important to me than good sex.

I promptly developed a routine I was comfortable with. I socialized *only* with wealthy older men. And to get what I wanted, I was willing to spread my legs as many times as I had to. I ate at the most expensive restaurants, my sugar daddies paid the rent on my cute little apartment, I rarely had to pay the note on my three-year-old Thunderbird out of my own pocket, and I shopped in the finest boutiques.

The more I learned, the more prudent I became in everything I did. But I still ran into a lot of obstacles anyway. One childless retired doctor, who had lost his wife to cancer, hired me to be his live-in caretaker. He was a dirty old man, so seducing him on the first night I moved in was a walk in the park. Less than a minute after I'd lowered my head down into his flabby, naked crotch, he immediately began to howl and yip like he had never been with a woman before in his life.

In less than a month, I had him right where I wanted him. He gave me a credit card and the keys to his Cadillac, which he was no longer able to drive anyway. I got so slap happy I did everything he asked me to do no matter how unpleasant it was. And there was nothing more disgusting than having to remove his diaper every time he wanted to have sex or get his dick sucked. He began to drop hints that he was going to make sure I was "well taken care of" when he passed. He was so frail and senile I expected to collect on my investment and be on easy street by the end of that year. When he went to sleep one night a week before Christmas and didn't wake up the next morning, I was elated. But my euphoria was short-lived.

Come to find out, that old goat was in debt up to his receding hairline. His creditors and the IRS took his house and everything in it. I had given up my apartment to move in with the retired doctor, and when he died and left me nothing, I had to move back in with Cynthia until I found another mark. But that didn't take long. A month later I was up and running again when I got a job as a waitress in the restaurant in a private gentlemen's club near the Houston airport. I got involved with a mysterious man who had told me up front that if he ever found out I was playing him for a fool, I'd be "real sorry." I immediately did some snooping around to see what I could find out about him. When I found out that he had beaten one of his previous girlfriends so severely they had to wire her jaw shut and that he had ties to the Jamaican mafia, I hauled ass. Despite the risks involved, my plan was still to find myself a wealthy husband, but I didn't want to die trying. I decided to search for a man in less threatening environments than gentlemen's clubs.

When I met Kenneth at a software conference a few months later, I knew I had hit the jackpot.

Since he and I were the only two black people present in a break room after one of the sessions ended, naturally we stood out. I was so glad I had removed the light blue smock that I had been told to wear by the temp agency I had signed up with. I was afraid that if Kenneth found out the only reason I was at the convention was to sign people in and pass out programs and name badges, he wouldn't have been interested in me.

"I don't mind attending these events, but I'm getting sick of eating nothing but finger sandwiches, crackers, and spinach dip," he said as he slid a cracker between his lips, smiling at me like he wanted to put me in his mouth next.

"I hear you. This being the South, you'd think somebody would suggest some fried chicken wings or something that folks like you and me can appreciate." I smiled and extended my hand. "I'm Vera Thigpen."

"Kenneth Lomax. And who are you with?" he asked, shaking my hand and squeezing it at the same time. He had a strong grip for a man who appeared to be in his early forties.

"Uh, I worked for a small company in Ft. Worth until they suddenly laid half of us off last month. Since I'd already made plans to be here, well, here I am. I had to pay for it out of my own pocket, though." Once I started spinning that tale, I knew I couldn't go back to the reception area and do what I was being paid to do.

"Oh. Was it a family-owned business?"

I shook my head.

"Well, I own my own business in California, so getting laid off or fired are two things I don't have to worry about," Kenneth said with a triumphant look on his caramel-colored face. He had nice white teeth (capped I presumed) and a strong jawline. Despite his age and thick, graying hair, he was not a bad-looking man at all. Generally speaking, he was tall, dark, and handsome. But there was a noticeable sadness in his small black eyes. He looked lonely and neglected, like a puppy nobody wanted. And if that was the case, he was talking to the right woman. I was elated! A lonely, rich, older man was within my reach and he was interested in me. I was tempted to lick my lips. I would suck his pecker until his balls deflated if I had to. Something told me that I had hit the mother lode, so I had to play my part to the hilt. But before I'd allow myself to get too involved, I had to do some investigating and make sure he was telling me the truth about being the owner of his business. For all I knew, he could have been one of the busboys! I decided to have a friend of mine, who had helped organize the conference, do a background check on this Mr. Lomax. If everything checked out to my satisfaction, then all I needed to know was what obstacles I was up against. Like a wife. Well, that was one thing I decided to ask about right away. I didn't want to waste too much time on this man and then find out he was married.

"Your being your own boss must make your wife very happy," I cooed, silently praying that he was divorced or a widower.

Kenneth cleared his throat and shook his head and said something that was even better than what I had prayed for. "I've never been married," he said shyly, his voice cracking. Then his mood changed as if he'd suddenly remembered a bad experience because a sharp frown was on his face now. "I've been looking for the right woman all my life, everywhere I go," he confessed. "I've met a lot of nice ladies over the years, but not one I cared enough about to marry. I get pretty lonely."

"Oh. I know exactly what you mean. I've never been married and I've had only one boyfriend. Last year, a week after he proposed to me, he died from an undiagnosed blood disease." I sniffed. "I haven't dated since."

"That's a damn shame, Vera." I was pleased when Kenneth blinked and looked at me with rapidly increasing interest. "But a pretty girl like you must have lots of admirers."

"Not really. My shyness turns men off."

"Hmmm. Well, I think shyness in a beautiful woman is a virtue. It keeps her humble."

Out of the corner of my eye, I noticed some of the other attendees leaving to go into another session. One of the other temp workers, who had also been hired to pass out programs and badges, gave me a puzzled look, so I knew I had to react fast. I needed my job and if I didn't have a chance with Kenneth, I needed to know that right away.

"Um, I don't know about you, but I think I've had enough of this," I said with a nervous smile. I nodded toward the exit. "I'm going to head over to Sissy's Soul Food. Today the special is deep-fried chicken wings, mac and cheese, collard greens, and hush puppies."

"Is that the greasy little hole-in-the-wall near that bowling alley on Royster Street?"

"You know about Sissy's?"

"Sure enough! I grew up in Houston. My family used to eat there when I was a little boy! That was one of my favorite restaurants back then."

I nodded and blinked. "Well, I'm countrified, so I am a fool for everything on their menu. Which is too bad for my hips . . . ," I mock complained. The minute I said *hips*, his eyes lit up like lightning bugs.

"Well, I'm still a down-home boy to the bone myself. Do you mind if I join you? You are talking about something good to eat." Kenneth looked at me like I was something good to eat too. I was so glad I had worn a tight skirt. His eyes kept roaming from my face to my hips. "Girl, you got me acting like a fool. Let me behave myself." He let out a snort and threw up his hands and bugged his eyes out like somebody had just pulled a gun on him. "I'm sorry. I'm being way too forward." He laughed and gave me an apologetic look. "Let me start over. I'm going back to Frisco tomorrow afternoon and I'd like to enjoy my last night here. I would like very much to have dinner with you this evening, if you don't mind."

I was amazed. Despite my bleak background—but because of my good luck, my charm, and my good looks—I had attracted the attention of a wealthy, middle-aged black businessman who lived in one of the wealthiest cities in the world. This man was looking more and more like a very big fish to me. If I gave him enough bait, I could hook him and reel him in. And since he was leaving the next day, I had to work real fast.

"I have a better idea. And I hope I'm not being too forward." I paused and took a deep breath. "Why don't we spend the evening in your hotel room? Sissy's delivers," I said in my most seductive voice. "That way we can get to know one another better."

"Hmmm," he replied, caressing his chin. "You're not being too forward. I like a woman who knows what she wants and is not afraid to go after it."

As soon as I got to his lavish hotel suite, I decided to give him a little more incentive to want to know me better.

I fucked the hell out of him that night.

The next morning when my friend told me that Kenneth really did own four stores and was about to open a fifth, I started making wedding plans.

Then I fucked him some more.

I'd been recalling my first encounter with Kenneth a lot lately. He had been my meal ticket ever since that day. I was not about to step aside now and let another bitch replace me.

I had received several more detailed reports and photographs from the private investigator I had following Kenneth around from time to time over the years. That horny pig had had a couple dozen more brief affairs since I'd canceled his relationship with Lois! I eventually ended the surveillance because I knew all I needed to know. And his new flings still didn't bother me too much anyway. Mainly because he never spent too much time and money on the same ones and he had not fathered any more children.

I was sure that as long as I continued to send Lois her monthly payments on time, I wouldn't have to worry about her. The lawyer that I had engaged behind Kenneth's back had handled everything with utmost discretion. A cashier's check was sent from his office to Lois's post office box the first of every month. I had advised her that if she was going to put money in the bank, not to have more than ten thousand bucks in an account at one time because the bank would report that information to the IRS. The last thing an ignoramus like her needed was to have to deal with the IRS and possibly steer them in my direction. From what my lawyer told me, she didn't want a bank account because she planned to collect welfare payments for her baby too. And even I knew how nosy and sneaky those devils were. It might take them a few years, but they would find out if she had an unreported bank account.

"She told me she'd hide the money she receives from you in an old pair of pantyhose and stick it up under her mattress," my lawyer said. That was so typical. He had not even bothered to suggest a safe-deposit box to her, and I was glad he hadn't. I was sure that if she had opened one, she probably would have done something stupid that would have involved an audit or a police investigation.

Anyway, the important thing was I hadn't seen or heard from her since our meeting. And neither had Kenneth.

My marriage was stronger than ever and I was too happy for words.

CHAPTER 5

KENNETH

My life got a little more complicated with each passing year. It seemed like every time I took an unexpected break from the office to get some much needed rest and relaxation, all hell broke loose in my absence. And it could be about anything, but usually it was something stupid and something that could have been avoided.

Last year when I took a well-deserved two-week vacation and went to Japan, a fire broke out in the break room in one of my smaller stores because some idiot had left the coffeepot heating on the hot plate all night. The damage had been minimal and the culprit had never come forward.

The most serious thing that had happened while I was out of the office had been some mild looting during the riots incited by the Rodney King verdict, back in '92. I had rented a penthouse in Puerto Vallarta, Mexico, that week, determined to get my wife pregnant.

Well, we had not made a baby, but I still enjoyed making love to Vera. And when we were away from all the hustle and bustle that went on around us in the city, I enjoyed it even more.

Nobody knew that Vera and I were in our cabin in Clear Lake for the upcoming new millennium weekend. We had left late Thursday night, and by the time the New Year arrived that Saturday, I had not checked my voice mail for messages or called up my secretary, Arlene Cunningham, the plump, plain grandmother I had hired to replace Lois almost sixteen years ago. I had no clue as to what was going on back in Frisco. But I had an uneasy feeling. It was not a bad feeling, so I wasn't expecting some form of doom to come my way. It was just a feeling that my life was about to change.

And I was right.

My dream of becoming a father was about to come true and in a way that I had never expected.

I'd been trying to get Vera pregnant ever since we got married. Not having children at my age was my biggest sorrow. Both Vera and I had been checked out thoroughly by more than one doctor. There was no reason why we couldn't have a child. It was a subject that she and I discussed often.

"I read about a fertility specialist in San Jose. Maybe we should pay him a visit and have him run a few tests," I told Vera after we had gotten our hopes up the last time her period was late about seven years ago.

"All we need to do is relax," she assured me.

"Well, it probably wouldn't hurt for us to get tested by the same doctor at the same time," I protested. "It's a sin and a shame that you've miscarried within the first trimester *six* times since we started trying." Every single time Vera miscarried, it happened when I was out of town. And since she was the type of woman who didn't want to worry her loved ones, she never told me until I returned home. By then she'd be too depressed to go into a lot of detail, so it was a subject I avoided as much as I could. However, there were times when I couldn't avoid it. "There's got to be a reasonable explanation as to why you can't carry a baby."

"This is too personal and sensitive for me, and I'd really like to stop talking about it so much. Especially after I've had so many miscarriages," she sobbed. "Maybe it's all the stress of us wanting a child that's ruining everything."

"I agree with you, but if we don't do something soon, we'll never know what it's like to be parents. If we wait too much longer, we'll both be too old to adopt. I would like to have at least one child before I leave this earth. There is nothing I want more than a child of my own."

"Me too, honey. We'll keep wishing, hoping, and trying," Vera told me.

I put the thought of being a father on a back burner again.

Sunday evening when Vera and I returned home from our romantic wine country getaway, the Friday, Saturday, and Sunday editions of the *San Francisco Chronicle* were on the end table in the living room stacked up in a neat pile. I rolled my eyes when I saw Friday's headline; a local politician I had known for years had been charged with fraud. I was in no hurry to read about that. About halfway down the page, the headline for another piece caught my attention:

Local Couple Dies in Crash on Highway 101

I was in no hurry to read that report either. People died in automobile accidents all the time.

An hour later, Cassius "Cash" Booker, Vera's cousin and the manager of customer service in my main store, called me up. I answered the wall telephone in the kitchen.

"Where have you been, bro?" Cash asked. He sounded frantic.

"Oh. I'm sorry we missed out on that party we told you we'd go to with you and Collette. Vera and I were up at the cabin. We wanted to bring in the New Year quietly and in a more intimate setting," I told him, speaking casually even though my heart had already begun to thump and vibrate as if a stout woman were dancing on it.

"Man, I've been calling all over the place for you! I got something to tell you that I'm sure you won't like hearing. And if you ain't already sitting down, you'd better."

"Oh, shit!" I immediately sat down in a chair at the kitchen table. "Hold on a second!" I yelled, reaching for the vial of heart pills I kept in my breast pocket. I popped one onto my tongue, but my mouth was so dry I couldn't even swallow it. Even after I chewed it, it took half a minute for me to get it down my throat. I could hear Cash breathing through his mouth on his end. "All right, Cash. What's the matter this time?"

"Remember that pretty little brown-skinned girl with the long ponytail and big legs that used to be the main office secretary some years back? The one that just up and quit one day without giving notice?"

My heart skipped a beat. I would never forget Lois Cooper and her abrupt and mysterious departure. I had often wondered what happened to her. "You mean Lois Cooper?"

"Well, she married some Mexican dude and became Lois Garcia." Cash paused.

"So? What's her getting married got to do with me? Did she send me an invitation or something and called you to find out why I didn't RSVP?"

"I doubt if she did that. She got married a few years ago. Anyway, a drunk driver broadsided the van she and her husband were in on Thursday evening during the commute hour. When I left work a couple hours after the accident, Highway 101 was closed down both ways for seven hours. I had to drive across the Golden Gate Bridge, then go through Richmond and Berkeley just to get back across the bay and into Frisco. The news about the accident was in Friday's *Chronicle.*"

"Oh. I glanced at it. I'll read the article right away. So Lois was married."

"Dude, can you talk?" Cash whispered.

"Sure. What do we need to talk about?"

"I knew about you and Lois. I knew you two were *getting busy . . .*"

"Oh. Uh, hold on." I took a deep breath and looked around to make sure I was still in the kitchen alone. We had just added a bar to the living room. Next to the lavish master bedroom on the third floor, it had become Vera's favorite spot in the house. I reached for my heart pills again, popping another one into my mouth. This one slid down my throat like a raw oyster. I set the telephone down on the counter and wobbled up off my seat. Then I tiptoed down the hall and peeped around the corner into the living room. Vera was behind the bar with her back to me. I could see she had a shot glass in one hand and a bottle of rum in the other. I scurried back into the kitchen and grabbed the telephone. "Cash, I'm back," I whispered, wiping sweat off my face. "So you knew about Lois and me all this time?"

"Uh-huh. All this time. But you don't have to worry about me. I'm a dude, so I know how we do and we have to look out for one another. I got your back protected better than a bulletproof vest."

A long moment of silence followed. Even though Cash had just told me he had my back, I was still scared. "Cash, my man, I want you to keep your mouth shut about this. I promise you I will make it worth your while." I had never been blackmailed before, but I was prepared to pay whatever was necessary to keep this damaging information from Vera. "How much do you want?"

"I don't want nothing, brother. You've already given me more than anybody else I ever knew. Even my own mama and daddy."

Cash had moved from Houston to California shortly after he finished high school in '78. He had spent a few months in L.A. pursuing an acting career that he had not been able to get off the ground with a crane. When he visited us one Memorial Day weekend, broke, unemployed, and depressed, I gave him a job and helped him find an apartment. He *owed* me, but if I had to pay him off to keep him from telling Vera about my affair with Lois, I would.

"Then if you don't want anything, why are you bringing this up? And how did you find out about Lois and me?" I asked.

"No, I don't want nothing. Honest to God, I don't. If I wanted something, I wouldn't have waited no fifteen, sixteen years to say something to you about it. But I knew what was up with you and Lois when I saw you and her coming out of that motor inn on Branson one evening. It was Super Bowl weekend."

"I see."

"I never said nothing about it to you because"—Cash paused—

"I was in that same motor inn for the same reason with this girl I'd met on the bus the week before. Me and Collette had only been married a few weeks and I wanted her, and you and Vera, to think I was a, uh, good husband. I couldn't bust you without busting myself. You know how women are when it comes to things like that. They don't know what it's like to be a man . . . know what I mean?"

"Yeah, I know what you mean. And thanks for bringing Lois's death to my attention. Had you not told me, I might not have even read that newspaper article. I'll send flowers and a sympathy card."

Cash grunted and cleared his throat. From that, I could tell he had more gloomy information to report—much to my dismay. I tensed up right away. "I think you might want to do more than that, Kenneth."

"What are you getting at? Have you been in touch with Lois? Does her mother need help paying for the funeral?"

"Dude, the article starts on the front page, but it continues on page D1. There is a picture of Lois and her family."

The silence that followed for about ten seconds scared me.

"Cash, what are you trying to tell me?"

"Remember when we attended that family reunion in Houston a few years ago, right after I got back to the States from the Gulf War?"

"Sure, I remember that event. What about it?"

"Not too many of your folks came, but your late brother's daughter was there."

I smiled. "Sonya Ann. That little girl looks just like me."

"Dude, Sonya Ann ain't the only little girl that looks just like you."

"Cash, please get to the point."

"Lois had only been with the man she married for four—oops! Excuse me, the newspaper said five years. The girl Lois gave birth to is fifteen now. That means Lois was either pregnant when she dropped out of sight or she got pregnant shortly after that."

"So? What's that got to do with me?"

"Get the newspaper and look real close at the picture of Lois's daughter. That girl and your niece Sonya Ann could be identical twins."

I don't remember what I said next. I just hung up. I went to the living room and retrieved the newspaper. I ignored the curious look on Vera's face and headed back to the kitchen.

Before I could turn to the page to check out the photograph of Lois's daughter, Vera pranced into the room.

CHAPTER 6

VERA

I HAD BECOME A DAMN GOOD LIAR. I HAD HAD SO MUCH PRACTICE over the years that I could tell more believable lies than most people. My husband told just as many lies as I did. The difference was, I knew when he was lying. When I walked into the kitchen a few seconds ago, he looked like he'd seen a ghost.

"Baby, what's the matter?" I asked, wrapping my arm around his waist. His body felt so tense I thought he was having another heart attack. He'd had several since our marriage. No matter how many times Dr. Cortez told him to stop putting himself in stressful situations, like working so much, he rarely took his advice. "Did something happen in one of the stores while we were in Clear Lake?"

"No . . . nothing is the matter," he stammered, sweating bullets. The light shirt he wore was so wet with sweat it looked like he'd just stepped out of the shower. He had a newspaper in his hand. He folded it and gave me a fake smile. "I think I drank a little too much wine this weekend."

"In that case, I won't offer you a drink now." I looked at my watch. "It's later than I thought anyway. How about a nice long hot bath, and after you finish I'll give you a massage."

"Okay, baby. Uh, I think I'll do just that," he blubbered. "I'll go take my bath right now."

I waited a few minutes before I tiptoed upstairs to make sure

Kenneth was taking his bath. Our bathroom door was shut and I could hear the water running in the bathtub. I eased back downstairs to take care of some urgent personal business.

We had several telephone lines throughout the main house. There was a separate line in the servant's quarters behind the mansion where our stout, middle-aged Salvadorian housekeeper/cook Delia Suarez and homely husband, Costa, our chauffeur and maintenance man, lived. The phone on the wall in the kitchen had a number of its own. I had had it installed for Delia to use while she was in the kitchen cooking since that was where she spent most of her time during the day. But another reason was so I could use it and not have to worry about Kenneth or anybody else in the house listening in on my private conversations on one of the extensions. I quickly dialed a number that I had memorized.

"Happy New Year, Tony. I tried to reach you the other day," I whispered into the mouthpiece as soon as he answered. I kept my eye on the door leading into the living room area and the door leading to our backyard. Living in a huge mansion, it was difficult to tell where any of the other residents were from one minute to the next.

"Happy New Year to you, too, Vera. I got the message you left telling me you were going to be out of town with your husband. So, did you enjoy your weekend in the wine country?" Tony asked in his deep baritone voice.

"Like a toothache!" I snapped. "Don't try to be funny."

"I'm sorry, sugar. Are you still coming to see me tomorrow like you promised? I'm sure you could use a good workout . . ."

"Oh shit! Don't you talk shit like that to me! Not tonight!"

"Why not? I do it all the time," Tony whined.

"Because I don't know when I can see you again. Kenneth's not feeling well, so I don't know if he's going into the office tomorrow."

"Damn! What's wrong with him this time?"

"It doesn't matter. He's not feeling or looking well, so I don't know if I'm going to be able to get away for a few hours these next few days."

"Well, when do you think I'll be able to see you again? I'm stretched out on my bed right now with my dick in my hand and this sucker is as hard as Chinese arithmetic."

I swooned just thinking about Tony lying on his bed naked with a hard-on. I had to fan my face and press my thighs together to control myself. I could feel the love juice pooling in the crotch of my panties. "I'll let you know as soon as possible. After what this old dinosaur put me through this weekend, I really need to see *you*. I'd like to celebrate the new millennium in style—uh, *doggie* style." Just the thought of Tony humping me from behind almost made me pass out. And it was no wonder. I was a desperate woman because I didn't get the sex I deserved at home. Making love with Kenneth when he was sober was bad enough. But making love to him after he'd had a few drinks was torture. No matter what I had done for him in our cabin, he still had not performed well or finished in a timely manner. Last night after he'd fumbled around inside and on top of me with a dick as limp as a wet noodle for one hour and thirty minutes (I knew because I had looked over his shoulder at my watch several times), I screamed. He was such a clueless oaf he had thought that I was screaming in ecstasy. And I'd let him think that. I was horrified when he said, "Don't worry, baby. I'm going to fuck you all night . . ." And he almost did. He didn't roll off me until 4:00 a.m.

"I really need to see you, baby. If old dude don't go to work tomorrow, can't you tell him you're going shopping or something?"

"Hmmm. I guess I could swing by Neiman Marcus and grab a few items so it would look like I went shopping. The only thing is, if he is too sick to go to work tomorrow, he'll want me to wait on him hand and foot."

"Well, if you can make it here to see me, cool. You don't have to go out of your way for me . . ."

"Now don't you pout again!" After all of the affairs I'd had with young men—most of them young enough to be my sons—I should have been used to pouting by now, but I wasn't. "Baby, you know I'll do my best."

"I hope so," he replied, still pouting.

"You know I'll make it up to you if I don't make it over to see you tomorrow. And I'll do my best to make it the next day or so. I'll bring you something real nice whenever I do come."

"Okay, baby. You are so sweet to me. And you know I ain't choosy, so anything from Neiman Marcus or Bloomingdale's will do."

CHAPTER 7

KENNETH

I LOCKED THE BATHROOM DOOR IN OUR BEDROOM IN CASE VERA DEcided to enter before I had finished reading the newspaper article about Lois's death. Sitting on the commode, I read about the fatal accident that had claimed the lives of Lois and her husband. I got so overwhelmed with emotion I began to cry and let out choking moans like an old woman. Even though I had never intended to leave Vera for Lois, I had really cared about that girl. I would have continued the affair indefinitely (or until Vera caught me) had Lois not run off.

I stared at the photograph of her and her daughter enjoying last year's Fourth of July in Disneyland. My heart was beating so hard I thought it was going to leap clean out of my chest. I stopped crying and moaning, but I had to take a whole lot of deep breaths to keep from passing out.

I was practically convinced that Lois's daughter was mine, but I needed to know for sure so I could do the right thing. And there was no way I could do that and not let Vera know. I desperately wanted to be a father, and it was not a role that I wanted to fulfill behind closed doors.

Despite the fact that the girl, whose name was Sarah, looked like she belonged to me, that could have been a coincidence. I had met strangers who looked more like me than some of my blood relatives. Cash already knew about my affair with Lois, and even though he was Vera's cousin, I didn't have to worry about him blabbing to her before I told her. He knew better than to betray me. He had too much to lose. To please Vera, I had hired that sucker seventeen years ago—even though he had only a high school education and a spoonful of experience—to manage the customer service department in my main store. With his lazy, ignorant ass, he wouldn't have been able to find another job on the planet paying him what I paid him for doing practically nothing. When he complained about his "boring-ass job," he took a break and joined the Marines about ten years ago. After eighteen months fighting in the Gulf War, he couldn't wait to get back to the "boring-ass job" in my store. He was so humble he would have mopped floors if I had asked him to. But because I liked Cash and wanted to keep him happy, I not only gave him his old job back, but I also hired his wife, Collette, a woman he'd met when he lived in L.A. She had attempted to establish a show business career like Cash. But Hollywood had had no interest in her either. She worked as a cashier in my main store now.

I almost tumbled off the commode when somebody knocked on the door. "Yes," I yelled right away.

"Baby, are you all right in there?" Vera asked. "With all that moaning and groaning you're doing, you must be *really* constipated this time. There's a fresh bottle of Maalox in the medicine cabinet. And some Ex-lax."

"Uh, I'm fine. I'm feeling much better, too, so you don't have to worry about that massage," I said. I needed a massage to ease some of the tension in my neck, back, and almost every other part of my body. But I didn't want to face Vera until I had composed myself. And the way I was feeling, I predicted it would be the next morning before I was able to breathe normally again.

"Can I get you something?"

"Uh, some warm milk if you don't mind. But you don't have to do it now. Give me about fifteen more minutes. I think I'll just lie here in this tub of warm water for a while."

"Okay, honey."

I waited a full minute before I looked at the newspaper article again. The funeral was scheduled to take place tomorrow and I had to go. I didn't care if I was too sick to get out of bed; this was one funeral I didn't want to miss.

I finally did get in the bathtub. After I had wallowed in the warm soapy water for about ten minutes, I stumbled out. I hid the newspaper under my robe. Right after I entered the bedroom, Vera came in with a large glass of warm milk.

"Baby, you don't look well at all," she said. "I've never seen your hands shake so hard."

"I'm fine," I lied. I drank some of my milk and gave her a big smile. "Now let's get to bed and get some sleep."

I slept for less than two hours that night. And when I woke up around nine the next morning, Vera's side of the bed was empty. I felt like I'd been run over by a train. There was no way I was going to be able to go to a funeral anytime soon, unless it was my own. The way I was feeling, that was a strong possibility.

As soon as Vera returned, I told her, "I think I'll stay home today." She had already applied her makeup and put on a beige pantsuit. As usual, she looked like a film star. I was surprised that she looked so disappointed by what I'd just told her. "But you don't have to babysit me," I told her. I had dressed and was sitting on the side of the bed. "I don't know why I bothered to put on my clothes. I may not leave this bed at all today."

"Hmmm. Well, I hope you don't mind if I go out for a little while. I'd like to make a run to Neiman Marcus and Macy's to pick up a few things. It shouldn't take more than a few hours," she told me, sitting down next to me on the bed. She put her arm around my shoulder and held me close. "I'll be thinking about you every minute while I'm gone." Then she kissed my cheek and massaged my balls.

My dick was as limp as a wet dishrag. I was such a mess even Vera couldn't excite me right now. And I didn't want her to keep trying, wasting her time and making me feel even worse.

"Then you go right ahead, honey. Delia will be here and I can always call Cash or Collette if I need anything before you get back."

"Oh, by the way," she said, rising. "Did you see last Friday's newspaper?"

"Huh?"

"Remember that girl named Lois who used to work for you about fifteen, sixteen years ago?"

I gave Vera a thoughtful look. "Lois who?"

"Lois Cooper! She was your secretary! The one who left so abruptly without giving notice or an explanation as to why she was quitting."

"Lois...Cooper...let me see—oh yeah! That was a long time ago and I vaguely remember her. Wasn't she kind of homely?"

"No, she was kind of pretty. Anyway, she and her husband died in a car crash last Thursday evening."

I had hidden the newspaper under my robe and placed both on the nightstand. I glanced to the side and saw that the robe and the newspaper were no longer there.

"I just glanced at the newspaper last night," I said. "I'll read the piece later after I read the sports section. Lois Cooper. Hmmm. I hope that poor woman didn't suffer in that crash."

"I hope she didn't either. Oh well." Vera yawned and looked at her watch. One day I planned to tell her just how much it irritated me for her to do that so often. She even did it sometimes when we were making love!

"Can I get you something before I leave?" she asked.

"I'm fine, sugar. You go on and do what you need to do and don't worry about me. I'm going back to bed," I said, already removing my clothes.

Vera kissed me on the forehead and patted my back and then she practically skipped out of the room. I was glad she was in such a good mood and I hoped she stayed that way. I loved my wife. She was the best thing that had ever happened to me. She was the first woman who really made me feel like a man. Before I met her, I had been with so many women I lost count. I knew they were using me, but I didn't care. I felt that I was using them just as much. And once they found out I had inherited the business from my daddy and was making money like it was going out of style, they tried to use me even more. It seemed like the more money I made, the more trouble I had with women trying to take it.

My money had not impressed Vera when I met her at a software conference in Houston some twenty-eight years ago. I had realized that right away when I offered to help her pay her rent after a friend she had loaned money to didn't pay her back that month. "I have never taken money from a man before in my life. Besides, I couldn't pay you back. But don't worry about me. I'll get out of this mess somehow," she told me. The fact that she didn't want my money made me want her even more.

I had returned to San Francisco the day after I'd met Vera. But I spent a couple of weekends each month in Houston so I could see her and visit some of the relatives I'd left behind. I had always wanted to live in California, so I moved the business to Frisco shortly after my mama and daddy both passed a month apart. But when I fell in love with Vera, I decided that I had to return my business to Houston or get her to move to California. She was a hard nut to crack, but I was determined to win her over—and I didn't care how much it cost me.

No matter how hard I tried to give Vera money, she refused to take it. Finally, when I was about to give up, she not only let me bring her rent up to date, but she also allowed me to pay it for the next two months. I didn't mind. I had more money than I knew what to do with anyway. I helped out my relatives from time to time, lending them money I knew they'd never pay back. Each year I donated thousands of dollars to various charities, I supported and paid for the college education of several children in third world countries and in the States, and I gave very generously to the black universities and colleges throughout the country.

Vera quickly became so important to me that I wanted to give her everything she needed, too, and I encouraged her to help me spend my money. Despite my generosity, she remained humble and reluctant. I wined and dined her in the most expensive restaurants in the country, but she preferred rib joints and chicken shacks. Four months after I'd met her, I talked her into quitting her dead-end temp job. She moved to San Francisco to be with me a week after she quit her job. She couldn't believe a black man lived in a mansion in San Francisco's exclusive Pacific Heights district. But that didn't impress Vera. That's just how humble she was.

Despite my obvious wealth, Vera continued to shop in discount stores and she still preferred to dine in rib joints and chicken shacks at the time. However, her frugality did not last long. Once she met some of my friends at the country club and realized what a position of privilege she was in now, she changed her tune and all hell broke loose! She began to spend money like it was going out of style. Within a month after I married her, she was spending more on one dress than all her other dresses put together. She went hog-wild in all the high-end stores, and she used my money to make herself over, starting with breast implants and a butt lift. But she was more than a vain, extravagant trophy wife; she was my savior.

Until Vera entered my life, I had not really lived or loved. I had always felt empty and lonely. Most of my family had passed, and I was afraid that if I didn't produce an heir, my family would become extinct.

As much as I wanted to find out if I was a daddy now, I couldn't bear the thought of losing Vera.

Just thinking about my predicament gave me the strength I needed to prop myself up in bed and call Cash.

"You may be right about Lois's daughter being mine," I told him, clutching the bedside telephone in my hand so hard my fingers got numb.

"Uh-huh. What about Vera?"

"She saw the newspaper. I don't think she remembers meeting my niece, or she would have noticed the resemblance between her and Lois's daughter. The funeral is today."

"Are you going to attend it?"

"I don't know, but I'm going to try. I need to see the girl up close before I say or do anything. And I want her to see me."

"Why do you want her to see you?" Cash paused. "Do you think her mama told her about you, showed her a picture of you or something?"

"Lois could have done that. I never heard from her after she called in and resigned that Monday morning, so I have no way of knowing whether she did or not. And I've never even met Lois's mama."

"I feel for you, bro. I don't think you should deal with this by yourself. If you want me to go to the funeral with you, I will. You might need a backup."

"Why would I need a backup?"

"For one thing, you don't know what Lois told her mama as to why she quit such a good job. She might have even told her you took advantage of her."

"I didn't take advantage of any damn body!" I hollered. "Lois was of age. She knew what she was doing!"

"True. But like I just said, you don't know what she told her mama. She might have even told her you raped her. And another thing: if you do go to that funeral, I'm sure people will be wondering who you are and why you're there."

"You're right. Okay. Let's assume Lois didn't tell her mama about her having an affair with me. If I go to the funeral and somebody asks me who I am, I'll tell them the truth. And as Lois's former boss, it wouldn't be out of the ordinary for me to attend her funeral. Last year I attended my bookkeeper's daddy's funeral. And the year before that I attended the funerals of two of my folks in sales."

"Yeah. If you change your mind and want me to go with you, just let me know by the end of today. And you know how Collette is. She'll be asking all kinds of questions and I'll have to tell her something eventually. If the child is yours, we might need to do some damage control in advance before you tell Vera, my brother."

CHAPTER 8

KENNETH

THE DAY WAS ALREADY GLOOMY ENOUGH. BUT WHEN THE RAIN started, it got even gloomier. I glanced out my bedroom window and saw that the sky looked like a dark gray blanket. There was thunder and lightning like never before. Within minutes it sounded like I was inside the belly of a military bunker complete with torpedoes. I felt doomed.

Somehow I managed to crawl out of bed around ten, but I was still aching from head to toe. My head was throbbing like it was about to explode. But the main thing I was concerned about was my heart. I had had rheumatic fever when I was eight and had almost died that year. The illness had left me with a weakened heart. That was the reason I couldn't play any football in high school like my friends or any other sport for that matter. My mother didn't even want me to ride my bicycle that often. "I ain't going to bury another child," she said, hugging me so hard I couldn't breathe. My older sister Louise had died a year earlier at the age of eleven. She had run in front of a speeding car with a drunk behind the wheel. Two years after my sister's funeral, my mother gave birth to my brother Alonzo. Sadly, she had to bury him too. He died in a boating accident in a city park when he was twenty-one, leaving behind a new wife and a baby daughter.

Losing two children had practically destroyed my mother. Her grief had caused her to quit her job as a seamstress, so money became very tight. Thank God my father was an enterprising man. He used the settlement money from my brother's accident and opened a manual typewriter sales and repair shop. He employed my brother's widow and a few other family members, including myself.

After the manual typewriter had bitten the dust and everybody started buying electric typewriters, Daddy reluctantly went with the flow. "If you can't beat 'em, join 'em," he said. For many years, we did quite well. And when the word processors entered the picture, we did even better.

Health issues kept me out of the military, so I focused more on my education. By the time I had completed some business courses at Texas State, my daddy was too old and senile to make good business decisions. My mother talked him into retiring and letting me take over. Both of my parents passed the following year. By then, computers had come along, so I started selling them too. The next adjustment I made was to move the business to California.

My brother's widow had remarried the year before, so she stayed in Houston with her husband and the baby girl she'd had with my brother. Sonya Ann was not just my niece; she was the daughter I had always wanted. A lot of people used to say that she looked more like me than her daddy. A few years ago, she married a young doctor from Belize whom she had met on a cruise ship. They moved to Belize shortly after they got married, and I no longer saw her when I visited Houston. We communicated by letter and telephone a few times, but after she started having babies, that stopped. I had not heard from her in years. That was why it was so important for me to find out if Lois's daughter really was mine.

Somehow I managed to get back up and dressed again before noon. Vera had told me she'd be back in a few hours, so I didn't have much time. I knew that if she returned before I made it out of the house, she would probably interfere with my movements. It had suddenly become very important for me to see Lois one last time, even if it had to be at her funeral.

It was still raining when I left the house. Then a traffic jam on 101 slowed me down considerably. It was 1:10 p.m. by the time I made it to the church on Third Street where Lois's funeral was supposed to start at one o'clock. The closest parking spot I could find was three blocks away from the church. And with the way I was limping around like a dying man, it took me another fifteen minutes to walk down the street and up a steep hill to the church.

For the first time in my life, I was glad that black folks had such a hard time being on time. Even our funerals often ran on what we jokingly refer to as "colored people's time." Lois's funeral had not even *started* by the time I entered the church fifteen minutes later.

There were not that many people present, so there were a lot of empty pews. I decided to plop down on one near the back in case I wanted to leave early. I was sure that none of these people would recognize me, but I was wrong. Five minutes after I'd sat down, an elderly birdlike woman wearing a hat that looked like a bird's nest sat down next to me.

"Ain't you the one that own Lomax Electronics in one of them strip malls going toward Ghirardelli Square?" she asked. "I seen you on a TV commercial one time."

"Yes, ma'am. I'm Kenneth Lomax," I mumbled.

"My grandson bought me my first computer from your store in South San Francisco. That was ten years ago. It still runs real good and it should—you charged enough for it." The old woman smiled. "It'll probably conk out in another year or so, but I don't care. I'll be dead by then. Me and my whole family used to buy our computers and TVs and stuff from Circuit City until we found out about you. When my neighbor's daughter started working for you, she told us to put our money back into the black community."

"Oh. Well, I appreciate your business, ma'am. Next time you see your neighbor's daughter, tell her that I thank her for sending me more business."

I glanced around and blinked hard a few times, hoping nobody else would recognize me. The old woman fished a handkerchief out of her large bamboo purse and wiped tears from the corners of her eyes.

"I won't be seeing that sweet child again until I make it to heaven myself," she told me, nodding toward the closed casket in the front of the church. "Poor Lois Ann. I remember when she got that job working for you. She was so happy, and everybody in the neighborhood was so proud of her. She had been all over town trying to find work, and you was the only one that gave her a chance. Bless your heart and soul."

"Oh," was all I could say at first. I had to blink hard again to hold back my own tears. "She was a good secretary."

"She was such a pretty young woman. She got so messed up in that crash—burnt to a crisp—that they couldn't even have an open casket service."

I looked toward the front of the church. Another elderly woman and a young girl, both dressed in black from head to toe, walked up to the casket. They were holding on to each other and sobbing hard and loud. Nobody had to tell me who those two were. It was Lois's mother and her daughter, Sarah. A grim-faced usher led them to the front pew.

About ten minutes later, the funeral finally started. An enormous young woman in a red wig began to play the piano, and a thin young man got up and sang four different hymns in a row. There was a lot of weeping and wailing going on. And before I knew it, I was crying like a baby myself. I hawked into my handkerchief every few minutes.

After the service ended, everybody went downstairs to the dining area. Nobody was weeping or wailing down there. The way some of those folks were pushing and shoving trying to be the first ones to get to the food, it resembled one of my kinfolks' family reunions.

I didn't have much of an appetite, so I didn't have to fight with the hungry crowd to get a plate. Lois's mother and daughter sat at a table near the front of the room. As soon as everybody stopped hugging them, I went over and introduced myself to Lois's mother. From the way she frowned when I sat down in a chair next to her, it didn't seem like she was happy to meet me.

"You the one that fired my baby!" she accused. "She needed that job!"

"Excuse me, ma'am. I didn't fire your daughter," I protested, one hand up in the air. "Lois called in one morning and resigned. That's all I know. I would have never fired her. She was one of my best employees."

"She sent my stepdaddy to one of your stores to buy me my first computer," the young girl said. "That was last year on my birthday."

"You must be . . . Sarah," I said, almost choking on my words.

"Yeah. I'm Sarah."

"I hope you're enjoying your computer."

"I was enjoying it until somebody broke into our apartment one night while we was sleep and stole it a week after I got it," Sarah said with a pout.

"Well, I am sorry to hear that. I'll make sure you get a new one." I smiled so hard my jawbones ached.

"Not unless it's free," the grandmother said sharply. "We fixing to get seriously behind with our bills this month. My daughter and that fool she married didn't have no insurance, so I got to use my little savings and ask for help from the church to cover this funeral."

"Grandma, can I go now? This is too depressing," Sarah whined, already rising and waving to another young girl near the exit.

Instead of answering, the grandmother dismissed Sarah with a wave of her hand and then quickly turned back to me.

"Mrs. Cooper, this is not the time or the place for it, but it's really important for you and me to sit down and talk," I told her, glancing around. I was glad I had not been approached by another customer who recognized me.

"What you need to talk to me about? Y'all turned me down when I tried to get some credit, so I know I don't owe you no money."

CHAPTER 9

VERA

I HAD NO LOVE FOR LOIS COOPER, BUT I WAS SORRY TO READ ABOUT her death. However, I was still angry about her sleeping with my husband and having his baby.

It made me sick when I thought about all of the new clothes and jewelry I could have bought and how much fun I could have had with my lovers with all the "hush money" I'd paid her the past sixteen years! Only another married woman who had to deal with her husband's mistress and their baby would know exactly how I felt.

I didn't know all the details of Lois's short life, but I knew enough to determine that she had had a miserable one. She'd been raised by a single mother in a low-income neighborhood and had struggled to get from one day to the next. But then so had I before I landed Kenneth.

I don't want to know what might have happened between Kenneth and me if Lois had not disappeared from his life and gone along with my plan. The fact that she was no longer in the picture meant a whole new outlook on life for me.

The newspaper had reported that Lois's teenage daughter, Sarah, lived with Lois's mother. The article didn't say but I assumed Lois's mother was one of those elderly sisters who had been beaten down by life in more ways than one and who had lost her man many years ago. So typical. Women like Lois got pregnant with babies they didn't need and the grandmothers or some other family member ended up raising those babies. The last time I got a call from my mother, she complained about how my three younger sisters left their numerous children in her care for days at a time. "I can't keep feeding all these kids with just my pension check," she informed me. Of course, the real reason my mother told me about her latest setback was because she wanted me to send her more money. I didn't mind helping out family. But it seemed like the more I did for them the more they expected. I had been sending money and expensive gifts to my mother and my sisters ever since I married Kenneth. It had begun to get on my nerves, so I had slowed down considerably. And what made the situation even worse was despite all of the financial aid I had provided, my mother and sisters were no better off than they had been before my help! It had made me quite bitter. I felt like I had been taken advantage of, which I knew in my heart was the case, but I never threw it in their faces. I had always felt that you didn't kick a person who was already down. You just got bitter and resentful. Paying all that money to Lois had made me even more bitter and resentful about "helping" people.

Sarah was no longer my problem. I was off the hook! I wanted to protect my investment in Kenneth more than ever now. I had no payment plan with Lois's mother, so she wouldn't be getting a plugged nickel from me.

I couldn't wait to speak to my lawyer and tell him to stop sending those cashier's checks to Lois's post office box. I didn't have my cell phone with me, so I called him up from a pay phone at the pharmacy I'd stopped at for condoms on my way to Tony's apartment. It was almost 2:00 p.m. I'd just come from a two-hour session at the spa where I'd enjoyed a Swedish massage. I always needed to be extremely relaxed when Tony got a hold of me or my body would take days to recover from all the ecstasy he put me through.

"Mitch, this is Vera Lomax. You can stop sending the checks to

Lois Cooper, effective immediately. I hope I caught you in time so I won't be out any money this month."

"Hello, Mrs. Lomax. Well, due to the holiday and my secretary being on vacation, we're a little behind. I am glad you called me today because this month's check was about to go out in this morning's mail. May I ask why you're making this adjustment?"

"She's dead. She died in an automobile accident last week."

"Oh for goodness sake! Well, my condolences. I am so sorry to hear that the child is deceased."

"Not the child, the child's mother."

"I see." My lawyer cleared his throat. "The child is still a minor, but you wish to discontinue the payments? Is that what you're telling me?"

"That's what I'm telling you. For all I know, that woman might not have even been using the money to take care of that child anyway! You're a brother from the hood, so I know you know how trifling some of our sisters are! Lois Cooper got married somewhere along the line and the grandmother's been raising the child for God knows how long." For the first time, I regretted that I had not communicated with Lois from time to time. Had I known she had married and dumped Kenneth's child on her mother, I probably would have modified our arrangement. As far as I knew, that heifer could have been using my money to help support the man she married!

"Hmmm. Well, come in so you can sign off on a few documents. I'm available this afternoon from about three p.m. to six."

"I don't like signing anything that connects me to that woman. I don't like leaving a paper trail. I told you that from day one."

"Mrs. Lomax, this situation is highly confidential. But for your own peace of mind, and mine, I'd like for you to sign a release form that will end this arrangement. And don't worry about a paper trail. You and I are the only ones who have ever seen any of these documents associated with Lois Cooper. My secretary has never even seen them, so you don't have anything to worry about."

"All right. Uh, I don't think I can make an appointment for today. I have an important engagement that I can't reschedule," I said, glancing at my watch. I could have kicked my own ass for not calling up Tony to let him know that I was going to be a little late. I was horny as hell, and I didn't think I could go another day without the kind of loving I needed. "I'll check my calendar when I get home and I'll call your secretary before the end of today."

I hung up and galloped back to my car. I was in such a hurry to get to Tony's apartment on McAllister Street I ran two red lights and drove down a one-way street to save time.

He was naked when he opened the door. I was pleased to see his enormous erection dangling in my direction. Because of the grueling workouts my personal trainer put me through four times a week, I was in better shape than most women my age. Tony had a fabulous body, too, but he was not that good-looking. His head reminded me of a globe, and his eyes looked like they belonged on a fish. His lips were so big one of his could cover both of mine. And he had bad teeth, so I rarely kissed him. But he made up for all his flaws in bed. He was the best lover I'd ever had so far.

"Where'd you park?" he asked, running his ashy reddish brown fingers through my hair. I turned my head to the side so that the kiss he aimed at my lips landed on my cheek.

I dropped my purse onto his living room coffee table next to an empty container from Taco Bell and several empty beer cans. "I left my car in a lot downtown. I took a cab over here," I replied. "Baby, this is going to have to be real quick. I have a lot of things on my plate today." I kicked off my shoes and began to unbutton my blouse.

He glanced at my hands and frowned when he saw all I was holding was my purse. "I see you didn't make it to Neiman Marcus." There was a disappointed look on his face. "Or did you leave the shopping bags in the car?"

"I didn't have time to go there, so I'll have to take a rain check." I grinned, wiggling out of my pants. "I really need to get back home soon. I have a situation with my husband that I need to take care of."

"All right, then. This won't take long." Tony took my hand and kissed it.

"Good! We'll make up for it the next time. Let's get down to business, baby," I said, almost out of breath. I slid my panties off, not taking my eyes off his.

CHAPTER 10

KENNETH

I HAD NOT BEEN INSIDE A CHURCH SINCE THE LAWSONS' DAUGHTER'S wedding four months ago. I had been feeling out of place and uncomfortable since I walked in the door of the Baptist church on Third Street to attend Lois's funeral.

Her mother's cold reception had made me feel even more uncomfortable. I couldn't wait to leave, but I couldn't do that until I completed my mission.

The old woman, who looked like an elderly version of Lois, gave me a guarded look before she adjusted the wide-brimmed hat she wore, which looked like a cross between a cowboy hat and a sombrero. The wig she had on must have been sewed into the hat because when the hat moved, the wig moved with it.

She grunted and began to talk in a slow controlled manner. "Look, Mr. Lomax. I don't know what's so important for you to discuss with me that we need to set up an appointment. Before today, I ain't never even laid eyes on you except on them TV commercials. Now, if Lois owed you some money, that's too bad. I didn't sign nothing, so I ain't responsible for nothing she left behind. I got enough bill collectors coming after me for my own bills. I ain't got no money, so I ain't about to pay nobody else's debts. Not even my daughter's."

"Your daughter didn't owe me any money, ma'am," I said quickly. "But the sooner we can discuss our business, the better."

"Well, you need to tell me what business you need to discuss with me and you need to tell me now."

I exhaled loudly and looked around some more. More people had entered the dining area. There were now almost twice as many mourners present as the number who had actually attended the service. Apparently the latecomers had come to get a plate and, I hoped, to offer their condolences to Lois's family.

Lois's daughter, Sarah, had joined some other young people near the exit. For a brief moment, she glanced at me. There was a puzzled expression on her face.

"This is about your granddaughter," I finally said, still looking around the room. "Ma'am, this is kind of sensitive. If you really need to talk about it now, I suggest we go to a more private location."

Mrs. Cooper shook her head. "I ain't going no place with no strange man. Now, either you tell me right here and now what you need to talk to me about and what it's got to do with my granddaughter, or you can get up out of my face."

It didn't take long for me to realize that I didn't have a choice, so I took a deep breath and formed the words in my head before they slowly rolled out of my mouth. "I think I'm Sarah's father."

Mrs. Cooper's mouth dropped open and she looked at me like I had just insulted her. "It was you? You the one that done it?" she asked, rotating her neck.

"Ma'am?"

"Some horny devil drugged my child and took advantage of her at a party one night. She passed out and when she woke up the next morning she was naked to the world. A few weeks later, she found out she was pregnant. Did you do it?"

Hearing the news that someone had drugged Lois and raped her horrified me. For one thing, it made me angry to think that someone would commit such a vile act. "Ma'am, I didn't drug your daughter and I didn't take advantage of her. She was over eighteen and more than willing to have a relationship with me."

Mrs. Cooper blinked and looked me up and down, frowning

and shaking her head. "You look old enough to be her daddy. What in the world did she see in a geezer like you? Why did you fire her?"

"Ma'am, I told you I didn't fire Lois. One day she didn't show up for work and she didn't call to say why. I tried to call her, but the number she'd listed on her application had been disconnected or changed. I don't know which. She called my personnel office and had the clerk mail her last check to a post office box, and I never heard from her again. I never did find out why she suddenly quit her job without giving me any notice. I didn't even know she was still living in the Bay Area. I didn't know she was married, and I didn't know she'd had a daughter. Now, your granddaughter looks exactly like my late brother's daughter. Because of that, my affair with Lois, and the time frame, well, what else can I think?"

"You telling me that my daughter lied to me? She lied to me all these years?"

I nodded. "I'm afraid so, ma'am."

"Why should I believe you? Where you been all this time? How come you never paid a dime to help support Sarah? You just another nigger to me, so why should I believe anything you say?"

"Ma'am, I swear to God I didn't know about Sarah until I saw her picture in the newspaper. Had I known about her before now and even suspected that I was her father, I would have taken care of her."

Before Mrs. Cooper could respond, Sarah returned. "Grandma Lilly, you all right? You look upset," she asked, a scowl on her beautiful cinnamon brown face as she looked at me. She reminded me of a doll with her big brown eyes and pert nose. Her thick black hair was braided and wrapped around her head like a finely woven basket.

"I'm . . . I'm fine, baby," Mrs. Cooper said. "Sarah, uh, me and you need to talk."

"We need to talk about what?" Sarah asked, looking from her grandmother to me. "I ain't done nothing!" Her voice was so loud, a huge man in a black suit and dark glasses walked over and stood in front of Mrs. Cooper.

"Everything all right over here, Sister Cooper?" the man asked, looking at me like he wanted to bite my head off.

"Everything's fine, Jimmy. Go on back to what you was doing," Mrs. Cooper said, waving Jimmy away. Then she turned to Sarah with a weary look on her face. "I ain't said you done nothing, gal. But, uh, this gentleman here, Mr. Lomax, he got something important to tell you."

"I don't think we should discuss this here," I insisted, my hand in the air.

"This man might be your daddy," Mrs. Cooper blurted out. She placed her hand on Sarah's arm and began to rub it.

"Nuh-uh!" Sarah hollered. Then she gave me a hot look and stated, "My mama didn't fool around with old men!"

"Well, she fooled around with me," I said firmly.

"Mama told me my daddy died in a plane crash!" Sarah snapped. The hot look on her face suddenly looked cooler. "Didn't he? She gave me a picture of him, and he didn't look nothing like you."

"I don't know anything about that. The picture your mother showed you was probably of a man she knew and he may have died in a plane crash. But he was probably not your daddy. All I know is . . ." I stopped talking and stood up, feeling more robust than I had in weeks. The thought that I had a child had brought out strength in me I didn't know I still had. A lot of the people, who were still gnawing on fried chicken and snatching rolls like they were pearls, kept glancing in my direction, giving me menacing looks. That scared me. I couldn't imagine what those people were thinking. Strange things often happened at black folks' funerals. During the service for my brother, a process server had stormed the pulpit and interrupted Pastor Morris so he could serve him with a summons that one of his creditors had initiated. Two of my rough friends escorted the process server out to the church parking lot and laid open his lip with a well-aimed fist. I didn't want that to happen to me. "I really do think we should go to a more private place to discuss this," I said. Two more very large men in dark suits and dark glasses were staring at me now.

"There ain't nothing to discuss!" Mrs. Cooper hollered, wobbling up from her seat. "Now, if you don't get out of my face, I'm going to have you thrown out!"

Sarah held up her hand. "Wait, Grandma." She turned to me with a pleading look. "If you are my real daddy, I need to know."

"I need to know too," I replied. The more I looked at this girl, the more I believed she really was my child. She even sounded like my niece and had the same slight gap between her two front teeth.

Another one of the dark-suited men strolled over and glared at me. "Sister Cooper, is this man bothering you?" he asked, removing his glasses. He made the first man look like a choirboy. I stared into the most evil-looking, bloodshot eyes I'd ever seen in my life. His huge hands looked like smoked ham hocks. I was no wimp myself, but this man was at least forty years younger and forty pounds heavier than me. He could have swatted me like a fly.

Before Sister Cooper could respond, Sarah piped in, "It's all right, Brother Whigham. I think this man is my real daddy."

"Say what?" Brother Whigham said, putting his glasses back on and looking me up and down.

"Can you leave us alone for a few minutes?" Sarah said in her gentle voice. "If this man is my real daddy, I want to know and I want to know now. Today's been a real hard day for me, knowing my mama is in that coffin and all. Other than my grandma, she was all I had left in the world. Now, if this man is my daddy . . ." Sarah sniffed and looked at the floor. When she looked up again, there was a strange smile on her face. "Maybe I won't be so alone in the world now."

"All right," Brother Whigham grunted. The hard look on his face had softened, but he was still a man I didn't want to tangle with.

Right after Brother Whigham slunk back toward the rest of the mourners and the food, Sarah looked at me. "You can prove you're my real daddy, you know. That DNA thing I keep hearing about on TV would prove it."

I nodded. "I didn't want to have this conversation here. Not right after your mama's funeral," I began.

"Then how come you didn't try to find out sooner?" Mrs. Cooper asked.

"Like I told you just a few moments ago, I didn't even know Lois had a daughter until yesterday when I saw last Friday's newspaper. I came as soon as I could." I placed my hand on Sarah's, covering and gently squeezing it. "I want to do a DNA test as soon as possible. I'd like to get on it *today* if you don't mind." I was so anxious to find out the truth, I knew I would not sleep again until I had at least put the wheels in motion. "I'll take you to a facility where we can have it done. One of my closest buddies is the head technician there, and I'm sure he'll accommodate us without an appointment. It could take a few weeks or even months to get the results, but I'm going to do all I can to speed it up." Then I turned to Mrs. Cooper. "If Sarah is my daughter, I will take care of her and I will make sure you are well taken care of too."

"You still operate all them computer stores?" Mrs. Cooper asked dryly.

"Yes, I do," I said proudly.

"Brother, you gots to be *real* rich, then. Where you live at? Not in the hood, I bet!" Mrs. Cooper hurled the words at me like rocks. "You probably live in the Marina district or up on Nob Hill or one of them other uppity neighborhoods with a bunch of white folks. You want your friends to know about us?"

"I live in Pacific Heights. And if Sarah is my child, I want the world to know about her," I stated.

"You got any other young'uns?" Mrs. Cooper asked. "You got a wife? What about them?"

"I don't have any other children—that I know of. Most of the family I have left still live in Houston where I grew up. I have a very beautiful wife. She's very understanding and supportive."

"I hope you still think your 'very beautiful' wife is 'understanding and supportive' when you tell her about Sarah," Mrs. Cooper quipped. "My husband left me for a girl who was working as his secretary almost thirty years ago. I'm still mad enough about it that if I ran into her on the street, I'd kick her tail from here to Timbuktu."

I wondered just how understanding and supportive Vera was going to be when I told her I'd had an affair with a teenager and possibly fathered a child. I wasn't going to say anything to her about it until the DNA test was completed. If it proved that Sarah was my child, then I'd beg Vera to forgive me. If she did, I would spend the rest of my life making this up to her.

CHAPTER 11

SARAH

I MISSED MY MAMA. SHE WAS ON MY MIND DAY AND NIGHT. AND WHEN she wasn't on my mind, Mr. Lomax was. I liked him. I would have been proud to claim him as my daddy, even if he wasn't.

Mr. Lomax had told me that it would take a while to get the results of the DNA test. We didn't hear from him until two weeks later.

Grandma Lilly and I had just come home from church that Sunday afternoon about twenty minutes before he knocked on the door.

Our apartment was located in a twenty-unit building in the crime-ridden district called Hunters Point. We lived on the fourth floor, and every window in our apartment had bars. But that still didn't stop the thieves. Our door had a dead bolt, but a thief had still pried it open one night when we were at church. He (or she) had walked off with a jelly jar full of coins, a camera that didn't work, and two packages of frozen smoked turkey necks.

I was kind of embarrassed for a rich businessman who lived in a mansion in one of the wealthiest areas in one of the world's wealthiest cities to see our tacky little apartment. The living room was only large enough to accommodate a couch and a few end tables. The small color TV we owned sat on the windowsill facing the couch. Our kitchen was just a corner by the door with a stove and a small refrigerator. Grandma Lilly had fried a catfish the night before. You could still smell it and the cabbage greens and pig ears cooking on a stove in our neighbor's apartment next door.

Mr. Lomax had a big manila envelope in his hand when I opened the door and waved him in. He looked like a high-class banker in his navy blue, pin-striped suit and white shirt and red tie. He had a nice head of hair for a man his age, even though most of it was gray and he had a couple of bald spots on the back. There was a big smile on his face as he pulled a document out of the envelope and handed it to me. I read it as fast as I could and then I started smiling too. "This . . . this DNA report says that out of a *trillion* people, you are the only one who could be my daddy," I said with a huge lump already forming in my throat. "Uh . . . I don't know how many a trillion is."

Mr. Lomax laughed. "It's more than the number of people on this planet." He laughed some more. "I'm very happy with this news."

"I . . . I . . . me too," I stuttered. I didn't know what to say next. All this time I thought my real daddy was dead, so this was a moment I had never allowed myself to even think about. "I hope you'll still be happy when you get to know me," I said, looking at my feet. We hugged and then we both started to laugh and talk at the same time. "You know, we got the same eyes!"

"Sure enough," he agreed, patting me on the back.

"Girl, what's going on out there?" Grandma Lilly yelled from the tiny bedroom we shared across the narrow hall from our bathroom. Before I could answer, she came trotting into the living room. She stopped in the middle of the floor when she saw Mr. Lomax. "What's going on out here?" she asked with her head whipping from side to side, looking from him to me.

"Mr. Lomax *is* my daddy!" I hollered, waving the piece of paper.

"Lemme see that thang!" Grandma Lilly yelled, rushing across the floor with her stroke foot and arthritic legs, stumbling like a drunken person. She snatched the document out of my hand and started to read. She moved her gnarled finger over each word and muttered under her breath, like a person who had just learned how to read. My grandmother was a real nice lady and all, but sometimes she acted real ghetto and mean. She had had a hard life and had to be a hard person in order to survive. Just like me. She looked at the paper for a couple of minutes, and then she slowly handed it back to my daddy. "Have mercy, Jesus," she wheezed. "Uh, why don't you have a seat, Mr. Lomax. I guess we need to talk." Grandma Lilly nodded toward our lumpy plaid couch. "You want something to drink? It's after the middle of the month, so all we got left is some Gatorade."

"No thanks," Daddy said to the drink. But he eased down on the couch.

"What your wife got to say about all this?" Grandma Lilly asked. She sat down on the other end of the couch, fanning her face and crossing her knotty legs like she always did when she was nervous or excited. I plopped down next to Daddy, and as soon as I did that, he put his arm around my shoulder and hugged me some more. I couldn't remember the last time I felt so special.

"I haven't told her yet," my daddy said, rubbing his knee and looking worried. "I'm going to go right home and talk to her about all of this." He stopped talking, took a deep breath, and looked at me real hard. "Sarah, I'm going to take care of you and your granny from now on. But if you don't want to have a relationship with me, I'll understand."

I gasped. "But you are my daddy! Why wouldn't I want to have a relationship with you?"

"Well, that makes me feel a whole lot better," he said.

"Me too. It'll be nice to get some help with all the bills we got," Grandma Lilly muttered. "It ain't easy raising no teenager in this day and age. This girl wants everything she sees . . ."

"You won't have to worry about that anymore, ma'am." Daddy leaned over and gave my grandmother a quick peck on the cheek that made her flinch.

My grandmother was still so mad about her husband running out on her she didn't care too much for men anymore. She wouldn't even go to male doctors, especially when it came to procedures related to the female body that she had to remove clothing for. She had not been with a man since her husband left, so she had not had sex since then. My dead stepdaddy used to tease my grandmother and tell her that all she needed was a good fuck. She'd always get madder at him for saying nasty shit like that in front of me than she would for him saying it at all.

"Whatever," Grandma Lilly said, rearing back and screwing up her face as if my daddy had just hauled off and pinched her. He looked away like he didn't notice what she did next, but I know he did. She brushed off her cheek where he had kissed her. "What do we do now?"

"I'll be meeting with my lawyer in a couple of days to revise my will. I want to do that right away so that you and Sarah will be taken care of," my daddy said. All of a sudden, a real sad look crossed his face. "I . . . I . . ." He stopped and stared at the wall. I assumed he was thinking about my mama's sudden and unexpected death. "We can be here today and gone tomorrow." He was right. I had lost eight close friends in the last four years to violence. Two of them were sister and brother, shot down like dogs in separate incidents a month apart. When I thought about my future, I didn't wonder what I'd be when I grew up. I wondered what I'd be *if* I grew up. "My brother and my sister died in accidents," he added.

"You ain't got no deadly disease or nothing, huh?" Grandma Lilly asked, looking at Daddy out of the corner of her eye. One thing I could say about old folks was that everybody expected them to say whatever was on their mind. Like little kids, people over forty just didn't know any better. "Is that why you so anxious to get involved with me and Sarah now?"

"No, I don't have a disease or anything. But I am anxious to get to know you and Sarah better as soon as possible," my daddy replied, clearing his throat, looking around. A fat roach crawled up the wall by the door, but he didn't see it. But a big fly buzzed around his head and then landed on his hand. "Uh, I guess I should be going," he said, shaking the fly off.

"Don't you want to stay for supper? I cooked some Chinese mustard greens and smothered a chicken before I went to church this morning," Grandma Lilly said, nodding toward the kitchen.

"Only if it's not too much trouble." Daddy sniffed.

"It ain't no trouble at all. We just waiting on them corn muffins to get done." Grandma Lilly got up off the couch and gave me a stern look. "Sarah, get in that kitchen and find a plate for your daddy that ain't got no cracks in it. And a clean glass so he can drink some Gatorade with his supper."

Daddy got up off the couch and stood in the kitchen doorway, still talking as Grandma Lilly and I fixed dinner. He told us how he was going to set up a trust for me and how he was going to make sure his accountant paid all our bills, rent, and everything else. He even offered to buy us a brand-new car, but my grandmother never learned to drive and I didn't have my license yet, so she told him to forget the car. After he'd told us everything he was going to do for us, he stopped talking all of a sudden and he got this weird look on his face. I thought he was having a stroke.

"I have a better idea than me paying rent on this place." He was talking so fast, he almost lost his breath. "How would you two like to live in a lavishly furnished condominium a few blocks from downtown? I am sure you'd like to move out of this dump."

I covered my mouth with my hand to keep from laughing. My grandmother's jaw dropped as she whirled around from the stove with a spatula in her hand. "Dump? Look, Mr. Perfect Negro, this dump here is my home and has been for more than *thirty* years," she growled, shaking that spatula at my daddy like she wanted to swat him with it. "I ain't going no place. Now, I'm glad you want to step up to the plate and take care of your daughter, but I don't appreciate you coming up in here insulting us!"

"I'm so sorry, ma'am. I didn't mean for that to sound as harsh as it did. I would never purposely say anything to hurt you or Sarah. It's just that . . . well, this is a violent, run-down neighborhood. I wouldn't want a goat I didn't like to live over here. I just assumed that anybody who had the chance to leave here would do so lickety-split. Last week alone three people got shot on this very street."

"Four," I corrected, my voice cracking. "Last night, the little eight-year-old boy in the front apartment on the first floor was in his bed when a bullet came through the wall from outside and hit him in the back. He might be paralyzed for life."

"My Lord!" Daddy hollered, shaking his head and rubbing the back of his neck.

I would have left Hunters Point a long time ago if I'd had the chance. I was sick and tired of living in fear. My mama and I used to live in the Mission District, which is just the Latino version of Hunters Point. Our apartment got broken into so many times we stopped locking the door. The man my mother was with then, a man from Mexico, didn't like kids. So he told her he'd marry her only if she "got rid of" me. Well, Grandma Lilly was glad to raise me. I loved her more than I loved myself and I wanted her to be happy. I swallowed hard and gave her a hopeful look. "I'd love to move away from here, Grandma Lilly," I admitted. "When that bullet came through my bedroom window last year, you said you hoped we'd be able to get up out of here before you died, remember?"

"Yeah," Grandma Lilly grunted with a wounded look on her face. "But I never thought we would." She set the spatula down on the counter and looked at my daddy. "You telling me you'd pay the rent for us to live in one of them fancy places near downtown? I used to clean for a white lady down there, two days a week, until my lumbago got so bad. I could look out her living room window right at the Golden Gate Bridge. The rent in them places must be as high as a Georgia pine tree."

"I own a condo in one of those buildings: three bedrooms, three bathrooms," my daddy told us. "You and Sarah can live in it rent-free for the rest of your lives if you want to."

"You *own* a place over there? I don't mean to be nosy, but how much do one of them condos cost?"

"Well, the one I own set me back a couple of million."

"Lord have mercy! You're going to let us live in a two-million-dollar place for nothing? Heh, heh, heh. I know God is real for sure now."

"I don't know any black folks that live in that fancy neighborhood," I threw in.

"You do now, sugar." Daddy laughed.

He was such a nice man. I couldn't wait to get to know him better. I was already proud to be his daughter.

"Well . . . I guess it would be nice for this girl here to live the good life for a change," Grandma Lilly croaked. "And I would like to know what it feels like to live in a place where I don't have to worry about no sex fiend raping me."

From the wide grin on my grandmother's face, I knew she was just as excited to move into a better place as I was.

"Uh, it's too bad I'll have to take two or three buses to get from our new address to that chicken shack I work for over here," Grandma Lilly pointed out, batting her eyelashes in Daddy's direction. "I got to work two more years before I can retire."

"No, you won't," Daddy said real fast, shaking his head. "Mrs. Cooper, you can retire right away. As a matter of fact, I insist you do just that. You've worked long and hard enough taking care of other folks' needs. It's time for somebody to take care of your needs for a change."

Right after Daddy stopped talking, Grandma Lilly looked at me and winked.

"This junk we got won't look too good in a fancy new apartment," I mentioned, hoping Daddy would take the hint and offer to buy us some new stuff.

"Like I said, the condo is furnished. Pack only the things you really need—clothes, pictures, and other personal items. I'll have some movers come over here to collect and dispose of the rest of this broken-down mess." Daddy gave my grandmother an apologetic look. "I hope I didn't sound too harsh again," he said with his hands up in the air. "I can be pretty blunt at times."

Grandma Lilly laughed. "Honey, if you going to do everything you say you going to do for us, you can be as blunt as a dull shovel for all I care." Grandma Lilly rubbed her palms together and pursed her lips. She always did that when she was happy. I hadn't seen her look this happy since she won a hundred dollars in a bingo game last year.

I laughed, too, but I was still kind of sad inside. I was afraid that my new life might not be the life I wanted. . . .

CHAPTER 12

KENNETH

My visit with Sarah and her grandmother lasted a lot longer than I thought it would. I had not enjoyed such a scrumptious meal since the last time I visited Houston, and I couldn't wait to get better acquainted with my daughter and her grandmother.

I got home around five that evening. Vera was in our bedroom taking a nap. She looked so innocent and peaceful lying on the bed on her back. For a brief moment I considered not telling her about my affair and Sarah. I had enough money to do just about anything a cheating man could do to keep his house in order. Vera didn't have to know about me taking care of Sarah and her grandmother. But the downside was that I could never have an open and honest relationship with my only child. I could never claim her in public, bring her to my house, or introduce her to my friends and family.

Vera stirred as soon as I sat down on the side of the bed. She opened her eyes when I caressed her chin. "Hello, beautiful," I greeted. "I've been thinking about you all day."

She gave me a strange look at first; then she touched my hand, which was still caressing her face. "Where have you been?" she asked with a yawn. "I was getting real worried." She sat up and stretched her arms. She wore a red see-through negligee with matching crotchless panties. And from the smell of fermented grapes on her breath, I could tell that she'd also sipped a glass or two of wine. "Why . . . what's the matter? You don't look so good." Vera felt my forehead. "Did you take your pills today?"

I nodded. "All twelve of those suckers," I said dryly.

"Good. I don't want anything to happen to you," she said with relief as she gently squeezed my arm. "I want you to be around for a very long time."

"Baby, we need to talk. It's real important," I began. My chest tightened and I wondered if I'd live through my confession. "I have something to tell you . . ." The words left a nasty taste in my mouth. I knew that everything else I said in the next few minutes was going to taste even nastier.

"What is it?" Vera's body stiffened. She pressed her lips together and blinked at me. "What's going on, Kenneth?"

"I don't know how to say this. First I want to say that if you want to leave me after I tell you, I'll understand. But I love you more than I love life and I hope you can forgive me."

"Kenneth, what did you do?" Vera didn't even sound like herself. Her voice, which was usually soft and mellow, was so hoarse and cold I thought I was talking to a stranger.

"Baby, I've done something real . . . uh . . . real bad," I fumbled.

Vera looked frightened. Tears formed in her eyes. "Well, what is it?"

"See . . . there was another woman." I almost choked on the words.

"Another woman? Kenneth, are you telling me you're having an affair?"

"Something like that," I said in a voice just above a whisper.

"Who is she?" Her voice was so soft and gentle now it scared me. "Do you love her?"

I shook my head. "I did at one time."

"But you don't love her now?"

"She's dead now."

Vera pressed her lips together again. I didn't like the look on her face now because I couldn't read it. She didn't look mad or hurt yet, so I really didn't know what was going through her mind.

"This other woman you were in love with at one time is dead?" She released the words in such a detached, mechanical manner she sounded like a lousy actress reading from a lousy script. "Did you kill her?"

The odd question caught me completely off guard and I almost laughed. "No, she died in an automobile accident." All of a sudden, I was itching in several different places. I snorted and scratched my nose and the side of my neck. But I was still itching. "Do you want the long version or the short version?"

"Give me the short version and then I'll let you know if I want to know more details." I still couldn't decide if Vera was mad or what emotion she was feeling. But she did look dazed. I had a strong feeling that I was going to be doing some serious damage control until the day I died. If Vera stayed with me, I'd let her do whatever she wanted. I wanted to keep my wife just that badly.

"I had an affair with Lois Cooper. I didn't know she was pregnant with my child when she disappeared. Maybe that's why she disappeared. Anyway, I went to her funeral and I met her mother and . . . uh . . . the child."

"She was the child in the picture that was in the newspaper?" Vera asked with her lips trembling.

"Yes. I knew when I saw that picture that the child was probably mine. She looks just like my late brother's daughter. I had a DNA test done to confirm it. Anyway, I'm going to take care of my child. I'm going to move her and her grandmother into the Davis Street condo. I'll be buying them all new clothes and everything else they need. I knew that sooner or later, you'd find out and I wanted to make sure you heard it from me first." I stopped talking and held my breath. I couldn't look Vera in the eyes. But when she touched my hand, I did.

The next few minutes were very tense. Vera cried, I cried.

"How could you do this to me, Kenneth? You . . . you bastard!" she exploded. "I've been a good wife to you! I don't deserve this!"

I opened my mouth to speak, but before I could get a word out, Vera lunged at me like a tiger. We tumbled to the floor with her on top of me. She pummeled my head with both fists and I cried even harder. Then she slapped my face, bit my hand, and beat on my chest like she was beating a bongo drum. I thought she was going to kill me. I took my punishment like a man. I didn't even try to defend myself. When she finished whupping me, I wobbled up off the floor and staggered into the bathroom. After I had pissed out what seemed like a quart of urine, I splashed some water on my face and cleaned off my wounds. I was glad that the bite marks and scratches were mostly on my lower neck and arms and other places where I wouldn't have trouble hiding them from inquiring minds. I waited a few minutes until I thought it was safe and then I went back into the bedroom. Vera was sitting on the bed, looking like a zombie. I braced myself for another attack as I eased down next to her with a cold pack on my face.

"Kenneth, I . . . I love you and . . . and I don't want to let you go," she blubbered. "I know you're only human and I know how some of these little girls behave around handsome, wealthy men like you." She leaned over and grabbed a Kleenex off the nightstand. "If you want a divorce . . ."

"A divorce? Woman, I don't want a damn divorce! I married you for life. I . . . I was a damn fool for cheating on you, and I swear to God it'll never happen again. But I have to do the right thing by my child. I want us to be a family. You know I've always wanted children, and I know how badly you want to raise a child. This may be our only chance."

Vera covered her face with her hands and sobbed very quietly for about a minute. And I felt like a piece of shit the whole time.

"Was Lois the only one?" she choked.

"Huh? Oh! Of course she was the only one! I was weak . . . I was going through that damn midlife crisis at the time, and that was the *only* reason I slipped up the way I did!" I couldn't believe how easily the lie slid out of my mouth. But my goose was already in the oven, and I didn't want to turn up the heat. The truth of the matter was, I'd been with at least two dozen women since I married Vera. "You're all I want and if you'll stay with me and forgive me, I promise I will make everything up to you."

The room got so quiet I could actually hear my sorry heart thumping against the wall of my chest.

"When will I meet your daughter?" Vera asked, her gentle tone back. Her question gave me hope.

"As soon as possible. I spent this afternoon with them, even had supper over there. They started packing before I left. I'm going to move them into the condo on Davis Street this week—if that's all right with you."

Vera sniffed and shrugged as she swiped her nose with a tissue. "I don't care. We hardly ever use the condo anymore and most of your out-of-town associates prefer hotels." She gave me a weak smile as she tossed the tissue onto the nightstand. Then she pulled me down on top of her. "Kenneth, I think we can get beyond this intact," she whispered. "We've put too much into this marriage to give up on it now."

"I'm so sorry, baby. I promise I will never cheat on you again," I whispered back. "Thank you for being such an understanding woman."

We made love that night like we'd never made love before.

CHAPTER 13

VERA

I'D BEATEN AND BITTEN KENNETH AS MUCH AS I COULD MANAGE without breaking one of my nails. After we had both stopped crying, I allowed him to pull me into his arms and tell me how "sorry" he was several more times as we lay on the bed.

I had acted appropriately for a woman who had just been told by her husband that he'd fathered a child with another woman. That much I already knew, but I was appalled that he had already decided to take care of that child and her grandmother before even discussing it with me.

After I had calmed down and composed myself, I "forgave" Kenneth. I even allowed him to fuck me so that he would think everything was going to be all right. And it would be for me. I was going to make sure of that. From the moment he told me that I was going to have to put up with his whore's child, I started planning my future. And it was not going to include Kenneth or his bastard child if I could help it!

Ten minutes after Kenneth had rolled his sorry ass off me, he was snoring like a moose. He was the only person I knew who could sleep through a tidal wave. I covered my ears so I wouldn't have to listen to the annoying way he ground his teeth in his sleep. A few more minutes later, I took a long hot shower. After I'd reapplied my makeup and fixed my hair, I slid into a pair of pants and a blouse. I left him a note on the nightstand to let him know that I needed to be away from him for a day or so. Then I crept downstairs.

I could hear Delia in the kitchen cleaning up after the lavish dinner she had prepared and served. She was humming some silly-sounding song in Spanish, the way she always did when she was in the kitchen alone.

"Delia, my cousin and his wife are coming to stay with us for a while. Get one of the bedrooms on the second floor ready for them."

"*Sí*, Senora Vera," Delia replied with a puzzled look on her face as I left the room.

I eased out the front door and ran to my BMW that I had parked in the driveway.

It was around eight o'clock when I arrived at Tony's place, a couple of hours after Kenneth had dropped his bombshell in my lap.

"I am going to make him pay through his asshole! I will never let him forget this!" I started hollering as soon as Tony opened the door for me and waved me into his living room. He cleared off his cluttered couch and trotted to his kitchen with me following close behind him, stepping on dirty clothes on the floor. No matter how often I tidied up his apartment when I visited, it always looked like a train wreck when I returned. Dirty clothes, dirty dishes, fast-food containers, and empty beer bottles were everywhere. There was no place to sit in the kitchen, so I stood in the middle of the floor waving my arms and stomping my foot. "I can't believe that man! He's going to pay for this!"

"Calm down, baby," Tony said. He lifted a shot glass off the counter and handed it to me. "I just poured this for myself, but it looks like you need it more than I do."

I snatched the glass out of his hand and gulped down the tequila in less than three seconds—and I didn't even like strong-ass alcohol like this shit unless it was in a margarita.

"Now tell me what the problem is? I have never seen you this upset before."

"He's got a daughter!" I screeched. "He's going to parade her to the world, making *me* look like a fool!"

"Who's got a daughter?"

"Kenneth. He fucked some little hoochie coochie bitch from the hood and got her skank ass pregnant. Oh, it would have been one thing if the bitch had had some class, some education, some breeding. I could have gotten over that a lot easier and sooner. But he had to get him some of that nasty Hunters Point pussy! It's a wonder he hasn't given me AIDS!"

"How did you find out?" I was glad to see that Tony had poured himself another drink. And I was glad to see that he was already half naked. He had removed his shirt, so all he had on were his pants and they were already unzipped. His crotch had such a huge bulge it looked like he had stuffed a large fist down his pants. I was glad to see that too. I was going to need a vigorous workout to let off all the steam I had in me.

"He told me to my face a couple of hours ago! I thought I would faint dead away! And I beat the dog shit out of his black ass!"

"Baby, you didn't know nothing about him having a child at all?"

"No, I didn't know!" There was no reason in the world for me to tell Tony that I had known about Sarah since before she was born. That was one piece of information I would take with me to the grave. That and the fact that I'd been supporting that child all these years.

"Shit! That's some knee-deep shit, if you ask me. Is he still seeing this woman?"

"Oh no. That heifer died in a car wreck a couple of weeks ago."

Tony froze. A profoundly sad look slid across his face and covered it like a veil. I knew that he was thinking about his four-year-old daughter who had died in a wreck with his ex last year. "What about the baby? Did she die with her mama?"

Unfortunately, she didn't! was what I wanted to say. But because of Tony's tragedy and the fact that I didn't want him to think I was that insensitive, I said, "Thank God that child didn't die with her mama. And now I'm going to have to deal with *that child* for the rest of my life! SHIT!"

"Uh, I know you're upset, but you don't have any reason to be mad with the child. She's an innocent victim."

I rotated my neck and gave him a hot look. "Whose side are you on?"

"I'm on your side, sugar," Tony assured me with a hug. "At least you didn't have to see that child all these years." He snorted and cleared his throat. "But, uh, will you and Kenneth be taking her in to raise now? You've been telling me for the longest time how desperate he is to be a daddy."

I almost choked on my tongue. "Hell no we're not going to raise that child! She's a teenager now and Kenneth will support her, but there is no way in the world *I'm* going to raise another woman's child that she got by fucking my husband! She lives with the grandmother."

"Oh. Well, I'm glad to hear that. That'll lighten your load, I guess."

"I don't know about that. Just knowing about it is a load that's way too heavy for me. He'll be bringing her to the house and I'll have to look at her, talk to her, and act like I care about her! And on top of that, Kenneth is moving her and the grandmother into the condo on Davis!"

Tony's face looked like it had suddenly turned to stone. "I thought you told me I was going to move into that Davis condo eventually. I'm ready to get up out of this pooh-butt shoebox I'm in now."

"I was going to let you have the condo, baby. You know I don't lie to you. But I'll hook you up with another place. One even nicer and bigger than the one on Davis! I'm going to make that motherfucker sorry he was born. By the time I get through spending his money, he'll be panhandling."

I slept at Tony's place that night. I was still too angry to be around Kenneth, and I was too drunk to get behind the wheel.

I got home on Monday afternoon, after I'd treated Tony to a shopping spree in several upscale men's clothing stores and signed a year's lease on a three-bedroom, lavishly furnished apartment for him near Fisherman's Wharf. Except for our housekeeper, the house was empty.

"Did Mr. Lomax go into his office today, Delia?" I asked as I limped into the kitchen. I immediately went to the refrigerator and poured myself a glass of tomato juice. I had a hangover that wouldn't quit and I was aching in several places throughout my body. After fucking Tony a few hours after I'd fucked Kenneth last night, the insides of my thighs felt like they were on fire. When I was twenty-one, screwing more than one man within hours of each other didn't bother me as much as it did now at the age of fifty.

"Yez, yez, *senora.* Senor Lomax go to office early in morning," Delia said in her heavy Salvadoran accent. "I fix you a lunch?"

"No, I'm not hungry. And when you get the room ready for my cousin and his wife, make sure you put all new linen on the beds," I ordered.

"*Sí.* Right away, senora," Delia said, no questions asked. As soon as she left the kitchen, I called up my cousin Cash at work. He answered on the third ring.

"We need to talk," I told him.

"What about?"

"Are you ready to move into a better location?"

"I've been ready to move into a better location since the day I got back here from the military. But I'm barely able to pay the rent where I'm at now. Why?"

"With Kenneth gone so much, I get real lonely over here sometimes. How would you and your wife like to move in with Kenneth and me? This mansion is way too big for just two people and . . . I'd like to have you closer to me, cuz. I did promise your mama I'd keep an eye on you when you moved out here." Poor Cash. He was the family fool. Without me looking out for him, there was no telling where he would be now. He looked like a frog and I was the only family member who made him feel special and he did the same for me. I rewarded his allegiance by making it possible for him to enjoy some of the benefits of Kenneth's money. In turn, he did whatever I told him to do. Last month when I lost control of my car and knocked over a mailbox, Cash climbed behind the wheel and took the blame. His license got suspended for thirty days, but I bought him a brand-new Ford Bronco for helping me out.

"It took you long enough to ask me. I've been in Frisco for almost twenty years."

"Don't get cute with me! It's better late than never. Now do you want to move in here or not?"

"Would I like to live in that palace? Woman, do a bear shit in the woods? What the hell is going on, Vera? I'd give my left ball to live in a mansion like the one you and Kenneth live in!"

"I'm going to get one of the bedrooms on the second floor ready with my own hands—and you know how much I hate doing housekeeping of any kind."

"Vera, you kidding me, right? What brought this on? When we asked you to let us rent a room in the mansion last year, you almost had a heart attack."

"Forget all that. I want you and Collette to move into the mansion as soon as possible. Start packing up your shit tonight."

Cash mumbled something unintelligible under his breath. "You trying to get back at Kenneth for something," he accused. "What's going on, Vera?"

"That motherfucker had a child with that Lois Cooper, that bitch who used to be his secretary. Now he's moving the child and her grandmother into the Davis Street condo we own."

"Holy shit!"

"Did you know about him and that bitch?"

"Who, me? Hell no, I didn't know a damn thing! You know I would have put a bug in your ear."

I knew my cousin was probably lying, and I didn't blame him. He was not about to jeopardize his relationship with Kenneth and lose his job. Just like I had not been stupid enough to blow up my marriage when I first found out about Lois and forced her into that arrangement. For all I knew, if I had handled that situation wrong, Kenneth might have left me for her!

"I know you would have told me if you knew, Cash. I can count on you."

"That's right. I don't get involved in nothing but what Kenneth tells me to do on this job. I need my job," he stated emphatically, proving my point. "What the brother did was some stupid shit." Cash was my mother's oldest sister's only child. I'd taken him under my wing when he was still in grade school. He had learned a lot from me. When it came to the art of deception, he was almost as devious as I was. Like me, he worked both sides of the street at the same time. And right now it was to his advantage for him to remain silent about his role in the mess Kenneth had created. He knew that as long as he respected me and did whatever I told him to do, I would never "encourage" Kenneth to fire him.

"Don't be no fool, cuz. Don't do nothing stupid. Not with the prenup you signed. I'd hate to see you going back to work for another one of them fly-by-night temp agencies like you did back in Houston. Please tell me you won't be divorcing Kenneth."

I hesitated for a few moments. "Divorce my foot! What's wrong with you, man? I'm pissed as hell for sure. But like they say, my mama didn't raise no fool. I've got a damn good thing going for myself and I want to keep it going."

"That makes two of us," Cash agreed.

CHAPTER 14

SARAH

THE DAY ME AND MY GRANDMOTHER MOVED INTO MY DADDY'S CONDO was the happiest day of my life since my mama died, and it was also the saddest. Some of my friends were happy for me; some were not. I couldn't believe how the people I'd known all my life could do so much hating.

"I guess you think you better than the rest of us now, huh?" Debbie Martin asked, looking around the spacious living room in the condo. She and her brother Marcus had taken the bus over that Saturday morning in February just to be nosy.

"I don't know why you think that," I snapped. I noticed how Marcus kept walking from room to room and looking at all the new stuff we had. He was nineteen and had been in and out of jail since he was fourteen. His specialty was breaking and entering. He had broken into half of the apartments in our old building. Last year he stole a blue suit from the man in the apartment next to ours. Then he had the nerve to wear the same suit to the man's birthday party a few days later. But Marcus had a few morals. He didn't rob elderly people, little kids, disabled people, or his close friends. When he knew of a good thing, he told his thug friends and they did the robbing. I didn't have to worry about him setting us up to get ripped off. Our new building had a security guard on duty twenty-four hours a day, cameras everywhere you looked, and an alarm system. That's why I didn't mind him casing our place. We were on the eighteenth floor anyway and unless his friends could fly or crawl up the side of our building, I wasn't worried. But I was worried about the way Debbie was talking.

"Girl, I can smell the money your daddy spent on all this stuff," she went on. "I don't even know how to act around you now." Debbie didn't try to hide the fact that she was jealous. The pinched look on her face and the way she kept rolling her eyes said it all. "I bet don't nothing but white folks live up in this bitch-ass *palace*," she added nastily, walking around the room, lifting pillows off the couch and feeling the drapes.

"So? I had white friends before. You and me both used to hang out with white girls," I reminded her.

"Bah! The ones we used to hang with was rednecks. Living with the kind of muckety-muck peckerwoods that live in buildings like this is a whole different ballgame. The first time something get stole, they'll be accusing you and calling you a nigger."

I rolled my eyes and shook my head. "I'll worry about that when and if it happens," I said with a laugh.

"Dang! Sarah C, you done come waaaay up in the world!" Marcus exclaimed, strutting back into the room. "That bathroom is hella cool! It's so spick-and-span, smell so rosy, I was surprised my pee didn't melt the commode!"

I was glad when Grandma Lilly came into the room from taking her bath in the bathroom connected to her bedroom. We had *three* bathrooms now. I was also glad my grandmother had on one of the fancy robes she had bought when my daddy took us shopping a few days ago.

"Debbie, Marcus, it's time for you kids to get to stepping," my grandmother advised, looking at her new watch. "You two don't need to be out in this neighborhood past a certain hour drawing attention. Especially you, Marcus. Look at all them tattoos up and down your neck! These white folks will call the cops for sure."

"All right, Miss Cooper. Thanks for inviting us over here," Debbie said in a wounded voice. "This is the kind of place I can get real comfortable in," she added, looking around the room some more.

Debbie and Marcus shuffled toward the door, and I walked

them out to the elevator. They gave me a hug and each one "borrowed" a hundred dollars from me. My daddy had already started giving me a huge weekly allowance, so my friends expected to share it with me. Every time I got with my friends now, they expected me to pay for everything and I did, from a trip to the movies to a shopping spree in all of the high-end stores in several different malls all in the same day. For one thing, I didn't want them to think I was stingy. And for another thing, I didn't want to lose my connection to the world I knew best. Of the few people Daddy had introduced me to so far, I didn't feel comfortable with them at all. I'd met some of the people who worked for him, some of his friends, but I hadn't met his wife yet.

"My wife is a lovely woman. But she still needs a little more time to get used to this," Daddy had told me last night when I asked him for the tenth time when he was going to let me and Grandma Lilly meet his wife. "We'll all sit down and enjoy a wonderful down-home dinner together at my house." I noticed he always got a dreamy look on his face when he mentioned his wife.

I wasn't really that anxious to meet the woman, but I knew that the sooner I did the better. I didn't expect her to welcome me into her life with open arms after what my mama had done to her. But I was going to try my best to be nice and friendly. Anyway, I was a lot more interested in seeing Daddy's big house than I was his wife. I think my grandmother felt the same way.

"I'll be glad when your daddy's wife is ready to meet us. I can't wait to tell the folks at bingo about your daddy's mansion," Grandma Lilly had said more than once.

Grandma Lilly never got the chance to see my daddy's mansion or meet the "lovely woman" Daddy was so crazy about. Three days before we were supposed to do that, my beloved grandmother went to sleep and never woke up. I didn't know she was already dead before I returned to school that Tuesday morning in February, the day after the President's Day holiday. We'd only been in our new home a couple of weeks. When I got home that night around eight (I'd treated some friends to a movie and dinner after school) and found her still in bed, I knew immediately that something was wrong. My hands were shaking so hard I kept dropping the telephone when I attempted to call my daddy. A woman answered.

"Is this Mrs. Lomax?" I asked in a loud voice. I knew Daddy had a housekeeper and since I'd never spoken to my new stepmother, I didn't know her voice.

"Yes, this is Mrs. Lomax."

"Um, I'd like to speak to Mr. Lomax, please."

"Who are you and why are you calling here for my husband?"

Since this lady sounded so gruff, I lowered my voice to a whimper. "Uh . . . I'm his daughter, ma'am."

"Oh," she said. She didn't sound so gruff now. But she sounded disappointed.

"I need to talk to my daddy right away. It's real important," I bleated. My stepmother didn't say another word. She didn't even give me a chance to explain why I was calling. About a minute later, my daddy was on the line.

"Lomax speaking. How can I help you?" he said, sounding distant and businesslike. I guess his wife didn't even tell him that it was *me* calling!

"Daddy, it's me," I sobbed. "Grandma Lilly won't wake up."

"Sarah? Is your grandmother ill?"

"I don't know. I just got home a little while ago and it looks like she didn't get out of bed today. She's just laying there with her eyes closed. And . . . and she's real cold and stiff, and she's not breathing."

"Oh my God! Don't you move! I'll be right there!"

CHAPTER 15

VERA

I HAD PUT OFF MEETING SARAH AS LONG AS I COULD. BUT WHEN KENneth brought her to the house the night her grandmother died, I had no choice. I groaned when I saw her suitcases. My finding out that she existed had been traumatic enough. Her moving in with us meant that I'd have to see her every day, talk to her every day, and worst of all, be her "mother" every day. This whole mess had become unspeakable and unbearable. I didn't know how I was going to get through this latest development. How I managed to smile at her was a mystery to me. But I did. I even hugged her as soon as she entered the living room.

"Sarah, I've been so anxious to meet you," I declared. I had to hold my breath to keep from smelling that loud cheap hairspray she had saturated her hair with. With her thick curly brown hair and her boxy, corduroy jumper and flat-heeled loafers, she looked like a black Orphan Annie. Why she was dressed in such a pitiful outfit was a mystery to me. What I couldn't understand was with all the money Kenneth was giving her these days, why was she still shopping in dollar stores?

"Yeah," she muttered, giving me a distant look.

"It's just that I've been so busy and sick these past few weeks," I lied. Every time Kenneth had attempted to arrange a meeting, I'd feigned one ailment after another. And he didn't dare dispute my claim. He didn't want to lose me (and Lord knows I didn't want to lose him), so he bent over backward to keep me happy.

Having Cash and his wife under the same roof now gave me more leverage. Whenever a dispute came up between me and Kenneth, they took my side and Kenneth backed down real quick. He knew he had to if he wanted to keep me happy. That was why he didn't even bat an eye when I told him I was thinking about bringing my cousin Bohannon Harper up from Houston so he could work at one of the stores. Cash and Bo were about ten years younger than me, but we'd always been close. I was the big sister they had always wanted and they were the brothers I used to pray for. Cash was a jackass, but Bo was a sweet, hardworking man who was just as easy to manipulate as Cash. That was fine for me, but other people took advantage of Bo's easygoing manner too. His wife, Gladys, was a greedy bitch who had him working two jobs to keep her happy. From the complaints I had heard from my poor cousin, even that wasn't working out. I had to do something for him.

The more of my family members I had around me—the acceptable ones, of course—the easier it was going to be for me to deal with Kenneth's child. Now that Kenneth had put his daughter in his will, I had to work overtime to make sure she didn't get what was mine. But last night when I called up Bo and asked him again if he wanted to move to California and work for Kenneth, he told me his wife had suddenly become a "changed woman" and he wanted to stay in Houston to work on his marriage. "I appreciate your generous offer, though, cuz. And I appreciate how you always put family first," he told me before we ended our conversation.

I used to look forward to family affairs. But that was a long time ago. Now that I had an unfaithful husband and an inconvenient stepdaughter, the word *family* had become like a double-edged sword in my book. I would never look at family the way I used to. That's why it was so important for me to keep Cash and Bo in my life.

But Kenneth and Sarah were not the only family members I resented these days. I didn't keep in touch too much with most of my blood relatives either, especially my sisters. Those jealous hussies couldn't stand the fact that I'd married a wealthy man, and they were still struggling just to make ends meet. It didn't matter how generous I was to them. They were never satisfied. Last year when I went to Houston, I bought my baby sister Darla a brand-new Altima so she would have a way to go out and look for a job. She let her man talk her into using her car to go visit his mama in Chicago, and he never returned. Since she had let the insurance lapse and she had put the boyfriend's name on the pink slip, there was nothing she could do. The car was his and she had to go back to riding her bike or using public transportation. When I refused to buy her another car, she stopped speaking to me. My other sisters eventually stopped speaking to me when I stopped sending them designer outfits and money. So now the only family members I helped were the ones who were still loyal to me.

Six months ago, when I went home for my mother's funeral, two of my sisters didn't even show up to pay their respects. Nellie, my middle sister, moseyed into the church twenty minutes late. She started whispering into her cell phone as soon as she plopped her bony ass down on the pew next to me. Not once did she shed a tear, and she didn't turn her phone off until the pallbearers had hauled our mother's coffin out to the hearse. That really pissed me off.

After my mother's funeral, I decided I didn't want to attend another one any time soon unless I had no choice. The minute Kenneth told me that Sarah's grandmother had suddenly passed, I knew that this was one I wouldn't be able to get out of.

"Sarah, I am so sorry about your grandmother," I told her with my arms still around her. "I only wish I could have met her before she died."

Sarah exhaled and moved back a few steps. "I wish you could have met her too." She was talking to me but looking at her daddy.

"Uh, Sarah, your stepmother has had a very busy schedule lately and she's been a little sick," Kenneth blubbered, mopping sweat off his face with a white handkerchief. "But she's feeling much better now, so I'm sure she's going to rearrange a few things on her schedule. Then she can spend time with you and help you get settled in." He paused and forced a smile. "Now let's get you upstairs and unpacked so you can pick out something to wear to your granny's funeral on Saturday."

Now here I was sitting on the front pew just a few feet from that old woman's casket. I had only looked at her a few times, and that had been all I could stand. Nothing freaked me out like being in the presence of a dead body. I couldn't believe how many people actually touched that old woman's remains. And a few even had the nerve to lean down and kiss her—even Sarah! I couldn't tell you what all that preacher babbled about or what songs that sorry off-key choir sang. It was all gibberish to me. My mind was a thousand miles away. Well, actually, my mind was only a few miles away. I was wondering what Tony was doing across town. I glanced at my watch and let out a loud sigh.

"Are you all right, sweetheart? You look uncomfortable," Kenneth whispered.

"I'm fine. But you know how I feel about funerals," I whispered back.

Sarah occupied the spot on the other side of Kenneth, boohooing up a storm. I had been crying a lot, too, but for a different reason. Having that child living in my house was going to be the biggest challenge of my life. Every time I looked at her, I would be reminded of Kenneth's betrayal.

CHAPTER 16

VERA

JUST WHEN I THOUGHT THINGS COULDN'T GET ANY WORSE, THEY DID. First of all, I was extremely disappointed that Bo was not going to move to California. He was a smart man but docile enough for me to keep him under control. I had manipulated him and Cash since they were toddlers. If Bo lived in San Francisco and worked for Kenneth, he could help me keep Kenneth and all of that money the business was making under control. And since I had no intentions of working for Kenneth (or anybody else for that matter) so I could keep an eye on him myself, I decided that Bo would be the next best thing.

One of the things racing around in my mind during Sarah's grandmother's funeral was my telephone conversation with Bo the night before and how stupid he had sounded talking about how his wife had changed. That woman had been fucking him over for years. Just last week when he and I spoke on the telephone, he was threatening to kill her! The more I thought about it, the more pissed off I got.

Then, after that old woman's funeral, two of Sarah's hoochie-coochie friends crawled into the limo with me and Kenneth and Sarah because they wanted to see Sarah's new home. Their names went in one of my ears and out the other; I just thought of them as Hoochie Mama One and Hoochie Mama Two.

"I want to see what kind of house gots *eight* bedrooms," Hoochie Mama One hollered. This one had spent most of the time at the funeral standing in the back of the church listening to her Walkman and flirting with a boy with several gold teeth and his hair in cornrows.

"I feel you," Hoochie Mama Two yelled back. Both of these bums wore outfits and hairdos I had only seen in nightclubs: tight skirts; see-though, low-cut blouses; fishnet stockings; and stiletto heels. Their weaves looked like they had been attached to their heads with staples.

I was horrified when one said to me, "Where you get your weave done at?"

"I don't have a hair weave," I snapped, patting the side of my hair. Yes, I did have a hair weave, but since mine looked so much better than theirs, I refused to admit to it.

"Well, who be doing your hair?" the same one asked, giving me a suspicious look.

"I go to Pierre at Tres Chic," I bragged. I was one of the few black women that Pierre Bardot—one of the most famous hairdressers in Northern California—worked with. Not because he didn't like to deal with black folks but because I was one of the few black women who could afford his prices.

"Ain't that some kind of French?" I was so detached from these two hoodlums I didn't even know which one was speaking now.

Kenneth sat facing me, looking disgusted and amused at the conversation I'd been dragged into. Sarah's head was on his shoulder. Every time one of her crude friends said something, Kenneth looked at me and rolled his eyes. I was glad to see that he appeared to be as annoyed with them as I was. Now, because of Sarah, kids like these two were going to be in my presence on a regular basis.

I was elated when the limo stopped in front of the mansion. I ignored the two hoodlums gasping and oohing and aahing like they'd just landed in Disneyland for the first time.

Kenneth had a headache, so he went upstairs to lie down as soon as we got inside. Sarah was grieving so hard she had a headache too. All she wanted to do was sit on the plush blue velvet living room couch with a long face. It was up to me to "entertain" the two hoochies, and that was one thing I was not too thrilled about. When I left Houston, I thought I was through dealing with people like these and their uncouth behavior. Now here it was again, in my beautiful mansion!

"Would you girls like some tea?" I asked, forcing myself to keep the fake smile on my face.

"*Tea*?" Hoochie One snickered, looking toward the bar on the opposite side of the room. "My grandmama don't even drink tea. You ain't got no Pepsi?"

"And what y'all got up in here to eat?" Hoochie Two wanted to know. She repeatedly turned her ashy neck from side to side like a marionette, looking around the living room at the antique furniture and original paintings that I'd picked out myself right after I moved in with Kenneth. "This is the first funeral I went to where they didn't have no real good stuff like fried chicken and some greens and corn bread. That's what we served at my baby daddy's funeral last month." She shook her head and mumbled more complaints under her breath.

"Whoever heard of black folks serving them itty-bitty ham squares and cheese sandwiches at a funeral in the first place?" Hoochie One complained.

I had helped Kenneth make the funeral arrangements. Had I left everything up to him, he would have ordered fried chicken and greens and corn bread. He had protested when I suggested cheese sandwiches and ham squares. But like always, I had gotten my way this time too.

I had given Delia the day off. I excused myself to go get a couple of soft drinks and some ham and cheese sandwiches that I'd asked her to make the night before.

Sarah offered to show her friends the rest of the house. They were so loud I could hear them even after I had entered the kitchen. Now that they were out of sight, I couldn't tell which one was doing the talking at all now. *"I ain't never seen no spiral staircase like the one up in this motherfucker!"* They kept babbling about how "cool" or "hella sharp" this or that was and asking how much things cost.

"What bus do we take to get home?" Hoochie One asked, walking back into the living room with her shoes in her hand. Her heavy thigh bumped against one of the end tables by the couch, almost knocking one of my exquisite ivory ashtrays to the floor.

"Bus?" I said the word like it was obscene. I would travel by skateboard before I got on a bus. "It's been more than thirty years since I rode on a bus. I don't know how they run or even where the bus stops are in this neighborhood," I replied, setting the ashtray on the mantel above the fire place.

"Dang!" the hoochies yelled at the same time.

"Can't we give them a ride home or get Daddy's chauffeur to take them home in the town car?" Sarah asked in a small voice. She was looking down at the floor when I whirled around to give her one of my meanest looks. But both hoochies saw it, too, and I guess that was enough for them to get the message.

"We can walk them nine or ten blocks to the bus stop," Hoochie One sneered.

By the time they left, stumbling out the door in those four-inch stilettos like two drunken streetwalkers, I had a headache. The insides of my nostrils burned from the unholy stench of their cheap cologne. I sprayed the entire room and the seats they had occupied with air freshener.

I was glad when Sarah got up off the couch and went to her room to continue her grieving. And I was glad that Kenneth was still upstairs lying down. I moved to the kitchen where I sat down in a chair at the large round red oak table that I'd ordered from an exclusive furniture store in Pebble Beach last month. It even had a lazy Susan in the center like the tables featured in some of my favorite old movies. We ate our informal meals here. Dinner was always served in our spacious dining room, which was located on the other side of the living room. I sat in my seat enjoying a glass of wine, going over the unpleasant events that I had endured on this gloomy day.

About an hour later, Cash and his wife, Collette, wandered in from their weekly movie date. Cash and I were first cousins and I loved him to death, but he was as oafish as they came. He looked like a dark brown frog, but his short, stout, pecan-colored wife looked even worse. She had a wide flat face, beady black eyes, and a nose that resembled a frozen meatball. The only attractive thing about her was her thick black hair. She practically kept the women who braided hair in business.

"How was the funeral?" Collette wanted to know, dropping down into a chair across from me. They had come in through the kitchen door. Each one was clutching a bottle of beer. Cash, still ghetto to the bone, was chomping on a hot link wrapped in a napkin.

"Pure torture," I moaned, rubbing my forehead with the balls of my thumbs. Then I told them about Sarah's two visitors and how much they had irritated me. "I'm so glad you two moved in here. I'm going to need both of your shoulders to cry on from time to time now. Otherwise, Sarah and her friends just might drive me crazy."

"Don't you worry about nothing, cuz. You know I always got your back," Cash assured me, giving me a warm look. He set his half-eaten hot link down on the top of the lazy Susan and gave it a few twirls, something you'd expect only a very young child to enjoy.

"And me too," Collette said, wiping beer suds off her lips. I liked my cousin's wife. She had been raised in a middle-class neighborhood in Long Beach. But she'd hung out a lot in Watts and Compton, so she was very much aware of the behavior of folks in the ghetto. She knew how I felt.

"I hope Sarah's friends don't come around here too often. We'll have to keep our eyes on them when they do and make sure they don't walk off with anything." A frightened look suddenly crossed Collette's face. She looked toward the ceiling. "Since we're on the subject, I'm going to lock my bedroom door from now on as long as that girl lives here. I am not even going to let my purse out of my sight when she's around or when any of her friends come to visit."

"I'm more worried about Sarah's homies doing a home invasion, hog-tying us, and cleaning us out," Cash added. "But I got something for them if they break in while I'm home." He lifted his denim jacket and revealed a gun in the waist of his jeans that I didn't know he owned.

"I hope you never have to use that damn thing," I gasped. "Uh, have you ever used it?"

"Not yet. But if I have to protect what's mine, I won't have no trouble doing whatever I have to do. I'll even kill me some niggers if they get out of line with me." Cash laughed but I knew he was serious. He had come a long way from the street gang in Houston he had belonged to when he was a teenager. But he still had some gangster blood in him, which was why I felt safer with him out in public than I did with Kenneth.

"Cash, have you ever killed anybody?" I asked.

"Yep. I blew away a few of them Muslim bad boys while I was stationed in the Middle East," he boasted.

I shook my head. "I didn't mean when you were in the marines."

"Oh, you mean around here?" Cash vigorously shook his head. "Oh no. I ain't never had no reason to hurt nobody here. But like I just told you, I'd kill me some niggers if I had to."

Cash's declaration stunned me. I had no idea that my cousin had it in him to be so cold-blooded. If he thought that he could kill somebody if he had to, I wondered how far I would go *if I had to.*

The room remained silent for a few moments.

Collette looked at Cash and frowned. Then she turned to me and shrugged. "Oh well. Look on the bright side of that girl being here, Vera. She'll be eighteen in three years, so she can get her own place. Or maybe she'll get caught up in the crossfire during a drive-by while she's roaming the streets with her thug friends and get blown away."

My mouth flew open. I was so taken aback by what Collette had just said, and the coldness in her voice, that it took me a few moments to respond. "Collette, that's an ominous thing to say."

I was glad to hear that Cash felt the same way. "It sure enough is." There was a concerned look on his face as he stared at Collette. I decided that maybe he wasn't so cold-blooded after all. "I'd hate to see the girl get herself killed. She done had enough misery in her life. She lost her mama and her granny. Maybe she'll find a husband real soon. Then she'll be his problem."

My breath got trapped in my throat. I thought I was having a panic attack. Somehow I managed to contain myself. "Now that's another thing we'll have to deal with—her men! Lord knows what kind of porch monkeys she's going to have coming to this house!" I shrieked. The thought of brooding young punks swaggering into my house with gold teeth, gold chains, nose rings, cornrows, and baggy clothes sent shivers up my spine. I never thought I'd have to deal with a problem of this magnitude. "If she's not already pregnant, it's just a matter of time before she becomes another baby mama or worse."

"Vera, I feel so sorry for you. You got a mess on your hands now," Collette decided, giving me a sympathetic look.

"That's true," I agreed. "But I don't care what I have to do, I am not going to let Kenneth's child ruin my future."

CHAPTER 17

SARAH

I DON'T KNOW WHAT MADE ME CHOOSE THE BEDROOM THAT WAS directly above the kitchen. But it was a good thing I did. For one thing, it had a great view of the Golden Gate Bridge. Even though my daddy's mansion was beautiful and very expensive and full of fancy furniture, it was an old house. It had one of those old-fashioned air ducts on the wall close to the floor near the side of my bed. The vent had to be opened and closed by hand. When I stood close enough to the air duct and opened the vent, I could hear the conversations taking place in the kitchen. If I crouched down and put my ear real close to the open vent, I could hear even better. That's how I found out just how Vera and Cash and Collette felt about me.

Grandma Lilly had just been buried a few hours earlier and since I believed in ghosts and stuff, I was sure her spirit was still near me. She had to have heard what Vera and those fools said about me, too, so she must have rolled over in her grave. I wanted to go downstairs and tell all three of them what I thought about them and that they could kiss my black ghetto ass! But I managed to control myself. I didn't like being in this mansion any more than they wanted me in it. But it was my daddy's home too. And because of him, it was now my home. However, if I had had someplace else to go, I would have packed up my shit and left that night.

I was glad I had only three years to go to reach eighteen so I could be on my own. I had never given much thought to going to college before, and I didn't think I was going to change my mind about that. It was a dream that I had given up on a long time ago. Very few kids in my old neighborhood dreamed that big. The ones who didn't get killed along the way got dead-end jobs or had a bunch of babies and got on welfare and did whatever else they had to do to make it. I didn't want to have any babies until I got married. The five boys that I'd already had sex with, beginning when I was thirteen, hated to use condoms. But I had told them all, "No condom, no nookie." And just to make sure I was doubly protected, I was on the pill too. And I was going to stay on it until I was ready to be a "baby mama."

My new bedroom, done up mostly in pink and white, had a lot of other cool stuff. I had a queen-size bed, a TV, a computer on a desk, and a closest full of new clothes. Even with all of that and my daddy paying so much attention to me, I didn't feel comfortable in this new place. I felt more like an abandoned baby in a basket that somebody had dropped off on a doorstep like in the movies. I slept less than four hours that night. I couldn't stop thinking about what Vera and those other two assholes had said about me.

I realized just how phony Vera was the next morning when she knocked on my door. I was still in bed. She entered my room before I could even respond.

"Good morning, sweetie," she purred, so much warmth in her voice a rock would have melted on her tongue. Even if I had not heard her trashing me last night, I still would have been able to tell she was as fake as the color of her partially fake hair. "I know you must still be tired from all you went through yesterday, but if you're up to it, breakfast is ready. Your daddy told me how much you like grits and hot links, so I had Delia go to the market this morning and stock up on them."

"Uh, I'm about to get up," I muttered, sitting up. I glanced at the clock on the nightstand. It was only 8:00 a.m. and this wench had on more makeup than Ronald McDonald. And she was dressed like she was going to be in a fashion show. "You look real nice, Miss Vera. You going somewhere?"

"Uh-huh. I have an important appointment this morning," she told me, looking at her watch.

Both of us remained silent for a few seconds. Finally I shrugged. "Daddy said something about a private school for me?"

"Oh that. Well, he thought it might be a good idea for you to get away from California for a while and clear your head. You've been through so much the past few weeks—losing your mother, your stepdaddy, and your grandmother so close together and now having to adjust to a whole new lifestyle."

That bitch! I knew she was lying. Daddy had already told me that *she* had suggested that I go to a boarding school because it would help "clear" my head. My head was already clear. I knew what time it was and it was not the time for me to act a fool and say what was really on my mind. Vera had a plan. Well, so did I. I was going to prove to her that she was wrong about me. I wasn't going to cuss her out or do any other crazy thing like she probably expected me to do. But I was still going to associate with some of my old friends and I was still going to fuck the boys I wanted to fuck. I hoped that by the time I turned eighteen, Vera will have changed her mind about me so I wouldn't feel so uncomfortable when I was around her. But I was not going to let her break my spirit. I was prepared to stand my ground, and I didn't care about the fact that she was my daddy's wife. I was his blood and as far as I was concerned, that gave me more leverage.

The first couple of weeks in the mansion were the hardest. Vera was like an angel to my face. But when she and Cash and Collette got together in the kitchen, they talked about me and the few old friends I still associated with like dogs. They were on a roll today, talking so fast and loud they sounded like they were speaking in tongues.

"I thought you said she was going away to some boarding school," Collette spat. That was followed by a loud belch, so I knew they were drinking too.

"She is. I'm working on the arrangements now," Vera mumbled. She was usually too demure to belch in front of people, but this time she let out one that sounded like it had come from a buffalo. "Excuse me!" she giggled.

"A boarding school in another country, I hope," Cash guffawed.

"No, it's in Iowa. Kenneth had suggested one in Switzerland, but I don't have the patience to wait several weeks for her to get a passport. I want her little ass out of my house now. It's just as well she's not going to Switzerland or somewhere else out of the country. That ignorant little bitch would be totally out of her element in a foreign school. Can you imagine her over there asking them to fry her some chicken wings?" Vera howled. "Lord have mercy. I took her to lunch at La Salle's Bistro last week and she had the nerve to order a cheeseburger!"

"La Salle's? You took a jigaboo like Sarah to a place like *that*? A piece of toast cost ten dollars up in that motherfucker! I can't imagine what a cheeseburger costs," Cash hollered.

"Thirty-five dollars is what that damn thing cost!" Vera screamed.

I rose up from off the floor and closed the vent, so mad I wanted to cuss out the world. I stumbled to my bed and flopped down, landing on my back. I had heard enough. Yes, I had ordered a cheeseburger—with extra onions—in that fancy restaurant Vera took me to last week. What was wrong with that? If it was so tacky to order a burger in a place like La Salle's Bistro, why did they have it on the menu in the first place?

A few minutes later, Daddy opened my door and quietly entered my room. He was the only one in the house who entered my room without knocking. Vera always knocked, but she always entered before I could invite her in. I was glad I had got up from the vent and moved back to my bed in time. Had I not, Daddy would have caught me listening to the conversation taking place in the kitchen and I knew he would have put a stop to that.

"Baby, Vera tells me you're all excited about going away to that nice school in Iowa," Daddy said.

"Uh-huh. I'm real excited about it," I said. I was so sad and confused that I didn't really care one way or the other. My only concern was doing whatever I had to do to keep my daddy happy.

"It'll be a big change from the schools I've been going to here."

"True. And a big improvement I might add! The life you lived before will make your new life with me seem like a totally different culture. Just think of all the fine young ladies you'll meet in that school. The exposure will do wonders for your future development."

I frowned. "Just promise me one thing, Daddy. I do not want one of those stuffy coming-out parties. . . ."

Daddy laughed. "Oh, you don't have to do anything like that. I'm just so excited for you, baby! And just think, you'll learn a lot more than what they teach the kids—or don't teach, I should say—in your old schools. I just want you to make us proud of you. Your mother feels the same way."

"My . . . *mother*?" Just hearing that word associated with Vera sent a sharp pain through my chest like a butcher knife with a poisonous blade.

"Honey, Vera is your mother now." Daddy suddenly looked so tired and hopeless, I wondered just how happy he was. From the conversations I'd already overheard, Vera thought of him as an "old fool" and a "stupid bastard." Lord how I wanted to tell him some of the things she'd said about him! But I couldn't. He was obviously madly in love with that woman. And maybe she had loved him at one time and that was why he chose to keep her. "She's my wife and I love her to death. I caused her a lot of pain by having that affair with your mother, but she was woman enough to forgive me. I promised her that I'd make up for my betrayal. I made a mistake and I intend to pay it off in full."

"I was a mistake?" I had been called a lot of things in my life, but nobody had ever made me feel like I was a mistake. Even though my daddy didn't mean it the way it sounded, he had still hurt my feelings. "You don't have to let me live with you. I got friends I can live with," I pouted.

"Oh no, baby! I didn't mean anything like that! You are a blessing to me, and I thank God you are in my life. It's just that, well, you were not conceived under the best of circumstances." He paused and offered me a smile. I smiled back. "Now let's look more toward the future. See, Vera loves you just as much as I do."

"But do I have to call her mama?" I grunted.

"That's up to you. Everybody in this house just wants you to be happy."

"I am happy," I mumbled, looking toward the floor. When I looked back at Daddy's face and saw his big smile, I actually did feel happy. But the only thing I was happy about was the fact that I was making him feel so good. "I can't wait to get to that boarding school."

CHAPTER 18

KENNETH

Two years later . . .

MY LIFE KEPT GETTING BETTER AND BETTER. I HAD EVEN MORE TO BE thankful for. My daughter and I had an even better relationship now. I was still in reasonably good health, and my business was booming. We couldn't count the money fast enough.

But there was at least one thorn in my side.

Things were somewhat strained between Vera and me. Some days when she didn't know I was looking out of the corner of my eye, I caught her glaring at me like she wanted to coldcock me. One night after we had gone to bed, I woke up a few hours later and caught her sitting up in bed looking at me with so much contempt in her eyes I was too afraid to say anything. That was a scary moment for me. Vera didn't say anything to me about it, but I didn't go back to sleep that night. To my dismay, she spent the next few nights in one of the other bedrooms.

Even though Vera said she'd forgiven me for having an affair and fathering a child with another woman, I still had some doubts. For one thing, she had not yet accepted my daughter to my satisfaction.

"I do care about Sarah, and I know that someday she and I will be close, but I need a little more time," Vera told me in an apologetic tone of voice. She sounded sincere enough, but things were still not the way I thought they should be by now.

Sarah had been away at school for almost two years. And so far Vera had not gone to Iowa with me to visit her—and I'd made the trip eight times. She had come up with one excuse after another as to why she couldn't accompany me. After the 9/11 terrorist attacks on the World Trade Center last year, Vera came up with the excuse that she was now afraid to get on a plane. When Sarah came home for spring break this year in April, which was just a month ago, Vera suddenly decided to go to Houston to visit the sisters she claimed she couldn't stand. I knew how much she despised her sisters, so her preferring their company over my child's made me sad. It also made me angry, but I didn't let Vera know that. I was still trying to make up for my most serious indiscretion. And, I was proud to say, I had not cheated on Vera since we found out about Sarah.

"Sarah asks about you all the time. The least you can do is send her a card or a letter every now and then. She will be coming home for good next year, and you're going to have to live with her," I told Vera.

"All right. I'll go with you the next time you visit her."

That same day, I made arrangements to visit Sarah the next day. And Vera went with me. From the way she carried on, you would have thought that she and Sarah were best friends. When Sarah came home for good the following year in June, Vera welcomed her with open arms. At least that was what it looked like to me.

"I'm glad your wife finally stopped treating me like a stepchild," Sarah confided in me during a moment when she and I were alone.

I chuckled. "But, honey, you are a stepchild to her."

She chuckled too. "I know. But you know what I mean."

"Baby, just be nice to her and I am sure she'll be nice to you." I gave Sarah a firm hug.

I couldn't believe how sweet Vera was to Sarah now that she was home for good. Each day Vera seemed sweeter than the day before. Several times a week, she took Sarah shopping at the best stores, lunch at the best restaurants, and she even took her to the theater. As far as I was concerned, I had the best of both worlds now.

As good as things were, there was still a thing or two going on in my house that didn't sit too well with me. Vera's spending habits had gotten out of control. I stumbled upon dozens of large shopping bags filled with expensive items with the price tags still attached. Not only was her bedroom's large walk-in closet full of these shopping bags, but she had also filled up the closets in two of the other bedrooms, two closets downstairs, and even the laundry room. She purchased a brand-new Ferrari that she drove for only two months. She traded it in on a different one just because she wanted one in a color that would match most of her outfits. She had had so much cosmetic surgery done on her face and body she looked and felt like a mannequin. I came home from one of my business trips last week and she had gotten rid of all the furniture in the house and replaced it with more expensive items. Every time I attempted to scold Vera about her spending, she reminded me about how I had "hurt" her by having an affair with Sarah's mother and that spending money pacified her. For that reason, it was easier for my peace of mind to let her do whatever she wanted to do.

Things went on like this for the next *four* years.

There was nothing I wanted more than to see my wife accept my daughter completely. I knew Vera was really trying, so I couldn't say anything or even make any suggestions as to what they could do to improve their relationship. But just knowing that they did go out and do certain things together was a step in the right direction. However, there were flaws in that endeavor too. One of Vera's complaints was that Sarah got bored on the six- to eight-hour trips to the malls and the boutiques. What was even worse was that when Sarah did want to go shopping, she *still* went to the same discount stores that she'd shopped in before she came to live with me.

"Kenneth, you need to talk to your child," Vera said to me after their latest Saturday shopping spree.

"My child? You told me you were going to treat her like she was your child," I chided.

"*Our* child," she said with a smile and rapidly rolling eyeballs. "I have bought our child clothes from the best stores in town. She prefers outfits she picks up in discount stores."

"Well, as long as what she wears is clean and has a pleasant smell, what's the problem?"

"Kenneth, what's wrong with you? I'm trying to teach the girl—our child—to have some class. What will our friends think?"

"They can think whatever they want to think. As long as Sarah's not wearing something that's offensive, why should they care?"

"You're missing the point, baby. We have an image to maintain. We can't do that if our only child is running around dressing like a bag lady. She wore some mammy-made polyester dress, with vinyl shoes, to Wilma Finch's daughter's wedding last Saturday. I was so horrified and embarrassed when she walked into that church! I knew I should have made her ride in the same limo with me," Vera told me.

I laughed.

"It's not funny, Kenneth."

"And it's not that serious. We can't expect Sarah to change overnight," I insisted.

"Overnight? She's been with us for *seven* years now!"

"Overnight, seven years, whatever. The bottom line is, we have to let the child be who she is."

"The child is no longer a child. She's a twenty-two-year-old woman. She should be more refined by now. And what about her friends?"

"So? What about her friends?"

"What if one of them tries to do something crazy to her? Her friends are the kind of people who like to take advantage of people like her."

"I don't know what you mean by all that, but Sarah is not stupid or blind. She's got enough sense to know when and if somebody is trying to take advantage of her."

"When Sarah's hoochie-coochie girlfriends go out with her,

who do you think is paying for everything? She is! And I've seen her hand money to a couple of those moochers more than once!"

"What's wrong with her being generous to her friends? So many of them have so little. I'm sure they appreciate anything they can get from Sarah."

"You're damn right they appreciate it! Who wouldn't? And you don't have a problem with that? You don't think they're taking her kindness and generosity for weakness? As crazy as people are these days, you need to be more concerned about what some of them will do to Sarah if they get desperate enough. She could be kidnapped and held for ransom!"

"Look, I don't like where this conversation is going, Vera!" I exclaimed, holding my hand up in the air. I rarely showed my anger to Vera, but she was pushing her luck. "I could say the same thing about you and your cousin and his wife."

"Huh? What do you mean by that?"

"Cash and Collette hang around with some pretty shady people. Are you just as worried about somebody kidnapping them?"

"That's different."

"No, that's not different. Let's not worry about Sarah unless she gives us something to worry about."

The conversation was over as far as I was concerned. Vera realized that when I turned and walked out of the room, even though she was still talking.

CHAPTER 19

VERA

THIS THING WITH SARAH WAS REALLY BOTHERING ME, AND I HAD TO do something about it. Most of the people I knew went to bars to drown their sorrows. I either went shopping or to the spa, or I paid a visit to one of my sexy young male friends. Some days I did all of the above—including a visit to one of my favorite bars. Well, this time I was only interested in some young male flesh.

I didn't mind being generous when it came to my lovers; therefore, they didn't mind doing whatever I wanted them to do. And I always made it clear from day one with each one where he stood with me, so I'd never had any "fatal attraction" experiences like another married woman I knew.

Shirley Biddle and I had similar backgrounds, except she was white. She had married Kenneth's tax attorney six months after I married Kenneth and we'd been casual friends ever since. We'd even swapped a few lovers. Last year she had attempted to "unload" her twenty-three-year-old Jamaican gardener off on me because he had become possessive and had even begun to stalk her. The last thing I needed was a stalker, so Shirley accused him of stealing from her and made such a fuss he got deported. Anyway, I had already decided to "give" her my latest lover, Andre Gaudeux, as a Christmas gift this year. He was as meek as a lamb, so he wouldn't cause her any problems. Since I was always looking for new thrills, I had become bored with this boy and was going to "fire" him before the end of the year. Until then, I planned to keep him on my payroll. . . .

Andre didn't answer his door when I rang the bell and that pissed me off. Unlike Tony, whom I'd discarded two years ago after he had stopped working out and his belly got bigger than his dick, Andre was the cream of the crop. He was nineteen and very hungry. Hungry enough to do anything I told him to. I liked men who had nothing to offer but themselves. Andre had been working as a cabana boy when I met him on the beach in St. Thomas last summer. Kenneth had taken me down there for our anniversary. While he was floating around on a fishing boat, I was getting my groove back in a very big way. Andre lived in a shack with his blind grandmother and his nine siblings and a goat tied to a tree in the backyard. Other than an amazing body and handsome face, he had nothing but a few cheap shirts, two pairs of pants, one pair of sandals, and a post card with the map of America on it that he carried in his back pocket like it was a rosary. He was just what I needed at the time. I literally scrubbed the ash off his body in my hotel Jacuzzi. I took him to the same tailor that the island politicians went to and had several new outfits made for him, all within a two-week period. And to make sure he wouldn't run off with his new wardrobe and his pocket full of my money, I booked him on a first-class flight to the States, a day before Kenneth and I returned home. He stayed at the Mark Hopkins in a deluxe suite until I found him a place he liked.

I really *needed* to see my boy today. I returned to my car, disappointed and horny as hell. Right after I got in and put the key in the ignition, Andre trotted up and tapped on my window.

"Haylo, bay-bee," he greeted in his cute Caribbean accent. He grinned and then patted his bulging crotch. "I got hard as soon as I saw your car."

"Where the hell were you?" I demanded. "You're not supposed to go anywhere without leaving me a voice mail to let me know."

"I only went for a ten-minute jog," he muttered, looking down at his feet. "You told me earlier you had plans for today, remember?"

"Yeah, well, my plans changed." I had planned to go out to dinner with Kenneth and that child of his. But she'd balked about going to a French restaurant in Sausalito and insisted on going to some rib joint in Oakland! That's what had started the latest argument between Kenneth and me.

I glanced at my watch and opened my car door. "I don't have a lot of time," I said as Andre gently took my hand and helped me back out. My knees buckled and I fell against him. "Damn these heels!" I mock complained, holding on to Andre's arm to keep from falling to the ground. Despite all of the surgeons who worked on my body, there was nothing any of them could do about my arthritis, and it seemed to get a little worse each year. I was still in fairly good shape for a fifty-seven-year-old woman. And until I got too old to get around on my own, I planned to enjoy every single minute while I still could. "I just need a good hard ten- or fifteen-minute fuck to loosen me up a bit. I hope you're in the mood for it."

Andre nodded and steered me into his apartment.

There were times when he was a little too docile for his own good. One thing I could say about my former boy Tony and the ones in between him and Andre was that they had a little more backbone than Andre. This boy was so submissive I had no idea what *he* liked in bed after all this time. It was always about me. But from the way he grunted and groaned and humped me all over his bed, I was convinced that he was having as good a time as I was.

We didn't waste any time. Andre took me into his bedroom and closed the blinds. By the time he walked over to the bed where I was, I was already on my back. He stretched out next to me. "You seem tense," he said as he unbuttoned my blouse. At least he was assertive enough to undress me once in a while.

"Honey, I am tense!" I hollered as I wrapped my fingers around his balls and began to grind myself against him.

"I will relieve you, m'dear."

"Relieve me my ass," I snickered. "If that's all I needed, I would have given myself an enema. I want you to fuck me."

When I got back home, I was feeling so good, Sarah could have walked in front of me naked and it wouldn't have bothered me.

CHAPTER 20

SARAH

I DIDN'T THINK MY STEPMOTHER WAS EVER GOING TO ACCEPT ME AND be sincere about it. She was all kissy-poo nice and sweet to me in front of my daddy and other people, but she wasn't so nice when she and I were alone. I always seemed to do something that irritated Vera. She criticized the way I talked, my friends, what I ate, and the way I dressed. "You have too much money to be looking and acting so *black*," she scolded one day. I had come home with a Tupac Shakur T-shirt in one hand and a half-eaten bucket of fried chicken gizzards in the other.

"Excuse me, but when I look in the mirror, a black woman is the only thing I see," I quipped, licking grease off my lips.

"You know what I mean," she insisted with a hand on her hip and a frown on her face. "When you have money, you can't afford to be too *ethnic*. It makes people nervous."

I brushed Vera off that time, and from that point on, I brushed her off every other time she said stupid shit to me. I no longer cared if she liked me. I decided that as long as Daddy was not complaining about me, that was all that mattered.

My life was somewhat boring, but I did everything I could to keep myself busy and out of Vera's way. I still wasn't ready to work, so getting a job was not on my agenda yet. Daddy had even offered to hire me as a cashier, but I turned that down. That sounded too boring for me! But I had to admit to Daddy that the real reason I didn't want to work was because I wanted to enjoy the luxury of lying around in a mansion not having to worry about money a little longer.

Feeling so out of place and unaccepted by Vera was one of the reasons I became so promiscuous. I went out with men I didn't even like just so I could get out of the house and away from her for a few hours, or a few days, at a time.

The following year I dated a lot of guys but none I liked enough to make a commitment to. Finally, I thought I'd found the man of my dreams. Two weeks after my twenty-third birthday, I started going out with this brother named Vincent Bruner. He worked for a company that made garage door openers. I had met him on a bus one day on my way to visit some of my friends in my old neighborhood. He was on his way to an appointment with his parole officer. He had no idea I was a "poor little rich girl" until I rolled up to his apartment in the projects in the Ferrari Daddy had bought for me last month.

"Girl, why do you be riding on a bus when you got a ride like this?" Vincent asked me, looking at my shiny black car like he wanted to kiss it.

"Uh, you know how bad parking is in this city," I said with a shrug. "Besides, I like riding on the bus."

"What kind of job you got?"

"I don't work. And I still live at home."

Vincent reared back and looked me up and down. "Your folks must be real well off, huh?"

"My daddy is real well off. Uh, he owns the five Lomax Electronic stores," I confessed with hesitation. I had kept this information from Vincent since I'd met him a month ago because I wanted to see if he'd still like me if I was broke.

Vincent's eyes lit up, but he tried to remain calm. All he said was, "No shit?" An hour later he asked me for a "loan" so he could take his mama out to dinner for her birthday. I gave him the money, which he was supposed to pay back a week later. I never heard from him again. Getting screwed like that was the only thing I hated about having money.

It was easy to see why some people thought having a lot of money was more of a curse than a blessing. Despite what I believed, I continued to be generous when it came to my "friends." Daddy didn't seem to mind, but the more I gave to my friends, the more it bothered Vera. And she didn't hesitate to let me know.

One day while I was in the living room, she spied on me from behind a bookcase in the hall that led to the kitchen. I had just given a thousand dollars to one of my homegirls so she could pay some bills. Cathy Proctor had practically run out the door as soon as the money landed in her hand. A few seconds later, Vera marched into the room with her hands on her hips. "Sarah, I know it's none of my business, but you need to be more careful about loaning money to your friends. You're going to regret it one day," she warned.

"They would do the same for me," I said. I was perched on top of a stool at the bar. "They told me they would."

"Ha! People like the friends you have will say anything they think you want to hear as long as it'll help them get your money. Honey, these damn freeloaders don't care about you. If you're not careful, they are going to bleed you dry. Your daddy works too hard for his money for you to keep giving it away. How come you don't socialize with some of those nice young girls I introduced you to?"

"I don't have much in common with those girls," I answered. I almost laughed in Vera's face. The girls she had introduced me to had treated me like dog shit on the bottom of their shoes. They knew about my childhood background, so that was reason enough for them to always treat me like an outsider. One girl had even asked if I had been in a gang before I came to live with Daddy. And most of them thought that I knew drug dealers who would sell drugs to me at a discount that I could pass on to them. I had never been in a gang, and the drug dealers I grew up with were all dead or in jail.

"Well, I'm telling you for your own good; you really need to be more careful about who you associate with!" Vera must have realized how mean she sounded because a few seconds later, she started smiling. Then she gave me a hug. "I don't mean to sound so harsh," she said, rubbing my back. "I just want you to be happy."

"I am happy," I declared.

"I know you don't know much about fine wine, but let's have some. It'll help you relax more than that cat-gut beer you drink."

I followed Vera over to the bar and she poured me and herself a glass of her finest red wine. "This is good," I told her with a burp as we moved to the couch and sat down.

"I love martinis and cosmopolitans, but this particular wine is my favorite. It's more expensive than that shit most black folks drink, but it's worth it. All of my friends back in Houston love it just as much as I do."

"Houston must be a cool place."

"It is." Vera reached for a photo album on the end table and placed it on top of the coffee table. "Let me show you some of my friends."

I couldn't think of anything more boring than looking at somebody's photo album and gawking at people I had never met and probably never would. There were pictures of homely babies, fat old women in outlandish hats and muumuus, and Vera as a teenager riding a bike. How lame was that?! Just as I was about to pour myself another glass of wine, I saw a picture of one of the most handsome black men I'd ever seen before in my life. He looked like a cross between Dwayne "The Rock" Johnson and Will Smith. Vera was in the picture with this hunk of black gold, and his arm was around her waist.

"Dang! Is this one of your old boyfriends?" I was actually enjoying myself now. But I wasn't going to let my guard down. Vera was still the same witch I overheard talking trash about me in the kitchen with Cash and Collette on a regular basis.

"That's my cousin Bo Harper," Vera said casually. "He's married to a woman who used to live across the street from my mama's house."

"Does he have any unmarried male relatives?" I laughed.

Vera laughed too. "Yeah, but most of them are a lot older than he is."

I shook my head and let out a loud breath. "Why can't I meet a man like your cousin Bo? His wife sure is a lucky woman."

"She doesn't think so. The marriage is on the rocks."

"Oh that's too bad," I said quickly, forcing myself not to sound too excited.

Vera gave me a sickly look. "The next time we all go to Houston, or if he ever comes out here for a visit, I'll make sure you meet him."

"I hope so." I sniffed. *Boy would I love to wrap my legs around his waist,* I thought to myself.

That night was the beginning of the end of the life I had come to know.

CHAPTER 21

VERA

"BO'S WIFE HAS BEEN THREATENING TO DIVORCE HIM FOR MONTHS. They've been having problems for years," I said quickly, wondering where this conversation was going and what was in it for me. "Poor Bo. That hussy he is married to is the Bride of Satan. She treats my poor cousin like a dog."

Sarah couldn't take her eyes off Bo's picture. "That sure is cold, Vera. Your cousin looks like a real cool dude."

"He is," I replied, trying to look and act nonchalant. The last thing I wanted was for her to suspect I was up to something. The thought that I could use Bo to "straighten Sarah out" had entered my mind immediately after she'd expressed her interest in him. He'd be good for her and she'd be good for him as long as I was the one in control.

"He's so damn cute." Watching Sarah swoon like a love-struck puppy was sickening, but it was worth it.

"His wife took him to hell and back. She grew up in some fancy neighborhood in Boston. She has this notion that people from that part of the country are better than the rest of us—especially people from the South like me and . . . people from California like you. That wench was so trifling she'd fuck her lovers in the same bed she shared with Bo."

"Ooo wee! That's what I call a straight-up skank!" Sarah snorted. She softened her voice and grinned. "So . . . uh . . . he's single now?"

"Oh yeah, the divorce is in the works. He put up with her as long as he could before he finally threw in the towel. Well, actually she's the one that moved out. She was screwing one of their neighbors who was also one of Bo's fishing buddies. When she left Bo, she moved in with the dude—in the house right next door." I sniffed and gave Sarah a serious look. "I wish he could meet a nice girl like you. He's somewhat older than you, but an older man can enrich a younger woman's life tremendously. Look at your daddy and me."

"Uh-huh." Sarah gave me a mildly incredulous look. Then she grinned like the Cheshire cat and blinked a few times. I could just imagine the wheels turning in her head. "I like older men as long as they're cute and not too broken down."

"Me too," I said. Had I known Sarah was this big of a fool over a handsome older man, I would have been on this case a lot sooner. I could have hooked her up with Bo a long time ago.

"Having his wife leave him for one of his friends must have been real hard on Bo," Sarah continued with a glazed look on her face. "If I were a dude and my woman disrespected me the way Bo's wife did him, I'd beat her ass."

This was getting so good I wanted to lick my chops. Instead, I just cleared my throat. "Tell me about it. She'd park her car in the dude's driveway so Bo had to look at it every time he left his house or looked out the window."

Sarah's eyes darkened and her brows furrowed with anger. "She sure was a bold soul sister."

"She's a lucky one too. Bo wanted to kill her. He'd even bought a gun. He probably would have killed her if Cash and I hadn't called him up every day and talked him out of it."

"Well, the next time you go visit your family in Houston, take me with you. I sure would like to meet your cousin."

"I'll keep that in mind, Sarah." Her interest in my long-suffering cousin had really piqued my interest. "Would you like some more wine?" I poured what was left in the bottle into her wineglass before she responded.

"Thanks, Vera. This stuff sure gives a smooth buzz." She took a long drink and then let out a sharp hiccup. I had purposely left the photo album open to the page with the picture of Bo. Every few seconds I looked at Sarah out of the corner of my eye and caught her staring at that same picture. "Want me to get another bottle of wine from the bar?" she asked, already rising.

"That's all right. I've had enough for now." Now that I had the ball rolling, I needed to focus on my own love life. My pussy was itching like I had fleas. I had to put Sarah on hold for a little while so I could go get myself taken care of. "Um, I just remembered I'm supposed to call up Mr. Beauchamp to discuss that fund-raiser for a children's home in South City that houses troubled kids."

"Huh?"

The fact that I did some charity work surprised a lot of people. But there was more to me than shopping and dining out and having affairs. During the year, I spent a few hours a week now and then at various inner-city churches or some youth facility, helping out any way I could. Those places had become havens for kids in low-income families and other bleak situations. Had it not been for places like that when I was growing up, I would have lost my way and ended up like my sisters.

"Why is a woman like you off into stuff like that?" The look on Sarah's face confused me. I couldn't tell if she was surprised or amused by what I'd just told her. "I used to help serve dinners to the homeless at our church on the holidays. And when I was acting up a little in my early teens, Grandma Lilly put me in a youth home for a few weeks and it sure straightened me out." Sarah gave me a pensive look. "You're the last person in the world I expected to be doing charity work or helping out with the troubled kids."

Her last statement stunned me. I didn't want her to spend too much time thinking about how I spent my time during the day. The last thing I needed was for Kenneth to start monitoring my movements.

"Well, I care about people, so that's why a woman like me is off into stuff like that!" I snapped.

"I . . . I didn't mean anything by what I just said!" Sarah fumbled defensively, rearing back in her seat. "What I meant was, you are such a glamorous, dainty lady. I just thought that when you weren't at some fancy country club or having lunch with one of your rich friends, you'd be hanging out at fashion shows and beauty parlors and stuff every day."

I only did enough charity work to make myself look good. But that was not what I wanted to discuss at the moment. I had a more important matter to address, but Sarah seemed to be so interested in what I did with my time, I decided to indulge her a little longer. My pussy would have to itch a little while longer. The more I got her into my corner, the easier it would be for me to keep her there.

"No matter how glamorous and dainty I am, I still enjoy helping less-fortunate people. I had a hard life when I was young, so I can relate to those people. It's a burden I accept without complaint. That's why God has blessed me so much."

Sarah looked at me in awe. "Dang, Vera. I think that is so hella cool! Is there anything at one of those places that I can do to help out? I'd love to help out less-fortunate people like I did at our church when I was younger. Now I can donate some of my money, too, especially now that I have so much of it."

Tell me about it, I said to myself. Sarah had already "helped out" enough less-fortunate people by being so generous with her friends. This conversation had taken a wrong turn. The last thing I wanted to do was encourage this stupid girl to give away even more of Kenneth's money. "Uh, yeah. I'll look into it. Right now we have more help than we need," I mumbled. I finally snapped my photo album shut. I glanced at my watch for the third time in the last five minutes. "Hmmm. I'd better go freshen up and use the bathroom before I call up Mr. Beauchamp. He's so long-winded he might keep me on the line for an hour." I was going to call Mr. Beauchamp—and Andre—but later. I had another call to make that was a little more important. I practically floated upstairs to my room so I could use the telephone in private.

Bo was the only person I knew who did not have call waiting on his landline. I got a busy signal for ten minutes. I finally called his cell phone, but it went straight to voice mail. After three more attempts, he answered his landline. I didn't want to waste any time putting my latest scheme into action. "We need to talk!" I yelled.

Bo greeted me with an exasperated sigh. "Look, Vera, I know I still owe you a couple of grand. As soon as I get myself sorted out with that bitch and her alimony, I'll break you off a payment. Now stop harassing me. Do you hear me?"

"I hear you and I don't appreciate you accusing me of harassing you."

"What else is it? You've called me five times this month asking me when I'm going to pay back the money I borrowed from you last month."

"Fuck that. As a matter of fact, you can forget about the money you owe me. Consider it a gift," I said in a low voice, my eye on the door. Sarah had a rude habit of entering my room without knocking. "Listen, I've got a proposition for you."

"I'm afraid to ask what it is," Bo replied with a groan.

"You told me one time you'd love to live in Frisco someday."

"So? I still do. Why?"

"Now that you and Gladys have finally called it quits, a serious change would probably do you a world of good."

"That's true. I even thought about moving up to Buffalo to start up a landscaping business with one of my old navy buddies."

"Buffalo gets real cold in the winter."

"So?"

"Well, it's warm out here most of the year. And we've got all these empty bedrooms in this beautiful mansion. . . ."

"Cuz, I know you, so I know you want something from me. You don't need to beat around the bush. Whatever is on your mind, you need to tell me and you need to tell me now. I have to get to my second job in a little while. That bitch left me so high and dry that I have to work two jobs now just to get by!"

"It would help if you didn't have to see her for a while. Is she still living right next door to you?"

"Yeah, she is! I'm going to start looking for a new place as soon as I can afford it. I'd rather live in a hole than stay so close to Gladys!"

"Bo, how would you like to live with us and work for Kenneth? You'll be earning way more money than whatever you're earning now. I'll see to that."

Bo was taking too long to answer.

"Bo?"

"I'm still here. What's going on, Vera? For you to be offering something that sweet to me, there has to be something in it for you. Now what the hell is it?"

"When will your divorce be finalized?"

"One month from today. And not soon enough for me! I will say this much—had I known how many headaches I was going to have as a married man, I never would have taken that step in the first place. I still think about shooting that heifer dead!"

"You stop talking like that! What good would it do for you to kill Gladys? And believe me, Texas is not the state where you want to commit murder. Those courts down there would love to fry another black man. Or at the very least, put your ass in jail for life." The words were rolling off my tongue so fast I had to pause for a few seconds to catch my breath. "Baby, let nature run its course. At the rate Gladys is going, you ought to know that somebody else is going to kill her sooner or later." Bo's ex had played several different men at the same time before he married her. One had attempted to choke her to death when he caught her screwing his brother.

"Going to prison for killing that tramp would be worth it to me. I can take care of myself."

"Bo, a pretty boy like you wouldn't last a week locked up with all those thugs. Some snaggletoothed redneck or some baldheaded brother from the ghetto would make you his bitch in no time. Just forget about that woman and move on with your life."

"I wish I could. I've never been hurt like this. I never thought losing my woman would hurt so much. I wish she was dead. If . . . if I can't have her, I don't want anybody else to have her."

"You married the wrong woman, Bo. That's all. There are a lot of other women available for you to choose from. And there are women you can trust who will treat you the way you deserve to be treated. A smart man like you should know that."

"I don't need you to tell me that."

"Well, then, move on with your life, cuz. Don't let what happened with your first wife turn you against women!"

"My first wife?" Bo guffawed and I could hear him snorting like a bull and clapping his hands like a seal. "Gladys was my first and *last* wife! I will never go through some shit like this again!"

"Gladys didn't have anything to offer you anyway," I said. "You brought so much more into that marriage."

"I don't need you to tell me that either. She even had the nerve to tell me that she married me because I was such a hard-working man. She saw me as a goose that laid golden eggs from the get-go. The money that I had saved up over the years, that bitch is taking half of it. And my retirement and 401K money too!"

"It's time for somebody to give you something, cuz. You deserve it."

"I deserve a lot. I deserve to be rich. I deserve to get my dick sucked on a regular basis. What are you getting at?"

"Now, I want you to listen to me and I want you to listen good. I'm going to get you back in the game. Honey, *have I got a woman for you!*"

Bo let out a loud and impatient sigh. "Now that's just great. I already feel like a pile of shit and now you're telling me I need you to help me find a new woman. I used to listen to shit like that from my mama! I don't want you or anybody else to pity me—or find a woman for me!"

"Calm down, sweetie! I do not pity you. I'm trying to help you."

"Thanks but no thanks. I don't need your help. If you are trying to dump off one of your homely friends on me, don't waste your time. I've seen a few of the women you associate with and I already have one dog."

"Stop trying to be funny."

"Vera, I'm not trying to be funny. I'm serious. I still know how to pick a woman on my own."

"I hate to remind you, but you didn't do such a good job when you picked Gladys."

"I guess I didn't."

"Will you just listen to what I have to say? That's all I want you to do."

"All right. I'm listening. And this better be good!"

"It is," I said with a triumphant sigh.

CHAPTER 22

VERA

"You remember me telling you about Kenneth's unmarried daughter, don't you?"

Bo grunted something unintelligible. Then he laughed. "Keep talking, Vera. I have a feeling this is going to be real amusing and I could use a few laughs."

"I hope you're not drinking. I need for you to have a clear head right now."

"I had a couple of beers a few hours ago, but my head is as clear as it can be now."

"Then listen and listen good. I think she's the one for you, Bo. She's up for grabs and so dumb and stupid she's a sitting duck for these scumbags out here. If some man's going to put his hand in her pocketbook, that man ought to be you. She's the answer to all of your problems."

"Kenneth's daughter? I remember you mentioning something about her. Is she the one he had with some file clerk he was fooling around with back in the day?"

"She was his secretary. Lois was her name. The child's name is Sarah and she's living with us now."

"Oh? Where is her mama?"

"She died in a car crash a few years ago. I thought I told you about that."

"You probably did, but I've had a lot going on in my personal life these past few years, remember? I've forgotten about a lot of things."

"Let me refresh your memory. The girl has no other relatives, so that's why she's living with us now. She was away at boarding school in another state for a while and doesn't want to go on to college, so now she's with us for good. Having her under foot has become a major burden to me! She's a pain in the ass if ever there was one. See, she still hangs out with people from her old neighborhood. Believe it or not, she was actually dating a man who hauls trash! And before him, she was fucking a cabdriver! He was some Nigerian tar baby with sneaky eyes. I had my friend down at Immigration check him out. That sucker came here to go to school and no doubt look for an American fool to marry so he can get a green card. He would have hit the mother lode had he convinced Sarah to marry him. It's a good thing I found out in time to stop that! She's too stupid for her own good. I'm going crazy trying to keep an eye on this girl, preventing her from getting into something she can't get out of on her own. Luckily, the Nigerian lost interest in her, but I'm sure some other maniac will take his place. It seems like trouble comes looking for this girl. Right now she's sliding around town with a man who is a . . . a fry cook in a fast-food restaurant!" I almost choked on those words.

"Well, give the girl some credit. At least she's not getting involved with drug dealers or pimps. She likes men who do honest work. I thought that was what every woman wanted."

"She's worth *millions*, Bo. When Kenneth dies, she's going to be worth even more millions. With that much money on the table, she needs to marry the right man. Every unattached, broke-ass man in this city will try to marry her once Kenneth is out of the way. She's just stupid enough to say yes to the first one who proposes to her. I need to help her get with the right man."

"You need to help this girl find a man? Hmmm. Well, what all is wrong with this sad sack? She must be one hell of a dog! And is she retarded or deformed too?"

"Nothing's wrong with the girl, Bo."

"Well, something's *got* to be wrong with her if the only way she'll get a husband is because she's filthy rich. She either looks like Godzilla or King Kong. Don't play with me, Vera. I am not about to let you set me up with a beast."

"No. Believe it or not, the girl is quite pretty. You remember Kenneth's dead brother's daughter? The one that accidentally spilled some punch on your foot at the family reunion a few years ago."

"Oooh yeah. I remember that juicy little cutie." Bo laughed again. "She had a nice pair of legs on her and butt for miles."

"Sarah looks a lot like her. They could almost pass for twins."

"Why are you telling me all this and I haven't even met the girl? How do you know she'd be interested in me?"

"Bo, she saw your picture a little while ago. The way she was drooling, you would have thought she was looking at a picture of Denzel Washington in the nude."

"Uh-huh. Well, I'm sure she's already got more men sniffing her scent than she can handle."

"That's the problem."

"What's the problem?"

"Are you listening to me or not?" I was more than a little impatient. But I was not ready to give up. "A lot of men are sniffing her scent. I don't want the next man she falls for to make a fool out of her."

"Vera, are you serious? You want me to move to California so I can hook up with Kenneth's old maid daughter?"

"Bo, like I told you, the girl is up for grabs and she's real interested in meeting you. Just a few minutes ago she told me to bring her to Houston the next time I come just so she can meet you."

"She's young. Young chicks say shit like that all the time."

"Quit being so damn stubborn, Bo! Don't look a gift horse in the mouth. Are you interested or not? You know Kenneth's got one foot in the grave, so he's anxious to marry her off before he kicks the bucket. She might just up and marry any old body just to please him. And what if it's some creep like the Nigerian who was trying to get a green card? If you marry this girl, you and I would be on easy street for the rest of our lives."

"For a minute, I thought you were just playing with me. But you really are serious, aren't you?" Bo exclaimed.

"Honey, I'm as serious as cancer. Now, the sooner you get out here the better."

"A new job is one thing. I could definitely use a change in that area. Uh, but I don't know about the part where I'd go after Kenneth's daughter. Something like that could backfire and a lot of folks could get hurt. Now, about this job working for Kenneth, what's up with that? Have you discussed it with him?"

"You let me worry about him and everything else. He's in the palm of my hand right now, so he'll do anything I ask him to, if I approach him right. He's got a few openings at all five of the stores, and he's not going to hold them open for too long. He's already interviewed a few folks. He needs a strong, personable brother like you to manage the office in his main store. You've got the education and the background. You'd be perfect."

"That job sounds real tempting, Vera. I'm not going to lie about that," Bo admitted. "But I don't know. Something that sounds too good to be true usually is. It might not be all you say it is."

I exhaled as loudly as I could. "Stop talking shit!" I wanted Bo to know how impatient and exasperated I was. "I'm offering you the life of a king on a platter—a job to die for and a rich, young, pretty wife. If you don't want a package like that, maybe I'll call up Cousin Lester in Detroit. . . ."

"Ow! That really hurt my feelings, cuz! Not only did Lester always get the jobs I wanted, but he always got the girls I wanted too."

"Well, don't let him pull the rug out from under you this time. Don't let him get his hands on Sarah."

"Uh-uh. You can forget about Lester. He changed after he left Houston. The only thing a black woman can do for him these days is lead him to the white women. He married some woman from Germany last month."

"I didn't know that. Oh well. You know what, forget I called you. Kenneth won't have any trouble finding the right person to hire and Sarah will eventually find the right man to marry. Don't say I never tried to do anything as big as this for you. But I will tell you now that I won't try to do it again. Have a blessed day—"

"Hold on! Don't hang up yet! Look, this would be a life-changing move on my part. You're asking me to give up a lot. I have a lot of good friends down here and a secure job."

"Your *two* jobs," I reminded him. "You wouldn't have to work two jobs out here. Honey, I'm offering you a lot more than what you have now. And you can make some new friends."

"Can I think about it?"

"Yes, you can think about it. But if I don't hear from you by this time tomorrow, you can forget it."

Ten minutes after I ended my conversation with Bo, he called me back.

"What kind of benefits go with the job?"

"You won't have to worry about any of that if you marry Kenneth's daughter!" I laughed. "But since you asked, the benefits include medical, dental, all the usual things. And a retirement plan that won't quit. You can't lose! You know how happy Cash is working for Kenneth and living in this beautiful mansion."

"Oh, please! Every time Cash and I talk on the phone, he reminds me of how 'blessed' he is because of you and Kenneth." Bo paused and let out a great sigh. "Okay. If we're going to move on this arrangement, we have to make it look real. Now, tell me—have you discussed any of this with Cash?"

"No, but I will eventually. That is if you go for it. We'll need him to watch our backs."

"Okay. I'm in, I guess. I'll need enough time to tie up some loose ends down here, though."

"What loose ends?"

"I'll need to get rid of my furniture and my car. I have to give notice at my jobs, in case I need to come back. Maybe I can rent a U-Haul and bring some of my stuff to Frisco with me."

As hard as I tried not to, I laughed long and loud. "Bo, I've seen the shit you have in your house. I know you are not thinking about driving halfway across the country with all of that *junk*!

What you can't give to Goodwill, leave behind. And I promise you, you won't ever need to go back to those dead-end-ass two jobs."

"Well, there's something else . . ."

"What?"

"I do have a new lady friend here, see. I was just getting to know her."

"Oh? What kind of work does she do?"

"She's between jobs right now. But she used to work in a car wash until she got laid off last week."

"A *car wash*? What the—Lord have mercy. How can you even consider passing up a gold mine like Sarah for a woman who worked in a car wash and is 'between jobs' now? If you are interested, you need to move on this as soon as possible. You know that I am not a patient woman."

"Just give me at least a week or two to get rid of my stuff and to break it off with Nelda." Bo paused. "I'd still like to think this through a little more."

"Okay. You have until this time tomorrow to make up your mind."

"Oh, all right! I know you won't stop until you get your way, Vera. I can handle the job, but if this thing with Kenneth's daughter blows up in my face, I am going to hold you responsible."

"Don't worry about her. She's a goose just waiting to get cooked and I'm the chef."

Bo and I laughed so hard, my sides were aching by the time I got off the telephone.

CHAPTER 23

KENNETH

I'D HAD A LOT OF AFFAIRS SINCE I MARRIED VERA, BUT I HAD ALWAYS been discreet. To this day, the only affair Vera was aware of was the one with Sarah's mother. Up until then, I never gave her any reason to think I was cheating on her. Had Sarah not entered the picture, Vera would have never found out that I had an affair with her mother.

I felt that if a person had to cheat, they should do it right. Make it as painless as possible, meaning try not to get caught. Hearing about how blatant Bo's ex-wife, Gladys, had been with her affairs made me mad as hell. People like her made it hard for people like me—the *old* me. I was through cheating!

And since Vera adored Bo so much, when he was in pain, so was she. I hated to see my woman in distress, so I comforted her as much as I could.

We were lying in bed that Sunday morning when I witnessed her latest meltdown regarding her beloved cousin. This was a subject that came up at the most peculiar times. I had just made love to Vera and she was still in my arms, naked and covered in my sweat. Her head was on my chest, bobbing up and down with every breath I took. It felt like I had a big rock sitting right on top of my heart, but I didn't complain. Vera was the kind of woman that a man would walk through fire for.

"Poor Bo," she said, almost in tears. "I can't believe how Gladys abused him!" She paused long enough to reach behind her to grab a tissue off her nightstand and blow her nose. "Every time I talk to him about this shit, I can feel his pain." She blew her nose again and choked on a sob. "She was also fucking another one of his friends before she left him for the one she's with now. She spent Bo's money on cocaine and in the casinos, and she made a complete fool out of him every other way possible. On top of all that, she was violent. She tried to run him over with his own car. She's such a good liar; everybody believes everything she tells them about Bo. She's beaten him over the head with skillets, but she's got everybody believing that he was the one beating her! Now he has to sit back and watch her traipse in and out of the house next door, all hugged up with that fool she left him for."

"That heifer! Shame on her!" I yelled.

"Tell me about it!" Vera yelled back. "And Bo was such a good husband. He reminds me of you. . . ."

Vera's last comment caught me completely off guard. It had been a long time since she had given me a compliment, so I was flattered. I was glad to hear that she still thought of me as "such a good husband" too. Especially after the way I had cheated on her with Lois. I knew a lot of women who would have left their husbands for just cheating on them, let alone fathering a child with another woman.

I shook my head and let out a disgusted groan. "Bo needs to get as far away from that woman as possible," I suggested.

"That's what I told him. I told him he'd be so much better off leaving Houston."

"I hope he listens to you. There is no reason in the world for him to put up with that kind of mistreatment. I'm surprised he hasn't killed that damn jezebel!"

"And that's another thing. I'm afraid he's going to snap one day and kill that woman if he doesn't put some distance between himself and her."

"If he kills her, or even hurts her, he'll spend time in prison. I sure would hate to see that happen. I hope he takes your advice and gets away from her before it comes to that," I said. "I like Bo. He's good people."

Vera let out a sharp yelp and sat bolt upright. "Baby, I just got a great idea!" There was an anxious look on her face. She was taking too long to reveal what her "great idea" was.

"Well, can you share that information with me?" I said impatiently, rearranging the pillows under my head. I was glad she had lifted her head off my chest, but now her arm was around my neck and that didn't feel too good either. I had had a neck spasm while we were making love and the muscles in my neck were still giving me a lot of discomfort.

"Bo's got great management and interpersonal skills. He's trustworthy, dependable, efficient, and a team player. He's just what you need to manage the main office!"

I pursed my lips and scratched my head. Running a business was hard work. Finding good people to help me run it was one of the most difficult aspects of the job. "Oh, I don't know about that," I replied, rubbing Vera's back. "I don't know anything about Bo's work abilities or his general habits."

"Well, I do! I practically helped raise Bo, so I know he's a righteous man. Honey, Bo would be perfect for the company," Vera insisted. I hadn't seen such a gleam in her eye in years. "He could be running a Fortune 500 company if he wanted to."

"Then why isn't he?" I asked. "If he couldn't control his woman, how well do you think he'd be able to manage the three dozen employees in my main store? And hell, half of those employees are women."

"That's different. Trying to control a crazy bitch would be hard work for any man, even you. It would be like putting perfume on a turd! No matter how much you spray it, it's still going to stink." Vera reared her head back and looked up at me with a hopeful expression on her face. "Baby, next to you, Bo would be the best thing to happen to the company. Please give my cousin the chance he deserves."

I didn't know Bo that well, but I'd never heard Vera say anything negative about him. Other than Cash, he was the only other one of her relatives that she communicated with on a regular basis. If he was half as good as she claimed he was, he was just what I needed. Since it meant so much to Vera (and since I was still trying to make up for my cheating on her), I had to give her request some serious consideration. "Is he currently out of work?"

"Uh, not yet. His personal problems have had a bad impact on his work lately. His boss has warned him more than once to get his shit together or he's going to be standing in the unemployment line. But he's so depressed, just being in Houston where he still has to see that woman all the time is ruining his life. She even has the nerve to still be going to Bo's church with her new man."

"Say what?" I gave Vera an incredulous look. Just as I opened my mouth to speak again, she cut me off.

"Baby, do this for me. If he doesn't work out, or if for some reason you are not happy with him working for you, he'll go back to Houston. I'll make sure of that." That hopeful look was still on her face.

"You really care a lot about your cousin, don't you? My goodness, you are such a compassionate woman." I kissed Vera's forehead and rubbed her shoulder. "That's one of the many things I love about you, baby." Even as I made this statement, I was still concerned about how Vera and Sarah were getting along. Things appeared to be going well, but I still had some reservations about that situation.

"Even Sarah wants Bo to move out here," Vera blurted. She really surprised me with that statement.

I sat up straighter. My hand was still rubbing Vera's shoulder. "Oh?" Both of my eyebrows shot up and formed arches above my eyes. "Sarah's never even met Bo."

"She saw a picture of him and got all worked up. She couldn't stop talking about him." Vera gave me a peck on my neck. Her warm, moist lips made my flesh tingle. "You know how girls her age are. Especially now that she's currently not dating anyone."

My jaw dropped and I let out a loud gasp. Then I chuckled.

"Well, if you're thinking about playing matchmaker, don't. Sarah's too young for Bo. She's twenty-three. He's well into his forties."

Vera stiffened. "I'm glad you didn't feel that way about age when we met! I was in my early twenties and you were well into your forties—just like Sarah and Bo! And didn't you tell me that older husbands make better husbands?"

"Yeah, you're right. I remember telling you that, and more than once," I admitted with a sheepish grin. "I can overlook the age difference, but I don't feel comfortable about my baby hooking up with a man who is still going through trauma with his ex-wife. Sarah's had a hard life, and now I only want the best for her. Especially when it comes to her men friends."

"Like that garbage collector she was running around with? Or that cabdriver?" Vera snapped. "And by the way, the Millers' cross-eyed chauffeur asked me about Sarah the other day. He wanted to know if she had a boyfriend. Don't you want our daughter to do better than that?"

It pleased me to hear Vera refer to Sarah as "our" daughter. She didn't do it enough, though. "Yes, baby. I want our daughter to do better than that. But if she loves a man who happens to be poor and he loves her, what's wrong with that?"

"Kenneth, you and I both know that Sarah would not be happy being married to a poor man. Of all the men she's been running around with since she came to live with us, not a single one of them could provide the lifestyle she's become accustomed to."

"But you know Sarah. She's not a materialistic girl at all. She still shops at Walmart and Target and the Dollar Tree, for God's sake. She's even been threatening to trade in her Ferrari for a Honda. I don't think she's comfortable being rich."

"Let me ask you this: Do you think if Sarah had the chance to move back to that hellhole she lived in with her grandmother, she'd go?"

That was something I had to think about. I must have been thinking about it too long because a few moments later Vera brought up another important point.

"Let me put it this way, Kenneth. If something were to happen to you and . . . say you left this world unexpectedly, would you want Sarah to go back to the ghetto?"

"Of course not. But I—"

"I doubt she'd want to stay in this house or have anything to do with me, if . . . God forbid . . . you should suddenly pass. She'd probably pack her bags before they even put you in the ground. With you out of the way, that garbage man or that cabdriver or some other opportunistic punk will milk her like she's a Guernsey cow. Do you want that to happen?"

I rubbed the back of my aching head. "I think we need to change the subject."

"All right. But I'm just trying to help. I'm going to pray for Sarah," Vera whined, wiggling out of my arms. "I guess I'll get dressed and see what fattening things Delia has cooked up for breakfast this time."

"Wait a minute, baby," I said, grabbing Vera by her arm. "I think we should look at things from a different point of view. First of all, we may be jumping the gun. We don't know what's going on in Sarah's head, but I hope she wants the same things in life that we want for her. Like a good solid marriage and a family of her own. She's considerably younger than Bo, but the big difference in our ages didn't stop us from getting together and look how happy we are. And even though I don't know Bo that well, I do like him. And I believe he'd be a good employee. But his love life, and Sarah's, are really none of our business. They are both grown and no matter what we want for them, they need to make their own decisions about who they want to be with. If they hook up on their own, all we should do is hope for the best," I said.

Vera's face lit up like a flashlight. "Does this mean you'll give Bo a job?"

"Well, first I'd like to talk to him and feel him out. I'd like to hear what he wants to do, and I'd like to hear it from him. If he wants to move out here and needs a place to stay until he gets sorted out, he's more than welcome to stay with us. But I don't want you trying to get him interested in Sarah. You are not Cupid, so I want you to stay out of their personal affairs. I don't condone people scheming when it comes to an intimate relationship. If they do get together, I want it to happen naturally like it did with us."

CHAPTER 24

SARAH

I HAD BEEN FANTASIZING ABOUT BO HARPER EVER SINCE VERA SHOWED me his picture a week ago. I needed a man like him. Last night when she told me that he was moving to San Francisco and would be working for Daddy, I went up to my room and danced a jig.

A couple of nights ago, I was rolling around in a bed at the Garner Motel off of I-80 in Berkeley with Steve Randall, an ex-con that nobody knew I was seeing. It was Bo I was thinking about when I came. And boy did I come! I scratched Steve's back, bit his cheek, and squeezed him so hard around the waist with my legs, I scared him.

"Damn, baby! I know I'm good, but I ain't that damn good! You 'bout to kill me," Steve hollered as he roughly pushed me away. "I can tell you ain't used to good dick like mine. But since I just got out the joint a few weeks ago, it's going to take me a little while to get used to a woman's body again. Don't spoil it with all that whooping and hollering and scratching and shit." He let out a disgusted breath as he rubbed the spot on his cheek where I'd bitten him. "And no woman never chewed on my jaw like you just done! If I wanted to get mauled, I'd go to the zoo and climb in a cage with a gorilla." Steve laughed.

I laughed, too, and slapped Steve on his back. Despite all the scratch marks I'd just decorated his back with, you could hardly see them for all the tattoos he had. There was a huge tattoo of a dragon that covered most of his back. There was another one of a ninja fighter that almost covered one of his arms completely. There was a tattoo of a python on his chest. My grandmother would have never allowed me to get involved with a man like this one—especially if she knew he had spent six years in San Quentin for beating and robbing a woman the same age as her. I knew better than to bring Steve to Daddy's house. Ha! Daddy would be cordial, but Vera would shit out a black brick.

My love life was so dismal.

But until my luck with men changed, men like Steve would have to do. However, after him I would not date another man with a prison record. I'd dated two and that was two too many.

"I'm sorry, Steve," I cooed. "It's been so long since I had some good loving, I just couldn't help myself."

"Well, what the hell," Steve snorted, dismissing me with a sharp wave of his calloused hand. "Uh, listen, baby, I need to borrow a few dollars."

"Again?" I felt like shit knowing that the real reason he had called me up and asked me to meet him was so he could "borrow" a few dollars—*again.* The sex had probably been an afterthought on his part.

"Will a hundred do?" I asked, reaching for my purse on the nightstand. I always kept my purse close by when I was with Steve. The first night I was with him, I saw him going through my purse when he thought I was asleep. I never mentioned the three hundred dollars he'd stolen from me. I pulled out my wallet and removed five twenties from a wad that contained a little over five hundred bucks in twenties, tens, and fives.

"A thousand would do better," he snickered, snatching the bills out of my hand. He frowned as he counted the money. Money I'd never get back from him. Then he snatched my wallet, flipped it open, and turned it upside down. "This all you got?"

"It's all I have on me right now," I replied.

"Damn!" he complained. He unzipped the change pocket in my wallet and dumped out all the coins and took that too. "Girl, I can't believe somebody like you goes around with nothing but chump change in her pocketbook. What's the point of you being rich?"

"Smart rich people don't walk around with too much cash on them," I stated. "That way, if they get robbed, the thief won't get much."

"Pffft! After that old hag blew the whistle on me, I ain't trying to rob nobody these days. Shit. And I wouldn't have to if I had a woman who knew how to take care of her man! What about a cash advance on your credit card?" Steve removed my Visa from my wallet and looked at it like it was the Hope Diamond.

"It's almost maxed out. I think there's less than a hundred dollars on it," I lied. Daddy had given me three credit cards. Each one had a twenty-five-thousand-dollar credit line.

"Look, Sarah, if you want me to stick around and be your man, you have to do a lot better than you been doing. I don't need no broke-ass woman. And you black women wonder why we brothers hook up with white girls!"

I had planned to stay with Steve for at least another hour. But after his outburst, I suddenly wanted to leave.

I finally realized I was tired of being a sugar mama to the men I dated. It was time for me to get involved with a decent, hardworking man like Bo with the same old-fashioned values my daddy had.

Last night when Daddy had come into my room and told me that Bo was moving to San Francisco shortly after Vera had already told me, I had tried to act nonchalant.

"Bo who?" I had asked, sitting on the side of my bed, blowing on my freshly painted nails. My heart was thumping like mad. I just hoped that Bo looked as handsome in person as he did in that picture.

Daddy sat down next to me and patted my knee. "Vera's cousin in Houston," he answered, giving me a suspicious look. "Vera told me she showed you his picture the other evening."

"Oh, him," I said, looking up at Daddy, nodding and still blowing on my wet nails as I spoke.

"Don't you mess with me, girl!" Daddy warned with a stern look that was so weak it wouldn't have frightened a gnat. "Vera told me how big your eyes got when you looked at that picture. Bo's a handsome devil, but don't be disappointed when you see him in person. He was still in his early thirties when that picture was taken."

I had not thought about that! What if I was getting myself all worked up over an old geezer that probably looked like a lizard by now?

"Oh. I didn't know that," I mumbled. Other "what ifs" crowded my mind. What if Bo turned out to be a grumpy old man with a lot of health issues? What if he didn't even like me? Worse than that, what if he was a meddlesome busybody that caused problems for me? "So, just how old is he now?" I still wanted to know.

"Bo's forty-seven. And like Vera, he looks at least ten years younger in person. I guess good genes run in that family." Daddy gave me a playful slap along the side of my head.

I breathed a sigh of relief. Forty-seven was not too old for me. I'd been in love with movie stars like Samuel L. Jackson and Denzel Washington since I was a preteen, and they were definitely over forty.

"And you can stop playing games with me. Vera also told me how you looked at that picture of Bo with such a hungry eye."

I giggled, but my face was burning with embarrassment. "Oh, Daddy! I was just playing with Vera. I just acted that way to impress her. I'm doing everything I can think of to get closer to her. Honest to God I am, Daddy."

"Well, you must be doing a damn good job. Vera seems more relaxed around you than she was when you first came. The bottom line is, she really cares about you."

"I know, I know," I said, dipping my head. "She's been real nice to me lately," I admitted. That was true. I still listened to her conversations in the kitchen with Cash and Collette through the air duct, and I hadn't heard her or them talking about me as much as they used to. "So why is this Bo coming out here?"

Daddy groaned. "Poor fellow. He's recently divorced. And his wife was a pit bull if ever there was one. I agreed with Vera that the man needs a change." Daddy gave me a pensive look. "I've already told Vera that if he doesn't live up to my expectations, I will not hesitate to fire him and send him on his way. Now I want you to be on your best behavior when he gets here. Be nice to him but don't act a fool. I know how girls your age can be."

"What do you mean by that?"

Daddy gave me another stern look, more serious than the one he'd given me a little while ago. "Baby, I told you not to play games with me. I know I don't spend a whole lot of time with you now because of my work. I don't know, and I don't want to know, what it was like when your mama was alive. I don't want to know what kind of men she brought around you and how they treated you. I know you love the boys and all, but you're not a child any longer. I want you to behave like a mature, intelligent young woman when it comes to men. They'll have a lot more respect for you if you do. Isn't that what you want?"

"Uh-huh," I muttered.

I got real sad and angry just thinking about some of the jackasses my mother used to fool around with. Before she married Joaquin Garcia, my Mexican stepfather—who was also a jackass—she'd had men marching in and out of our apartment like soldiers. There were a few that weren't so bad, but the ones she kept around the longest were the ones I couldn't stand. Mama worked a lot of low-paying dead-end jobs, but she always had a lot of money. She was cheap, though. That's why she refused to move us to a better neighborhood or shop in the high-end stores. Being a cheapskate didn't keep my mama out of the casinos two or three times a month, but she managed to keep a roof over our heads and food on the table. I assumed some of the boyfriends were helping her out financially, even though most of them had low-paying dead-end jobs, too, if they had jobs at all. So far, I'd been spending time with some of the same kind of losers.

Well, I was ready to make a major adjustment in my love life. I wanted a good man. If he didn't have millions of dollars, that was all right. I had enough for both of us. But I didn't want a man who wanted me because of my money. With the exception of him cheating on me and getting another woman pregnant, I wanted a man just like my daddy.

It was because of Daddy that I felt better about myself than I used to. Before he'd entered my life, no other man had ever made me feel like I was worthwhile. But even the best daddy in the world couldn't fulfill every need a woman had. Because I had grown up without a positive male figure consistently in my life, I had developed a hole in my heart. And it was the kind that a daddy could not fill no matter how hard he tried.

"I'm sure I'll marry a man you'll like, Daddy."

"I certainly hope so. If you end up with one that makes a fool out of you, it'll break my heart clean in two. And I would die if I ever found out one hurt you in some way." Daddy looked so old and sad sitting there, looking around my room. "You're the most important person in the world to me now." For a minute, I thought he was going to cry.

"Daddy, you don't have to worry about me. I wouldn't stay with a man who hurt me in any way," I vowed. "I want a man just like you."

That must have been exactly what he wanted to hear. He smiled and gave me such a loving look, it made my head spin. Then he gave me a big hug.

CHAPTER 25

KENNETH

It took a lot to make me cry. But when my daughter told me she wanted a man just like me, I almost did. I had to blink real hard to hold back my tears.

"Uh, Bo will be here tomorrow. I've spoken to him by telephone, and he's anxious to get here and get to work," I reported.

"You're going to hire him without interviewing him in person?" Sarah asked. She looked bored now. I guess it had something to do with me bringing up Bo's age. "Cash told me you do background checks on everybody that works for you. Even the maintenance crew and the security guards."

"In Bo's case, I'm going to bypass all of that. I'm just going to take Vera's word that he's a good fit for us, and the fact that he has been working for the same company since he finished college. That's good enough for me. Besides, he's family. Regardless of all that, I did call up his supervisors at both places he currently works for. Each one gave an excellent reference."

The plane Bo flew in on was two hours late, and then there was an accident on the freeway involving several cars. Vera and I didn't get back home until around two the next morning. Sarah was in bed. But, as usual, Cash and Collette were perched on top of stools at the bar with drinks in hand when we entered the living room.

"My man!" Cash leaped off his bar stool and ran to his cousin.

They bumped fists and then Cash gave Bo a bear hug. I noticed how awed Bo seemed to be as he looked around the room. "Boy am I glad to see you. Man, you are going to love California."

Collette didn't budge from her stool. Bo strolled over to her and gave her a peck on the cheek. "I see you don't travel with much luggage," she remarked, looking at the duffel bag in Bo's hand. "How long are you going to stay?" There was a concerned look on her face.

"Well, I don't—"

Vera jumped in and answered for Bo. "He's staying permanently!" she chirped. "Cash, do you mind getting the rest of Bo's luggage out of the car?"

Cash slipped into his shoes and trotted out the door without hesitation. But Collette didn't look too happy. Her lips were pressed together so tightly it looked like they had almost disappeared into her mouth. And I didn't like that at all. For one thing, I had made it possible for this woman to live a very comfortable life. She didn't have to pay rent or any other household expenses. And she was enjoying other luxuries that most people only dream about. She used my chauffeur much more than Vera and I—even to drive her to the nail shop! I rarely chastised people, but I did when I felt the need. I cleared my throat real loud, and when Collette looked in my direction, I gave her a hot look. Like magic, a smile broke out on her face.

Vera had told me the other day that Collette was worried about Bo being groomed to take over Cash's job. When Vera told her that Bo was coming in as a senior manager in my main store, she got even more worried. It bothered her that Bo would be making more money than Cash. But she knew not to say anything to me about it. Who else would put up with her? She had dropped out of school in tenth grade. She had been working as a telephone psychic when Cash met her in L.A. when they were both trying to break into show business. And when she got fired from that job, nobody else wanted to hire her. She had thanked me profusely when I hired her to work in one of my stores. It was the smallest of my five locations, so I figured she couldn't get into too much trouble working there. Despite her many flaws, I liked the girl. I'd eventually transferred her to the main store so she could be closer to Cash. I guess I was a fool when it came to the underdog or people going through a rough time. That was the main reason I had hired Bo.

Bo couldn't have looked happier if he'd won the lottery. There was a grin on his face that had been present since he walked into the airport baggage claim area. "This sure is a nice house. This living room alone is bigger than the whole house I just moved out of," he said, looking around. "I can't thank y'all enough."

Cash stumbled in with Bo's two large suitcases and set them on the floor. "Brother man, you ought to see how Vera fixed up the room you'll be staying in," Cash said, wiping sweat off his face.

Bo held up his hand. "I really don't mind staying in a motel until I find a place." He looked from Vera to me, still grinning like a kid in a candy store. "You folks are doing too much for me too soon." I admired that he was so modest and humble. It was no wonder Vera was so proud of him.

"Motel my ass! You will do no such thing!" I boomed. "You're family and we have plenty of room here. We're glad to have you. Now, I know you had a rough flight and with the time difference, you probably just want to get some rest now." I gave Bo a quick hug and clapped him on the back. "Any more of that pot roast we had for dinner left?" I asked no one in particular, but I had turned to Collette. She gave me a tight smile and a weak nod. I returned my attention to Bo. "Are you hungry?"

"Yes, I am. But if I don't get some rest soon, I'm going to fall out," Bo said, his voice getting noticeably weaker. "Kenneth, you won't regret giving me this wonderful opportunity. I promise you won't regret it."

"Oh, I already know that!" I gave Bo a dismissive wave. "I know a good man when I come across one."

"Uh, where is that lovely daughter of yours I've heard so much about?" His voice sounded mighty strong now.

"She's in bed," Collette offered. "She got tired of waiting for you all to get home. She's really looking forward to meeting you, Bo."

Bo looked dazed for a few seconds. "Oh! Well, I'm looking forward to meeting her too."

"Come on, sugar. Let's get you unpacked," Vera said. She took Bo by the hand and led him to his room upstairs. Cash followed with the luggage. Collette finally hopped off the bar stool and walked up to me with her arms folded and a frightened look on her face.

"What's the matter?" I asked. "You got a problem with Bo being here?"

"I just don't want him to ruin things for Cash. Cash told me that Bo used to boss him around when they were kids. He would do everything Bo told him to do, including his homework and chores around the house. Bo's mama was as big a bully as Bo was. That's the reason Vera's sisters turned out to be so hostile. They used to spend more time with Bo's mama than their own. I don't want Bo to make a fool out of my husband at this stage of his life. He's already sensitive about being so close to fifty."

"I wouldn't worry about Bo making a fool out of Cash. Cash is a strong man. Everything is going to be just fine for everybody. Now you stop worrying about Bo changing things around here. That's not going to happen as long as I'm alive. All right?"

"All right." Collette nodded. But the frightened look was still on her face.

CHAPTER 26

SARAH

I HAD WAITED AROUND FOR HOURS LAST NIGHT, HOPING THAT DADDY and Vera would get back to the house with Bo before I went to bed. Well, they didn't. And since I could barely keep my eyes open, I had gone to bed. I got up early and applied my makeup and put on one of my cutest dresses. But by the time I made it downstairs to the kitchen area where we always ate breakfast, Daddy and Bo had already left the house.

"I know Daddy don't expect the man to start working already," I wailed, looking from Cash to Collette to Vera. They were all enjoying an elaborate breakfast with tall flutes of champagne like they did a few mornings every week before Cash and Collette went to work.

Vera's daily activities varied from one day to the next. Some mornings when I got up, she would have already left to go shopping or to see one of her plastic surgeons or wherever it was she went almost every day. One thing I noticed was that she never bothered to hook me up with any of the charities she worked for, even though I had mentioned it several times. And whenever I brought up me helping with her charities in front of Daddy, she quickly changed the subject or made it sound so unappealing Daddy suggested I not get involved. Therefore, I had a lot of time on my hands. That was the reason I visited my old friends so much. But that was getting to be too expensive. I was sick of "lending" money to my friends. And I was tired of fucking men that I didn't have a future with. I still wasn't ready to start looking for a job yet, and since I didn't have to work anyway, I decided to enjoy my leisure time as long as I could. Unlike most of my friends who were trapped in boring jobs, I was living the life of Riley. When I was not out shopping, I lounged around the house reading street lit and romance novels and watching game shows on TV most of the day.

"No, he's not going to start working until next week. Kenneth just took him out to the main store to introduce him to some of the more important members of the staff. They'll be back here in a little while. Once Bo gets settled in, I want you to help me make him feel at home," Vera told me.

"Oh, I'll make him feel real welcome," I replied quickly. "I want him to be so happy here, he'll never want to go back to Texas."

Cash had the usual stupid look on his frog face, but Collette rolled her eyes. I didn't care what they thought about Bo. If the man was nice to me, I was going to be nice to him.

I was glad they left the kitchen a few minutes later, burping and picking their teeth with toothpicks. Breakfast was more enjoyable when I ate alone.

Before I finished my breakfast, Daddy strolled into the kitchen with Bo behind him. I almost choked on the hot link in my mouth.

"Hello, sweetie," Daddy began. He came up to me and kissed me on the cheek. Bo had stopped in the middle of the floor. I hugged Daddy, but I was looking over his shoulder. When Bo's eyes met mine, I looked away and pulled away from Daddy. He glanced from me to Bo and back. "Honey, this is Bohannon, but we call him Bo. He's Vera's favorite cousin." Daddy covered his mouth with his hand. "Oops! I'd better not let Cash hear that!" he laughed. "He thinks he's Vera's favorite cousin." He turned to Bo again and beckoned for him to move closer. "This is Sarah Louise, my princess." I rose up out of my seat like a Phoenix.

When I'd heard that Bo was moving to California, I had prayed that in person he still looked exactly like his picture. I thought that would make it easier for me to be nice to him.

God didn't answer my prayer. Bo didn't look exactly like the man in the picture I'd seen. He looked even better! And he looked at least ten years younger than his actual age.

I couldn't wait to see how things would develop between him and me. I was glad I had put on a dress that showed off my curves.

"Hey, Sarah," Bo said, squeezing my hand. "I've heard so much about you."

"Hi, Bo," I said shyly. The way he looked into my eyes with so much intensity, I had to blink and look away to keep from giggling like a teenager. "Welcome to California. I hope you like it here."

"I'm sure I will," he said. He winked at me and my blood rushed up to my face.

"Bo and I have a lot to cover today, so we're heading right back out. I just wanted to swing back by here first because it'll be somewhat late when we get home tonight. We'll let you finish your breakfast, baby," Daddy said, already walking toward the door.

I was already worried about Bo spending as much time at the store as Daddy, who was there ten to fourteen hours on most days. Doing what? I never could figure that one out. Whenever I asked Daddy why he had to work such long hours, his answer was always something vague and confusing. Like, "I need to make sure things are being handled accordingly."

"It was nice meeting you, Sarah." Bo cocked his head to the side and gave me a mysterious smile. "I can't wait to get to know you."

"Uh-huh. Me too," I squeaked. I was glad he left when he did. My mouth had begun to water.

It was almost midnight when Daddy and Bo returned. I had turned in for the night, so I didn't see Bo again until the next day when we all sat down to eat breakfast. He nodded at me and "good morning" was all he said to me the whole time. He chatted with Daddy and Vera about world events, work, and other mundane things. Then he argued with Cash about some stupid sports events. He didn't even look at me again and my seat was directly across the table from his! Then I decided that he had not winked at me the day before. He must have had a piece of lint or something in his eye and he'd winked to get rid of it. I wasted no time trying to convince myself that maybe Bo was too old for me after all.

I was the first one to leave the table, and I couldn't get out of that kitchen fast enough.

An hour later, as I lay across my bed reading the latest issue of *Ebony* magazine, somebody tapped gently on my door. I assumed it was Delia coming to clean my room because she was the only one who bothered to knock these days.

"Come on in," I yelled, rolling onto my side.

"Sarah." It was Bo.

My breath caught in my throat as I stood up ramrod straight, dropping my magazine to the floor.

"I didn't mean to startle you," he said with one hand in the air and an apologetic look on his handsome face. "I was just wondering if I could borrow your car today if you won't be using it. Kenneth needs his car to drive to Daly City this morning for a meeting with his lawyer. Vera has a doctor's appointment. And Cash is taking his car to the shop for an oil change."

"Oh! You want to drive my car?"

"If you have plans, don't worry about it. I can take a taxi. I want to check out some dealers, compare prices. I'll have a vehicle of my own as soon as I find one I like. Thanks to your generous daddy."

"What about Costa, our chauffeur? He can drive you anywhere you want to go."

Bo waved his hand. "I don't like the idea of somebody driving me around. It makes me feel less independent."

I wished some of the men I'd been fooling around with had felt that way. Every chance one of them got, they had me arrange for Costa to haul them here or there. Then I had to bribe our driver with a lot of hush money so he wouldn't blab to Daddy or Vera.

"Yeah, you can use . . . uh . . . use my car," I stammered.

"Now, if *you* want to drive me around, I wouldn't mind that," Bo said, sliding his hands into his pants pockets. Then he winked again. "But you probably have plans for today. . . ."

I smiled. "I don't have any plans for today. I'd be glad to drive you around." I had an appointment to get my hair done, but I could do that later.

That was how it started, the beginning of the end.

I took Bo to three car dealers and he chose a brand-new Range Rover that Daddy had agreed to pay for.

That Friday, Bo took me to dinner at my favorite restaurant in the downtown area, which was Tad's Steakhouse. We talked about everything from our favorite foods to our favorite movies. After dinner, we rode around and I showed him some of the most popular parts of San Francisco. He liked action movies, so I took him to some of the locations where Clint Eastwood had filmed some of the scenes for *Dirty Harry*. Bo was like a kid in a candy store. And so was I. He was so damn fine, I had to force myself not to grab him.

He was still being trained at the store, so some days Daddy had him come in for only a few hours. Friday evening when he got home from the store a little after four, we went to Fisherman's Wharf. We walked along the pier acting like tourists and munching on jumbo prawns on a stick. He held my hand and draped his arm around my shoulder the whole time. We rode the cable car back down to Powell Street, where he had parked his brand-new SUV in a nearby garage.

When we got back to our neighborhood, I pointed out Danielle Steel's sprawling mansion a few blocks from ours. There was a shiny black stretch limo parked out front. "She's as gorgeous as the women she writes about," I said with a sigh.

Bo gave me a confused look. "Who is Danielle Steel?" he asked, staring at her mansion.

"You don't know who Danielle Steel is?" I gave him an incredulous look. He looked puzzled as he shook his head. "She's one of the most successful romance writers on the planet. I have most of her books if you want to read one."

Bo blinked and shook his head. "When I read, it's usually nonfiction or something related to business and finance," he said seriously. "I have never read a romance novel." He laughed. "But it's nice to know we live around people like one of the most successful romance writers on the planet."

The following week when Bo started working full-time at the main store, he got home early enough to take me out to dinner three nights in a row.

I got the feeling that Collette was jealous of all the attention I was getting from Bo. Every time she saw me leaving the house with him, she got this tight look on her face. And last Saturday night, as I was dressing to go to a jazz club with him, she eased into my room and plopped down on my bed. "You look real nice, Sarah."

"Thanks," I replied, struggling to get into my dress.

I was surprised when Collette ran up behind me and zipped up the back of my dress. "You know Bo is still in love with his ex-wife," she warned, giving me a guarded look as she sat back down on the bed. "Cash told me she's the only woman that man has ever loved. Cash also told me that Bo took the breakup so hard, he actually bought a gun and talked about killing Gladys. Knowing a man would go that far scares me."

"It doesn't scare me," I said sharply. "I know how to treat a man."

"Well, at least you know about Bo's past. He sounds like he's got some serious issues with women."

"So?" I shrugged. "Most men have serious issues with women."

"Yeah, but Bo's the kind of man who has a problem with women who disappoint him. A man like that can be real dangerous. Especially one that went out and bought a gun. That doesn't scare you?" she continued with even more conviction in her voice now.

"Collette, I appreciate your concern, but please let me take care of my business and I'll let you take care of yours. I can take care of myself when it comes to men. When I was still living in Hunters Point, I used to go out with dudes that would bash a girl's face in if she even thought about getting out of line—which I did with more than one of my boyfriends. And I'm still here," I said proudly, stabbing my chest with my finger. "Besides, as long as my daddy is alive, I don't have to worry about some man hurting me."

"Your daddy is getting older every day."

"So am I. So are you. Who isn't?"

Collette gave me a frustrated look. "Your daddy might not be around to help you when you need him, you know. Or he may come around when it's too late. I really do care about you, Sarah, whether you believe me or not."

It was my turn to give her a frustrated look, and I gave her one that was so severe it made her shudder. "Collette, what is your problem? Why do you care about what happens between Bo and me?"

"Well, I'm just trying to look out for you. You've become like a little sister to me."

I had to hold my breath to keep from laughing.

"If I were you, I wouldn't get too involved with Bo," she advised, placing her hands on her hips. It was only eight o'clock and she was already in one of the many ugly nightgowns she owned. This one was plaid with ruffles on the end of each sleeve. "Girl, I am telling you, if his ex decides she wants him back, he'll be up out of here lickety-split."

"I'll worry about that when and if it happens. Until then, Bo is my man."

The following Monday, Bo came home early enough to take me out again. He always enjoyed the rib joints and chicken shacks that I took him to. But on this particular night, we dined in one of the most expensive Italian restaurants in the Bay Area. I couldn't tell if it was the potent wine or if we were both ready to take our relationship to the next level, but we made love that night in my room.

We did the same thing the next night, and the next. . . .

If that meddlesome-ass Collette had not barged into my room, or if I had locked my door, things might have turned out differently. I looked over Bo's shoulder as we lay in bed, naked and humping like rabbits, to see Collette standing in the doorway with her mouth hanging open.

"Collette—shut that damn door!" I ordered, glaring at her.

"I knew it! I knew it! I knew you two love birds were getting busy," she said with a smirk. She kicked the door shut and folded her arms, looking like she was some kind of warden or something. "I see I was right!"

"Shit!" Bo hollered, scrambling to get under the covers.

"It's okay, Collette. Bo and I are getting married," I announced, grabbing his hand.

I couldn't tell who was more surprised by what I'd just said, Bo or Collette.

CHAPTER 27

KENNETH

SARAH AND BO CAME INTO MY BEDROOM HOLDING HANDS THAT SUNday morning. He had been in Frisco six weeks. And when I saw Collette trailing along behind them, I didn't know what to think.

Vera was sitting at her vanity applying makeup and fussing with her hair. She had had the bags removed from under her eyes two weeks ago, so now she looked more beautiful and younger than ever. As far as I was concerned, the woman was flawless, even with bags under her eyes. But whenever she felt the need to do something to make her feel better about herself, I encouraged it. More than anything I wanted to keep the two most important women in my life happy. But when I saw the strange look on Sarah's face, and the fact that she and Bo were holding hands, I got curious real quick.

"What's the matter?" I wanted to know.

Collette, being the busybody she was, spoke first. "Sarah has something to say." I ignored the smirk on her face.

"Daddy, you know Bo and I are real fond of each other," Sarah began.

"Mmm-huh. I figured that out already. You two have been out almost every night since he got here," I said with a chuckle. My daughter was glowing like a two-hundred-watt lightbulb, and that made me feel so jubilant I could barely contain myself.

Vera stood up, still holding a powder puff in her hand. She looked puzzled. Just as Sarah was about to speak again, Collette started waving her hands. "I think it's way too early for them to be talking about getting married!" Collette said.

"Who's getting married?" Vera and I said at the same time.

Out of the corner of my eye, I saw Bo look at Vera and nod. She nodded back. I didn't know what to make of that, but then I didn't know what to make of anything else that had just occurred in the last few moments.

"Bo and I are in love," Sarah blurted, leaning her head on Bo's shoulder. He put his arm around her and started to caress her shoulder. "We want to get married."

I adored Bo. He reminded me of myself when I was his age. When I recalled how Sarah had told me she wanted to marry a man just like me, I couldn't have been happier about him and her getting together now. Despite the fact that they had hooked up quicker than most people, I didn't let that bother me. I knew the first moment I laid eyes on Vera that she was the only woman for me.

"This is kind of soon to be talking about marriage," Vera suggested, giving me a sharp look. She must have suddenly remembered how fast she and I had decided to marry after we'd met. "But I guess there is such a thing as love at first sight." She gave me a big smile. I smiled back and gave her a knowing wink.

"Vera's right. There is such a thing as love at first sight," I agreed. "But things are different now than they were when she and I rushed into marriage. Times have changed. It's a big step that nobody should rush into nowadays."

"I tried to tell them that," Collette snarled. "Bo, don't you think you should wait for the ink to get dry on your divorce papers?"

"Collette, don't *you* think you should mind your own damn business?" Sarah snapped.

Cash padded down the hall and into the room. He was still in his pajamas. "I was wondering where everybody was. What's going on here?" he asked.

"Sarah wants to marry Bo," Collette told him. "Can you believe this girl?"

"Excuse me?" Cash's eyes got big and an amused expression spread across his face as he looked from Sarah to Bo. He slapped his hands onto his hips. "Is this some kind of a joke?" He laughed. "Don't you two think you should get to know each other better first?"

"I know all I need to know about Bo," Sarah insisted. "Daddy, I hope you will give us your blessing." Then she turned to Vera. "You, too, Vera. But . . . we've made up our minds. I'm over twenty-one now, so we're going to get married no matter what anybody says," she said, looking from Collette to Cash as she made her last statement.

"Baby, all I want is for you to be happy. If you and Bo want to get married, you have my blessing." And I meant every word. Sarah was a strong-willed young woman. I knew right after I'd first met her that she was the kind of girl who was going to live her life the way she wanted to. She'd been doing just that so far. If she wanted to get married, I was glad it was to a man like Bo and not one of the lowlife characters she had been involved with in the past few years. And I knew Vera felt the same way.

"Uh, I hope you two getting married doesn't mean you'll be moving out of the house," Vera mumbled. There was a worried look on her face and that worried me.

"Vera, if they want a place of their own, that's their business," I threw in quickly. "Newlyweds need their privacy."

"What I want to know now is when you two plan on getting married? Do you plan to do it in a church, or what?" Vera asked. I was glad to see that the worried look was no longer on her face. Now she looked downright giddy. But that worried me too. Vera was a complicated and mysterious woman who never ceased to amaze me.

"We don't want to spend weeks or months planning something real fancy. We're going to fly up to Reno and do it there in one of those cute little chapels," Sarah announced. She was already glowing like a bride.

"Girl, you must be pregnant!" Collette hissed with a harsh look on her face.

Sarah didn't even bother to look at her. She only had eyes for Bo. "No, I'm not pregnant," she said demurely, and then she snickered. "But we're working on that."

CHAPTER 28

VERA

I WAS MAD AS HELL! I COULDN'T WAIT TO TALK TO BO! I WANTED TO wring his goddamn neck with my bare hands!

I didn't like that he wasn't following my plan. I had told that fool to court that dumb-ass girl for at least three or four months to make it look good. I told him to treat her like a queen, lick her pussy all day long if he had to, and spoil her so rotten she'd have to be weaned like a baby to get back to normal. *Then* he was to ask her to marry him, not six *weeks* after he met her!

Bo managed to avoid me all day Sunday and he left for work Monday morning before I got up. I called that hardheaded jackass at work five times before noon. I left a message each time, but he hadn't returned any of my calls. It was after 1:00 p.m. when I finally caught up with him. And that was only because I had pressed *67 before I dialed his number so my name wouldn't show on his caller ID.

"We need to talk," I hissed into the telephone.

"Hi, cuz. Sorry I haven't been able to return any of your calls. I was in a payroll meeting all morning. Kenneth and I just returned from lunch with a rep from an account we're trying to land." I couldn't believe how casual he sounded.

"Negro, don't you go there! You know I don't give a good goddamn about a fucking rep. I know you've been dodging me and you know we need to talk about that little stunt you and Sarah pulled yesterday."

"I'm kind of busy at the moment," Bo claimed, sounding nervous now. And that did not surprise me. He had to know I had a bone to pick with him. "We can talk when I get home."

"We'll talk then, too, but we need to talk *now* before I blow a gasket."

"I'll be home early. We can talk then."

"How do you expect us to talk with Sarah clinging to you like a vine as soon as you step into the house and Kenneth lurking around like Turkey Lurkey?"

"All right. Hold on just a second." Bo put me on hold for about five minutes, which was four and a half minutes too long. By the time he returned to the phone, I was seething. "Where are you now, Vera?"

"I'm in my bedroom. I've been trying to reach you since this morning!"

"I told you I received your messages, but I was too busy to call you back."

"Look, dear cousin, if you want to stay busy and keep that job, you'd better straighten up and fly right."

"What's that supposed to mean?"

"You know damn well what it means. I moved your pitiful ass out here for a reason."

"Yes, you did. You moved me out here to work for your husband."

"Correction, I brought you out here to take care of Sarah. The job was just a smoke screen. I initiated this thing between you and Sarah and I—"

"Hold on now. You can stop right there. I happen to be in love with the girl."

"Only in a pig's eye!"

"No, I really do love her. I know you and I talked about a . . . uh . . . a setup, but things didn't work out that way after all. She's . . . well, she's a good woman and she has a lot to offer a man."

"Tell me about it! She's worth millions and will be worth even more someday—"

"Vera, I'm glad Sarah is rich, but there is a lot more to her than her money. If I had met her under different circumstances, I probably would have fallen in love with her anyway, even if she didn't have a plugged nickel to her name."

"If you really do love her, why the rush to get married? I told you to court the bitch a few months, not a few weeks!"

"Vera, please calm down!"

"Calm down my pussy! This is my future and my life you're playing with! I have come too far and worked too hard to let you ruin things for me!"

"I am not going to ruin anything for you, woman. And I don't appreciate you talking to me like I'm some kind of flunky. I'm forty-seven years old and nobody tells me what to do!"

"I don't believe my fucking ears! What do you think Kenneth would say if I told him the *real* reason you moved out here?"

"I moved out here to work for him. That's the real reason," Bo said flatly. "Listen, we're not going to lose a damn thing by me marrying Sarah this quickly. You'll still be in control of Kenneth's money. I will be married to his daughter and I will be in control of her. If she's this anxious to marry me now, I want to strike while the iron is hot! What if I had held out for a few months like you wanted me to and Sarah lost interest in me? Then I would have moved out here for nothing but the job after all."

I had to consider Bo's words. What he'd just said made me calm down. "I just wish you had discussed it with me before you asked her to get married."

"I didn't ask her. We hadn't even discussed anything that serious. Cuz, you know me well enough to know that I wouldn't have made such a bold move on my own. I would have discussed it with you first."

"What? Do you mean to tell me Sarah proposed to you?"

"Not exactly. She didn't *ask* me to marry her. I guess you could say she *told* me that's what we were going to do. She had already made up her mind and the first I heard of it was yesterday morning when she led me to you and Kenneth's bedroom. Uh, a few minutes before that, Collette had barged into Sarah's room and caught us in her bed taking care of business."

"What the hell . . ." My voice trailed off. A few moments passed before I continued. "Oh. I didn't know any of that," I said in a low, apologetic voice. "But why didn't you tell me that getting married was her idea?"

"Why didn't you give me a chance to tell you? I was going to take you aside and talk to you this evening when I got home."

"Shit. Well, I guess you really should marry her as soon as possible now before she changes her mind."

"I agree with you on that. I do love the girl and I think she and I can have a good life together, even though she is kind of immature and impulsive. This is going to be a real challenge for me."

"Tell me about it. But you're the best man for Sarah if she's so anxious to get married. You should have seen some of the creatures she had coming to this house!"

Bo laughed and I laughed right along with him.

"So, are you still mad at me, cuz?" he teased.

"I guess not. I feel a little bit better. Just don't screw things up. Marry her and treat her nice. She's just as gullible and stupid as her daddy. But she's so crazy about you anyway, I'm sure she'll do whatever you tell her to do."

"All I want her to do is be good to me."

"Don't worry. I'm sure she won't do anything to disappoint you. If she makes a fool out of you, you'll know how to deal with her."

Bo was taking too long to respond.

"Bo, did you hear what I just said?"

"I did," he said quickly. "I just hope she doesn't make a fool out of me the way Gladys did. If she does . . . I don't know what I'll do this time."

CHAPTER 29

KENNETH

Vera and I and Sarah and Bo flew up to Reno on a private jet the following weekend. The flight was only about forty minutes long, but during that whole time, Sarah couldn't stop grinning and fawning over Bo.

Just seeing them together reminded me so much of my first years with Vera and how giddy we had both been. It looked like history was being repeated and I could not have been more pleased. My marriage was a big success, so I had every reason to believe that my baby's would be too. However, I did have at least one mildly disturbing thought dancing around in my head. Bo being a man, he no doubt possessed some of the same flaws as other men, especially ambitious men like me. He would probably lose his perspective on life from time to time, which I had come to believe was normal. Men made more mistakes than women. I just didn't want Bo to put my baby through what I'd put Vera through. It was unrealistic for anybody to think that any man on this planet could be married to a woman and be one hundred percent faithful to her throughout the duration of their marriage. That was such a bunch of baloney. It made me want to laugh every time I thought about it. However, a good man learned from his mistakes. I was proof of that. I just prayed that if Bo involved himself with other women along the way, my daughter would never find out. If she did, I hoped that she would handle it with the same level of dignity that Vera had.

But this was supposed to be a happy day, and I didn't want to ruin it for anybody. I cleared my mind and plastered a smile on my face.

My baby girl married the love of her life in a little chapel with a life-size statue of Cupid propped up on the front entrance steps. I had never seen Sarah look more beautiful and radiant in my life, and I prayed that she would remain that way.

"If he ever hurts her, I'll die," I told Vera in our luxurious hotel suite later that night, a few hours after the ceremony. "She's the most important thing I have in the world, and I wouldn't want to live if something happened to her."

"What about me?"

"What about you?"

"You just said Sarah's the most important thing you have in the world. What about me?"

When I realized how insensitive my comment must have sounded to my wife, I wanted to bite off my own tongue. I had never put my foot in my mouth so deeply before in my life! "Oh, baby. You know what I mean. You're my wife and I have never loved a woman as much as I love you. You should know that by now. You're just as important to me as Sarah. But nobody's going to hurt you as long as I'm alive. I'm responsible for your welfare. And now that Sarah belongs to Bo, she's his responsibility. That's what I meant."

"Bo would never hurt Sarah. As much as his ex put him through, he knows what real pain feels like, but he never put his hands on Gladys. Sarah's a nice, quiet girl who goes out of her way to please people. She's nothing like that witch he used to be married to, so I doubt if there is anything Sarah could do that would make him snap."

"I know, baby. But I'm a daddy and that's just the way our minds work. We worry about our kids no matter how grown they get, and we don't want to see anything happen to them. And I'm not just talking about something physical. I'm talking about emotional hurt too."

"Look, as bad as Bo's ex treated him, he never hurt her physically or emotionally. As long as Sarah stays with Bo, she will be just fine. Now, I thought you were going to take her down to the gaming area so she could try her luck at the roulette wheel."

I jumped off the bed. "Shit! Thanks for reminding me." I froze in my spot. "I'd better call her up first. I'd hate to interrupt them." I laughed as I dialed the honeymoon suite. Sarah answered on the first ring. "Baby . . . uh . . . I hope I didn't interrupt anything," I said quickly, feeling embarrassed. My daughter was a grown woman. I didn't know—and didn't want to know—about her sex life. Just knowing she would be sleeping with Bo every night now made me cringe.

"Oh, Daddy. Please don't go there. It's only five-thirty and Bo and I have the whole night ahead of us. Are we still going to the roulette table?"

"That's what I was calling about."

"I'll meet you downstairs in ten minutes."

Vera stood in front of the mirror on the huge dresser facing our king-sized bed, putting on a new face. "Honey, I won't be gone long," I told her. I walked up behind her and placed my hands on her hips. She pressed her body into mine and started a slow grind. My dick jumped to attention right away. The more she moved, the harder it got. "Aw now, baby. You know I can't leave this room with this blue-steel brick in my pants!" I teased, pulling Vera to the bed. She giggled as she lay back, spreading her legs open like a pair of scissors.

Sarah was meandering around the gaming area by the time I made it downstairs twenty minutes later. Vera had declined my invitation to join Sarah and me. She was craving a few margaritas and was convinced that the only place in Reno that made her favorite drink the way she liked it was a nearby Mexican restaurant called Bertha's. She had invited Bo to join her and he had reluctantly agreed.

"What took you so long?" Sarah asked, hands on her hips.

"I had to return a call to the store. And I had told my staff not to bother me this weekend!" I fibbed, trying to sound annoyed.

"I thought you told me you advised everybody to call Cash if they had any problems?"

"I did," I responded, leading Sarah by the hand to the gaming area. Harrah's casino was as busy and crowded as ever. We had to squeeze our way into a spot at the roulette wheel. "But somebody had a question Cash couldn't answer." I didn't like to lie to my own child. But I was not about to tell her the real reason I got held up.

One thing I loved about Vera was that it didn't take much to satisfy her in bed. Oh, she used to need more bedroom maintenance years ago, but like me, age had slowed her down. The last time she sucked my dick, I got off in less than thirty seconds. I had gone from being a minute man that night to a half a minute man. We had both laughed about that.

Sarah and I didn't have much luck at that damn roulette wheel. So we played a few games of blackjack. After we lost a couple of hundred bucks at that in just a few minutes, we went to the casino bar to have a few drinks.

"Baby, I just realized that this is the first time in years that you and I have had a drink together, just the two of us."

"I didn't realize that. I enjoy drinking with you, Daddy."

Sarah hauled off and kissed my cheek. I noticed a wrinkled white dude accompanied by an equally wrinkled white woman looking at us with puzzled expressions on their faces. They kept their gaze on us too long for me, so I gave them a harsh look until they looked away.

I had already gulped down a few drinks in the room with Vera, so I was already tipsy. But I swallowed a double shot of bourbon right away and it hit me like a ton of bricks. My head felt like it was swimming in a bowl of quicksand. I blinked and looked around the room. The wrinkled couple had left. I looked around some more and shook my head. "Baby, don't look now but there's a dude directly across from us that looks a lot like me. And he's with a sweet young thing too. I know folks will stare at them the same way that couple was staring at us a few minutes ago. They are probably thinking I'm some dirty old man taking advantage of a cute young chick." I laughed, but I didn't laugh long. There was a sad look on Sarah's face.

"That's us, Daddy," she said gently.

"Huh?"

"That's a mirror on that wall. That old dude and the sweet young thing you're looking at are us."

"Oh." I pushed my empty glass to the side and covered my mouth to stifle a belch. "I guess I don't need anything else to drink if I'm too drunk to recognize my own self and my own child in a mirror."

"I don't need anything else to drink either," Sarah said with a mild belch. She had drunk only half of the piña colada she'd ordered. The sad look was still on her face.

"What's the matter, baby? You don't look like a woman who just got married a few hours ago."

"Daddy, I hope everything works out between Bo and me. I hope he treats me the same way you treat Vera."

That statement sobered me up considerably. "What do you mean?"

"Well, for one thing, you're old enough to be Vera's daddy, but you treat her like you're both the same age. I have never seen you treat her like a child the way some old men do when they marry young women. I just hope Bo always treats me the same way you treat Vera."

"Don't you sit here and tell me that you're having doubts about your marriage already!"

"I'm not having doubts. It's just that . . . everything happened so fast."

"Then why didn't you wait like Vera suggested? If you're not pregnant like you said, there was no reason for you to rush into something as serious as marriage."

"I'm not pregnant. I wanted to do it fast because . . . uh . . . I was afraid that if I waited too long, Bo might go back to his ex."

"Honey, you don't have to worry about that. Bo told me that he wouldn't reconcile with that woman if she came back in a gift-wrapped box." I gave Sarah a big hug. "I'm just glad to know that Bo was just as anxious to get married as you were. I will rest in peace when the time comes."

Sarah gave me an exasperated look and said, "I wish you would stop doing that!"

"Stop doing what?"

"Talking about death."

"Well, it's the one thing we'll all have to face one day."

"I know that, but I wish you wouldn't talk about it. It worries me."

"Well, you can stop worrying. I'm going to be around for a long time. As long as nothing bad happens to you."

"What do you mean by that?"

"I told Vera that if something really bad happened to you, it would kill me." I had a smile on my face, but I was dead serious.

"Daddy, nothing bad is going to happen to me. Bo is going to take real good care of me. He promised."

"I know he will," I said, standing up. "Bo's a man's man, and I couldn't have picked a better man for you if I had tried. You landed yourself a real big fish."

"I know I did, Daddy."

"Well now! I'm glad that's out of the way." I took a deep breath and patted the pocket I kept my money clip in. I was mad that the wad of bills I had brought to gamble with was a lot thinner now. It was time for me to get the hell up out of Reno. "Vera and I are going home tomorrow so you can enjoy the rest of your honeymoon alone with your husband."

CHAPTER 30

VERA

WHILE KENNETH AND SARAH WERE ON THE CASINO FLOOR LOSING money at the roulette wheel, Bo and I were sharing a pitcher of margaritas at Bertha's, an old-school Mexican restaurant a few blocks from the main strip.

"Is she on the pill?" I asked. I took a sip from my glass and plucked a couple of tortilla chips out of the bowl on the table. I loved Mexican food, but I didn't have much of an appetite. I had too many things on my mind and one of them was to make sure I stayed on top of my plan at all times.

Bo gave me a confused look. "Is who on the pill?" he asked dumbly.

I looked at him like he had just lost his mind. Apparently my cousin was not as sharp as I thought he was. I had begun to suspect that the morning he and Sarah strolled into my bedroom and announced that they were getting married. I was surprised when Bo told me that Sarah had been the one to initiate this hasty union. But I was not surprised that he had gone along with it without question or protest. At least not in front of Kenneth and me that morning. Poor Bo. The biggest flaw in his personality was that he was like putty in a woman's hand. That weakness had contributed to the breakup of his first marriage. What if Sarah steered him in a totally different direction from the one I had established? That would derail my plans, to say the least. I had to keep things under control no matter what.

I forced myself to smile at my clueless cousin. "Sarah, that's who. Who else would I be asking this question about?"

Bo hunched his shoulders and replied in a dry voice, "I don't know if she's on the pill or not."

"Do you mean to tell me that you started fucking that girl not knowing if she was taking care of business or not?"

"It happened so fast and unexpectedly that I didn't have time to think about anything like that. But she always had a fistful of condoms anyway and so did I. I've used one every time we made love."

"Humph! Well, I'm glad to hear that. With all the action she was getting from those other bums, it was just a matter of time before she caught some disease that no doctor can cure."

"If you mean AIDS, she and I talked about that," Bo said. "She told me two people in her old neighborhood died of it, so when she became sexually active, she protected herself from day one."

"Hmmm. I guess she's smarter than she looks. I'm glad to hear she's got enough sense in that regard. But we need to find out about her birth control."

"Well, the condoms are good to prevent her from getting pregnant too. I'm sure that's the main reason most people use them." Bo shifted in his seat and took a drink. "Why are you asking me about birth control anyway? This subject is kind of personal, you know."

"If she has your baby, that'll lock you into her life for good. Kenneth will treat the child like royalty, just like he treats her."

"From what I've observed, he treats you like royalty too." Bo snickered and gave me a cheeky look.

He knew that I didn't like to be teased. And I reminded him of that by speaking in an angry tone of voice. "Well, he should! Being married to him is no picnic!"

Bo flinched. "Well, excuse me for asking you that. But I have to ask you something else you probably won't like. Why do you stay married to a man you talk about like he's some creature that escaped from a horror movie?"

I pursed my lips and cocked my head to the side. "Honey, you might be crazy, but I'm not. I would never leave a man with the kind of money Kenneth's got. And he's a fool when it comes to money, thank God. A grandchild would send him into a whole new level of fool. I want to be front and center when that happens."

"I see. Well, if you think that, how come you never had his baby?"

I looked at the ground and sniffed. When I looked back up at Bo, there was a look of concern on his face. "Did I hit a nerve? You look like you want to cry."

"I'm all right. It's just that . . . well, there is a reason Kenneth and I never had a child. He caught an infection in one of his testicles several years ago that left him practically sterile. Not having a child is my biggest regret." I choked on a fake sob as I dabbed at my eyes with a napkin.

"Oh. I didn't mean to upset you." Bo gave me an apologetic look and squeezed my hand.

"I desperately wanted a child, even more so than Kenneth. We had just started to talk about adopting one when Sarah came into our lives. By that time, my baby-producing days were over." I sniffed and blew my nose into the napkin. "Sarah is enough for me."

"Yeah, but she was already almost grown when you got her. Wouldn't you have adopted a much younger child or an infant so it would seem more like a child you gave birth to?"

"There were other reasons. I was happy to settle for a child Sarah's age and not consider adoption anymore. It made more sense under the circumstances. You see, Kenneth's not a young man anymore and he's dying of a bad heart. He was concerned about not being around to help me raise an infant or a very young child."

"Pfft!" There was an amused look on Bo's face as he waved his hand in the air. "Kenneth's been dying of a bad heart for over twenty years! You told me that right after you introduced him to me, remember?"

"Oh, yeah. Well, he's still alive and kicking, but you wouldn't believe all the pills he takes and all the visits he makes to his doctor. He's had several mild heart attacks and it's happening much more frequently now. He *could* drop dead any day now. . . ."

"Well, we all have to go sometime. But I'm sorry to hear that the two of you didn't have a child together, and long before now. Maybe you'd feel different about Sarah." Bo rubbed his neck and glanced slowly around the room, as if trying to hide the melancholy look that was on his face now.

"Why is that look on your face?"

He looked embarrassed now. "I just had a thought." He snorted. "Since we're talking about babies, I would love to have at least one of my own. I just hope it happens before I get too old. Most of my Houston male friends my age are already grandfathers; some have been for years." An angry look suddenly covered his face like a shroud. "Gladys didn't tell me until after we got married that she had no desire to have children. That was our biggest problem. Not only was she on the pill, but she also made me use condoms every time we made love just to be extra safe."

We remained silent for a few moments.

"Where does Sarah keep those condoms?" I asked.

"In her purse I guess. Isn't that where all women keep items like that?"

"I wouldn't know," I muttered. I didn't know where other women kept their condoms, but I was not stupid enough to keep mine in a place where somebody could find them. I always left my stash with my lover.

"Anyway, every time she came into my room looking for some action, she already had a few in her hand. And when we hooked up in hotels, she pulled a pack out of her purse. Why?"

"First find out if she's ready to make a baby. If she is, we don't have to worry about that. But if she gives you the runaround about wanting to wait and shit, we have a lot of work to do."

"What work would we have to do if she's not ready to be a mother?"

"Condoms don't always work. Some come from the manufacturer with defects. Holes. I knew a girl back in Houston who wanted to trap some dude by getting pregnant. She went behind his back and pricked holes in the condoms with a straight pin before he put them on."

Bo gasped. "Come on now! You don't think I'm going to stoop that low, do you?"

"Ha! If you stooped down any more, you'd be lower than a snake's belly!" I said in a loud voice. A sharp-nosed woman at a nearby table looked at me and laughed, so I lowered my voice. "It's too late for you to be getting all holier-than-thou."

"Vera, I was not joking when I said I really do love Sarah," Bo said in a small voice.

"And what the fuck does that have to do with anything?"

"I don't want to hurt her."

"What the fuck are you trying to say? Hurt her how? As long as you don't beat her or let her catch you fucking another woman, how would you hurt her?"

"You know what I'm trying to say. I would never want her to know you wooed me to come out here mainly to marry her just so you could gain control of Kenneth's money. Now here you are telling me I need to get her pregnant so she can have a baby so that you—and me, too, now—can gain even more control of that money. Sarah's a sweet woman. I realize that now. She doesn't deserve to be hurt."

"Humph! If you don't want that money, that's fine with me. That's more for me. But if you don't keep her happy and she divorces you, you'll be out in the cold. All you'll get is whatever she agreed to give you if the marriage fails." A large lump suddenly formed in my throat. "Shit! I didn't talk to you about the prenup! See, that's the problem when people rush into things!"

"Speaking of prenup, when Kenneth brought it up, Sarah got crazy and boo-hooed so hard, he dropped the subject."

"Do you mean to tell me you don't have any kind of financial arrangement at all?" It was bad enough that Kenneth made me sign a prenuptial agreement before he would marry me. According to that damn thing, if our marriage ends in divorce, no matter which one of us files, I will walk away with only the car in my possession at the time, my jewelry and clothing, and a modest allowance for just *a year.* I wouldn't even inherit any shares in his business, the mansion and its contents, the other cars, or any of his other assets. There were only three ways for me to benefit. I had to stay married to Kenneth or become his widow. The third way was for me to have some serious control over Sarah after Kenneth's demise. As her husband, Bo would automatically move up to the top of the food chain. A child would secure his position even more. And as long as Bo remained my puppet, I was in good shape.

"I don't have any type of financial arrangement with Sarah because I am going to do everything I can to make this marriage work. I know you and I originally planned a sham marriage between her and me. But I don't look at it that way now. Besides, if she ever found out that's what we had planned from day one, she'd be pissed! I don't want to experience another divorce—I wouldn't survive another traumatic experience like that. And, like I said, I really do love the girl. I can't tell you that enough." I couldn't stand the dreamy-eyed look on Bo's face whenever he told me how much he loved Sarah. Like now. He looked like he was so love-struck he'd be willing to eat a bowl of her shit.

"Sure you love her. Who wouldn't? If I had a dick, I'd love her too."

"Vera! You stop that! A classy woman like you should never even think such a raunchy thing, let alone say it!"

"Just don't forget I'm the only other person who knows why you moved to Frisco. I'm sure you don't want Sarah or Kenneth to know."

"You're not threatening me, are you?"

"No, I'm not threatening you. I just want you to remember that no matter what happens, you owe me. If Kenneth divorces me for some reason, and you're still with Sarah, I expect you to take care of me. Understand?"

Bo nodded and finished his drink.

CHAPTER 31

SARAH

THE FIRST FEW WEEKS OF MARRIED LIFE WERE SO WONDERFUL, I FELT like the luckiest girl in the world. No, I felt like Cinderella in living color. My story was an urban fairy tale. I had been a broke little girl living in the hood with my bitter, elderly grandmother who had raised me to be "realistic" about life: "Baby, don't expect nothing because this is as good as it gets for black females. We get the jobs nobody else wants and the black men that the white women don't want," my grandmother had told me, and on a regular basis at that.

Back then I had assumed I'd marry one of the shady boys next door, have a bunch of doomed babies, collect welfare, or get a low-paying dead-end job. Then I'd spend the rest of my life trying to keep my kids out of trouble and my man out of jail and away from other women.

One of my former female friends had joined the army and fallen in love with a high-ranking officer. He had married her and adopted her two-year-old son, so she was doing all right. But most of the other girls I had grown up with were living the bleak life that I had once envisioned for myself. *Look at me now!* I often said to myself. I had it all. My new husband was the icing on the cake.

On our wedding night, Bo had promised me that he was going to pamper me like a baby and treat me like a queen. He took showers with me just so he could wash my back. He gave me foot massages. He cut my toenails. And some mornings he brought me breakfast in bed. He gave me large bouquets of fresh roses when I least expected it. We made love as often and as vigorously as porn stars.

I loved waking up in bed next to Bo. He had wanted me to move into his bedroom at the end of the hall, but since mine was larger and had a better view, I convinced him to move into mine.

Daddy was happy because I was happy. He didn't look so tired now. And his health seemed to be much better. His eyes were brighter and he didn't even complain about his frequent chest pains. His arthritis didn't bother him that much anymore, so he didn't stumble around like a drunken sailor the way he used to from time to time.

The way Vera pranced around the house grinning and joking with me and Bo, you would have thought that she was a newlywed too. "You and Bo sure do spend a lot of time in the bedroom," she commented with a wink one Sunday morning. "It wouldn't surprise me if you two haven't already put a bun in the oven."

A baby? Me? I wasn't exactly ready to become anybody's "baby mama." I wanted to enjoy more of my young years first. But I had decided to keep my thoughts on motherhood to myself for the time being. "Not yet. My period just came on this morning," I told Vera, kind of embarrassed.

I didn't like talking about my sex life or anything related to sex with my parents. Things had improved considerably between Vera and me, so I really did think of her as my mother now. However, I still didn't trust her completely. When it came to her, I was never going to let my guard down. That was the main reason I wanted to remain in the bedroom that was directly above the kitchen, so I could continue to hear when people were down there talking about me. I wasn't worried about Bo or the housekeeper hearing the conversations through the air duct. For one thing, you had to squat down close to it and the vent had to be open. I always made sure it was closed before Delia cleaned my room and I'd instructed her to never open it without my knowledge or permission. The room rarely got cold enough to require heat. And when it did, I cracked the vent open just far enough to allow the minimum amount of heat to flow up. Now that Bo shared the room with me, I only opened the vent all the way when I was alone and wanted to eavesdrop.

It had been a couple of weeks since I had eavesdropped on the conversations in the kitchen. Most of the yip-yapping that I'd heard lately had been either something I'd already heard or something too petty to upset me. But since my status had changed, I suspected that Vera and her backstabbing crew had a lot to say about that.

Bo and I had been married a little over a year when I decided to resume my position at the air duct vent on a daily basis instead of a few times a week. And it was a good thing I did.

One Monday morning, when I got out of bed, Bo and Daddy had already left for work. They had to attend a breakfast meeting with a vendor. Since Vera was the ringleader, she was the one I had expected to initiate the latest bash aimed at me. But it was Cash and Collette who began to talk about me like a dog as they ate breakfast that morning. Harsh voices floated up to my room along with the heat and the pleasant smell of bacon.

"Humph! I'm sure Miss Thing really thinks she's hot shit now. I wouldn't be surprised if she started throwing her weight around even more. Next thing we know, she'll be treating me like I'm her ugly stepsister and you like her ugly stepbrother. The bitch," Collette fumed.

"I feel you! She's on her way to becoming a straight-up fishwife all right. She rolls her eyes more than a gambler rolls his dice. Just last night when I borrowed a few bucks from Kenneth, she had the nerve to roll her eyes at me like it was her money he was giving me!" Cash complained.

"Well, I hate to keep reminding you, but in a way it is her money too."

"No! Kenneth was the one who reached into his wallet and gave me that money. She didn't!" Cash boomed.

Collette hawked and let out a disgusted sigh. She did that a lot, especially during her conversations with Cash about me. "Cash, you jackass! Don't you realize that what's Kenneth's is hers? Do you think that when Kenneth dies things are going to be the same for us? She'll probably evict us before they even put him in the ground! And where would we go? Back to that hole we were living in on Joost Street before Vera made Kenneth let us move up in this highfalutin motherfucker? Not me. Between the two of us, we don't make enough money to continue living the way we live now."

"I don't think we have to worry about that right now."

"Why not?"

"For one thing, we're family!"

"We're *Vera's* family. We don't mean a damn thing to Kenneth. I wouldn't be surprised if he only left us a few thousand dollars in his will."

"Collette, we don't even know if he's leaving us anything in his will."

"Before that little witch came here, we were. Vera told me just last month that Kenneth had provided for all of us in his will. Even his housekeeper and his chauffeur."

"Well, then, what are you worried about? Did she tell you how much he's leaving us?"

"She didn't tell me that and I didn't ask. For one thing, I doubt if she knows. She didn't know all the other times we asked her. All she said the last time I discussed the will with her was that Kenneth still had us in the will. But the thing is, he keeps changing it!"

"Well, let's just be patient. Even if he doesn't leave us anything, we've had it good so far, living rent-free, getting that new SUV, and so on. But I don't see any reason for Kenneth to cut us out just because he put his daughter in the will. There is more than enough money to go around." Cash sounded really worried.

Before he or Collette could speak again, Vera joined them. She greeted them by saying, "I guess Her Highness is still stretched out in that twenty-thousand-dollar brass bed her daddy bought her for a wedding present," she snarled. "I do not trust that girl. Who knows what scheme she's got up her sleeve!"

"There's just no telling! She's full of surprises! I knew she was a pig in a poke the first time I met her," Collette said with a piercing laugh.

"Cuz, Collette just told me that Kenneth has changed his will a few times. Did he leave me and Collette in good shape?" Cash asked Vera.

"I hope he did. But we won't find out until he dies. He won't let me near that damn will. Pass the bacon, please." Vera paused and muttered profanity under her breath for a few seconds. Then she yelled, "All this greasy-ass pork bacon! Two times a fucking week! I thought I told Delia to buy only beef bacon now! There goes her next bonus." She paused again, a little longer this time. Then she spoke in her normal tone of voice. "Kenneth is a very generous man," she declared, chomping like a cow on the same greasy-ass pork bacon she found so offensive. "Now, we all know what a good man Kenneth is too. But he's unpredictable. He might be good to everybody in his will and he might not. He has a flesh-and-blood daughter in his life now. She's the only one I know he'll be real generous to. He'll leave her a pretty penny."

"I'm glad Sarah's his only child," Cash said.

"Well, the only thing he wants before he bites the dust is a grandchild. That's all he talks about these days. It's become an obsession with him. I hope Sarah and Bo don't wait too long to have a baby. If they do, Kenneth might not be around to enjoy it. He even dreams about being a grandfather. He said that it's the only thing left on his bucket list."

"You sound like you want her to have a baby," Collette threw in.

"Oh yes. Kenneth will treat that baby like royalty. And it'll have my blood, so that'll be some points in my favor."

I stumbled as I rose up off the floor. The moment that Vera had begun to speak, I had pressed my ear to the vent so close, it was aching like mad now. But what she had just said about Daddy's desire to have a grandchild made me smile.

I had to make his dream come true if I could. But it saddened me to hear that Vera thought a baby would benefit her financially. Well, it was Daddy's money. What he did with it was his business.

CHAPTER 32

VERA

BEING A BITCH WAS NOT EASY. ESPECIALLY ONE LIKE ME, WHO WAS determined to be successful and productive in everything I did. The only time I was not plotting and planning was when I was asleep. I had cooked up a real doozy this time. My latest plan was to "encourage" Sarah to get pregnant as soon as possible.

I wasted no time putting that plan in motion.

After Kenneth had left for work the following Tuesday morning, I refused to leave my bedroom. I ate my meals in bed and then I ordered Delia to make the bed with me still in it. I had remained in bed most of the day thinking about the conversation I'd had with Cash and Collette the morning before. Just the thought of Sarah edging me to second place on Kenneth's list was enough to make me cry, and that's what I had been doing, crying like a baby practically the whole day.

When Cash and Collette arrived home from work around 6:00 p.m., Delia told them I was so upset about something that I couldn't even get out of bed. They rushed to my room immediately and wanted to know why I was crying. I refused to tell them.

"Vera, why don't you tell us what's the matter so we can help you," Collette suggested. She and Cash stood over me as I lay in bed, looking like they wanted to cry too. I had almost emptied a whole box of tissue.

"It's awful! Just awful. But I don't want to talk about it!" I wailed before I hawked into another tissue. "Please leave me alone!"

I was still crying that evening when Kenneth got home around 7:00 p.m. By then I had moved to the living room couch, but I was still in my nightgown.

"Baby, what's the matter? Cash called me at the office and told me you were hysterical when he got home. I got here as soon as I could!" Kenneth hollered. He slid his suit coat off and draped it across the arm of the couch and loosened his tie. I had not looked in the mirror all day. But from the way my eyes were aching, I could imagine how bad I looked. "Your face and eyes are so bruised and red and swollen—did somebody mug you? You look like hell! Are you sick? Baby, what happened to you?"

"Delia said she didn't leave the house today," Cash said as he entered the living room and walked over and stood next to Kenneth.

Kenneth leaned down and placed his hands on my shoulders and gently shook me. "You tell me before I go crazy!" he demanded, shaking me a little harder. "Cash, pour her a shot of brandy!"

"Kenneth, please don't hate me," I sobbed, wrapping my arms around his neck. I pulled him down onto the couch next to me. As soon as Cash handed me the brandy, I stopped crying long enough to swallow the entire shot. I had to hold my breath to keep from belching.

"Baby, I could never hate you. Now tell me what's wrong." Kenneth squeezed me so hard it was a struggle for me to catch my breath.

"Kenneth, I . . . I don't know how to tell you." I sniffed, turning to Cash. "Cuz, do you mind letting me talk to my husband alone?" Cash gave me a blank look, but he left the room immediately.

"Tell me what?" Kenneth asked with a wild-eyed look. I didn't like to upset a man with a bad heart, but this time I did what I had to do. "Whatever it is, you just need to tell me. I'm sure it's something we can fix if we work on it together."

"Dr. Lott called me up this morning. Right after you'd left for work."

"Your gynecologist?"

"Uh-huh. I knew it had to be serious for him to be calling me at home so early in the morning."

Kenneth's jaw began to twitch. "How serious?"

"Baby, we may never have a child of our own! He had received the results of my last test yesterday and it was too late to call me then."

"What tests?"

"Uh, the tests that confirm what I suspected—I can never give you a child."

Kenneth gave me a curious look and then he scratched his chin. "Baby, you're *fifty-nine* years old. I thought you went through menopause already."

"I thought I had too. Come to find out, I'm in the last stages. I had a period last month, so it's possible I could still get pregnant, or so I thought." I blew my nose again and gave Kenneth the most desperate look I could manage. "I didn't tell you because I wanted to surprise you."

"Vera, I don't know who you've been talking to, but you are not making much sense. If you get pregnant now at your age, you will be surprising me and everybody else in the world," he said distantly. "Tell me more about these tests so I can try and figure out what gave you the notion that you could have a baby."

"There is a new and controversial procedure that involves shots and a special tea that they've been using in Asia for a few years. A few doctors in America just started using it on an experimental basis. Dr. Lott has had some success with a couple of his patients who had not been able to have a child. One woman was fifty when she finally got pregnant."

Kenneth was looking so curious by now I decided to jump ahead a few steps. The truth of the matter was, the suspense and predicting his final reaction were killing me. "I volunteered to let him test me to see if I'd be a good candidate."

"Vera! You had no business agreeing to something like that without talking to me about it!"

"I know, I know. I was going to tell you if the tests were good. That's just it—they were not good, so it's something we can't consider."

"Is that all? Is that why you're so upset?" Kenneth immediately looked relieved. He reached for a tissue, but the Kleenex box was empty, the second one I'd emptied since I'd come downstairs. He reached for his jacket and removed a handkerchief from his pocket and wiped a ribbon of sweat off his forehead. He handed the handkerchief to me and I honked into it.

"Hmmm." Kenneth scratched his head. "I always thought a doctor had a patient come into his office to hear something this serious in person." There was a worried look on his face, so I had to think fast.

"They usually do. That's why he called me this morning, to tell me to come in. But I wouldn't get off the phone until he told me the reason." I sniffed and blew into the handkerchief again. "When he told me that even this new procedure wouldn't work for me, I balled up on the bed and couldn't get back up for hours."

Cash eased back into the room. "Is everything all right?" he asked, looking from me to Kenneth.

"Everything is fine, Cash. You can let Collette know that Vera was just having a bad day. Something about her hormones running amok," Kenneth said, waving him back out of the room. Kenneth turned back to me. "Vera, we've been married all these years and have been trying all this time with no luck. I had come to the conclusion a long time ago that we'd probably never have a child of our own. I finally accepted that and gave up hope."

"I had thought the same thing myself. But I never accepted it and I never gave up hope. I desperately wanted a child and I prayed about it year after year."

"Well, sometimes prayer is not enough, baby. And be realistic. It's *way* too late for you to have a baby under normal circumstances."

"I know. And . . . and that's why I had taken further action before I even let Dr. Lott test me for this other procedure."

Kenneth's eyes got big. "What further action? I hope you didn't consider doing anything else drastic without talking to me about it! I read about a woman who fooled her husband and everybody else into thinking she was pregnant. When it came time for her to deliver, she bought a baby from a woman she'd met through some black market adoption outfit on the Internet!"

"Oh, Kenneth. I would never do something as deceptive as that! This is way too important to me for me to trick you!"

"Tell me now, exactly what is this 'further action' you just mentioned?"

"Uh . . . I took some of the most potent fertility pills on the market for years behind your back."

"What? You took fertility pills and still didn't get pregnant?"

I looked up into Kenneth's eyes and blinked.

"Every doctor I went to assured me that there was no reason I couldn't father a child. And you told me the doctors you went to told you the same thing. But if you took fertility pills for years and still didn't get pregnant, something is seriously wrong with one or both of us. And the thing is, the older we get, the more unlikely we'll ever have a child, so we don't have any time to lose. Miracles do happen. So we should move on this straightaway!"

"Huh? Move on what?"

"I recently heard about a doctor in Switzerland who has helped a lot of childless older couples have children. They do some kind of procedure very similar to in vitro. They'll fertilize one of your eggs with my sperm and incubate it for a period of time in some kind of device they've used to clone animals. Then they put the egg in the woman's womb. It's a very delicate operation and risky. That's why I never mentioned it to you before now. I don't know if everything I heard is true or not, but if it is, one woman was almost your age when she got pregnant. I'm going to have my secretary make some travel arrangements for us. And since you're still in the final stages of menopause, we just might still have a chance."

"Baby, that won't help. Dr. Lott told me that it didn't matter what I did now. I can't even try something like the in vitro procedure. You see, my womb has shifted. And now it's . . . tilted permanently. Not even surgery can correct the problem." I paused and looked in Kenneth's eyes again. They were almost as wide as saucers. His mouth was hanging open.

"What the hell does that mean, Vera?" Poor Kenneth. He looked so confused I could have knocked him over with a feather.

"It's a rare condition, but it's common among women in my age group. Even if I got pregnant through in vitro or that similar procedure you just mentioned, I couldn't carry a baby full term with a tilted womb. As a matter of fact, my womb is in such a precarious position, the baby would have a difficult time ingesting necessary nutrients. If I somehow managed to carry the baby to full term, he or she would probably be born with severe defects and die within a few months anyway. I could even die from the stress on my organs!" Even if my womb was not tilted, and it wasn't as far as I knew, I still couldn't have a baby no matter what age I was. I had had my tubes cut, burned, and tied. And so far, this particular procedure was irreversible. The *only* way I could claim a newborn baby as my own was to steal one.

"I see." Kenneth stared at me so long and hard I got scared. It was obvious from the hopeless look on his face that he was severely disappointed. "Baby, I know how much this subject upsets you, so we don't need to talk about it now that we know the problem. If you want to, maybe we can look into paying a surrogate mother to have our child. I think my sperm is still potent enough for that. I just read about a sixty-five-year-old woman who was a surrogate mother for her daughter. She gave birth to a healthy baby boy."

"A surrogate mother? Um, honey, please don't make me consider that. A woman who used to do my hair was a surrogate mother and she got such a bad infection she died a horrible death. I had nightmares about it for months and I promised myself I'd never ask another woman to do something like that for me." I was making shit up as I went along, and it must have sounded real good because Kenneth continued to comfort me.

"Baby, let's stop talking about this. It's not the end of the world.

We've been happy all these years and now that we have Sarah, somewhat late I'm sorry to say, we are still parents. And that's good enough for me." Kenneth's voice cracked and the disappointed look was still on his face. "In my opinion, the happiest moment in a man's life is when he hears he's going to be a daddy for the first time."

"But I—"

He held up his hand and cut me off. "I meant everything I just said. Now let me finish. The *second* happiest moment in a man's life is when he hears he's going to be a grandfather for the first time."

It was time for me to deliver the coup de grâce. "With this new development now in my case, I hope and pray that Sarah and Bo make a baby while you and I are still young enough to enjoy it." I sniffed. "I'm tempted to just come out and tell them to make us a baby!"

Kenneth laughed softly and squeezed my hand. "That sounds good enough to me. I just might suggest it to them myself."

CHAPTER 33

SARAH

I HATED BEING ALONE WITH CASH, COLLETTE, AND VERA. SO RIGHT after I'd eaten a light dinner in their company on a Monday about a month later, I excused myself and rushed up to my room. Bo and I had a large TV facing our bed and a mini-refrigerator, and I had plenty to read so I could hole up in our bedroom for long periods of time. Just being away from Vera and her crew was a reward that made me smile every time I thought about it. There was a huge smile on my face when Bo came into the room about an hour later.

"I'm glad to see somebody's in a good mood," he remarked, tossing his suit jacket onto the bed next to where I had propped myself up on four king-size pillows. He sat down next to me. Right after he removed his shoes, he gave me a quick kiss. "Boy was it a rough day. Two women, both wearing wig-hats that looked like a black sheep's ass, entered the store right after we opened this morning. They browsed for about an hour. They were rude to the clerks who tried to help them—and even accused them of following them around because they were black! Can you believe that shit? We're talking about a black-owned company where half of the staff is black and these two nitwits had the nerve to accuse us of racism." Bo paused and shook his head. "You would think that by now, most criminals would know how hard it is to leave a store with stolen merchandise. Well, these two didn't. They walked out the door and when the alarm went off, you should have seen the surprised looks on their faces!"

"Did you have them arrested?" I asked with a yawn and an indifferent expression on my face.

"I would have if we had been able to detain them. The lazy-ass security guard that was on duty was useless! He was outside around the corner smoking a joint. Today was not the first time that security guard was not on his job. I fired his ass on the spot. On top of everything else now, I have to hire another security guard as soon as possible. Those two women got away with some of the most expensive games and cameras in the store."

"They got away?"

"Those two witches ran like linebackers and were twice as big. One's wig fell off and the other lost one of her flip-flops."

Bo was obviously angry, but I wanted to laugh. Just a month ago when I drove my girl Lynn Turner to Target so she could "return something," she stole hundreds of dollars' worth of merchandise without my knowledge while I waited in my car. Just as I was checking my makeup in my rearview mirror, I spotted her sprinting across the parking lot with two big security guards right behind her. Lynn weighed more than anybody I knew, but she was as light on her feet as a jackrabbit. She made it to the car and jumped in and I sped off, praying that those security guards didn't write down my license plate number. I had never stolen anything before in my life, and I didn't want to get in trouble because of what somebody else did. I severed my relationship with Lynn that day. Now I had even more time on my hands.

"I hope you have better luck with the next security guard."

"I hope we do too. Baby, you look bored." Bo leaned forward and gave me a firm hug. "Do you feel all right, baby doll? You look a little peaked too."

"I'm all right, I guess. But since you brought it up, I am so bored I could scream!" I hollered. "I don't know what to do with myself when you're not around." Shopping and going out to lunch had become old to me. Every day when I got out of bed, I had to decide what to do with myself. Some days the boredom was so intense I had to go outside and walk around to keep from losing my mind.

"Maybe you should get a hobby outside of the house or a job," Bo suggested.

"I can't think of anything interesting enough to me that I'd want to take it up as a hobby. And I'm still not ready to go to work."

"Baby, there has to be *something* you want to do."

I closed my eyes for a moment. When I opened them, I looked at Bo and grinned. "I can think of something." I cleared my throat and looked at my husband like he was the most handsome man in the world. And at that moment, he was. "I think it's time for us to have a baby. Daddy and Vera told me it would make them the happiest couple in the world. I always knew Daddy wanted a grandchild, but I was surprised when Vera told me she couldn't wait to be a grandmother."

"Huh?" From the look on Bo's face, I got the impression that he liked the idea. He hugged me again, kissing up and down my neck. "Do you think you're ready to become a mother? That's a real big step, you know."

"I've taken more than one big step these past few years. Moving here, getting married. Sometimes I have a hard time remembering who I really am and my real purpose in life."

"And do you think having a baby will remedy that?"

"I think it will. I'd have something better to do with my time than looking for things to do every day. I'm a housewife, but since Delia does all the cooking and cleaning, I don't even get to do any of the things that a regular housewife does," I whined.

Bo gave me a weary look. "I think we should get our own place. That might help bring you out of the doldrums. We won't hire a cook or a housekeeper, so you will have plenty to do."

"Uh, we don't have to move," I said quickly. It would have been nice to have my own house so I wouldn't have to deal with Collette's meddling and Vera's mysterious ways, but I wasn't ready to leave my daddy's house yet. I wanted to stay as close to him for as long as I could because I was worried about him. Besides that, I still needed to be able to keep tabs on Vera, Cash, and Collette, and that would be hard to do if I moved out. They hadn't said anything too mean or stupid about me in a few days, but I knew it was just a matter of time before they had another "bash Sarah session" in the kitchen. "I love living in Daddy's house. I feel comfortable and safe here." I coughed to clear my throat and then I gave Bo a pleading look. "I'm so ready to have a baby." I sighed. "I don't like to bring up the subject of age, but I want you to be young enough to do things with our children that you won't be able to do if we wait too much longer."

"You've got a point there," Bo agreed. "Lord knows I'm beginning to feel my age."

"Then let's do it!" I squealed, teasing him by fondling my breast and sliding my tongue across my lips. "Let's do it now!"

"That's fine with me." He grinned as he rose up off the bed.

Bo unzipped his pants and flung them halfway across the room. Then he jumped on the bed and began to undress me. When he got down to my panties, he removed them with his teeth.

We spent the next hour making love. Bo was so tired afterward, he went into such a deep sleep so fast that I thought he had slipped into a coma.

After I'd made sure he was still alive, I got up and removed my birth control pills from the medicine cabinet and flushed them down the toilet.

CHAPTER 34

VERA

"THINGS ARE WORKING OUT JUST GREAT! ONCE SARAH GETS PREGnant, we won't have much to worry about. That baby will be *our* permanent link to Kenneth's fortune! All you need to do is make sure you keep her happy so she won't ever think about leaving you before you get her pregnant," I told Bo. I didn't like to discuss this subject with him in the house unless I had no choice. That was why I'd met him at a coffee shop a few blocks from the house right after he and I and Kenneth had had drinks in the living room that Thursday night around nine.

I couldn't believe that Bo had just made love to Sarah for two hours straight and had come *four* times! Whoa! That was a record in my book. I had never enjoyed a session that lasted that long or resulted in that much pleasure—with *any* of my men! Hopefully, Sarah was fertile enough and Bo's sperm was potent enough for her to get pregnant soon.

"Kenneth will be on top of the moon, so the sooner the deed is done, the better." I took a sip of my frappe and wiped sweat off my forehead with a napkin. Kenneth was at home in bed, as inactive as a corpse. I had just come from having a quickie with Ricky, my newest and best lover, and my crotch was still tingling.

"It would be nice to have a baby around, I guess. It would give Sarah something to occupy her time and keep her company. She's always complaining about how bored she gets when she's stuck in the house with just the housekeeper." Bo sipped his coffee; then he gave me a thoughtful look. "By the way, what do you do with your time every day? I've been meaning to ask you that ever since I moved here."

"What do you mean?" I asked, already in my defensive mode.

"For one thing, I know you spend a great deal of your day out of the house. I've called you from my office dozens of times and you're hardly ever home during those hours."

"I have a lot of things on my plate during the day, every day," I replied, giving Bo a reserved look.

He rolled his eyes and snickered. "I'll bet!"

"For your information," I began with a smirk, "I go to the gym and work out several times a week. I go to the spa. I shop and I visit friends. I even go by Reverend Cecil's Glide Memorial Church every now and then just to help out feeding those homeless people." Bo didn't laugh at that.

"No shit? I never would have guessed *you* would get involved in something like *that.*" He nodded and looked at me in awe. "I assumed that you spent a lot of your time running from one shoe and dress store to another, wrapped up in a towel in some fancy spa, the hair dresser, getting your nails and toes done, and whatnot. But helping feed the homeless—I'm impressed!"

"Well, since you asked, that's how I spend some of my time during the day, Bo. I'm a very private person. I don't like to toot my own horn about something like that, so not too many people know about it. I like to do certain things somewhat anonymously. Sometimes when the wrong people know you're generous with your time and money, they come begging. What's the big deal anyway? What's it to you?"

"Aw, Vera. You know I'm just messing with you."

"Don't mess with me, Bo. I have feelings and I resent you or anybody else implying that I'm a shallow woman, because that's not the case."

"I'm sorry. And I have to say you really impressed me. I admire you for helping give back to the community by donating your time to worthy causes. One day when I'm not too busy, I'd like for you to introduce me to the famous Reverend Cecil Williams. I've been reading about him for years."

"I'll do that," I said. Reverend Williams was well known, and he knew a lot of people. But he wouldn't know me from Moses. I had only met him once when I actually worked on a project that Kenneth had initiated for low-income families to get meals and other assistance from Reverend Williams. That had gone so well, Kenneth got slap-happy and donated dozens of computers and other electronics to some local low-income families. "As soon as I can set up something, I'll let you know. But it could take a while. Cecil Williams is a very busy man."

"And we'll take Sarah along with us. I'm sure she'd love to meet the reverend, too, and help him with his causes. She could be just as busy as you are. Maybe she won't feel so bored then."

"Sarah's not interested in doing the things I do. And besides, I don't want her tagging along with me too much. It's like dragging along a little kid. When she goes shopping with me and Collette, she gets impatient real quick."

"You can at least encourage her to do more things that women do on her own. Like getting her nails done and getting weekly facials. That would certainly take up a lot of her time."

"Pffft!" I gave Bo such an abrupt wave of dismissal my arm felt like it was going to fall off. "She's very low maintenance. She still gets her nails done at some Spanish hole in the belly of the barrio on Mission Street where they probably use the same drill for everybody. I wouldn't take a skunk to some of the places Sarah still goes to. And anyway, she'd rather do things like that with her old friends. You know what they say, 'you can take a person out of the ghetto, but you can't take the ghetto out of the person.'" I laughed. Bo didn't.

"Sarah's my wife now. I want you to remember that, Vera."

"I'm just kidding."

"I would appreciate you not kidding about my wife."

I sucked in my breath and glared at him. "You've changed since you moved here," I accused. "You're not the Bo I used to know. We're supposed to be a team shooting at the same target. What's the matter with you?"

"We are shooting at the same target and there is nothing the matter with me," Bo said.

"Something is wrong with you. Because with all the blessings you have now, you don't even look happy," I told him. He shrugged. This conversation had become awkward, but I had to see it to the end. "I hope you don't think that I think I'm better than Sarah, because that's not the case. She's slow and simple, but she's good people. And, to tell you the truth, I kind of like her now. If some of the things I say about her hurt your feelings, I'm sorry. But you know I've never been one to hold my tongue."

"It's not something you said about her that's bothering me at the moment. I have other things on my mind." Bo swallowed hard and gave me a wan look. Then he dipped his head and started talking in a low, controlled voice, looking at me with a strange look on his face. Between him and Kenneth, I couldn't decide which one gave me the strangest looks. "One of my boys back in Houston called me at work today. You remember Bobby Delaney?"

I let out a disgusted snort. I couldn't stop myself from rolling my eyes too. "How much did Begging Bobby want to borrow this time?"

"He didn't ask for money this time. He called to tell me that Gladys has been calling everybody who knows me, trying to get my phone number."

My jaw dropped and my blood pressure shot up. "That bitch! She took everything you had and you're depositing her alimony payments into her checking account on time every month! What else does she want? Hasn't she caused you enough problems? Why does she want to talk to you now that you don't have a damn thing left to give her? As far as I know, she doesn't know you're working for Kenneth and living like a king and all. Unless that damn long-tongued Cash blabbed to one of those long-eared dogs back in Houston."

"I don't know who Cash has been talking to back in Houston.

And I don't know what Gladys knows about how well I'm doing out here. I haven't told my old friends much about my new life."

"Then why does she want to talk to you?" The look in Bo's eyes said it all, and I was not trying to hear it! "Do you mean to tell me she wants you back?" I shouted, balling my fist.

"She told Bobby she misses me and wants to talk. . . ." Bo looked like he had lost his best friend. If he went back to his ex, or even *talked* to her, he would lose his best friend—me. I would never forgive him!

"Look, Bo, if you take that low-down bitch back after all she's done to you—and after all I've done for you—I will never speak to you again. And you'll be frying fish for a living! What about Sarah?"

Bo held up his hand and shook his head. "Hold up now! Don't bust a gasket until you hear all I've got to say. I told Bobby to tell Gladys to go to hell. I don't want anything else to do with that woman. Not now," he said. "I gave her too many chances, and besides, I have everything I want now. You made it all possible and I will be in your debt forever." He smiled and that reassured me.

"I'm glad to hear you say that." I was so relieved I wanted to jump across the table and kiss him. "You know how much it pisses me off when you mention Gladys, so you didn't even have to tell me about that call from Bobby, you know."

"I know I didn't, but I don't like to keep things from you. You've been too good to me. Had it not been for you, I'd have never met Sarah."

"Do you really and truly care about her?"

Bo shuddered and gave me an incredulous look. "Of course I do. I've already told you that so many times I've lost count. It started out as a plan to secure your future and mine, but as it turned out, I got the best of both worlds. Security and a woman I love. And things are only going to get better."

I nodded my approval. I was beaming. I didn't care if Bo loved Sarah or not, as long as everything continued to go well for me. It was not even going to bother me to be called "Grandma," and I was going to dote on that child when and if it ever arrived. "So, Sarah was the one who brought up having a baby?"

"Uh-huh. And all of a sudden too. I guess Kenneth must have dropped a few hints. He's desperate for a grandchild. She told me she wants to give him at least one before . . . before it's too late. I don't know if you've noticed, but Kenneth has been looking real run-down lately."

"Not run-down enough if you ask me," I snapped. "He's getting on my nerves so bad I can barely stand the sight of him. When he touches me, my skin crawls." Bo gave me such a long, hard look it made me squirm. "Why are you staring at me like that?" I narrowed my eyes and stared back at him.

He took his time responding. "I guess I'm just trying to figure you out, cuz." He shook his head and rolled his eyes and that made me squirm even more. "I'd like to say something, but I want you to stop me when you think I've crossed the line. I don't want to offend you."

"You can say anything you want to say to me. I've been offended before."

"I want you to know up front that I admire and respect Kenneth. He's done a lot for me and he is my wife's daddy. But I realize how much he's getting on your nerves. I know a lot of that is because you two have been together so long and the flame of romance is probably a lot dimmer." Bo stopped talking and let out a loud sigh.

"Don't stop talking now. Tell me everything that's on your mind," I advised. "And by the way, that flame you just mentioned, it burned out years ago."

Bo looked around the coffee shop, then back to me. "Have you ever thought about having an affair?"

I covered my mouth with my hand to keep from laughing. "Are you encouraging me to have an affair, cuz?"

Bo held up his hand again. "Yes and no. I mean, my first wife cheated on me left and right. I never cheated on her and to be honest with you, I don't think I could live with the guilt if I cheated on my woman."

"But you think an affair would help me?"

"I didn't say that. If what that Dr. Ruth and all of those other TV sex doctors say is true, you're still in your prime and you need sex more than ever now. And you're not getting it from Kenneth."

I did laugh this time. "I never said Kenneth was not making love to me."

"Well, I just assumed—oh shit. I can't keep secrets from you after all you've done for me. Men talk, see. Kenneth has shared a few things with me. He told me he wasn't doing so well with you in the bedroom. And he's too proud to use Viagra."

"Tell me about it. He tries to please me and that's part of the problem. Sex with an old man, who has a body like a dolphin, is no fun at all."

"Hmmm. Kenneth was old when you married him. Was the sex with him ever good?"

"I'm sure it was to some of those whores he fooled around with."

"Oh. I didn't know Kenneth had fooled around that much. I thought Sarah's mother was the only one."

"She wasn't. He's had more affairs since we got married than five men put together."

"Well, in that case, if you have one or two brief no-strings-attached affairs, it would even the score and probably make you feel better." Bo paused and gave me a dry look. "It would be one thing if you had let yourself go and looked like the typical hag, but you're still good-looking and sexy for a woman your age. I'm sure you wouldn't have any trouble at all finding somebody. And maybe you should find a *young* man. I know it's been a long time since you had a relationship with a man your own age and you probably don't even remember what a firm young body feels like. But you're a . . . a . . . real *mature* woman now, so I suggest you have a fling with a college-age dude—as long as he's eighteen or over." I looked at Bo and blinked as he continued. "If you are careful, you won't have to worry about getting caught. Just make sure you make him use a condom every time he lays pipe. You should at least give it some thought. I have a feeling a good fuck is what you need."

I finished my frappe and gave my cousin a big smile. "You know, I just might take your advice. . . ."

Sex was always on my mind. A good fuck was what I needed. But right now Sarah having a baby was on my mind even more. I would give up Ricky and all of my future boy toys if it meant Sarah producing just one gold-plated grandchild before I got too old to reap the benefits.

CHAPTER 35

SARAH

IT WAS HARD FOR ME TO BELIEVE THAT *TWO* MORE YEARS HAD PASSED and I still had not become pregnant. Bo and I had made love several times a week during all that time! We had almost given up hope. But Daddy's long face and the way he got misty-eyed around other people's grandchildren was the main reason we kept trying so hard.

My last two periods had been very light and I'd been feeling light-headed and weak a few times during those two months. But I had experienced similar symptoms before, even when I wasn't sexually active, so I hadn't given it much thought. My annual visit to my OB/GYN for a routine checkup was coming up soon, so I made a mental note to mention my symptoms to him.

On the day of my appointment, I treated my friend Mabel Cunndiff to lunch at the E&O restaurant, one of the best places in town when it came to exotic Asian cuisine. Mabel and I had attended the same boarding school. She had recently married and moved to the Bay Area.

"You look so tired and puffy," she said as we enjoyed our fried rice, veggies, and blackened prawns and white wine. Mabel's husband was a doctor, so she paid close attention to things like how other people looked. "Are you all right?"

"I hope I am," I replied as I speared another prawn with my fork. "But if something is wrong, I'm sure Dr. Parker will tell me when I see him this afternoon. I have been feeling funny, though.

It seems like no matter what I do, I ache somewhere," I said, chewing on the prawn even though my jawbone was aching now. "I've had this weird, sharp, burning pain in my stomach for the past two days."

Mabel's big brown eyes got even bigger. Her sharp little nose began to twitch like a rabbit. She gave me such a mournful look you would have thought that I'd just told her I was dying. "Uh-oh! That's the same kind of pain my mother had just before she died," she warned. "I feel sorry for you."

I froze. I suddenly lost my appetite, so I set my fork down and pushed my plate to the side. "I thought your mother died of cancer."

"She did. That weird, sharp, burning pain in her stomach was cancer of the intestines."

"Nobody in my family has ever had cancer," I pointed out.

"So?" Mabel shoved a huge forkful of bok choy into her mouth. I couldn't believe she was still able to eat like a hog and at the same time talk to me like I was about to be embalmed. "That doesn't mean anything. Nobody in my family ever had cancer either before my mother. You know us black folks. With all the greasy pork and cow parts our ancestors ate, we are bound to inherit some of the ailments that killed them."

"Yeah," I mumbled. I was glad I had ordered a huge glass of wine. The buzz I had made it easier for me to listen to Mabel's morbid comments without going into panic mode. "Like I said, my doctor will tell me what's wrong with me." I couldn't eat anything else, but I ordered another glass of wine.

After we left the restaurant, Mabel hugged me like it was for the last time.

It was the middle of July and the weather was so nice I walked the four blocks to Dr. Parker's office.

I was extremely nervous throughout the exam. When it was over, I got dressed so fast, I put my pantyhose on inside out. Dr. Parker entered the room and he was not smiling. But he didn't have the typical grim look you'd expect to see on a doctor's face when he was about to give you a death sentence. I didn't know what to expect.

"Congratulations, Mrs. Harper!" he said, rubbing his hands together. "You're going to be a mother." A huge smile formed on his weather-beaten, fake tan face.

I was so elated I almost kissed him.

I regretted drinking the wine with my lunch. I didn't want to do anything that might hurt the baby inside my belly. I was even afraid to walk the six blocks back to the lot where I'd parked, so I took a taxi.

I couldn't wait until everybody was in the house. I wanted to tell Bo the good news first, but getting him alone was not easy. I had called him at his office from my cell phone before I left the parking lot. And even though I had left a message that I had something very important to tell him, he hadn't returned my call by the time I decided to head for home. I'd left the same message on Daddy's voice mail and he had not returned my call either.

The closer I got to home, the more I didn't want to be in the house alone with Vera. I was afraid I'd break down and tell her I was pregnant. And I certainly didn't want to tell her before I told Bo and Daddy. I was too excited to go shopping, so I just drove around for a while.

After about an hour, I reluctantly headed home. Costa was in the driveway waxing our rarely used town car. I parked beside him. When I got out of my car, he nodded and tipped his black chauffeur's cap. "Costa, we may be using the car this evening," I told him.

"As well, Senora Harper," he replied with another nod.

I was hoping that we'd all pile into the town car and go out to dinner to celebrate.

When I got inside the house, I stopped in the foyer and took a deep breath. I moved quietly toward the entrance to the living room. I peeped in before entering, expecting to see Vera slumped on the couch or on a bar stool with a drink in her hand. She was not in the living room, but before I could breathe a sigh of relief, she came swishing in from the kitchen.

Her eyes got wide as soon as she saw me standing in the middle of the living room floor. "How was your visit to the doctor?" she asked. She had her purse and car keys in her hand, so it was obvious she was on her way out. That made me happy. I wanted to savor my feeling of elation about the baby. That would have been hard to do with Vera lurking about the house. "Is everything all right?"

"I'm just fine," I answered with a smile I couldn't hold back.

"Hmmm. That's nice. But that pinched look that's been on your face for the past few days is still there. You look constipated."

"Uh, I am constipated, but Dr. Parker gave me a prescription to take care of that."

"Good! Now I have to run. I will be back in time for dinner. I told Delia to cook lamb. I'm looking forward to it." It didn't look like the family was going out to dinner tonight. Vera ran out of the room like a dog was chasing her. I prayed that Bo and Daddy would get home before I went to bed.

Dinner was served at 7:00 p.m. I was glad Daddy and Bo had come home early enough to eat with the rest of us. Moving like robots, we seated ourselves and began to fill our plates with some of the lamb concoction Delia had prepared.

"Sarah, how did your appointment go today?" Daddy asked, using both of his hands to break a roll in two.

"I tried to call you this afternoon," I told him. Then I looked at Bo. "I tried to call you too."

Bo opened his mouth to speak, but Daddy beat him to it. "Oh? Is there something we need to know?"

"Uh-huh," I said, deliberately taking my time now. I could feel the sudden tension and anxiety in the room. And I enjoyed watching Collette and Vera shift in their seats. I looked from one face to the other. I didn't speak again until I was looking directly into Bo's worried eyes. "I found out something today that you all need to know," I announced, looking around the table some more.

Collette glanced at me with her eyes narrowed. Vera's face froze. Cash didn't even look up from his plate. Bo began to blink rapidly. His lips curled up into a smile that seemed like it had been waiting all day to form on his face. He reached across the table and grabbed my hand. "Baby, are you . . ." He didn't even finish his sentence. I nodded.

"What is it, honey?" Daddy asked, looking from me to Bo and back.

"I'm going to have a baby," I gushed. My eyes were still on Bo, but I heard Daddy let out a gasp. When I looked at him, he was beaming like a flashlight. "My doctor confirmed it this afternoon. If it's a boy, I'm going to name him Kenneth Bohannon Harper."

Bo dropped his fork and reared back in his seat. Then he looked at me with his eyes bugged out and his mouth hanging open.

Daddy choked on his wine. Bo slapped him on the back a few times. After Daddy stopped coughing, he wobbled up out of his seat and stumbled over to me, leaning on the table like a man with one leg.

"You could name my grandchild Donald Duck for all I care, and I'd be just as happy," he managed, looking so overjoyed you would have thought that he was the one pregnant.

"When are you due?" Collette asked stiffly, giving me a look I couldn't describe. After all these years, we tolerated each other at best. I was convinced that she resented me because she still thought my presence was a threat to the sweet position she and Cash occupied. Now that I was pregnant, my child and I would be a double threat.

"According to Dr. Parker, I'm due the twenty-third of February—that is, if I don't have any complications." Daddy was still standing by my side with his hand on my shoulder.

"What kind of complications?" Cash asked. "You look as healthy as a new mule to me. And as long as you lighten up on that wine and don't do nothing too extreme, having a baby ought to be a piece of cake for a young woman like you."

"Sometimes things happen to the healthiest and youngest women when it comes to having a baby. If I gain too much weight, or lose too much weight, I could have some problems. My mama and my grandmama told me they had all kinds of problems when they were pregnant. That's why they each had had only one child."

Daddy started sweating and coughing again. Vera jumped up and guided him back down into his seat. "Well, we are pleased to hear this wonderful news, baby. I'm sure everything is going to be just fine," he wheezed.

After a few more comments about my condition, we finished dinner. Cash and Collette rushed off to go bowling. Vera told Daddy he looked like a wreck, so she escorted him to their bedroom, where he could lie down for a while.

Bo and I headed to the living room, holding hands all the way. "I'm going to start working on the nursery tomorrow," I told him as soon as we sat down on the couch, still holding hands. "And I think we should move into your old bedroom. We'll put the baby in the one we're in now. I'll have fun turning it into a nursery."

"But the room we're in now is the largest one on the second floor. A baby won't need that much room."

"Bo, I know that, but I would like a change of scenery too."

"Do you want to move into one of the rooms on the third floor? I'm sure Vera and Kenneth won't mind us occupying a room that close to them."

"I'd rather stay on the second floor. But I do want to make our current bedroom into a nursery," I insisted.

"Suit yourself, honey. It's not that big of a deal," Bo said with a shrug.

I was glad Bo didn't seem too interested in my sudden desire to change bedrooms. But I had a valid reason—and it wasn't only because I wanted to turn the room into a nursery. I wanted to make sure nobody else discovered the fact that if you got close enough to the air duct and opened the vent, you could hear everything going on in the kitchen. Last night when Bo dropped one of his cuff links, he squatted down on the floor to retrieve it. It was just my luck that it had rolled dangerously close to the air duct—which I had forgotten to close after my last eavesdropping mission earlier that day. I scurried across the floor like a frightened cat and grabbed the cuff link before Bo could crawl too close to my secret "intercom system." I knew that if he could hear people talking downstairs, he'd say something about it. And there was no way that Vera, Cash, and Collette would continue to run their mouths so freely then.

Bo and I moved into his old bedroom a few hours later.

The next morning I was standing in front of Macy's when they opened. I purchased over a thousand dollars' worth of baby clothes and items for the nursery.

CHAPTER 36

VERA

NOW THAT SARAH WAS PREGNANT, SHE WAS DOWNRIGHT GIDDY. BUT she was not any more annoying to me than she usually was. However, because her head was in the clouds, she was a whole lot easier to tolerate. I was convinced that I could make her putty in my hands as long as I kept my wits about me.

But Sarah's pregnancy was not all peaches and cream. She quickly gained a lot of weight and didn't like the way she looked. I didn't like the way she looked either for that matter. Her skin glowed and her eyes sparkled like jewels. Everybody, even strangers on the street, commented on how beautiful she looked. When I was with her, it was like I was invisible. Nobody noticed how beautiful I looked, so I didn't get the compliments that I had grown accustomed to. Sarah didn't know how to take compliments. She always said something stupid like, "I'm so blessed—even with all this extra weight!"

I gloated in silence when she began to experience some of the discomforts of being pregnant. She had backaches, strange food cravings, and some days she would just bust out crying for no reason at all.

By her sixth month, Sarah didn't feel so *blessed.* "I'll be glad when I drop this load. I feel miserable and I've been eating like a cow," she complained, gnawing on a smoked turkey leg. "And I must look like one by now." That was true. She had already gained over sixty pounds. Most of the weight was in her stomach and ass, but her ankles and legs looked like tree stumps.

I thought it was to my advantage to convince her that she was as beautiful as ever. "No, you don't! You look just fine, honey. I wouldn't worry about gaining a few pounds if I were you. Besides, you're young. After you have the baby, you'll lose the weight and get your figure back in no time," I told her, rubbing her back as she sat humped over like a bear in hibernation next to me on the living room couch.

"I miss not being able to have a glass of wine or a margarita," she whined, poking her bottom lip out so far it looked like a second nose on her bloated face. "I hate all of these aches and pains that go along with being pregnant! Yesterday it was my neck. Today it's my back."

"Honey, you are still so blessed. In the long run, all of the discomforts you're experiencing now will be worth it. But I can't imagine how uncomfortable being pregnant must be! I'm so glad I never had to experience it."

Sarah sat up straight and looked me in the eye. There was a look of sorrow on her face. I wasn't sure if it was meant for her or me until she spoke again. "Is that why you never had any kids?"

Her question caught me completely off guard. I had to think hard because I wanted to make sure that what I told her was consistent with what I'd told Kenneth and everybody else. "I tried for years, though," I said hoarsely. "Unfortunately, the good Lord hasn't blessed Kenneth and me with a child of our own . . . yet."

"Oh. Maybe you *can't* have kids, huh?"

I gave Sarah a hopeless look. "I've been to several doctors and they've all told me there is no reason I can't get pregnant."

"Hmmm. Poor Daddy. He loves kids and I know he wanted more than one. He's told me so several times."

"Tell me about it," I muttered, staring at the wall. I was being sarcastic, but she was too dense to realize that.

"Oh well. It's way too late for you now anyway."

I whirled my head around so fast to look at Sarah that my neck felt like somebody had just tried to twist it off my shoulders. "What do you mean by that?"

"Aren't you like, uh, in your forties or fifties?"

"I'm sixty. That's like the new forty," I insisted.

"*Sixty*? You're *that* old?" Sarah asked with a sharp gasp. You would have thought that I had just told her I'd sprouted a dick. "Yikes!"

"As much TV as you watch and with all the reading you do, you should know that women my age—even though it is extremely rare—can still get pregnant. Medicine has come a long way. They've come up with some interesting new ways for older women to have babies." My voice was stiff and detached. It was a struggle for me to restrain myself because I wanted to slap the smug look off Sarah's face. "So *me* getting pregnant is *not* impossible in this day and age."

"Oh yeah. I saw something in the *Enquirer* or one of those other tabloids that run weird stories, about this real old woman that got pregnant. She was fifty-five, I think. But she went through something like that in vitro thing. Or that artificial insemination thing. Whatever it was, she didn't get pregnant the normal way." Sarah paused and yawned. Then she gave me a look of such extreme pity I wanted to slap that off her face too. I was the last woman in the world who wanted to be pitied. "Well, I would not want to be walking around pregnant if I was even close to forty. An older woman has to deal with a lot of aches and pains and arthritis and shit anyway, so dealing with pregnancy pains would be too much. I'm glad I didn't wait too long to get pregnant with my first baby."

I'm glad you didn't either, I thought.

I had to remind myself that I was partially responsible for Sarah getting pregnant and that it was all part of my plan. The thought of all the benefits I would eventually reap made it easy for me to smile at her now. "Well, to me, being a grandmother to your baby is almost as good as being a mother myself," I told her. "Now, let's go out and get some lunch. Barbecued ribs sound good."

Sarah had been complaining a lot about how little time Bo spent with her. Like Kenneth, he had begun to spend even more time at the store. The fact that I had tolerated that from Kenneth for so many years was one thing. I didn't want to be around him too much anyway. But I felt sorry for Sarah. She really loved Bo and wanted to be with him as much as possible. Every time she complained about it to me, I gave her my undivided attention because I didn't want her to take her complaints to her daddy. It was a major sacrifice for me not to spend as much time indulging myself with my usual activities so I could spend more time with Sarah. But that's just what I did. I had too much of a vested interest in her not to. Every chance I got to talk to Bo in private, I let him know in no uncertain terms how I felt about him being away from her so much.

"The girl is your wife now and she's about to have your baby. The least you can do is spend more time with her. We have to keep her happy," I told him. We occupied the same table in the same neighborhood coffee shop I took him to when we needed to talk. It was a Saturday morning in mid-December.

"I know, I know. After the holidays are over, things will slow down and I can spend more time with her. But she knows how demanding my job is and how important it is to keep her daddy happy," Bo told me.

"You don't even call her up from work or invite her to come meet you for lunch that often anymore," I pointed out. "A wife needs attention, you know."

"Oh yeah? It's mighty strange I don't hear you complaining about all the time Kenneth spends away from you." I didn't like the smirk on Bo's face, but I chose to ignore it. "He's with you less than I'm with Sarah."

"That's different. Kenneth is an old man and we've been together a lot longer than you and Sarah. There was a time when I resented him working such long hours, but I'm used to it now."

Bo suddenly gave me a conspiratorial look.

"What's the matter, Bo? Why are you looking at me that way?" I fished my compact out of my purse and checked to make sure I had not smeared my lipstick or that a sesame seed from the bagel I'd just eaten was not stuck to my lip or between my teeth.

"Vera, I know you better than you think. I *know* you can find a lot of things to do with all the time you have on your hands. If you know what I mean . . ."

I rotated my neck and blinked hard. "What do you mean by that?"

"You know damn well what I mean by that," he chuckled.

"If I knew, I wouldn't be asking," I snarled.

"Are you going to take my advice and find a young stud and have an affair? Or have you already done so?" He paused and snickered for a few seconds. "Is that why it doesn't bother you anymore that Kenneth is gone most of the day?"

I stared at Bo in mock slack-jawed amazement. "I don't know what you're talking about," I squeaked. I was so flustered I caught my finger in my compact when I snapped it shut. "And let's stay on the subject. We were discussing you spending more time with your wife."

"Maybe I don't want to spend more time with my wife right now. I like having my own space."

"Maybe that's why your ex divorced you."

That remark really rattled Bo. He squinted his eyes in such an odd way, his eyebrows almost touched the top of his eyelids. "Except for what I told you, you don't know a damn thing about me and my ex!"

"I didn't mean anything by that. I'm sorry," I apologized, waving my hand. "I know you were a good husband to her and you're a good husband to Sarah."

Bo swallowed hard and blinked a few times so that his eyes looked normal again. "I'm a man who loves harder than the average man. Before I met Gladys, I had only been with three other girls, and I never even thought about cheating on Gladys once we got together." There was a tight-lipped smile on his face now. It made him look downright shy, a characteristic he'd once told me was a weakness when associated with a man. I guess he must have suddenly recalled telling me that because a few seconds later a much more serious look suddenly crossed his face. I was amazed at how fast he could shift from one display of emotion to another. "A woman can cause a man a whole lot of grief!"

"True. But that's only when a man picks the wrong woman."

"Bullshit! Women keep talking about not being able to find a good man. Well, not that I'm bragging, but I'm a damn good man! Not only do I treat my woman with a lot of respect, but I also don't cheat on her. Other than Nelda, the girlfriend I left back in Houston, the only other woman I've made love to since Gladys dumped me is Sarah. And I will tell you here and now that I am *not* going to go through another divorce. I don't care what I have to do. I will *never* let Sarah go."

Bo's ominous words sent shivers up my spine.

CHAPTER 37

KENNETH

Each day I felt a little more blessed. Now I had a grandchild on the way. On top of all my blessings, I had more money now than I could ever spend in my lifetime. And since I couldn't take it with me, I was going to leave my fortune to the people who deserved it the most. I had just set up an appointment with one of my attorneys to amend my will. I wanted to continue taking care of my loved ones from beyond the grave.

I really loved my wife and I wanted to make sure she was well provided for, should I die before her. But without her knowing it, I had already decided to make some special provisions for my child and my grandchild, and any additional grandchildren after my death. Most of my estate, including my beloved mansion and my business, would go to Sarah because I felt she was the one who deserved it the most. Even though I loved my wife with all my heart, I had made her very happy since we met. But my mama didn't raise no fool. I was particular about *who* was going to enjoy my money after I died. Even with my busy schedule, I kept up with what was going on in the world. In addition to the *New York Times* and the *Wall Street Journal*, I read the local newspapers, I watched the news on a portable TV in my office, and some nights when I couldn't sleep I watched some of those true-crime TV shows. But I didn't need all of those sources to tell me that some people were out for everything they could get. My wife didn't like being single, so she would remarry in a heartbeat upon my death. There were so many con men and tricksters on the loose; she'd be a sitting duck.

I had always been generous, even when I was a boy growing up with limited funds. I'd split a baloney sandwich out of my brown paper bag lunch with kids who didn't have any lunch at all. The more I gave, the more blessings I received. That was why I was more generous than ever now.

And more blessings for me meant more blessings for my child.

I prayed that Bo and Sarah would spend the rest of their lives together. However, praying about my daughter didn't stop me from worrying about her. But being a businessman, I had to be realistic. Anything could happen, even in the strongest relationships. I was well aware of the divorce rate in America. There was no guarantee that my daughter and her husband would stay together. Bo had already been married once and had endured a very nasty divorce. That was something I thought about almost every day since he and my daughter got together. I was worried that Bo might have a flashback and take out his frustrations with his ex on my daughter and divorce her. Then she'd be up for grabs and the hounds would come sniffing. My daughter could be victimized by some gold-digging scoundrel and so could my grandchild. I'd seen it happen in other families.

But the bottom line was, I had to leave my huge fortune to somebody. Had Sarah not come into my life, I would have left most of my estate to charity and enough to Vera for her to live comfortably. These were things that I didn't like to think about too often because they were too disturbing. So I concentrated on all of the good things in my life.

I didn't think anything could go wrong. Unfortunately, things were going so well that I got a little too comfortable too soon and I should have known better. A man my age should always be prepared for the worst, no matter how well things were going.

When I least expected it, I got a reality check that literally brought me to my knees.

About six weeks before Sarah was due to deliver her son, she lost him. And she lost him in the most horrific way.

It was a Friday evening, two weeks into the new year. Bo and I had taken an important client out for a two-and-a-half-hour lunch, and we had run from one meeting to another before and after that. When Sarah dropped by unexpectedly, we didn't even know she was on the premises. Bo and I had almost concluded our last meeting of the day with one of my senior sales representatives around 4:00 p.m. when one of my cashiers burst into my office.

"Sarah's in trouble!" Tami yelled.

Bo and I reacted immediately. We sprang up out of our seats at the same time. My sales rep, a heavy-set female who got hysterical quicker than anybody I knew over the least little thing, fell to the floor trying to get out of her seat so fast.

"What the hell happened?" Bo yelled, already running for the door.

"Some dude snatched a handful of batteries and ran out the door. Sarah was on her way out, too, and he knocked her down!" Tami reported, talking as she ran along with Bo and me and my sales rep. "It looks like she's hurt real bad!"

I was huffing and puffing so hard I could barely breathe. I held my hand over my heart. It was beating so hard, it felt like it was going to pop right out of my chest. A small crowd had formed by the time Bo and I reached the front entrance.

"Mr. Lomax, please don't go out there!" yelled one of the floor salesmen as he parted the crowd for us. "You don't want to see your daughter the way she is!"

"Get out the way! I'm going out there to see my child!" I shouted. For an old man with a bad heart, I was very strong at times. I mowed down the salesman and two other employees who tried to prevent me from going outside. Sarah was stretched out on the ground by the entrance door with her eyes closed. She was writhing and moaning and rubbing her stomach. It was a sight that would haunt me until the day I died. The next thing I knew, I collapsed like a straw hut in a hurricane.

"My baby, my baby!" I managed. My hand was still over my heart. Massaging it didn't do much good because it was still pounding like a drum. My blood pressure had shot up so high it felt like blood was going to spurt out of my ears.

Curtis Thompson, the new security guard that we'd recently hired, was leaning over Sarah, fanning her face with a magazine. The thief who had knocked her down trying to escape lay on the ground unconscious. A large ugly black bruise had already formed on his knotty bald head.

"I've already called for an ambulance, sir!" Curtis hollered, looking at me, then at Bo.

Bo stood rooted in his spot like a tree. It looked like he was in a trance. A split second later, he crouched down on the ground. He fanned Sarah's face with his hand and Curtis continued to fan Sarah's face too. She slowly opened her eyes, but she was still rubbing her stomach. "My baby, my baby," she whimpered. These were the same words that I had just whimpered. A patch of skin had been scraped off one side of her face. Her shoes and the beret she'd been wearing, as well as her purse, had landed several feet away from her, right next to the batteries that the thief had attempted to steal. Tears were rolling down her face and I could see the large red stain in the crotch of her white maternity pants, which told me that she and my unborn grandchild were in serious trouble.

Curtis had coldcocked the thief. Two other employees stood guard over him. If I had not been present, they probably would have roughed him up even more. The cops arrived a few minutes before the ambulance. One of the officers had to slap the thug's face to rouse him so they could cuff him and throw his sorrow ass into the back of the squad car.

Bo rode in the ambulance with Sarah and I followed them to the hospital in my car. My heart felt like it was on fire and I was so light-headed I had to stop twice along the way. I knew that when and if I made it to the hospital in one piece, I was going to need some medical assistance too.

I prayed to God that I would live long enough to make sure my child was going to be all right. Now more than ever, I knew that if something really bad happened to Sarah, I would die of grief.

CHAPTER 38

SARAH

When I woke up, I thought I had died and gone to heaven because it was so quiet and the atmosphere was so serene. And everything was white. The ceiling, the walls, and my bedding. I was lying on my side in a loose, white hospital gown and two pretty white women dressed in white stood by the side of the bed, looking down at me. From the sad looks on their faces, you would have thought they were viewing a corpse in a coffin, which is why I thought I was dead at first. My mind was so jumbled I couldn't even think or see straight. I blinked several times, but my vision was still unfocused. Then I heard Vera.

"Welcome back," she said in the gentlest voice I'd ever heard her use.

I turned to the other side. Standing next to Vera was Bo. It was obvious he'd been crying. I could see the tracks of the tears on his face. Vera looked sad, but it didn't look like she'd lost too many tears, if any at all. Her eyes were as clear as a glass of mineral water.

"What happened to me?" I asked. My head was throbbing. My cheeks ached when I spoke.

"You were involved in an accident, dear," one of the pretty nurses told me.

"I'm in a hospital? Is my baby—" I didn't even have to finish asking my question. I could tell just from the sad looks on every other face in the room that I had lost my baby. "My baby's dead," I stated.

Then a doctor entered the room. He was so dark I assumed he was black. But when I heard his accent and saw his name tag I realized he was Dr. Ram Gupta, the same Indian doctor who had removed Grandma Lilly's gallbladder fifteen years ago. "We did everything we could," he told me. "I am so veddy veddy sorry, Mrs. Harper."

"You're young and healthy, so you can have plenty more babies, Sarah," Vera assured me. I couldn't understand why she was the only one in the room with a smile on her face now. The expression on Bo's face was so grim he looked like a pallbearer.

"Where's my daddy?" I looked from Vera to Bo.

"Uh, he's at home resting," Vera answered. "He, uh, he held out until you were out of danger. But the incident was real hard on him. His doctor told him to stay off his feet for a few more days. That's the only reason he's not here."

"How long have I been here?" I asked, rising even though it was painful for me to make even the slightest movement.

"You were brought in five days ago," the doctor said.

"I've been unconscious all this time? Well, what kind of accident was I in?"

"It was a criminal matter at the store," Bo said quickly. "We'll tell you the rest of the details in time."

"And the culprit is in custody," Vera added.

"Somebody tried to kill me. Why would somebody want to kill *me*?" That thought made me feel unbearably sad.

Bo's mouth dropped open and a look of horror appeared on his face. "Kill you? Baby, why would you say something like that?"

There was a horrified look on Vera's face. "Who would want to kill you, Sarah?" she croaked.

I shrugged and shook my head. "So nobody tried to kidnap me or anything like that, then?"

Bo and Vera looked at each other, then back to me. "No, that's not what happened. We'll tell you everything you need to know when you're feeling better," Vera said. "Now you need to get some rest."

I nodded in agreement. Bo leaned over and kissed me. My lips were so numb I could barely feel his. Vera gave me a pat on the shoulder and then they left the room. All I wanted now was to be alone.

I found out the next morning from Vera exactly what had happened. I cringed and shuddered when I heard the details. By the time she got to the end of the story, she was in tears. "If it hadn't been for that security guard, you might have been hurt even more. A witness said that that creep had grabbed you by the arm and was pulling you toward the parking lot. During the struggle, a gun fell out of his pocket." She sniffed, dabbed at her eyes, and blew her nose into one of her fancy monogrammed handkerchiefs.

"Well, whatever that security guard's name is, I hope Bo and Daddy do something real nice for him."

Cash and Collette came by while Vera was still with me. She was still boo-hooing a little. By now her handkerchief looked like just another snot rag. Collette brought flowers and she had to mention how much she'd paid for them. Cash brought me a green plant and a get-well card. Bless his heart, he had also smuggled in a bottle of beer for me in a brown paper bag. After he and Collette left, Bo returned and Daddy was with him.

"Bo, I'm so sorry I lost our baby!" I wailed.

"Honey, it was not your fault," he assured me. "We can start on another one as soon as you get well."

I looked at Daddy. "Daddy, I'm going to give you more grand-babies than you can stand," I vowed. "One a year until I'm no longer able to have children!" I immediately realized just how ridiculous that sounded.

Daddy laughed. "I don't need that many." He moved closer to the bed. "What's important now is you getting well. I've spoken to your doctor and he's confident you'll be up out of here in a day or so. Baby, you're going to be just fine." He gave me a quick peck on the cheek.

I looked at him and squinted my eyes so I could see him better. "And what about you?" I felt fairly well, but I was more concerned about him now.

"Me? I'm okay, I guess," he said hoarsely." He didn't look okay to me. There were deep dark circles around his eyes and lines all over his face that I had never noticed before. "Yep! I'm doing just fine! Fit as a fiddle!" Daddy had spoken too soon because he suddenly bent forward and began to cough so hard, Bo summoned a nurse. In less than a minute, a large pug-ugly nurse, who looked more like a prison guard, steamrolled into the room with a wheelchair and hauled Daddy away in it.

"Bo, I . . . I'm scared," I fumbled, clutching his hand. "I can't lose my baby and my daddy at the same time."

"Honey, everything is going to be just fine. Your daddy got so upset about what happened to you, he's just having some bad flashbacks. But Vera has spoken to his doctor and they've assured her that he's in good shape for an eighty-year-old."

"An eighty-year-old what?" I asked. "Horse, cow, goat, or what?"

"Excuse me?"

"Daddy looks way older than his age and he's been having one health problem after another the last couple of years. A man his age can't be in good shape with all that going against him."

"Honey, I don't know what you want me to do or say. Things could be a lot worse. Just be thankful they're not."

"Yeah, I guess you're right." I exhaled and then sucked in some fresh air. "Vera told me all about how that thug knocked me to the ground and how I passed out. I can't get that out of my mind. I just wish Daddy had not been there to see me lying on the ground unconscious and bleeding. Maybe he wouldn't have taken it so hard."

"I agree with that," Bo said, giving me an affectionate look.

"Well, I'm all right now. How is that security guard doing? Is he going to be okay too?"

"What do you mean?"

"He didn't get hurt trying to protect me, did he?"

"Oh no! Curtis is a big, strapping dude. He's a youngblood, like you. It would take a lot to hurt him. He's just fine." Bo laughed. "I sure would hate to tangle with that brother!"

"I'd like to thank him in person."

"I think that's a great idea. As soon as you get out of this hospital, we'll have him over for dinner."

I couldn't wait to meet the man who had possibly saved me from a much worse fate. I didn't think I could wait until I got home. And I didn't have to. Shortly after Bo left, a nurse ducked into my room.

"Excuse me, Mrs. Harper. There's a gentleman here to see you, but he wanted to make sure you're up to more company today," she told me.

"Yeah, I guess. Who is it?" I was almost feeling like my old self again, so I was sitting up in bed watching a *Deal or No Deal* rerun. I had finished the beer that Cash had snuck in for me, and I'd wrapped the bottle in some newspaper and dropped it into the trash can. I was glad I had rinsed my mouth out thoroughly with Listerine a few minutes ago. The last thing I needed was for the hospital staff to be buzzing about me having alcohol on my breath.

"It's the security guard who came to your assistance," the nurse told me, waving a tall handsome black man in a gray uniform into my room.

"Hello, Mrs. Harper," he said in a voice that seemed too gentle to belong to such a husky man. He had gentle eyes, too, and he was built like Mike Tyson. His eyes were the most dazzling thing about him. They were almond shaped and a light shade of hazel with long, jet-black lashes. His beautiful smile revealed bright white teeth. With his wavy dark brown hair parted on the side, he looked more like a TV soap opera heartthrob than a security guard. "I'm Curtis Thompson." He set a vase of red roses on my nightstand. The nurse gave me a big smile before she left the room.

"Oh," I mumbled. "Well, uh, I thank the good Lord you were at the store that day, Curtis."

"I thank the good Lord that I hadn't left at my regular time." He sucked in some air and then pulled a chair over to the side of my bed. "My shift had ended and I was supposed to meet some friends for drinks. But Mr. Harper asked me to work a little later to help move some equipment around in the storeroom. Had I left at my regular time . . ." His voice faded out.

"Thank you again, Curtis." I stared into those hazel eyes and felt warm all over. This man may have saved my life, so he would always have a special place in my heart now. "Uh, you look real familiar. Have we met before?"

Curtis nodded. "A real long time ago. We were both in Mrs. Grant's English class in ninth grade. Morgan High."

"Oh yeah! You didn't come back after the Christmas holiday."

"Well, I had to drop out and go to work to help Mama with the bills."

"A lot of kids had to do that."

"I see you did all right for yourself, though. I used to wonder what happened to you."

"I guess I did do all right," I said shyly. "Uh, my husband said we're going to have you over for dinner when I get home. We have a cook from El Salvador. My daddy, my husband, and my stepmother like to have her cook up a lot of weird exotic stuff. There's no telling what kind of bizarre concoction they'll have her prepare when you come to dinner." I smiled and gave Curtis a conspiratorial wink. "You know how some black folks get when they get money."

He nodded and snickered. "Tell me about it. But I'm pretty flexible when it comes to food. When I was eight, the neighborhood bullies made me eat a live grasshopper, so I'll eat just about anything now." Curtis made a face and then he snickered again.

He had such a jolly laugh. Just being in his presence made me feel so much better. . . .

"But if you don't mind, I'd like to treat you to a nice lunch or dinner on my own too." I lowered my voice to a whisper. "I hope you like that rib joint on McInnis."

"I do," he whispered back.

CHAPTER 39

VERA

Bo was really upset about the loss of his son, but Kenneth was almost inconsolable. It was bad enough he was on bed rest, but in some ways he had become like a baby to me. He even had to be spoon-fed and he didn't want me out of his sight for one minute. He balked when I told him that I was going to hire a temporary nurse, but I hired one anyway. There was no way I could do it all by myself.

"VERA!" Kenneth yelled my name every time I left his sight, even when the nurse was standing by the bed. I had just left the room to go use the bathroom. I had postponed all of my regular daily activities and a few appointments for the rest of the week and I didn't like that at all. One of my breast implants had shifted and roamed almost up under my armpit. I had made an appointment for this Wednesday to have it repositioned. But because Kenneth had so many demands, I had to postpone that appointment too. I was not happy about having to walk around with a lopsided breast. The bottom line was, when Kenneth was awake, the only place I could go without him throwing a hissy fit was to the hospital to visit Sarah.

I finished my business in the bathroom and trotted back out into the bedroom.

"Vera, baby, don't leave me alone," he blubbered, drool sliding down the side of his mouth, tears rolling down his cheeks. Traces of fresh puke, snot, and tears covered the front of his nightshirt. I had already cleaned him up and dressed him in fresh bedclothes three times since I got out of bed that morning.

"I'm right here," I said with a heavy sigh, rushing over to the bed on wobbly legs. I was dog tired, but I tried not to show it. I'd been running back and forth for one reason or another for hours.

"I opened my eyes and you were gone! I don't like being alone!" he wailed, ignoring the big Jamaican nurse I'd hired standing by the side of the bed, looking bored.

"I won't leave you alone, baby," I assured him. I snatched a Kleenex out of the box on the nightstand and wiped his face.

The weary look on my face was more for my benefit than his. I couldn't wait for Sarah to come home so she could help share the load. Since Kenneth didn't like the nurse and refused to let her bathe him or help him use the bedpan, I had to do it. I had not washed somebody's ass, other than my own, since I had been forced to take care of my younger sisters. But bathing toddlers was nothing compared to bathing a grown-ass, overweight man who was as fussy as a toddler and as clumsy as an ox. My marriage had become a nightmare within a nightmare.

A few minutes after I had returned to the room, Kenneth motioned for the bedpan. The nurse and I managed to hoist him onto it in the nick of time before his bowels moved and all hell broke loose. I had to run back to the bathroom to puke.

I had no idea how long this situation would last or how much more I could stand before I snapped.

They released Sarah the following Wednesday. Just having her back in the house was like an elixir to Kenneth. That same day he got up and took a shower on his own. That Thursday morning he went back to the office and worked almost ten hours. The only reason he came home at a decent hour on Friday was because that security guard who had helped Sarah was having dinner with us.

"I hope you like crabmeat," I said, looking at Curtis. He occupied a chair next to Sarah. Bo was on her other side. One thing Kenneth and Bo apparently forgot to mention to Curtis was that we dressed for dinner. I wore one of my most beautiful and expensive hostess gowns. Curtis was still in the dull gray uniform Kenneth's security guards wore. A toothpick was dangling from the corner of his mouth. It didn't even move when he spoke. He tucked his napkin into the collar of his shirt, used the wrong utensils at the wrong time, and he chewed like a billy goat. The boy was ghetto to the bone. Oh well. He didn't know any better. Despite his crudeness, I gave Curtis the benefit of the doubt. I liked him anyway and since I would never have to "socialize" with him again, I figured I could survive this one event intact.

"My family is from New Orleans, so I grew up eating a lot of seafood," Curtis told us, looking around the table. He rested his eyes on Sarah, too long in my opinion. And it looked like Bo felt the same way. He raised an eyebrow and cleared his throat. Then he draped his arm around Sarah's shoulder as if to mark his territory.

"Curtis, I can't thank you enough for coming to my wife's aid," Bo said, putting so much emphasis on each word you would have thought he was reciting a speech. "I've entered a letter of commendation in your file and I've initiated a generous bonus that will appear on your next paycheck." Bo looked at Kenneth for approval. From the surprised look on Kenneth's face, I figured the bonus was a decision that Bo had made on his own. But since Kenneth nodded and smiled, he obviously approved of Bo's actions.

"Aw shucks. I appreciate that and I sure could use the money, but you didn't have to do all that. I was just doing my job," Curtis said, glancing at Collette. I didn't like the look in her eyes. She was looking at Curtis like he was something good to eat. And I could see why. He made my pussy itch and I planned to sneak out of the house and get it "scratched" again as soon as Kenneth fell asleep tonight. Despite Curtis's crudeness, he still looked delicious. Just the type I liked. But he was certainly off-limits to me. Not only did I have too much to lose, but I was also happy with my current boy toy. I assumed Curtis had a few women already and probably more babies than he could afford to support. "I'm just so sorry about Mrs. Harper losing her baby. I know how important a first child is. My son died with his mama during Hurricane Katrina. He was three."

Everybody at the table gasped at the same time. "My goodness, Curtis! That's a damn shame!" I wailed, giving him a mournful look for good measure.

"Do you have any family still down there?" Sarah asked.

Curtis shook his head. "After Katrina, none of my folks wanted to stay in New Orleans any longer. They had lost everything anyway, so there was nothing to keep them there. They live all over the place now—Frisco, Detroit, Brooklyn, and one of my cousins even moved up to Vancouver, Canada."

"Do you like living in California, son?" Kenneth asked.

Curtis let out a loud sigh before answering. And then a look came over his face that I will never forget. He looked like a man who had lost his will to live. "Yes, I do, sir. I've been here since I was nine. I'll like it even more when I can afford to move into a better neighborhood." He stopped talking long enough to let out another sigh. The next thing I knew, he began to regale us with some of the most frightening information I'd ever heard. "I spent two years in Iraq when I was in the army. I dodged a lot of bullets. One day I almost stepped on a land mine, but a buddy pushed me out of the way in the nick of time. I saw men get blown to bits and pieces. Somehow, I made it back home in one piece. The *same day* I got back to Frisco, two dudes robbed me at gunpoint on the street right in front of the building I live in now. A month after that, somebody broke in on me and my mama in the middle of the night and pistol-whipped me because I wouldn't turn over the drugs they thought I had—which I didn't have. I don't mess with drugs. Not long after that, somebody attacked me from behind with a blunt instrument that left me unconscious for two days." Curtis paused and looked around the table. "I have a few enemies in the hood. I'm one of the few residents brave enough to speak out against the drug dealers and other criminals. I was a witness in a trial a couple of weeks ago. I testified against four brothers who had broken into the apartment of the young single mother next door to me. They shot and killed her dog, locked her kids in the bathroom, tied sister girl up, and raped her. I was coming home from work as they were running out the girl's front door, laughing and covered in her blood. I was able to identify them and I called the cops right away. From that day on, I received telephone death threats until I changed my number. Now I get the threats in writing. Two days ago somebody slipped a note under my front door telling me my days were numbered."

"My Lord," Kenneth exclaimed. "How can people live in an environment like that?"

"Some of us don't have a choice," Curtis pointed out. "I'm good with my hands when it comes to cars. I work a part-time job helping a friend who owns a body shop. Someday I hope to own my own shop and have a bunch of mechanics working for me. My mama works the nightshift in a furniture warehouse. We're able to sock away a few dollars every week. Hopefully, by this time next year, we'll have enough to move to a safer location." When Curtis paused this time, he chuckled. "If I live that long."

"What do you mean by that?" Sarah asked.

"The boys in the Hunters Point district don't play. Pissing them off is like signing your own death warrant. I've been to a lot of funerals for the people who stood up against the gangsters like I'm doing now. Just last Friday night after I'd called the cops and ratted out the dealers selling crack in front of my building, somebody slashed the tires on my car. And they wrote 'you next' on the windshield in black spray paint. Sarah, I'm sure you haven't forgotten how it was when you lived out there."

"And I hope I never will forget," Sarah responded, blinking hard in Curtis's direction. "I went to quite a few funerals of murdered friends myself."

"Hey! Let me stop talking about this gloomy stuff. I don't want to put a damper on this lovely dinner! I'm sorry." Curtis's decision came a few minutes too late. His grim report had already put a damper on our "lovely dinner." I was sorry I had encouraged Kenneth and Bo to bring him to dinner. I decided right then and there that if Kenneth or Bo ever mentioned inviting this man into our home again, I would not allow it.

The room had become uncomfortably quiet. From the expressions on each face, you would have thought we were at a funeral. I decided to steer the conversation in a more pleasant direction. "How many other babies do you have, Curtis?" I asked.

He didn't waste any time responding to my question. "None." Then he chortled. "At least none that I know of."

"I feel you on that one," Cash said with a sheepish look on his face. Collette shot him a scathing look, but she wasted no time turning her attention back to Curtis and plastering a smile on her face.

"Are you married now, Curtis?" Sarah asked. All eyes went to her. Why she was interested in his marital status was a mystery to me.

"No, not anymore," Curtis replied dryly. "I'm single and looking . . ."

I didn't like the smug look on Sarah's face as she gazed at him. I could feel the vibes between the two of them. I had an ominous feeling about Sarah's obvious fascination with this man.

Curtis was a nice enough young man, but he didn't have a goddamn thing to offer. He was just a security guard—a dead-end-ass job if ever there was one. The man had no class, no money, and he lived in one of the most run-down and dangerous areas in San Francisco *with his mama.* He drove a Ford *Escort* that was almost as old as he was. I didn't know jalopies like that were still on the road! It was in the shop, so he had come over on the bus and that was how I assumed he was going to go home. After we had finished dinner and enjoyed a few highballs, Sarah volunteered to give Curtis a ride home since she was the only one who had not drunk any alcohol. I was horrified. But for some strange reason, Bo and Kenneth thought it was a great idea.

"You need to get back into the swing of things, baby. The fresh air will do you good," Bo said, vigorously shaking Curtis's calloused hand like it was going to be the last time and thanking him again for being so helpful to Sarah.

"Yeah, you do need to get some fresh air and get your bearings back. And Bo and I need to spend a couple of hours together in my study to go over a few new contracts," Kenneth said, coughing. He rose from the table and shook Curtis's hand, too, and clapped him on the back. "You're a real asset to the store, son. I hope you'll be with us for a long time to come." Then Kenneth turned to Sarah. She looked as gleeful as a cheerleader. "You drive carefully now, honey."

"I'll go with her," Collette volunteered, jumping up out of her chair so fast it almost fell over. "If you don't mind, Sarah. I was going to run out to Walgreens to get a few things anyway."

"No, I don't mind at all." Sarah grinned. Even though the baby was no longer in her belly, she was still quite round around her middle. And her legs and ankles were still kind of thick. But she looked good in her loose black dress with her hair in a French twist. The way Curtis was looking at her made me uncomfortable. But since Bo didn't seem to notice or care, I set my feelings aside.

After everybody had left the dining room, I padded into the kitchen and dialed Ricky's number. He answered on the first ring. "I'm coming to see you tonight. I need to pick up some condoms—in a store across town, of course—so give me an hour or so," I told him. I never asked him if he wanted company or even if he had company already. When I wanted to see him, that was all that mattered to me. I always got what I paid for.

"I'll be naked when you get here," he told me.

It was no wonder I loved this sweet young thing so much! We were always on the same page.

I was going to hold on to this one for a little longer than I'd kept my other boy toys.

Maybe even permanently.

CHAPTER 40

SARAH

THERE WERE SEVERAL WALGREENS BETWEEN MY HOUSE AND CURTIS'S apartment. But I stopped at one downtown because it was big and always busy. Collette claimed she only needed to pick up a few items. But because of the mob of other customers and the slow cashiers, I knew she'd be in the checkout line for a while. That would give me more time to talk to Curtis without her listening in on our conversation. There were things I wanted to say to him that needed to be said in private.

I waited until Collette had entered the store before I said anything to Curtis. He occupied the backseat directly behind me. "So," I began with caution, turning around so I could see him better, "when can I take you to lunch or dinner, Curtis?"

He gulped and gave me a surprised look. "Huh? Oh! Mrs. Harper, you don't have to take me to lunch or anything else. I was glad to be of some assistance to you. Like I said, I was just doing my job."

"I know. But it would make me feel a whole lot better if you'd let me do something nice for you," I insisted.

"You've already done that as far as I'm concerned. Inviting me to have dinner with you and your family was more than enough. And the food was off the chain! I haven't eaten such a screaming good dinner since my grandmother died. I'm glad I spent the first half of my life with her."

"Oh? Your grandmother raised you?"

"Off and on, I should say." He smiled.

"Where were your mother and your daddy?"

Curtis stopped smiling. "My daddy died of a stroke when I was four. Mama was around. Well, to be more specific, she was all over the place. Sometimes I wouldn't see her for weeks at a time. She was a pretty woman, so she had a lot of admirers, if you know what I mean."

I didn't know what he meant, so I was glad he told me. "We lived with her pimp for two years."

"Oh. I'm sorry to hear that." Not only was I shocked, but I also felt truly sorry for this man. He had endured a rough life, just like me, and deserved so much more. Just like me . . .

"She didn't stay in that life too long. Thank God she had enough sense to realize how destructive it was. Anyway, I didn't like the way my mama's men treated her and they didn't like me. So my grandmother took over and moved me in with her. She passed when I was twelve and then I moved back in with Mama."

"We have something in common. The man my mama married didn't like me, so my grandmother took me in."

"Hmmm." Curtis gave me a strange look. "Uh, why did you move in with your grandmother? I know it ain't my business, but your daddy is one of the richest black men in the state. Where was he at the time?"

"I was ten when my mama married my stepfather. My real daddy didn't even know about me until my mama died in a car wreck a few days before the new millennium rolled in. I didn't know about him either. My mama had told me some off-the-wall bogus story about my daddy dying in a plane crash. Anyway, Daddy came to my mama's funeral, saw me, and put two and two together. I look just like his dead brother's daughter. But he still had a DNA test done to be sure." I snorted. "He didn't waste any time stepping up to the plate. He started taking care of me and my grandmother right away."

"Old brother Kenneth Lomax sounds like a righteous dude."

"My daddy is an angel in my book. He was real generous to me and my grandma. Right after my mama's funeral, he moved us into a real fancy condo he owns near downtown. He took us to fancy restaurants with names I couldn't even pronounce. One time he even picked us up in a stretch limo. My grandma died not long after he had moved us into his condo, so he brought me to live with him. He sent me to a real fancy boarding school in Iowa where I learned good manners and how to speak better English than that gibberish most of those ignoramuses back in the hood use. And when I graduated from high school, he bought me my first car—a BMW—and a different new car every year." I looked toward the door again to make sure the coast was still clear. "He bought me a Jaguar this year. It was real hard for me to go from living in the hood to living in Pacific Heights."

"I'll bet it was. Well, everything worked out for you anyway, Mrs. Harper." Curtis patted my shoulder.

"Please, call me Sarah," I told him.

He smiled and gave my shoulder a firm squeeze. "Sarah." He sniffed. "We have something else in common. Sarah was my daddy's mama's name."

I grinned. "Look, I really would like to take you to lunch. It's always nice to connect with people who grew up the way I did." I looked away for a moment. "Sometimes I feel so lonely. I spend so much time on my own. That's why I was in the store the day I had my accident and lost my baby. I just wanted to be around people. The mansion is so big and sometimes the only people I talk to all day are the housekeeper, our chauffeur, or the maintenance people who come around from time to time."

"Hmmm. What about your stepmother? Is she good company to you during the day? Or does she go to a job every day?"

"Puh-lease!" I rolled my eyes so hard it hurt.

"Oops! Excuse me. I didn't know it was like that." Curtis laughed.

"Vera's a hot mess, if you ask me. She has more on her plate than a glutton. She spends hours at a time, several days a week shopping. She goes to the spa, the gym, the shows in Vegas, and buys three-hundred-dollar lunches. And she goes to the hairdresser and plastic surgeons so often, I'm surprised she hasn't turned into a bionic woman with all of the fake things on her body! She even goes around helping churches feed the poor, so she says. And even when she is in the house with me, we don't have that much to talk about. She's as shallow as a duck pond. So, no. She's not good company to me."

"Don't you have any friends?"

"Not really. I hung out with my homegirls from the old neighborhood as long as I could. But I got tired of them asking me for money or making stupid, jealous remarks about me living in Pacific Heights. Daddy sent me to that fancy boarding school so I could learn how to act like I had some class and fit in better with other wealthy people. But that didn't really help. I still feel like a fish out of water. You saw how dull the conversation was at the dinner table this evening. . . ."

"Now that you mention it, it was pret-ty booooring."

We both laughed. "Pret-ty booooring is right." I coughed to clear my throat. I felt so comfortable talking to Curtis. He seemed like the kind of man I could say just about anything to. "You already told me you like barbecued ribs. . . ."

Curtis laughed again. "All right, Mrs. Har—uh, Sarah. I'll let you treat me to lunch."

"When? How about tomorrow?"

Curtis raised an eyebrow. "I have to work tomorrow and I don't get but an hour for lunch. We'd have to do it on one of my days off, which is Wednesday and Thursday."

"All right. We'll go to lunch next Wednesday."

"You tell me the address of the place and I'll meet you there. I should have my car out of the shop by then."

"Oh, I don't mind picking you up," I said quickly. "Why don't you give me your telephone number? I'll call you the day before just to confirm everything."

"Cool." Curtis pulled a pen out of his shirt pocket and eagerly scribbled his telephone number on a matchbook cover and handed it to me. "If a woman answers, don't get nervous. Mama usually answers the telephone."

I glanced toward the store again. It was foggy now, and I couldn't see the door. A few seconds later, Collette slunk out of the fog and strutted toward the car with a pinched look on her face.

"Uh, I don't know if you realized it or not when we were eating dinner, but my folks are . . . uh . . . not normal. I mean, they don't get loose like I do."

"Oh, I picked up on that right away. Vera must have mentioned the names of all the high-end stores she shops in twenty times. Cash and Collette seem more like stowaways. And, your husband . . . well, his mind seemed to be everywhere but at the dinner table. What a crazy setup you live in!" Curtis let out a loud groan and rubbed his nose. "And excuse me for saying this, but I couldn't wait for that dinner to end so I could get away from them."

"I feel like that every day. Some days I feel so uncomfortable at that dinner table I can barely get my food down," I complained.

Curtis gave me a serious look. "Other than your daddy, the only other interesting person at that dinner table was you. You are one special lady, Sarah."

A compliment like that coming from a man like him made my head swell. "Thank you," I mumbled. "By the way, I don't think they need to know about me treating you to lunch next Wednesday."

"I feel the same way," Curtis said with a nod. "Just promise me one thing."

"What?" I held my breath. Collette was just a few feet from the car now.

"After you treat me to lunch next Wednesday, the next time we get together you let me pick up the tab."

The next time we get together? "Oh! Yeah. That'll be fine with me," I gushed.

Collette snatched open the front passenger door and plopped down in her seat, groaning like an old woman. "You look like a cat that just swallowed a canary, Sarah." She gave me an accusatory look out of the corner of her eye. "What's up with that big-ass smile on your face?"

"Nothing," I replied, glancing at Curtis in the rearview mirror. I was not the only one who looked like I'd just swallowed a canary. He looked like he'd swallowed one too. The man's face was glowing like a lightbulb.

What am I getting myself into? I immediately asked myself as I started the motor.

CHAPTER 41

VERA

THE FOLLOWING WEDNESDAY MORNING, SARAH PRANCED INTO THE kitchen a few minutes before eleven. There was such a smug look on her face you would have thought she was King Solomon's favorite mistress. She wore a pair of jeans and a T-shirt with the words HOT STUFF printed across the front in once-black letters now faded by too many washings. She looked like she was on her way to a fashion show at the Salvation Army.

"Why are you dressed like that?" I asked. The frown on my face got even bigger when I saw she had flip-flops on her feet, showcasing ashy feet with toenails that looked more like bear claws.

"I'm going to lunch with Lupe Menendez, a friend that I haven't seen since she came out of her coma." Sarah's eyes glistened like raindrops.

"Excuse me?"

"Lupe. She used to be one of my main homegirls. She got into a fight with a girl when we were in eighth grade and the other girl had a gun in her backpack. She shot Lupe in the back of her neck. Lupe's been in a coma all these years until last week," she explained. To me, Sarah looked unusually cheerful for somebody whose friend had been the victim of such a cruel act of violence.

The knowledge that Sarah still associated with people like this Lupe amazed me to no end. "I hope the girl that shot your friend went to jail."

"No, she didn't. Before the cops could find her, Lupe's older brother, Javier, tracked her down and blew her face off with a sawed-off shotgun. He's in jail, though."

"My God, my God. Well, I hope your friend is going to be all right now and that she has family to look after her."

"Oh, Lupe's fine now. Her daddy got shot and killed a few years ago trying to rob a drug dealer in Mexico City. But her mama and her seven brothers and sisters still live in the building Grandma Lilly and I used to live in."

I groaned and let out a mournful sigh. "If you're going to your old neighborhood, you're dressed appropriately, I guess. You don't need to wear any of your nice clothes and draw attention to yourself. Those desperate, broke-ass people over there are just waiting to cook a goose like you." Sarah didn't like it when I implied that she might become a kidnapping victim someday. The same disgusted look that always appeared on her face when I brought it up was on her face now.

"Vera, don't you think that if somebody wanted to kidnap me they would have done it by now?"

"Just be careful. Your daddy has enough to worry about." I shook my head in exasperation. "I hope you're not driving your car over there. Let Costa drive you."

"No, I'm driving my car," she giggled. "I really would draw attention to myself if I rolled up in front of Lupe's building in the town car with a chauffeur behind the wheel."

"Humph! Just make sure that that can of mace I gave you is still in your purse."

I left the house a few minutes after Sarah did. I had a lot of things on my agenda for the day, but the most important thing I had to do was go to the bank and open a new savings account in my name only. Kenneth and I had several joint accounts and numerous credit cards. Our accountant took care of our bills and other expenses related to the business, but I took care of our personal expenditures. I had opened several credit cards in my name that Kenneth didn't know about. With all the gifts I purchased for my lovers, some months I had to rob Peter to pay Paul. But as long as Kenneth didn't know how out of control I was when it came to money, I was not going to worry about it.

I opened the new bank account with five thousand dollars that I had squeezed out of the monthly household expenses last month. My plan was to siphon out a few thousand dollars from the household money every month and funnel it into my new account. In a few years, I'd have at least a million dollars or close to it. So if Kenneth dumped me and if I had managed my money well, I'd be all right until I landed another wealthy husband.

Despite my increasing paranoia, I had no reason to believe Kenneth was going to divorce me. However, I still felt more comfortable having something to fall back on in case he did.

"Would you like to add someone to this account, Mrs. Lomax?" asked Mr. Garra, a molelike little man who looked more like an undertaker than a bank employee.

I didn't answer right away. I was so busy organizing my thoughts that I had almost forgotten where I was. I looked around the plush bank office, admiring the healthy-looking green plants in every corner. There was a file cabinet behind Mr. Garra's red-oak desk. On top of the file cabinet was a framed picture of his family—two adorable children and an attractive, decades-younger blond wife. She probably loved the puppy her son was holding more than she loved her homely husband. She had the kind of smirk on her face that made me think she and I shared the same secret. And we probably did. Women like me can usually spot another woman with the same motives.

Mr. Garra cleared his throat to get my attention back. "Mrs. Lomax. Will you be adding someone else to this account?"

"Huh? Oh, no. Not at this time." I smiled. "You have a beautiful family," I commented, nodding toward the photograph.

"Well, there's nothing like family. Each day is better than the last."

"You're right." I nodded. "There is nothing like family." I should have shut my big mouth while I was still ahead. I didn't like telling strangers too much of my business. I didn't realize I was doing just that until it was too late. "I have a wonderful husband and a daughter and son-in-law. We're all very close."

Mr. Garra lifted his chin and gave me a dry look. "I see. In that case, you should definitely include a beneficiary on this account. Heaven forbid, but if something were to happen to you, the state will take over your estate unless you provide beneficiary information for this account in your last will and testament. Otherwise, your family will have to struggle through probate and other forms of red tape for years before they can gain access to whatever is still in this account upon your passing."

"Never mind all that!" I snapped. I didn't like to get excited unless I was having sex. Excitement usually made me have a hot flash. One of the worst ones I'd ever experienced suddenly shot up from my feet to my face. It felt like somebody had just shoved me into an oven, face-first. I gasped for air and I fanned my face with my hand.

"Are you all right, ma'am? Would you like a glass of water?" Mr. Garra was around my age, so I figured he probably thought I was having a senior moment. And that was probably true. My memory had rapidly begun to fade. Last week when I went shopping downtown, I couldn't remember where I had parked my car. I had wandered around like an Alzheimer's patient for an hour before I located it. Getting old was a bitch. That was another reason why I had to ensure my future. And if Bo and Sarah had another child—and I prayed that they would make another one soon—at least I'd have a rich grandchild to fall back on. In the meantime, I had to do what I had to do.

"I'm fine, thank you," I insisted, rising. I stuffed my copies of the documents I had just signed into my purse and scurried out like a burglar.

CHAPTER 42

KENNETH

I WAS GLAD TO BE BACK TO NORMAL. WELL, NORMAL FOR ME. I STILL didn't feel as well as I used to, but I felt well enough to return to work.

It was a typical foggy Frisco morning when I left the house, driving with both hands on the steering wheel and squinting my eyes like that old cartoon character Mr. Magoo. Even though I stayed in the slow lanes all the way, impatient motorists behind me kept honking their horns for me to speed up, but I refused to do so. The last way I wanted to end my life was in an automobile accident.

By the time I pulled into my personal parking stall behind the store, I was aching in several places on my body, short of breath, and dizzy. I had to sit still for five minutes to compose myself. After I had taken several deep breaths, massaged my chest, and swallowed a few pills, I felt better. I wobbled out of my Lexus and stumbled into the building through the employee entrance.

In spite of what I told people, I felt like a dead man walking and I tried to hide it. I didn't want anybody to feel sorry for me, which most of them did anyway. People looked at me with pity and a few held their breath when I approached them. The same day I returned to work, half a dozen people came into my office to check and make sure I was still breathing. No matter how many times I told them to stop worrying about me, a few continued to do so. Finally, I closed and locked my office door. And it was a good thing I did that. I fell asleep sitting at my desk several times and once I tumbled from my chair and hit the side of my head on the corner of my desk. Luckily, nobody noticed the small knot that had immediately formed on my head and remained there for three days.

I went about my normal routine. Within a week, I had resumed all of the duties that I had put on hold during my time off. By then people had stopped looking at me like I was already dead. They had even stopped asking me about my health. Life was good again.

It had been a couple of weeks since we'd invited Curtis to the house to have dinner with us. In addition to the hefty bonus we'd given him for being such a hero, I'd taken him to lunch a couple of times. That Friday I strolled out of my office and approached him at the front entrance, which was where he spent most of his shift. "Hello, Curtis," I said, bumping his fist with mine. "I'd love to take you to lunch again today. And you can pick the place this time." I pretended like I didn't see the relieved look on his face when I told him to pick the place. I assumed he was tired of eating at the sushi place and that Indian place I had taken him to the other times. He was a country boy to the bone and it was time for me to start treating him like one. "How about a place that sells some down-home grub?"

"Yes, sir! I can go for that!" he said with a hearty grin. "Excuse me, sir." He looked off to the side of the front entrance and greeted an incoming regular customer with a nod. I admired how courteous he was and I gave him a huge smile when he returned his attention to me. "I love me some ribs."

"I still love me some ribs too," I told him. "My daughter loves them more than I do." I stopped talking and shook my head. "That girl can eat half a slab in one sitting. Her favorite rib joint is Smokey Moe's Rib Palace."

"I know."

"You know what?"

"Oh! Your daughter did mention to me how much she enjoyed

the ribs at Smokey Moe's that evening she drove me home after I had dinner at your house. She told me they were the best ribs she'd ever eaten."

"Well, the girl wasn't lying. Hold on. I'm going to call her up and ask her to meet us for lunch. I'm sure she wouldn't mind. After all, she owes you a lot." I stepped off to the side and whipped out my cell phone, hoping Sarah had not already left the house.

She answered the telephone right away.

"Baby, would you like to have lunch with your old man today?" I asked.

"I would, but I already made an appointment to get my hair done," she told me, sounding disappointed. "How about tomorrow?"

"I'm having lunch with some vendors tomorrow." I sighed, disappointed too. "All right, then, baby. I just thought you'd like to spend a little time with Curtis and me. That boy enjoys ribs as much as you do, so I offered to take him to that Smokey Moe's place that you go to all the time. Besides that, I thought you'd like to see Curtis again."

Sarah must have loved those ribs more than I thought because as soon as I mentioned them, she changed her tune real quick. "Uh . . . yeah, I'd like to join you for some ribs!" she said quickly. "I can get my hair done another day."

Sarah had already arrived at Smoky Moe's Rib Palace on McInnis Street by the time Curtis and I walked in the door. She was sitting in a booth facing the exit, sipping on a Coke in a glass that had once contained jelly. I shook my head when I noticed the large clock on the wall had stopped running and the calendar next to it was from last year. That was the kind of place this joint was. But since my visits were rare, none of that bothered me.

"This is the kind of place where you don't sit with your back to the door," I whispered to Curtis as we made our way to the booth. "On a Friday night, this low-rent neighborhood is like the Wild Wild West. And since the thugs got better firearms than the cops, the cops take their time coming out here when the gunfights start."

"I know. I live around the corner from here," Curtis said with a look on his face I couldn't interpret. I didn't know if he was embarrassed or offended by my comment.

"Oh. Well, I'm happy to hear that there are still some decent law-abiding folks living out here." Sarah stood up and gave me a big hug. Even though my baby girl and I lived under the same roof, we both thought it was important to display our affection for one another on a regular basis. As crazy as the world had become, I never knew when it'd be the last time I saw her. Death was a subject none of us could ignore, especially for a sickly old man like me. My failing health was one thing, but there were other factors involved. The murder rate in San Francisco was higher than ever. A lot of the crimes were random and sometimes the shooter mistook one target for another. It got worse. One of my business associates had lost his wife to random violence; a drug-crazed boy had shot her just because he wanted to see what it felt like to kill somebody. Sarah didn't say it often, but I knew she was worried about me up and dying any day just as much as I was. But I was even more worried about something fatal happening to her.

"Thanks for inviting me to join you guys," Sarah said. Her arms were still around me, but I turned my head in time to see her grinning at Curtis. He was grinning back at her. Curtis was one of my most well-liked employees. Even my most difficult staff members adored him. The men liked him because he was always willing to trade shifts or work an extra shift when one of them wanted to take off. It was obvious why the women liked him. The boy was handsome, charming, and single. And during a conversation last week when I took Curtis to lunch, he told me that he had not been involved with a woman in weeks. I laughed and gave him a dismissive wave when he assured me that he was not gay and was anxious to find a nice woman. "Then you're ripe for the picking," I'd joked. I had several attractive cashiers—single and married—who were hot to trot. And a lot of bold women customers who came in just to browse only "browsed" Curtis. I knew that it was just a matter of time before one of those brazen man-eaters got her hooks in Curtis.

"Hello, Curtis, how have you been?" Sarah released me and shook his hand.

"I've been just fine, Mrs. Harper. Thank you for asking." Curtis had good manners and a lot of class for a man on his level.

I slid into the booth next to Sarah on one side, and Curtis slid in on the other. The important thing was, all three of us were facing the door. I had noticed some pretty shady-looking dudes meandering about outside, so this was going to be a quick lunch.

"I've already ordered, so our plates should be here in a few minutes," Sarah announced. "Three rib orders, with baked beans, coleslaw, corn muffins, and a pitcher of beer."

The first couple of minutes were awkward. We took turns clearing our throats and making mundane comments about everything from the food to how proud we were of Obama. I took it upon myself to get the conversation up on its feet.

"Baby, did you know Curtis went to the same high school you went to?" I said. "I'm surprised you two didn't know each other."

"Uh, I had to drop out and go to work," Curtis said.

"That's a damn shame. It's almost impossible to get a job these days without at least a high school education."

"I got my GED and I put that information on my job application. You can check," Curtis said defensively with a frightened look on his face.

"Pffft! I know that. I went over your application with a fine-toothed comb. We did a background check and we verified your references." I sniffed. I quickly redirected the conversation back to the original subject. "You and Sarah are both so easygoing and likeable; I'm sure you could have been real good friends back then in school if you'd gotten to know one another," I remarked. I loved my son-in-law and I knew Sarah loved him too. Had Bo not entered the picture, I would have been proud to have Curtis in my daughter's life. However, I would have done something about his line of work by grooming him for a more prestigious position. I didn't see anything wrong with a man being just a security guard, but I was glad my daughter had not married one. For one thing, I wanted my baby to be with a man who could provide for her. And I wanted her to end up with a man who had a decent education and a bright future. As much as I liked Curtis, he was going nowhere. He had nothing to offer a girl like Sarah. She would have been better off with a cat. The thought of my daughter being with a man like Curtis, or any other man living a life as dismal as his, made me grimace. I was glad that none of her previous relationships had panned out. Bo got to her in the nick of time. Had he not, I might have ended up with a cabdriver or a fry cook for a son-in-law.

"Daddy, I know that look on your face. You're constipated again. You haven't been taking all of your pills," Sarah accused. She looked more than a little concerned.

"Yes, I have been taking all of my pills," I defended with a laugh and a gentle tap along the side of her face. "Curtis, this girl cares more about other peoples' health than her own. Sometimes I worry about her." I paused and got more serious. "I bet she would take a bullet for one of her friends if she had to."

Despite my Southern roots and all of the ghost stories I had heard when I was a boy, I did not believe in premonitions or any of the other superstitious riffraff black folks were known for. But right after I'd made that last statement, a cold chill crawled up my spine like a poisonous snake.

CHAPTER 43

SARAH

Daddy had called me up a little while ago and invited me to have lunch with him and Curtis, and I had accepted without hesitation.

When I walked into the kitchen on my way out, Vera was on the telephone giggling like a teenager to whoever it was on the other end. "The things you say make my ears burn! You're spoiling me, honey," she said, still giggling. I cleared my throat to get her attention. When she whirled around and saw me standing in the doorway, her face froze. Her being so fair skinned, she blushed like a white woman. Her face went from a light brown to a candy-apple red. She blinked at me and then pointed to the telephone, frowned, and shook her head. "I have to hang up now. And I hope I don't have to call you again or come down there in person. Now, I expect you to have my dry cleaning ready by this coming Monday! Do I make myself clear?" Then she slammed the telephone back into its cradle on the wall and turned sharply to face me. "Those damn Jamaicans! Incompetent to the bone! I'm going to start taking my dry cleaning to the Chinese people. They are the only ones who take cleaning clothes seriously."

I gave her a puzzled look. "Then how are the Jamaicans spoiling you?"

Her face froze again when she realized I'd overheard that part of her conversation. "Oh! I was just being sarcastic!" I could see that Vera was flustered. Beads of sweat dotted her forehead and she started blinking like she had something caught in her eye. She looked me up and down. I had on my jacket and my car keys were in my hand. "You look like you're going somewhere."

"I'm meeting Daddy for lunch at that rib joint on McInnis," I told Vera. "You want me to bring you a plate of ribs?"

"A plate of ribs?" The way she said it, gasping and screwing her face up like she'd just tasted something bitter, you would have thought I'd just offered to bring her back a plate of shit.

I cocked my head to the side and gave Vera a weary look. Next to Collette, Vera was the most exasperating woman I knew. I had been trying for years to "like" them, but so far, the most I could say was that I only tolerated them. Had it not been for Daddy, I probably would have moved out of the mansion by now. "I'll see you when I get back." I couldn't get away from Vera fast enough.

It was a short drive to the restaurant. But I had enough time to think back to last Wednesday when I took Curtis to lunch at the same place I was on my way to now. I had told Vera that I was taking Lupe Menendez to lunch to celebrate her coming out of the coma she'd been in since eighth grade. Since Vera couldn't verify that, I wasn't worried about getting busted.

Curtis had met me in front of the restaurant. He looked more handsome than ever, standing in front of the window where there was a crudely printed sign noting Smokey's Moe's business hours (which they rarely stuck to). He looked as happy to see me as I was to see him.

"You seem nervous," I told him right after we'd received our orders and started eating.

"I am nervous. It's been a while since I was out in public with a beautiful woman," he said shyly, sliding what was left of his ribs to the side of his plate with his fork.

"Thank you. I needed to hear something like that." After the comment he'd just made, I had to force myself to continue eating.

He gave me a sideways glance. "Come on now! I'm sure you hear things like that from your husband all the time."

I shook my head. "I don't remember the last time my husband told me I was beautiful. He spends more time at the store than with me and . . . and it's beginning to get on my last nerve. I didn't know being married to a workaholic was going to be this . . . this bad. And not just that but the man frustrates the hell out of me sometimes. My stepmother treats him like a puppy she trained personally for her benefit, and he just goes along with whatever she says."

"I'm sorry to hear that. But that's really none of my business."

"I'm sorry, Curtis. I don't mean to dump my marital problems on you."

We didn't have much to say about anything else and before I knew it, we had drifted back to the subject of my marriage.

"Sometimes I still feel like a single woman," I complained. "I don't know how my stepmother can stand Daddy spending so much time at the store and leaving her by herself."

"Have you tried to talk to your husband about the way you feel?"

"He's hardly ever around!" I snapped. "When he is, we rush through everything. Conversations, meals, and even sex! The last time we made love, he came before I even got out of my clothes!"

"Damn." Curtis bit his bottom lip and I think it was because he didn't want to laugh at what I'd just said.

"Let me hush. I'm embarrassing you. You feel me?"

Curtis stared at me for a moment, giving me a dreamy-eyed look. "Oh yeah . . . I feel you, Sarah." That look was still in his eyes. He tilted his head to the side and stared at me so hard it felt like he was looking through me, not at me. "Sarah, I wish I had met you before."

"Before what?"

"Before Bo."

I suddenly felt awkward, but I still managed to say, "I wish you had too. Uh, I'm ready to leave when you are." I wiped the barbecue sauce and the juice from the baked beans off my lips and neatly folded the paper napkin.

Curtis let out a loud breath. Then he gave me such an inviting look, which included a wink, I wanted to throw him to the ground and mount him like a horny dog. "I think about you all the time." He sighed. "I want you to know that."

His confession stunned me, but it also made me feel warm all over. I smiled demurely and looked into his eyes. "Curtis, are you hitting on me?" I teased.

He dropped his head and began to twiddle his thumbs. When he looked back up at me, he said very slowly, "Yeah . . . I'd like for us to know one another better. A *lot* better, if you know what I mean."

"I'm glad to hear that," I admitted. "I would love to know you a lot better. And I do know what you mean."

"So are we going to do anything about it?"

It took me a moment to compose myself and get the picture of me humping him on the floor out of my mind. "I hope so," I said slowly.

"Look, baby, if you want me to stop, you'd better tell me now. Otherwise, I'm going to take you to my place and once we get there I won't be responsible for my actions."

Curtis's threat intrigued me and I didn't waste any time responding. "I'd like to go to your place. And, whatever happens, happens."

CHAPTER 44

SARAH

I HADN'T SEEN CURTIS SINCE THE DAY HE HAD TAKEN ME TO HIS apartment after our rib lunch. He'd made love to me on his mother's living room couch. He had held me in his arms and pumped into me until I was so overwhelmed with ecstasy that I screamed like a woman being murdered. That thought had been on my mind day and night ever since. No lover had ever made me feel so special! Not even Bo.

The fact that I was rapidly losing interest in my husband and developing more interest in Curtis was something I could not ignore. I knew I had to do something about it, but what? Bo had told me more than once that he would never let me go.

He had come home early yesterday, and right after dinner we went up to our room and made love at his insistence. Despite my relationship with Curtis and the fact that my marriage was probably on its last leg, I still wanted to give my daddy at least one grandchild. Also, I thought that a baby by Bo would please Daddy a lot more than a baby by Curtis. That was the reason I had made Curtis wear two condoms at the same time when we made love.

Instead of Bo falling asleep right away, he propped his head up on some pillows and watched two of his favorite episodes of *The Sopranos* that he had previously recorded. The only time he spoke to me the rest of the night was when he told me to get him another beer.

* * *

Now I was about to see Curtis again. With Daddy present this time, I had to make sure I didn't say or do anything stupid. And it was not going to be easy. Curtis was irresistible.

I sat in my car a few minutes after I had parked. I could smell the aroma of barbecue wafting out of the cracks in the wall and windows in the building where Smokey Moe's was located. I took a deep breath and entered the restaurant and placed our orders. The way some of the other patrons were staring at me made me uncomfortable, especially the ones sitting at a table by the window who had seen me roll up in my Jaguar. I felt a lot more comfortable when Daddy and Curtis showed up about fifteen minutes later. The patrons stared even harder at them. And it was no wonder. Daddy wore one of his Italian suits and Curtis was still in his uniform.

I was glad to be in Curtis's presence again so soon, especially since we were in the same place where we'd had our first lunch together and decided to "get to know each other better."

Daddy dominated the conversation. He loved to tell people how hard he had worked to become a multimillionaire. "Hard work, perseverance, and being in the right place at the right time. That's all it takes to succeed in this country," he said, winking at Curtis. "And having a beautiful woman by your side."

"I hear that," Curtis said with a nod. I didn't even bat an eye when he reached under the table and massaged my knee.

Curtis was probably thinking the same thing I was thinking: I wanted to make love again. Him rubbing my knee was making me squirm, so I had to say something to keep my thoughts under control. "Daddy, your hair looks like the crown on a woodpecker," I said. "You should either keep it cut shorter or start wearing some of those hats you own. The way it's sticking up and pointing away from your head now, it looks like you've been flying." I gently kicked Curtis's foot, hoping it would make him move his hand away from my knee. It didn't so I shot him a hot look. He gave me a sheepish grin, but he did stop teasing me with his hand on my knee.

"I didn't realize it was that windy outside." Daddy patted the sides and top of his head and rose. "I'm going to step into the men's room. I hope there's a clean mirror in there," he added, still patting the side of his head as he walked toward a door in the back of the room with a sign that read TOILETS: NO SMOKING, NO DRUGS, NO WEAPONS, NO SEX.

"Curtis, I've been thinking about you a lot since the last time I saw you," I said in a low voice.

"I've been thinking about you too," he growled. "I hope that wasn't a one-time thing."

"I don't know yet."

"Let me rephrase that. Is there a possibility that I will see you again?"

My mind was a ball of confusion. I didn't want to say the wrong thing and hurt Curtis's feelings and discourage him from wanting to see me again. At the same time, I didn't want him to get too hopeful about us getting serious. "What about my husband?"

"Pfftt! What he doesn't know won't hurt him."

"What about your job? If we get caught, you'll be looking for another job."

"I can get another job."

I looked Curtis in the eye and asked, "I'm not just another piece of ass to you, am I?"

His eyes got big and his mouth dropped open. He looked angry and sad at the same time. "Listen to me, Sarah. You mean more to me than a piece of ass. I can get that anywhere. But I care about you. If you were my woman, I wouldn't trade you for five of the other women I've been with." He stopped talking and sucked on his teeth for a few seconds. He surprised me by what he said next. "But since you mentioned it, you are a pretty nice piece of ass."

I knew he was being funny, but I was not the least bit amused by what he'd just said. "I hope you don't think that I'm the kind of woman who will jump into bed with other men as quick as I did with you, because I am not."

"I hope you're not that kind of woman, but if you are, that's your business." Curtis winked at me. "I'm just glad that you hopped into bed with me. Or onto my mama's couch, I should say." He laughed, but I was not amused by that either.

"I've never . . . I never thought I'd cheat on my husband so soon into our marriage. And especially with somebody like you."

"Somebody like me?"

"I didn't mean that in a bad way. It's just that you're so down to earth and I can relate to you. I enjoy your company more than the people I spend time with now."

A few moments of silence passed. I didn't know about him, but I was racking my brain trying to decide what to say next. In cases like this, I usually said something stupid. This time was no different. "I had a crush on you in school. One time I even copied your answers on a test that I hadn't studied for."

"Oh? That's interesting. I didn't think you even noticed a thug like I was back then."

"I noticed you," I eagerly admitted.

"But not enough to even talk to me about it?"

"I gave up my cherry to a guy whose name I don't remember."

"Hmmm. I guess he didn't make much of an impression on you, huh?"

I shook my head. "I only went with him because he looked a little like you." That comment made him grin like a Cheshire cat.

"Baby, you just made my day," he told me.

Curtis glanced around again. Some nosy-ass, backstabbing individuals hung out in this restaurant. It was no wonder that the neighborhood drug dealers and other criminals were always killing a few for snitching. I recognized a heavy-set married woman who lived on the same block that my grandmother and I used to live on. She occupied a table against the wall. The man she was with was not her husband, and by the way he kept squeezing her hand and tickling her three chins, he was more than just a friend. Every time I looked in her direction, she was looking in mine. I knew a lot of unhappy wives cheated on their husbands. In the cases I knew about firsthand, the women had husbands who didn't appreciate them or have time for them. I had become one of those women.

"What would you say if I told you I wanted to come back to your place tonight?" I asked. My knee was shaking and not because Curtis had begun to massage it some more. I told myself that I was enough woman for Bo and Curtis, hoping it would make me feel less guilty. It did.

"You won't have any trouble getting out of the house?"

"I don't live in a prison. I can come and go as I please. I would like to see you again."

Curtis gazed over my shoulder, then back at me. "What time can you make it, baby?"

I shrugged. "You tell me."

I didn't look around, but I heard Daddy complaining to one of the waitresses about how foul smelling the bathroom was.

"Nine o'clock?" I said quickly.

"Nine o'clock," Curtis confirmed. He raised his hand and crossed his fingers. "Don't be late."

"I won't," I assured him with a slow lick of my bottom lip and a naughty grin. "Oh—what about your mama? Will she be home?"

"She works a night shift. She won't be home until seven in the morning. When nine o'clock rolls around, I want you knocking on my door. You feel me?"

I nodded so hard my neck ached.

Daddy plopped back down onto his seat with a groan. "That toilet was filthy! The stench was so unholy it would gag a mule. Flies as big as shot glasses buzzed around my head like a halo. Sitting on that commode was like sitting on a hole in the ground!" Daddy mopped his brow with one of the few napkins on the table that we had not saturated with barbecue sauce. "I don't like to rush, but I need to get up out of here. I need to get back to my office so I can use a decent restroom and spray my hind parts with some butt spray. Lord, I hope I didn't catch anything off that toilet seat." Daddy looked from me to Curtis, then at our plates, which still contained several ribs. "I can't eat anything else in this place," he declared, signaling for the waitress to bring the check.

Daddy paid the check, leaving a huge tip in spite of his complaints about the restroom accommodations, and we left.

I had parked on the street right in front of the restaurant's entrance. Daddy had parked directly behind me. I shook Curtis's hand again and gave Daddy another hug before I got into my car. It was a good thing we had decided not to stay any longer. A group of rough-looking young men stood a few yards away from Daddy's Lexus and my Jaguar, looking at both vehicles like they wanted to eat them.

"Baby, we are going to follow you until we make it out of this jungle," Daddy told me, making sure my doors were locked. "I don't want you cruising around over here by yourself."

A few minutes before 9:00 p.m., I drove back into the same neighborhood. I parked in a lot a block from Curtis's building. I eased out of my car, looking around to make sure nobody was lurking too close, and then I bolted. I sprinted all the way to his building. When I got inside and made it to his apartment on the fourth floor at the end of the hall, I pounded a tattoo on the door. He snatched it open immediately and gave me a long, hard kiss.

"I couldn't wait to get here," I said hoarsely, leaning my head away from his. He had kissed me so hard my lips were aching.

With a grunt, he scooped me up into his arms and carried me to the living room couch.

CHAPTER 45

VERA

I WAS IN THE LIVING ROOM SPRAWLED ON THE COUCH, RELAXING WITH a glass of wine. My feet were on the coffee table. It had been a strenuous day for me, so I deserved to kick back. I had spent an hour on the treadmill at the gym, something I didn't do often enough. A lot of parts on my body felt like they had taken on a life of their own, so I had to do all I could to keep myself looking and feeling good. My plastic surgeons couldn't do it all.

My last liposuction procedure eliminated twenty pounds off my body a few months ago, which had made me look almost like a supermodel. But the loss of weight had also made other areas on my body suffer. My breasts had a slight droop to them now. I didn't even want to bother getting them lifted again, even though that would have corrected the problem. But since I wanted to go from a C cup to a D cup, getting a brand-new pair was a better solution.

While I was enjoying my solitude, Cash moseyed in and plopped down on the wing chair facing the couch. He had come home from work early that Friday, around four. Kenneth and Bo were still at work, as usual. "Girl, you look like you don't have a care in the world," Cash teased.

"I don't," I said with a smirk. "That's what happens when you keep up with your game." I got up and padded over to the bar and poured him a glass of wine. As soon as I handed it to him, he took a long swallow and belched like an ox.

"I feel you." Cash looked at me and smiled. He paused long enough to finish his wine and let out another loud belch. "I remember when we were young kids. You always looked ahead. If it wasn't for you, there's no telling where me and Collette would be now. Cuz, I know you said we don't have to pay any rent or anything else to stay here, but sometimes I feel like a freeloader. I know I probably don't say it enough, but you're a beautiful person, inside and out. You got Kenneth to hire me and my woman so we can pay our way . . . if we have to."

"Why are you bringing this up? Did Kenneth say something about you and Collette living here rent-free?"

"No, he didn't. But lately Sarah keeps reminding me and Collette how lucky we are to be living in this beautiful place *rent-free.*"

"Her cheesy black ass is living here rent-free too!" I hollered, drinking more wine.

"I just don't want you to think we don't appreciate your generosity. I mean, if you ever want us to move out, all you need to do is let us know."

"Look, one thing you need to get in your thick skull is that you don't look a gift horse in the mouth. As long as I'm controlling the situation, you don't have to worry about anything. Fuck Sarah—that heifer! But just to be on the safe side, I hope you and Collette are banking part of your paychecks."

"Oh, we put aside most of our money every time we get paid. I know all good things eventually come to an end. We've been worried ever since Sarah got here that if something happens to Kenneth, she might get all legal and shit and derail our gravy train."

"And that's why we all need to milk the cow as long and as hard as we can. I've said it before, but I'll say it again: Once Kenneth kicks the bucket, there is no telling how Sarah is going to behave," I said. "With me being related only by marriage, I have no idea how she will treat me. She might even get crazy enough to mess with the business, sell it or something. Kenneth keeps changing his will and even I don't know how generous he's going to be to me and the rest of us now that he's got a blood relative in the mix. He just might leave everything, or most of it, to her. I am not counting on Sarah to do the right thing and split up that money fair and square!"

"Neither am I. If you, the *wife*, ain't even sure what Kenneth is going to leave you, me and Collette can't even guess how generous he'll be to us. He's not the same man he was before Sarah came. And since we are on the subject, what's the word on Sarah these days? I hope she's not putting bugs in Big Daddy's ears, encouraging him to change his will in a way that'll shortchange us or set it up so we don't get *nothing*! Are you keeping your eye on her and what she's doing when she's around him?"

"As much as I can," I sighed, shaking my head. "Some days that little fool is like a fart in a windstorm, so keeping an eye on her can be a lot of work." I blew out a disgusted breath. "My life was so much easier before she came here! And it doesn't seem like she's ever going to produce a baby by Bo that will save our asses."

"At least since Bo married her she's been a little easier to digest."

"By the way, where is your lovely wife? You two usually come home from work at the same time."

"She dropped me off, then took the car and went to some girl's house to get her hair braided."

"Listen, uh, I've been meaning to mention something that's been on my mind for a little while."

Cash began to fidget like a cornered roach. That made me think that he was doing something he should not be doing. Since we shared the same DNA, which was thick with high levels of deceit, there was no telling what he was doing on the sly. But as long as it didn't interfere with my game, I didn't care. "What's that, cuz?"

"Have you noticed how odd Sarah's been acting all this month?"

Cash looked relieved. "Oh, is that all that's been on your mind?" He chuckled. "Sarah acts odd all the time. What's your point?"

"I think she's up to no good," I said, drinking more wine. "Maybe she's pregnant again," I said hopefully. "I just hope she's not having an affair."

Cash whipped his head from side to side. When he looked back at me, he looked scared. "I sure as hell don't think that the stupid girl is *that* stupid! After what Gladys put Bo through, he would never get over Sarah putting him in the same trick bag. She's asking for trouble if she is fucking another man!"

"I just hope she isn't."

"You better do more than hope. Bo would have a fit that would never end and only God knows what he might do to Sarah."

I snapped my fingers. "Calm down. Let's not jump the gun now," I suggested, holding up my hand. "I said she might be having an affair, but I'm probably wrong."

"If you think you're wrong, why did you even bring it up in the first place? Has she given you any reason to think she might be fooling around?"

"Not really. But since she's been acting so strange lately, I just thought I'd mention it. Oh well. Even if she is, most married people who have affairs don't leave their spouses," I declared. "Especially if their marriage is as solid as mine. Now look at Kenneth and me. When he told me about his affair with Sarah's mother, I got mad, but I didn't get mad enough to cut off my nose to spite my face. I beat his ass, but I got over it and he's been going out of his way ever since to make it all up to me. Looking back, I wouldn't change a thing. I'd never tell him, but his affair made me stronger and more aware. And smarter. If something happens, say he leaves me for another woman, I will land on my feet no matter what."

Cash looked even more relieved now. "Vera, you are one amazing woman. Kenneth had his fun and made a baby with another woman, but you forgave him and stayed focused on your marriage. The world would be a much better place if all women were as sensible and loyal as you. I hope Sarah is learning how to be as phenomenal a woman as you are, don't you?"

"Uh-huh," I said. "I'm doing my best to help her keep her life on track."

CHAPTER 46

SARAH

I COULDN'T BELIEVE I'D FALLEN IN LOVE WITH CURTIS IN JUST ONE month. But I had. He was the first thing on my mind when I woke up each morning and the last thing on my mind before I went to sleep every night.

I loved Curtis, but I still loved my husband too. I didn't want to hurt Bo or Curtis. I wanted all three of us to be happy. I didn't see why I couldn't have them both as long as I didn't get caught. I knew that it was wrong for me to be cheating on my husband, but it was easy for me to justify my actions.

I wasn't the first married person to cheat and I wouldn't be the last. Cheating was all around me. Bo's first wife had cheated on him. Daddy had cheated on Vera with my mother. Most of his married friends had cheated on their spouses. And the way Cash stared at women's butts and titties when we were out in public, I knew he had probably had an affair or two. He could have been involved with another woman now for all I knew. And Collette was so sneaky she was capable of doing just about anything. I had seen her checking out other men in public. The only person that I was sure had *not* had an affair and probably never would was Vera. She seemed to have eyes only for my daddy and I knew she really did love him. With the exception of her devotion to Daddy, Vera was too much in love with herself to share any more of her affections with another man. There were times I actually envied her. I wished that I could be more like her when it came to being a faithful wife. That way having a part-time husband wouldn't have bothered me so much. Bo left me alone too often, and I was one woman who didn't want to be ignored by her man.

Yesterday, Daddy and Bo left the house to go to the office before Vera and I even got out of bed. I had no idea where Vera had spent her day, but I'd spent some time with Curtis after I'd shopped at the Dollar Tree and Target for a couple of hours. I had picked him up on his lunch hour in the alley behind Daddy's main store. I forced myself not to look at Daddy's and Bo's cars in the employee parking lot as I barreled past them toward the freeway.

We stopped at a liquor store and picked up a bottle of wine and some condoms. There was a McDonald's close by, so we picked up two Big Macs. We checked into the first motel we came to, which was only half a mile away from Daddy's store.

After our little rendezvous, I dropped Curtis off where I'd picked him up. Then I drove to the Mission district to get my nails done. I left the nail shop about an hour later and went to a movie. When I got home that evening around six, Bo and Daddy had already come home. I was shocked when I saw both of their cars parked in the driveway. My first thought was that something had happened to Daddy. I parked my car behind Bo's silver Range Rover and jumped out. I ran into the house with my heart racing about a mile a minute.

There was nobody in the living room, so I started yelling out names. "Daddy! Bo! Vera! Where is everybody?" I checked the dining room next. It was empty. I almost collided with Delia as I ran down the hall toward the kitchen. She must have been cooking up a storm. She smelled like onions and baked chicken and there was flour all over the crisp white apron that hugged her barrel-shaped body like a second layer of flesh. "Where is everybody? Did something happen?" I asked. Delia was not the kind of servant like the ones on TV. She usually knew everything that was going on in the house, but she never stuck her nose into the family business. She knew better. She was careful not to say or do anything to jeopardize her job. She and her crusty old husband, Costa, and a few of her relatives who came to help out on an as-needed basis, had been with Daddy ever since he'd moved his business to California.

"Um . . . everyone is in kitchen. I believe they wait for you," Delia told me, her voice cracking. The worried look on her face caused me to worry.

I continued on down the hall. When I got to the kitchen doorway, I stopped in my tracks. Bo, Daddy, Vera, Cash, and Collette were sitting at the breakfast table. It looked like they were about to have a séance. They all looked up at me at the same time. I moved toward them with caution.

"What's going on?" I stopped a few feet from the table and looked from one face to the other. "Why all the long faces? Did something bad happen?"

"That's what we'd like to know," Daddy snapped.

"Huh? What do you mean?" I asked dumbly. I had made sure nobody saw me pick Curtis up and drop him off, and there was no way in the world they could have found out already that I'd spent time with him in a motel a few hours ago.

"Sarah Louise, what have you been up to?" Daddy asked, his voice cracking.

I opened my mouth to speak, but before I could get a word out, Cash yelled, "What's wrong with you, girl?"

"What?" I asked dumbly.

"Karen Gorman braids my hair," Collette offered.

"So?" I said with a shrug. "She does a good job."

"Karen lives in Hunters Point," Bo said quickly. His eyes were red.

"I have a feeling somebody's trying to tell me something and I don't have any idea what it is," I said, glancing at Daddy. I didn't like the somber look that was on his face now.

"Sarah, why were you seen coming out of Curtis Thompson's apartment last night?" Vera asked in a low voice.

My jaw dropped. "Who said I was at Curtis's place last night?" I wailed, rotating my neck and waving my arms defensively. I had spent time with Curtis in his apartment the night before today's motel tryst.

"When I left Karen's place last night, I saw a car exactly like yours parked on the street in front of her building. I didn't think it was your car because as far as I knew, you were supposed to be at a bingo game in Oakland. Anyway, I decided to check it out. For all I knew, somebody could have carjacked you. I peeped in the window, and on the backseat I saw that red Windbreaker you wear sometimes. I went back into the building lobby and saw Curtis's name and apartment number on his mailbox. I was about to leave when the elevator door opened and you walked out. I didn't want you to see me, so I ducked into the stairwell."

"So what if I was over there?" I snapped. "I still visit people over there all the time. If you saw me last night, how come you waited until now to say something about it?"

"I wasn't going to say anything at all until . . ." Collette stopped talking and looked directly at Bo. "When I saw Curtis piling out of Sarah's car in the alley behind the store on my way back from lunch this afternoon, I got real suspicious. I don't want the wrong person to see her coming out of a man's place and get the wrong idea."

I was tempted to say that the "wrong person" had already seen me coming out of a man's place and got the wrong idea. Collette could stir up a hornet's nest quicker than anybody I knew. But I decided to remain as calm as I could. "I had lunch with Curtis today," I said, looking to Daddy for support.

"How come you didn't mention that to anybody?" Bo asked, glaring at me. If looks could kill, I would have dropped dead on the spot. I had never seen such a severe look of disgust on his face before.

"I go to lunch with my friends all the time, and I don't mention it to anybody!" I said. "I, uh, chat with Curtis when I visit the store. I'm still thankful for what he did for me. What's wrong with me taking him to lunch?" I looked at Daddy again. "Daddy, you enjoyed lunch with Curtis that day we went to the rib place, didn't you? You said you liked him."

"He's a good old boy," Daddy said with some hesitation.

I wondered how come Vera was being so quiet now. Each time I looked at her, she looked away.

"But what about you coming out of his building *last night*?" Bo barked. "What were you even doing in that neighborhood by yourself at night?"

"I wasn't by myself!" I lied. "I had run into Lorna Moss, the girl who used to braid my hair. She asked me to give her a ride home. I didn't even know she lived in the same building as Curtis. She insisted on giving me some gas money, but she had to collect the ten dollars Curtis owed her first. I went to his place with her. That's why I was coming out of Curtis's building last night."

"I still don't understand why you didn't mention it to me," Bo said.

"I was asleep when you got home last night. I was still asleep when you left for work this morning. When I called you around ten this morning, you were in a meeting. When could I have told you?"

"Sarah, we don't want anything bad to happen to you. Curtis is a nice dude and a good employee. But you and he are from two different planets," Daddy said in a gentle voice.

I could not believe my ears. "What's that supposed to mean?" I asked.

Daddy looked so miserable and that bothered me. He was the last person in the world I wanted to hurt. "It's okay to be friends with people like him, but it's not too smart to be *too* friendly. He's got too many enemies. There is just no telling what one of them might do to you if you happen to be with him the next time he gets attacked. And when that happens and if those people know whose daughter you are, you'll really be in a pickle."

"I've been telling Sarah that for years," Vera muttered, talking to me but looking at Daddy.

"I'm twenty-six years old," I reminded.

"And you're my wife," Bo said sharply. "Besides, none of us really know Curtis that well. Who knows what is really on his mind? He could be cooking up all kinds of schemes to get his hands on your money."

"Curtis doesn't want any money from me." I guess that was the wrong thing for me to say. Vera gasped, Collette snickered, Daddy's jaw dropped. But Bo's reaction concerned me the most. He just stared at me with a blank expression on his face.

"If Curtis don't want money, maybe he wants something else from you," Cash suggested with a sneer.

"I don't know what's gotten into everybody—" I stopped talking in midsentence, threw up my hands, and shook my head. "What the hell! I'm going to bed." I started to leave the room, but I stopped when Daddy rose.

"Sarah Louise, I don't want you going out in public with Curtis. Do not go to lunch with him again unless Bo or I"—Daddy paused and looked from Vera to Collette to Cash—"or somebody else goes too."

"Oh, so now I need a babysitter? Nobody trusts me anymore?"

"Sarah, if Curtis tries anything with you, I'm going to hurt him." Bo's words gave me a chill. It wasn't just what he said; it was also the cold, threatening tone of voice he used. "He'll regret the day he was born." Bo was normally a mild-mannered man. I had never seen him angry except when his ex-wife's name came up in a conversation. That was why what he'd just said disturbed me so much.

"You don't have to worry about that. I won't even speak to the man again, even when I come by the store." I blinked. "That is, if he still has a job with you now."

"He's still got a job. I always give people the benefit of the doubt and that includes Curtis," Daddy said quickly. "As long as nothing inappropriate is going on between you and him, he can work for me as long as he does his job right."

"Okay." I sighed. "I don't want to get the man in any trouble, and I don't want him to lose his job. He's got enough problems, so I hope this conversation stays between us."

"I don't intend to mention anything about our concerns to him," Daddy said. Then he looked at Bo. "I think we've made our point."

"Uh-huh." Bo nodded. "This case is closed."

I breathed a long sigh of relief this time. But because Bo and

Daddy had come home from work early and confronted me as soon as I walked in the door, I knew this was more serious than it looked. And I sure didn't like everybody talking to me like I was a rebellious teenager. Living in a house with nothing but folks over forty-five had turned into a nightmare.

Maybe my home was a prison after all. It suddenly felt that way.

Well, I had weaseled out of a tough spot this time. My explanation had sounded believable, even to me. But I had to do something and I had to do it before somebody got hurt. If I continued to see Curtis, sooner or later Collette or somebody else would see us together and I might not be so lucky the next time.

Now I knew what I had to do: I had to make a choice between my lover and my husband.

CHAPTER 47

KENNETH

I KNEW THAT NO MATTER HOW WELL YOU THOUGHT YOU KNEW A PERson, you could never know everything there was to know about him or her. The fact that I'd cheated on Vera for years without her suspecting anything was a good example. I knew that Sarah was not perfect and I expected her to make mistakes, just like everybody else. On one hand, I wanted her to learn from her mistakes like I had. On the other hand, I didn't want her to make mistakes that she would regret and ones that would hurt other people. Bo was a good husband and as long as he remained a good husband, I was going to do whatever I had to do to keep them together.

I didn't like to meddle in other peoples' business, but when it involved my child, I made an exception to that rule. She didn't have to know about me keeping my eye on her. Well, I'd keep my eye on her as much as I could, but I had suddenly decided to move it up a notch. The Monday after we'd had that discussion in the kitchen about her prowling around Curtis's neighborhood, I left my office around noon. I told my secretary I had an appointment with my tax attorney, but the truth was, I had an appointment with a private investigator named Tim Larkin.

"I want you to follow somebody," I told him after he had shut the door to his office and motioned for me to sit down. As soon as my butt hit the chair facing his desk, I got so anxious my knees began to knock against each other. I had never hired an investigator before in my life and it was something I didn't feel comfortable doing. But I had decided that if I wanted to stay on top of things, I needed to know what was going on around me. Especially when it involved my only child.

"You've come to the right place, big guy." Tim Larkin was a slightly built white dude I'd met at a reception back in November of '92 to celebrate Bill Clinton's win. We had a lot in common. He and I both loved our work and families more than anything. We played racquetball together every now and then, and we attended a lot of the same social events. Tim had a baby face and curly blond hair, so he looked a lot younger than seventy-two. Unlike me, he worked out several times a week, he was a vegetarian, and he only drank in moderation. I assumed that was what helped keep him looking and feeling so much younger. I should be so lucky.

Tim knew all about my past and he had never attempted to get in my business like some of my other male friends had. His office was on the twentieth floor of a high-rise in the financial district where the rent was extremely high. With a beautiful young secretary sitting in front of his office dressed to the nines, all the fancy furniture and exotic original paintings on the walls, a brand-new Cadillac every two years, I knew that Tim was doing better than some of the other private investigators in town. For one thing, he didn't play by the rules, whatever they were. Some of the things he did were probably illegal to say the least. But he'd been highly recommended to me by a colleague who had hired Tim to spy on his mistress, a predatory she-devil who had once made eyes at me.

"Who is the subject?" Tim asked, handing me a cigar, which I eagerly accepted. I didn't light up around Vera because she hated the smell of any kind of smoke. But when I was with my male buddies, I was happy to indulge myself.

"I want you to keep an eye on my daughter," I said quickly, bile rising in my throat. The cigar smoke floating into my mouth helped hold it back.

"Your daughter?"

I nodded. "Sarah Louise."

"Is she mixed up with the wrong crowd or something? Drugs?"

"I don't know about any of that. If she is, I want to know that too. But right now, I'm more interested in her other activities. She's got a damn good husband and I don't want her to lose him."

"Hmmm." Tim paused and scratched his chin. "Is there another man involved?"

"Yes and no."

"Can you be a little more specific? Is she involved with another man, or is she not? It can't be both."

"Remember that incident at the store when one of my security guards intercepted an assault on my daughter by a would-be thief?"

"Oh, I remember that all too well. That hit you pretty hard. Your daughter lost her baby," Tim said with a nod and a grimace. He took a drag from his cigar and flipped the ashes into a gold-plated ashtray on his desk, next to a picture of his beautiful redheaded wife, his two divorced sons, and his three teenage grandchildren. "Is the man involved the one who attacked her?"

"Uh, no. She and the security guard who assisted her, they have become quite friendly."

"I see. Is it possible they've become *too* friendly? Or that they might become too friendly?" Tim paused again and shook his head. "If you know what I mean . . ."

"I know exactly what you mean and that's what I need to know. I love her to death and I'm quite fond of her husband and the security guard. I don't want to see either one of them get hurt."

"I doubt if I can help keep that from happening. But I can guarantee you that I will get all the necessary information and photographs that you and your son-in-law will need to take whatever action you have a mind to."

"That's another thing."

"What's another thing?"

"I don't want *anybody* to know about this. My wife and especially my son-in-law. I don't want to look like an overprotective father, even though that's exactly what I am." I laughed, but Tim didn't.

"You can rest assured that whatever business we conduct is confidential unless you advise me otherwise. Now that that's out of the way, tell me: do you think your daughter is capable of cheating on your son-in-law?"

"That's what I need to know. The more I know, the more I can do to keep her from ruining her life. I know she's a grown woman, but . . . well, you know. Our babies will always be our babies and it's our nature to protect them from harm."

"As a father and a grandfather, I agree with that assessment one hundred percent. If I had my way, I'd still be tucking both my middle-aged sons into bed each night." Tim rubbed his nose and snorted and then he gave me a tentative look. "Is there anything else I can do for you? I know you've had to fire a few dishonest employees over the years. Do you want me to tail any of your current staff or anybody else?" Tim cleared his throat and shifted around in his high-back leather chair, which looked way too big for a dude his size. He looked to be only slightly larger than my daughter and she was a size eight. "This is a crazy world we live in, my friend. I hope I don't come off sounding like Big Brother, but men like us, we can't afford to be made a fool of. Had I been more diligent, my wife would still be with me. . . ."

"Oh? You and Sherry are no longer together?"

Tim shook his head. There was an unbearably sad look on his face.

"She's probably the finest Caucasian woman I've ever seen in my life! She reminds me of my beautiful bride. When did you separate?"

"Last month. I was so distraught I couldn't even talk about it to my friends. Otherwise, you would have been the first to know. She moved out while I was in Baja on a weekend fishing trip with my grandsons. She served me with divorce papers a few days ago." I gave Tim a sympathetic look. From the way he was looking, I could tell that he was still distraught. "The bitch!" he blazed. He slammed his fist down so hard on the top of his desk, everything on it rattled.

"Man, I am so sorry to hear that Sherry left you! *What did she catch you doing?*"

Tim's mouth flew open and his small blue eyes rolled up in his head. "Me? What did she catch *me* doing? She didn't catch me doing a goddamn thing! I found a package of condoms in her purse one day last month. Well, it didn't take me long to find out the reason she needed them and it wasn't for me. She's banging her masseuse and has been for years! That . . . that BITCH! And the killer thing is, I found out the day of our anniversary. I devoted forty years to that woman and look how it ended!"

"Now that's some cold shit, Tim. I'm so sorry for you."

"I'm sorry for me too. Sorry I didn't find out a lot sooner. I'd be a lot richer! I had just bought that whore a brand-new Cadillac two days before I busted her." Tim held his breath and gave me a wan look. "Hey, I'm sorry. I didn't mean to go off on a tangent. Now let's get back to you and Vera. All right? Now, don't take what I'm about to say the wrong way, but no woman can be trusted these days. . . ."

I pursed my lips and gave Tim a stunned look. "Hold on now, buddy!" I shouted, holding up my hand in protest. "I disagree with you on that point. I *know* I can trust my wife."

Tim nodded and gave me a tight smile. "I trusted my wife too. Both of my sons trusted their wives—all the way up until they caught them with other men."

I looked at Tim and blinked. "My wife has no reason to cheat on me."

"Uh-huh. Let me ask you this—did you have a reason to cheat on Vera with the woman who gave birth to your daughter?"

I shrugged. "I didn't need a reason to cheat."

"Exactly."

Tim had just given me another disturbing situation to think

about. What was the world coming to when a man couldn't trust his wife?

I had felt like hell when I first arrived at Tim's office. Now I felt even worse. "Well, now that you mention it, I think I'd like for you to keep an eye on my wife too."

CHAPTER 48

VERA

KENNETH WAS IN A STRANGE MOOD WHEN HE GOT HOME FROM WORK that evening around seven. He offered me a halfhearted greeting and told me he would not be having dinner. "Baby, is everything all right?" I asked, my arm on his shoulder.

"Yeah. Why wouldn't it be?" he mumbled, removing my arm as if it had the cooties. He quickly turned his head when I attempted to kiss him on the cheek. Then he brushed past me like I was a bothersome salesclerk and went upstairs to our bedroom. The way he was dragging his feet, I was worried about him walking up two flights of steps to reach the third floor. No matter how much I fussed about him exerting himself, he didn't want to relocate to one of the bedrooms on the second floor. One of his arguments was that other than sex, climbing two flights of steps each day was the only regular exercise he got these days. He used to be a lot more active. He had always enjoyed playing golf or racquetball with some of his friends and business associates, but he rarely did those things anymore. This was the first time he'd gone to bed without dinner in years.

Bo was still at the store, so it was just me, Cash, Sarah, and Collette at the dinner table.

"What's up with Kenneth? He's been acting strange most of the day. Even stranger than usual. He stayed in his office alone for hours after he came back from lunch and even missed that inventory meeting," Collette said, spearing her prime rib with her fork.

She was the only one enjoying the dinner that Delia had prepared.

"He's got a mighty big plate and there's a lot more on it these days," I said. "A lot of his loyal customers have been going to Best Buy for their electronic needs."

"So what? Our sales are still going strong. We don't have to worry about Best Buy," Cash said.

"I bet Circuit City said the same thing a few years ago. And then they shut down all of their stores," Collette pointed out. "And don't forget about how Blockbuster video came along and ran a lot of the little mom-and-pop video rental stores out of business. Now that Netflix and Redbox have come along and put such a dent in Blockbuster's business, I'm surprised they're still open."

"Kenneth is not worried about being run out of business by the competition. But he has to really stay on top of things to make sure that doesn't happen. And he's got other issues to deal with. He's concerned about the state of his health and I don't blame him. Some nights he thrashes around in bed like a seal and moans and groans in his sleep for hours on end. And a few relatives back in Houston keep hounding him for more loans." I paused and looked at Sarah. "That niece he hasn't seen in years, the one who looks like you, she's been calling him begging for money so she can buy a beach house in Cabo San Lucas. With everything that's going on in his life right now, I'm not surprised Kenneth doesn't act strange more often."

"Kenneth is not the only one acting strange," Collette commented, grabbing her third roll off the platter next to the prime rib. "Sarah, you're acting mighty peculiar this evening too. You must be depressed about something. Did all the rib joints close down or what?" she snickered.

"I wouldn't know," Sarah hissed. "I haven't been near the rib joints lately."

We finished our meal in silence. Cash and Collette moved to the living room. Sarah went upstairs to her room, I assumed. I checked on Kenneth, glad to see that he was asleep. One thing I liked about him was that when he turned in for the night and went to sleep, he slept like a log and usually didn't wake up until morning. He'd been feeling fairly well lately, but he had not attempted to make love to me in over a week. And that was fine with me.

I desperately wanted to visit Ricky, but a sharp pain in my lower abdomen had been bothering me all day. And even though I was as horny as a blue goose, I didn't think that one of Ricky's vigorous sex workouts was in my best interest. As a matter of fact, I was worried about the pain I was experiencing. It was something that I had never felt before. Last year during my routine visit to my gynecologist, he told me that I had a few medium-sized fibroid tumors, which were common among black women, especially in my age group. "These little boogers are nothing to be concerned about," Dr. Lott had assured me. But I was mildly concerned anyway.

I swallowed a couple of Advil and the pain eased up considerably. Then I took a long hot bath and gave myself a douche. After I'd dried myself off and was about to put on a clean pair of panties, I noticed blood on my thighs. It wasn't the first time and I wasn't really that concerned about it. Dr. Lott had told me that it was because of the fibroids. He also advised me to refrain from sexual intercourse whenever I saw blood. That was the *only* reason I didn't pay Ricky a visit that night.

Cash and Collette had gone to bed by the time Bo came home around 10:00 p.m. I had returned to the living room and curled up on the couch with a glass of wine.

"What's up, cuz?" Bo asked, entering the living room with a bouquet of roses. He looked toward the stairs. "Is Sarah home?"

"Yes, she's home. She's been in her room since she ate dinner. What are the flowers for?"

"I feel bad about the way we all came down on her the other night about her relationship with that security guard."

I stood up and slapped my hands onto my hips. "You feel bad? She's the one that fucked up! She ought to be bringing *you* flowers!" I yelled, glancing at my watch. "And where have you been all this time? It's ten o'clock."

"What the hell is it to you, Vera? You're not my wife," Bo snapped.

"You'd better be glad I'm not your wife," I shouted. "I asked you a simple question and the least you can do is give me a simple answer. People do worry about you and you could have called to let somebody in this house know where you were."

Bo gave me a wide-eyed look. "You know damn well where I was! I was at work. What's gotten into you?" He dropped the flowers onto the coffee table. I followed him as he made his way to the bar and poured himself a double shot of Jack Daniel's. "Shit! I have enough problems as it is. I don't need you riding my ass too."

"I'm sorry. I was just worried about you." I got another drink and then I returned to the couch and dropped back into the same spot I'd been occupying most of the evening.

"Well, you don't need to worry about me." Bo sipped his drink, loosened his tie, and flopped down on the couch. "Did Sarah leave the house today?" he asked, crossing his legs.

"I don't keep tabs on your wife," I replied. "If you care so much about her comings and goings, how come you don't spend more time with her? Especially now that you know she might be getting too friendly with that security guard."

"We're going through inventory at the store all this week. You know that either Kenneth or I need to be present at all times during this procedure."

I was surprised that Bo had ignored my last comment. "Well, I doubt if inventory is more important than your marriage. I'm telling you that if you want to keep your woman, you'd better find out what she's up to or else."

I didn't like the way Bo was looking at me. His eyes had darkened. And the way he furrowed both his eyebrows, they looked like two sleeping caterpillars. I knew what was on his mind before he even said it. "Or else what? She'll become like you?"

His comment compelled me to drink some more wine. "Become like me? What do you mean by that?" I asked, wiping wine off my lips with the back of my hand. "If you are insinuating that I'm fooling around with another man, you are wrong. I love my husband too much to cheat on him. And I don't appreciate you saying some shit like that to my face. And to think that one time you even suggested I have an affair!"

Bo gulped down the rest of his drink and gave me a look that I would never forget. His face tightened and it looked like he was in pain. That was why I was surprised by what he said next. "Vera, what if Sarah is fucking another man?"

"If she is, you'd better do something about it—but quick. I would hate to see you melt down the way you did when you found out Gladys was playing you for a fool." Bo's eyes darkened even more and his jaw began to twitch. "I know it sounds like I'm getting all up in your business."

"Sounds like?" He leaned his head back so far I was surprised it didn't roll off his shoulders. Then he had the nerve to give me an amused look. "If you got up in my business any more, we'd be conjoined twins." I had to laugh at that myself.

I cleared my throat and shook my head. "Let's get serious. Come into the kitchen," I suggested. "I don't like to say too much in here. You never know when somebody's going to sneak up on us."

We set our glasses on the coffee table and Bo followed me to the kitchen. As soon as we got there, I whirled around and said to him, "By the way, since we're on the subject of Gladys *again*, she called. . . ."

We stood by the back door with our eyes on the entrance. If somebody came toward the kitchen from another part of the house, we'd hear their footsteps approaching on the hardwood floor in the hallway. I liked having my most sensitive conversations in this location because it was the most private room on the first floor.

"Gladys called? When? How did she get this number?" Bo asked anxiously.

"She called Cash's number at the store."

"When?"

"Today. He was out of the office when she called, so your nitwit secretary called here looking for him."

"Madeline didn't give Gladys the number here?"

"Madeline is a dingbat sure enough, but she knows better."

"Did Gladys leave a phone number for Cash to call her back?"

"Yeah, she left a phone number. Madeline told me she'd give it to Cash when he returned to the office. And that's not all."

"What else?"

"A little while ago when I told Cash she called, he came clean."

"Came clean how?"

"He told me he had called her back before he left work. Then he told me that he had received a letter from her, also today, and in it she begged him to tell you to call her up. She included a note in the envelope for him to give to you."

"She's sending mail out here?"

"Don't worry. She didn't send it here. She doesn't have our address. She sent it to the post office box Cash rents."

I didn't know how to interpret the look on Bo's face. His eyes were glassy and his nostrils were twitching. "Let me go talk to Cash." I noticed his hands were shaking. "Excuse me," he said in a scratchy tone of voice. He wobbled across the floor toward the door like a man who had had a few drinks too many. Then he stopped and turned back around and looked at me. He looked so helpless and confused, I felt sorry for him. He kept glancing toward the door and shifting his weight from one foot to the other. "I need to know what's going on. I guess I won't find out unless I talk to her. I'm going to go upstairs and talk to Cash. I want to see that letter."

"Bo, you know as well as I do why Gladys is trying to get in touch with you. I'm sure she knows you've remarried, but she doesn't give a damn about that. She still wants you back. You'd better watch your step now. You've got a good thing going with Sarah. Don't mess it up. You forget about Gladys and I'm sure Sarah has already forgotten about that security guard. She looked like a scared rat that day in the kitchen. If she was considering doing something inappropriate with him, she won't now. Not now that she knows all eyes are on her."

We left the kitchen and returned to the living room. I sat down on the couch while Bo paced back and forth in front of me a few times. "I love Sarah. If she ever leaves me, I'm going to kill her."

"Don't talk like that! Take it back! Take it back right now, Bo. You're scaring me."

"All right, I take it back," he muttered. Then he laughed. I laughed along with him. When he left the room to go upstairs, I put what he'd just said about killing Sarah out of mind and fixed myself another drink.

I remained in the living room for another hour wondering exactly what Cash and Bo were talking about upstairs. When I finally went to my room, Kenneth was snoring like a moose with asthma.

The next morning when he nudged my rump with his knee, I ignored him. "Baby, you still asleep?" he whispered, coughing to clear the phlegm out of his throat. "How about a little squeeze? It's been a while and I know you need some good loving as much as I do." His foul morning breath on the back of my neck made me cringe. I held my breath and continued to play possum until he got up and went into the bathroom to take his shower.

I wasn't going to go downstairs until I was sure Kenneth had left the house. I needed more time to think and organize my thoughts.

There were a lot of things rolling around in my head that morning, especially what Kenneth had said before he left the room. He was right; it had been a while and I did need some good loving.

And I was going to do something about it *real soon.*

CHAPTER 49

SARAH

I HAD STARTED ON MY WAY BACK DOWNSTAIRS TO SEE IF ANY OF THAT prime rib we'd had for dinner was left when I heard Bo's voice. He and Vera were in the living room. I had no idea what they had been discussing before I got to the stairs, but when I heard her tell him to go into the kitchen with her, I whirled around and made a beeline to my old bedroom. All of the nursery items I had put in there were still intact, awaiting the baby I still hoped to have someday.

As soon as I shut and locked the door, I ran to the air duct and opened the vent. I was horrified by what I heard this time!

I was not surprised that Bo's ex wanted to get in touch with him. She had probably finally realized what a good man she had lost. But I was surprised that he seemed so interested in what she had said in the letter to him that she'd sent to Cash. And whatever it was, I needed to know. For one thing, if Bo was not going to let another man cause problems in our marriage, I was certainly not going to let another woman—especially Gladys—do it. Every doggone thing I'd heard about the woman was nasty. She had treated Bo like a dog! Why would he even want to *talk* to her again?

I had not seen Curtis since the day Daddy busted me in the kitchen in front of everybody. I had called him up the next day, though. "I'm really sorry, but I don't think I can see you again," I had told him. "Somebody saw me coming out of your apartment building."

"Do they know anything?"

"No. All they know is that I was there. I told them I'd been over there dropping off a friend. But they are not stupid. I have a feeling they *know* we're sleeping together."

"I see. Well, the last thing I want is for you to get in trouble, Sarah. I care too much about you to let that happen. It's not worth it. And anyway, it really bothers me having to sneak around to be with you."

"I know. I don't like sneaking around either. And I know you need your job. I just wish . . . I just wish things were different."

"Different how?"

"Like if Bo gave me a real good reason to see you, I mean."

"You're married to the man. If you don't love him, you need to leave him. If he's good to you, well, good men are hard to find. You women have been saying that loud and clear for as long as I can remember. Don't throw all that away for me."

"But I care about you, Curtis. When I'm with you, I feel like a different woman. A woman who is appreciated. I don't feel that way with Bo anymore."

A long, uncomfortable silence passed before either of us spoke again.

"I only want the best for you," he told me.

"Do you want to see me again?"

"Sarah, be serious. You know how I feel about you. If it was up to me, I'd move you in with me today."

"I'm happy to hear you say that. We can still see one another and just be more careful."

"We were being careful and some busybody still saw us. What do you think would happen if your old man found out for sure that we've slept together?"

"I don't know."

"Well, I don't want to know. Now, if things change, maybe we can see each other again someday."

Curtis's last statement brought tears to my eyes. I knew I had to hang up before I broke down and cried. "I guess there's nothing else to say, so I'll let you go. Good night, Curtis," I said quickly.

"Good night, Sarah. If things change, let me know."

"I will," I managed.

When Bo and Vera left the kitchen, I closed the vent and ran back to my bedroom, praying I wouldn't bump into Bo on his way to Cash's bedroom at the end of the hall.

I was in bed when Bo came into our bedroom about fifteen minutes later. My last conversation with Curtis was still on my mind as well as the conversation I'd just heard between Bo and Vera in the kitchen, so I felt like shit. I would have pretended to be asleep if Bo had not leaned over and tickled my neck.

"Hi, baby," I said with a fake yawn. "I heard your car pull up a while ago. What took you so long to get up here?"

"Huh? Oh! Um, as soon as I got in the house, Vera hung me up for a few minutes and then I had to discuss some business with Cash."

"What kind of business did you have to discuss with Cash that couldn't wait until tomorrow?"

Bo removed his jacket and placed it at the foot of the bed. He took his time answering my question. "Uh, some inventory issues, that's all. Kenneth and I will be visiting the other four stores tomorrow and after that, we'll be in meetings the rest of the day. I needed some information from Cash beforehand." I could see that he was nervous. He kept scratching his neck and clearing his throat. "I'm going to take a quick shower and get some of this funk off me," he said, smelling under his arms.

I waited until I heard him turn on the shower. Like a jackrabbit, I hopped off the bed and ran to his jacket. I found the letter from Gladys in the first pocket I checked and read it in record time. I couldn't believe how corny her words were!

My Dearest Bohannon,

I really would like to talk to you. I know you're not happy with that cow you married and from what Cash has been telling me, how pitiful you look without me. I know I hurt you, but you didn't let me explain my actions so that's why I left when I did. And I was afraid that if I stayed, you would have hurt me like you had threatened to do so many times before. I still work at the same place and you know the number. I can meet up with you next week if you go to L.A. with Kenneth for that software conference that Cash told me about. My cell phone number is still the same so I'd like to hear from you.

I love you Bo and I always will.

With all my love and blessings, your Gladys

What the fuck? Who signs a letter "your Gladys"?

It was obvious that Cash had been telling this witch all kinds of shit about me. How else would she know enough about me to call me a cow? And Cash—with his two-faced, backstabbing self—had bashed *her* in my presence as much as Bo and Vera had!

I was tempted to rip the letter to shreds, but I didn't. I folded it up, tucked it back into Bo's pocket, and climbed into bed. He came out of the bathroom a few minutes later with a towel wrapped around his naked body.

"Vera decided she is not going to L.A. with Daddy for that software conference next week," I said, waiting with bated breath to hear his response.

"She told me." He sniffed and then started drying his wet hair with the towel. Seeing his naked body didn't excite me the way it used to. It only made me cringe.

"I'm worried about Daddy going off for almost a whole week by himself, so maybe I'll go with him."

"Oh no. You don't have to do that. I know how much you hate things like those damn conferences," Bo protested. He sat down hard on the bed, pulling me into his arms. "Uh, well, I've decided to go after all." The way his voice cracked and the way he was sweating—after just coming out of the shower—was enough to convince me that he was up to no good! For one thing, he had already told me that the last thing he wanted to do was attend another conference so soon. He and Daddy had spent four days in Vegas at another one two months ago. Now here he was telling me he was going to another anyway. "If it's all right with you," he added.

"Uh-huh. Well, you go on to L.A., then," I said stiffly. Our marriage was already in the toilet bowl. I just didn't know which one of us was going to flush it down. "I hope you have a lot of fun."

Bo made love to me that night. His body was so stiff and tense it felt like I was fucking a tree. He didn't even kiss me like he usually did when we made love. When I looked into his eyes, he didn't even acknowledge me. It was like he couldn't even see me. That made me think that Gladys was the woman on his mind when he rammed into me so hard my head hit the headboard. If so, that made us even because when I came, Curtis was the one on my mind.

Bo and Daddy left for L.A. the following Monday morning. They were supposed to be gone for five days. That Monday evening I called up Curtis again. I almost hung up the phone when a woman with a husky voice answered.

"Hello, is Curtis available?"

"Speak up! I can't hardly hear you! And hurry up! I got things to do!"

I thought I'd dialed the wrong number. "What number did I reach?" I asked.

"Pffft! What's wrong with you, girl?! You reached the number you just dialed!"

"Is Curtis available?" I asked again, and much louder.

"Naw! He ain't here!" I had encountered a lot of angry black women in my life, but this one sounded like she was on fire.

"Do you think he'll be home soon?"

"He might be, and he might not! You have to call back if you really want to know! Shoot!" She hung up before I could tell her who I was. I called four more times that day until Curtis answered.

"Hello, Sarah. Mama told me you called."

"I didn't even leave my name!" I gasped. "How did she know it was me?"

"She didn't. You're the only woman who calls me here these days." He laughed. "When Mama said some 'proper-sounding gal' called, I knew it had to be you."

"Can I come see you?"

"Sarah, we've talked about this. Have you already forgotten our last conversation? You said that you didn't want to see me again because of your husband."

"I might not be with Bo too much longer."

"You what?"

"He's probably going back to Houston to get back with his ex."

"Probably? So you don't know for sure if he is or not?"

"No, I don't know for sure. But there is a chance that he will."

"So it's just a chance that he might be moving back to Houston?"

"A chance is better than nothing!"

"Look, Sarah. I don't know what's going on between you and your husband, but I don't want to get caught in the middle. He's been giving me some mysterious looks lately, so I need to watch my step."

"Well, I don't know why he's been giving you mysterious looks."

"I don't want to find out. The thing is, I don't think we should see each other again. Especially now that you think Bo suspects we're involved."

"All right," I replied slowly. As much as I knew I needed to end this call, I still wanted to prolong it as long as possible. "If that's the way you want it, I won't call you again."

"Wait! Don't hang up yet. I just thought about what you said about Bo possibly going back to his ex-wife. What makes you think that? He loves his job, so why would he want to give it up to move back to Houston and start over again?"

"I don't know."

"Has he been talking to his ex?"

"She sent him a letter through Cash."

"Oh. Did you see the letter?"

"Yes, I did. I think Bo changed his mind about going to L.A. so he could meet up with her there."

"I'm surprised to hear that. You told me she had been the wife from hell to him. Going back to a woman like that is not something a smart man like Bo would do."

"Maybe Bo's not as smart as you think he is." I sighed. "Well, I'll let you go now. And you don't have to worry, I won't bother you anymore."

"Sarah, wait! Don't hang up yet. Um . . . you know I want to continue seeing you, but things are kind of hot right now. It wouldn't be too cool for you to come over here. I have some nosy-ass neighbors, and the less they see you over here, the better."

"So you do still want to be with me?"

"I do," he muttered, releasing a long, drawn-out sigh.

"Do you want to meet me someplace else other than your apartment?" I didn't give Curtis a chance to answer my question. "We can get a room across the Bay."

He took his time responding. That made me even more anxious to see him. If he still wanted to see me . . . "Uh, let me think about it."

"Don't make me wait too long, Curtis. I've waited long enough."

"I won't," he assured me. "I've waited long enough too."

CHAPTER 50

VERA

EVEN THOUGH DR. LOTT HAD TOLD ME NOT TO WORRY ABOUT THE bleeding, I was worried now because I'd been bleeding every day for a week. I had already gone through menopause and had not had a period in over ten years. I hated walking around with a bloody pussy again after so many years, so I was anxious to have something done to end it. The main reason was that I wanted to get on with my sex life.

I believed that the longer I let this unpleasant issue go, the worse it would get. Yesterday I had bled so heavily, the tampon I'd inserted had been useless. I'd found that out at the most inconvenient time. I had gone to a specialty market in Chinatown to pick up a few gourmet items, like some black goat cheese and caviar. While I was standing in the checkout line, I got this funny feeling between my thighs. It felt like I was peeing on myself. Anyway, I looked down and was horrified when I saw blood dripping onto my handmade Italian sandals, not to mention my silk-wrapped toenails. I almost fainted. I didn't even wait around to pay for the items I had picked up. I dropped them onto the counter and flew out the door like the place was on fire.

I didn't want to mess up the seat in my spotless Ferrari, so I ran to a newspaper rack on the sidewalk and got four copies of the *San Francisco Chronicle.* I used the newspapers as padding on my car seat. I made it back home and into my bathroom by the skin of my teeth. Not only had the blood soaked through my tampon, it had pushed the tampon completely out. It sat in the crotch of my panties along with a blood clot the size, shape, and color of a plum. I immediately called my doctor's office. Dr. Lott was on a conference call, but I made such a fuss, his receptionist put me on hold and a minute later Dr. Lott was on the line.

"Look, Dr. Lott, I've been bleeding like a damn hemophiliac all day!" I roared. "I'm scared to leave the house or sit on anything for more than a few minutes because I'm flowing so heavily. Blood dripped through my underwear and down my legs while I was in a checkout line a little while ago."

"Hmmm. Well, in addition to a tampon, for more security try wearing a maxipad as well," the good doctor said in a calm voice, which was easy for him or any other man to do. There was not a man alive who could truly understand what we women had to go through with our bodies. Not even the men who had undergone that sex change operation that turned them into women. "That should take care of the problem. If it doesn't, we'll consider other protective options."

"Other protective options? Bah! If you're talking about adult diapers, no way. Now, there has got to be something you can do to end this mess! I need to take care of this problem immediately!"

"Mrs. Lomax, calm down. I've explained to you that this is a very common problem among women your age—"

"Bullshit! I don't care if it is. I want it to end and I want it to end NOW!"

"As I've told you, we can do a minor procedure to eliminate the problem. I can remove the fibroids that are causing the bleeding. But that would be like going after a fly with a shotgun. I've also told you that because you're at the postmenopausal stage, all of your fibroid tumors will eventually shrink to a point where they will hardly even be detectable. As a matter of fact, the last time I examined you, I noticed they had already shrunk considerably from their original size. However, if the bleeding becomes more serious within the next day or so and begins to disrupt your usual activities, including ones of a, uh, sexual nature, let me know."

My sexual activities had already been disrupted long enough. I wanted to see Ricky as much as he wanted to see me. And the one thing I knew about young men was that if they got too horny and couldn't control themselves, they'd stick their dick into the first available female if they had to. The bleeding got so bad after I got off the telephone with Dr. Lott, I called him back twenty minutes later and told him he had to do something or I was going to change doctors.

He modified his schedule and arranged for me to have "emergency" surgery the following day, which was a Wednesday. I'd check into the hospital in the morning and be out by the middle of the afternoon.

Kenneth and Bo had left for L.A. the day before. I saw no reason for me to tell either one of them, or anybody else, that I was going to have the surgery. My numerous and frequent cosmetic surgeries were no secret, but when I had to deal with a female-related issue, I chose to keep that information to myself. For one thing, I didn't want Kenneth to cut his trip short and come back home. And I didn't want Collette to know because I didn't like the way she always brought up my age whenever I had a medical issue, even my cosmetic surgeries.

Despite the fact that having a few fibroid tumors removed was a minor surgery, Dr. Lott had made it clear that afterward I couldn't drive myself home or be sent home in a taxi. Our chauffeur was on vacation, so he couldn't drive me to and from the hospital like he did when I had my cosmetic procedures. Since I didn't trust any of my few female acquaintances, Sarah was the only person I could turn to. She had nothing but time on her hands these days and I knew she'd keep her mouth shut if I told her to.

"Are you sure you don't want Daddy to know about you having surgery?" she asked as she drove me to the hospital that Wednesday morning. "What if something goes wrong? You could die like James Brown's wife did during her minor surgery. Kanye West's mama died during surgery too. And what about Usher's ex-wife? She almost died, too, when she—"

"I am not going to die, Sarah. I've been having surgeries done most of my life and I'm still here. Besides, Kenneth has enough to worry about without me adding to it."

My surgery went well. As soon as the anesthesia wore off, I tumbled out of the hospital bed and hobbled to the bathroom. I was delighted not to see even a speck of blood. I was as good as new.

Sarah picked me up a little after 4:00 p.m. and drove me home. As soon as I got inside, I scrambled up the stairs to the third floor, puffing like a dying horse. I scolded myself because I had not insisted on Kenneth having an elevator installed so we would not have to climb so many damn steps to get to our bedroom. Sarah was right behind me yelling, "Vera, stop running! Take it easy before you hemorrhage or something."

I ignored her command. I didn't stop running until I reached my bedroom bathroom. "You can have these," I said to Sarah with a chuckle, handing her what was left in the box of tampons and heavy-duty Kotex I had purchased. I exhaled and was smiling until I saw my reflection in the mirror over the sink. I didn't like what I saw. Without makeup, I looked like an old hag. I was anxious for Sarah to leave my side so I could resume my normal daily activities. And the first thing I wanted to do was take a long hot shower and put on some makeup.

"I probably won't need any of those things for a while," she told me with a faint smile. I had started to walk away, but Sarah's words made me stop in my tracks.

"Why not? Are you pregnant again?" I asked, wanting to cross my fingers.

"No. I just got off my period yesterday. But when Bo gets back home, I want to get started on getting pregnant again."

"Oh," I said, smiling to hide my disappointment that she was not pregnant. "I hope you'll get pregnant again real soon."

Dr. Lott told me I had to wait a whole month before I could have sex again. It was going to be one of the most difficult things I ever had to do in my life. And since Ricky was so damn irresistible, I knew

I couldn't even be in his presence without wrestling him to his bed. I decided to not even visit his apartment for that month.

"Aw shit, baby. What am I going to do for a whole month? It's already been too long since the last time we had some fun," he whined when I called him up and told him. I had called him from my cell phone in my bedroom. "Can't you even come by and just *play* with me a little bit?"

When it came to sex, I didn't "play." I didn't do hand jobs because I had decided when I was a young girl that that was beneath me. That was for teenage boys, inmates, and perverts. I gave a mean blow job, but I didn't even want to visit Ricky tonight if that was all I could do. There was nothing in a blow job for me. And my pussy was too sensitive from the surgery for me to let him eat me out. It would be hard, but I could survive for a month. Then I would make up for all the lost time. The very thought of all the fun I was going to have made me tingle.

"I'll see you in a month," I promised, spreading my thighs and gently fingering myself to make sure I was still dry. "But I'll call you up every day."

"Will you talk dirty to me when you call?"

That was another thing. "Talking dirty" was beneath me, too, but I didn't mind doing it if it turned my man on. I especially didn't mind doing it when Ricky was on top of me, but I couldn't see myself sitting with a telephone in my hand talking trash. I hadn't done anything that vile since some of my desperate girlfriends and I had worked as telephone sex operators in high school.

I'd find something to keep myself busy for the month, which meant I'd do some serious shopping.

An hour after Sarah had brought me home and fixed me some hot green tea, she left the house to go get her nails done, or so she claimed. I prayed, for her sake, that she was not still sniffing after that lowlife security guard or anybody else. I didn't know what kind of sex life she had with Bo these days, but if she was half as frustrated as I was, I could understand her going outside of her marriage. I just hoped that she was as sly as I was and didn't get caught.

I couldn't stop thinking about something Bo had told me after we'd confronted Sarah about getting too friendly with Curtis. *"If she ever leaves me, I'm going to kill her."*

I didn't think he'd go that far. But if he did, we would *all* be up shit creek without a paddle.

CHAPTER 51

SARAH

A couple of hours had passed since I'd brought Vera home from the hospital. Since she was in the living room at the bar, and had been for the past hour, I assumed she was doing just fine. I wasn't, though. I needed to go somewhere I could be completely alone. My head had so many disturbing thoughts and questions floating around in it, I had to sort them out as soon as I could before I lost my mind. I couldn't even think clearly with her lurking about. And I didn't want to hole up in my bedroom or any other room in the house.

Vera saw me leaving. But from the way she kept her cell phone glued to her ear as she waved me toward the front door, I had a feeling she wanted to be alone for a while too.

At first I just cruised along, meandering from one street to another, thinking about one thing after another. I couldn't stop thinking about the letter Gladys had sent to Bo and how he had not told me about it yet. Was he going to meet with her in L.A.? If so, would she talk him into reconciliation? And even if they didn't get back together, what if he made love to her while he was in L.A.? If he did and I found out, I was going to be pissed and our marriage would be over for sure. If he didn't, the respect and trust that I had lost for him in the last few months would be somewhat restored.

And then there was Curtis. Despite his apprehension about continuing our relationship as long as I was still with Bo, he had admitted that he wanted to see me again. I hadn't spoken to him since our conversation Monday evening right after Daddy and Bo left to go to L.A., but I planned to call him up again real soon. I needed to know for sure if there was a chance that we'd have a future together. If I lost Bo to Gladys, would Curtis still want to be with me? I wanted to keep Curtis so I'd have him to fall back on in case Gladys took Bo away from me. On the other hand, if Curtis decided he didn't want to continue his relationship with me, I wanted to have Bo to fall back on.

In the meantime, I'd continue to be with Bo and Curtis as long as I could get away with it, like I had originally planned.

And there was another important factor in this equation: I had to produce a baby by Bo to keep Daddy and Vera happy. And to keep Bo happy, too, in case I ended up settling for just him and severing my relationship with Curtis. Besides, I really did want a child. I thought that motherhood might help me decide exactly what I wanted to do about my future and which man I wanted to share it with.

I finally got tired of driving and decided to go get my nails done.

As I sat in Maria's Nail Shop on Valencia Street in the Mission District waiting my turn, I fished my cell phone out of my purse and called the Marriott airport hotel that Daddy and Bo had checked into. Since it was so late in the day, I assumed they'd be out of their meetings by now. Daddy answered his line right away.

"It's me, Daddy. I was thinking about you and decided to call so I could hear your voice." I sniffed. "How's the conference going?"

"It's going just fine. The speaker, a gentleman from Harvard, is a real visionary when it comes to being more innovative in the world of business. I'm glad I brought my tape recorder with me. I wish you could have come with us."

"Hmmm. Well, maybe next time I'll go with you."

"Baby, is everything all right? You sound sad. Is something the matter?"

"No, everything is just fine, Daddy." I bit my bottom lip. "Where's Bo?"

"He's in his room, I guess."

"Has he been with you all the time? Are you keeping an eye on him?"

Daddy hesitated and grunted under his breath before he answered my questions. "Girl, why are you asking me something like that? Bo is a grown man, so why do I need to keep an eye on him?"

"I was just wondering if you and him were spending a lot of time together."

"We're not on a vacation, honey. We're down here on business. I see him during the sessions, of course, but after each one ends, it's every man for himself. I'm having dinner with an old friend from college who lives in L.A. now."

"Don't go to an Italian restaurant. Bo will be farting for days."

"Bo's not going with us. I invited him, but he's going to hook up with an old friend too."

An old friend?

I knew that if the "old friend" was Bo's ex, he probably would not have mentioned it to Daddy. But I had to ask anyway. "Who is this old friend Bo's going out with?"

"He didn't tell me. He just told me a little while ago. All I know is that it's an old friend of his from Houston. But if I see him in time, I'll tell him not to do Italian. I do enough farting for the both of us." Daddy chuckled.

I slid my tongue across my bottom lip, fuming. The old friend from Houston had to be Gladys. My lips began to quiver while I tried to decide what to say next.

"Hello? Sarah, you still there? You got mighty quiet all of a sudden."

"I'm still here, Daddy. Will you tell Bo I called?"

"Baby, he's your husband. Why don't you just call his room and tell him yourself. I'm sure he'd love to hear your voice."

"Okay, I will."

"Sarah, is there something going on that you don't want to tell me about?"

"No, nothing is going on."

"Then why did you call me before you even called up your husband? He told me he left you two messages yesterday and so did I for that matter, and you're just now calling back. But you should be calling him instead of me, don't you think?"

"I figured he was probably busy. . . ."

"Well, I could have been busy, too, but you still called me." Daddy laughed again. "Honey, there's a lot you need to learn about marriage." He paused and then all of a sudden he sounded like a love-struck schoolboy. "By the way, where is my beautiful bride? Lord do I miss that sweet little woman!"

"Vera? She was watching television when I left the house. Daddy, I hate to rush off the phone, but the girl is ready to do my nails. I'll talk to you later." The girl was ready to do my nails, but I signaled for her to give me a few more minutes. I immediately called the hotel operator again. I had her patch me through to Bo's room. He didn't answer and I didn't leave a message. I hung up and dialed the hotel operator again. "Can you tell me if a Gladys Harper has checked in yet?"

"One moment please." The operator put me on hold for about ten seconds. "Yes. She checked in last night. I'll transfer you to—"

"That's okay!" I yelled. Then I hung up.

I didn't really want to talk to Vera, so when I called the house and she didn't answer, I was glad. I left a voice mail message and told her I was going to the movies. I even drove to the Metreon theaters downtown and bought a ticket (for a movie I'd already seen) so I'd have a stub in case I needed it. I returned to my car, hopped in, and barreled toward the freeway that would take me to Curtis's neighborhood in less than ten minutes.

I was going to call him up first to make sure he was home and alone. The last thing I wanted to do was drop in and find him with company, especially a female. Even his mama. When I got to his block, I pulled into the parking lot of a nearby liquor store and dialed his number. His answering machine was supposed to pick up on the fourth ring, but it didn't. On the seventh ring his mother answered, sounding as hostile as ever.

"HALLO!" she growled. "Who is this?!" I was tempted to hang

up without saying anything. Curtis had caller ID, so she would know who was calling—if she could read.

"I'm a friend of Curtis's," I said in a meek voice. "Is he home?"

"Nope. He gone somewhere."

"Do you expect him to return soon?"

"I don't expect nothing but to go take my bath like I was fixing to do when this phone rung!"

"I'm sorry I interrupted your bath, ma'am." It took all of my strength for me to remain civil. "Would you please tell him that Sarah called and I'll call back again?"

"Just don't call back here while I'm taking my bath! This is my only night off this week and all I want to do is relax!" The woman slammed the telephone down so hard I heard a popping noise in my ear.

After I got my nails done and left the shop, I did some window-shopping along Mission Street. It was after nine, so most of the businesses had closed for the day. I called Curtis's number two more times on my way home. Each time I was harshly told by his mother that he was "gone somewhere."

I turned my telephone off.

When I got home and into my bedroom, I turned it back on. There was a message from Bo. He had also left a message for me on the landline. He was the last man in the world I wanted to talk to at the moment, but I called his room anyway. He didn't answer, so I called Daddy again.

"Have you seen or spoken to Bo since I talked to you today?" I asked.

"I ran into him in the elevator on my way up a little while ago. He was on his way back out to meet his friend from Houston again. Boy was he in good spirits! He was grinning from ear to ear." I heard some muffled voices on Daddy's end. "Baby, I have to go. I'm supposed to meet a few folks for drinks downstairs and I'm already late."

I didn't even bother to look for Vera. Her car was in the garage, so I assumed she was in her bedroom. I went back downstairs and

Cash and Vera were in the living room watching some reality show.

I returned to my room, took a hot shower, and climbed into bed. Now that I knew Gladys was in L.A., my thoughts were not as unclear as they'd been earlier in the day. I pretty much knew what I wanted to do now. Because of Bo's actions, and the way he was keeping important information about his ex-wife from me, it was going to be easy for me to choose. If he wanted to get back with Gladys, I was not going to stand in his way. I didn't believe in fighting for a man. If he didn't want to be with me, I didn't want to be with him.

It looked like Curtis was the man I was going to be with after all.

CHAPTER 52

KENNETH

THE NEXT MONTH WENT BY QUICKLY. I WAS GLAD I HADN'T HEARD from Tim. But I was tempted to call him just to make sure he had nothing to report on Sarah or Vera. But the fact that he had not called me told me all I needed to know. I told myself that if either of them was guilty of anything, they would have slipped up by now.

Or so I thought.

I was in my office at the store relaxing after a three-martini lunch with my accountant. I had a meeting to attend in a few minutes and I was going to make sure it was a short one. I planned to leave the office early so I could pick up some flowers for my lovely bride and take her to a French restaurant in Sausalito that she liked so much. It was a Friday and I planned to spend the weekend doing as little as possible. I was in such a good mood, I was whistling. When my private line rang and I saw Tim's name on the caller ID, I stopped whistling and answered the call immediately.

"Thank God I caught you," Tim began.

"Tim . . . hey, buddy. Good to hear from you," I greeted in a tentative tone of voice. "What's up?" I unbuttoned the top buttons on my shirt, slid my hand inside, and placed it over my heart. It had already begun to thump like mad.

"Can we talk?" he asked. "Is this a convenient time for you?"

"I have a meeting to go to, but I can spare a few minutes." I glanced at my Rolex. I was already late for the personnel meeting I had had my secretary schedule, but that was of no importance to me right now. Even though Tim and I were close friends, he usually didn't call me up unless he had something important to talk to me about. Since I had retained him for his services, I knew that was the case. I had been dreading a call from him because I was afraid he would tell me something I didn't want to hear. "I presume you have some information for me?" I asked with my heart beating about a mile a minute. I took my hand from my chest and balled it into a fist.

"Yes, but not much."

I was relieved to hear him say that. "Oh? That's good to hear." My heart immediately slowed down and I was even more relieved.

"Well, I've got some good news and some bad news."

Shit! Just hearing him mention "bad news" got my heart to beating like hell again. "Tell me the good news first."

"The good news is, I don't have anything on your wife. She's been a very good girl. Other than some serious shopping and some expensive lunches, that's about all she's been up to this past month. She made a few trips to City Hospital, and whatever goes on there is highly guarded. But I don't think there's anything to worry about there. I caught a glimpse of her physician, and I don't think she'd get involved with a gnome like him." Tim laughed.

"She spends a lot of her time and my money on plastic surgeries," I chortled. "I know all about her frequent trips to various hospitals and clinics."

"Hmmm. Two days after you and your son-in-law left for L.A., she checked into San Francisco General Hospital in the morning and checked out in the afternoon. Your daughter took her there and picked her up." Tim paused and shuffled some papers.

"That's the good news?"

"I'm not sure if it is or not. When she exited the hospital, she was in a wheelchair. Apparently she'd had another procedure performed."

"Whatever it was, it couldn't have been too serious. She would have told me about it. She probably had her titties tuned up again with *another* lift. Otherwise, they wouldn't have released her the same day. Right?"

"Right."

"Now what's the bad news?"

"Your daughter made several trips to an address on Third Street this week." Tim shuffled papers again. "The apartment—a dump I wouldn't house a dog I didn't like in—is leased to a Maggie Mae Thompson. According to the information I was able to obtain, this woman is quite the battle-ax, always in a dispute with her neighbors. Does her name mean anything to you?"

"Maggie . . . Thompson. Hmmm. You got me. I don't know a woman by that name. She's probably one of Sarah's friends from back in the day. And she must be a pretty ferocious battle-ax if Sarah hasn't brought her to the house like her other old friends."

"Well, this Thompson woman is a lot older than Sarah, so it's unlikely she's a friend. But Thompson has a son the same age as your daughter."

"Oh?"

"He's the same security guard who works in your main store who assisted Sarah the day she lost her baby. Do you think she may be going there to see him?"

"Oh Lord, it's Curtis! I knew it! I knew it in my heart! I think she's fooling around with that boy!"

"I don't know about that. Each time she visited this address since I got on the case, she knocked but no one answered the door. Either the gentleman in question refuses to see her, or he's out and about more than most people."

"He works the day shift at my main store, but he's been off for a few days. Some elderly uncle or cousin or something in Detroit passed and Curtis and his mama had to go take care of the funeral and sort out his business."

"That's about all I have for you right now, my friend. Your wife is not fooling around. And I don't have any concrete proof that your daughter is either. At least not at this time."

"Let's give it one more month. But I'd appreciate it if you check in with me on a weekly basis."

"You got it, buddy."

I was happy to hear that Vera was not cheating on me, not that

I even remotely thought she was anyway. My main concern was Sarah. Especially since I knew she'd been back to Curtis's residence.

I was already late for my meeting, so I didn't think another few minutes would matter. I locked my office door and called the house. Vera answered. She promptly informed me that she was late for an appointment and was on the way out the door, so I only chatted with her long enough to tell her I needed to speak to Sarah. Sarah came on the line about a minute later.

"Yes, Daddy? What's up?"

"I'd like to write up a little report to keep in my files about that incident that happened."

"You mean about that jackass who made me lose my baby?"

"Yes."

"That happened weeks ago! Why did you wait until now to write up a report? And what about the police report? Can't you just get a copy of it from them?"

"I could but I'd rather get something directly from you. I'd also like to get a few words from Curtis."

"You want me to come down to the store and dictate something to your secretary, or do you want me to throw something together on the computer here?"

"You can compose something for me at home. When and if Curtis comes back to work, I'll get something from him then."

Just as I expected, Sarah remained silent longer than she should have. I knew she was thinking about what I had just said about Curtis. To my surprise, she didn't react to that.

"Oh. Okay, then. I'll type up a few pages and have it ready when you get home this evening."

"Thanks, baby. Like I said, I'll get something from Curtis when and if he comes back."

She took the bait this time and ran with it. "When and if he comes back? Where is he?" Sarah was sly, but she could not hide the curiosity and concern in her voice.

"He's in Detroit with his mama. Some relative passed away. I think he told me it was his elderly uncle. He's supposed to return to Frisco this evening. But before he left work the other day, he told me his mama is thinking about moving to Detroit to be closer to her family. If she goes, I wouldn't be surprised if he packed up and followed her. He's real close to his mama. . . ."

"Oh. That's nice." I was surprised that Sarah didn't have more to say about Curtis possibly moving away. But I could still hear the curiosity and concern in her voice. "So Curtis might be moving to Detroit. Hmmm. Well, I'm sorry his uncle died."

"Yeah, I'm sorry too. Listen, sweetie, I have to run off to another meeting now. I'll see you when I get home." I called Tim back. "I want you to keep a real close eye on my daughter for the next few days," I told him. "Starting tonight."

Five days later, Tim called me again. "We need to talk!" he hollered into the telephone. His voice was so loud it sounded like he was standing right next to me.

"You've got something for me?" I had a dreadful feeling that he was really going to tell me something I didn't want to hear this time, so I braced myself by taking a deep breath.

"Dude, I'm so sorry to tell you that I do."

"Humph! My daughter is fooling around with my security guard, isn't she?"

"I'm afraid so."

"Is she sleeping with him?"

"*Excessively.*" Tim let out such a disgusted snort you would have thought Sarah was his daughter. "She entered his apartment three nights ago while the mother was working a night shift at a warehouse in Alameda. She stayed for two hours. When she exited, he walked her to her car where they kissed very passionately before she got in and drove off. They got together last night at a motel near a truck stop where the rates are charged by the hour. The hookers do their business there with the truckers. Anyway, after they left the motel, they had a romp in the backseat of your daughter's car parked in an isolated spot behind the Cow Palace."

"OH, HELL NO!"

"Take it easy, dude. These things happen," Tim said calmly.

"How can I take it easy after what you just told me? I can't believe my ears!"

"Well, you'll believe your eyes when I show you the pictures."

"Pictures?" That word flew out of my mouth like a loose tooth. "You've even got pictures of her with Curtis? Well, when I confront her, she won't wiggle her booty out of this one!"

"I have pictures of them going into the motel and coming out a couple of hours later. I took some really good shots of them in an adult toy shop two days ago. You wouldn't believe the unique devices they purchased—made me blush and you know I'm not a prude."

"Sarah didn't see you in that place taking pictures of her?"

"Oh, I didn't go inside. My associate steps in when we need close-ups. I remained a safe distance the whole time."

"Oh Lord in heaven!" I had to stop talking long enough to catch my breath and rub my aching chest. I fanned my face for a few seconds, but I was still as hot as a six-shooter. "I suspected she had a crush on Curtis, and I'd even confronted her about it not too long ago—right in front of her husband and the rest of the family. She denied that anything was going on. I should have known she was screwing that man even back then. Well, I'm going to put a stop to it for good this time! I am not going to stand by and let my daughter ruin her life over a security guard! THAT NASTY HEIFER!"

"Dude, I'm not finished."

"Oh? Is she giving that sucker my money too?"

"Not that I can tell. His pockets are obviously not very deep, but he manages to cover the motel rooms and he pays the check when they go out to eat. It doesn't look like he's after her money. At least not yet. But that's not something you should be worrying about right now." Tim paused and released a loud breath followed by a groan. "Let's move on to your wife."

"What about my wife?"

"Buddy, this is the part of my job I hate. Especially when the client is a close friend such as yourself."

"Tim, what about my wife? Is she . . . did she . . . *Is she screwing around too*?" My head felt like it was going to explode. But I had not heard the worst yet.

Tim didn't mince words or soften the blow. He hit me in the gut with a punch so brutal I thought I'd pass out on the spot. "Your wife's lover is a twenty-two-year-old unemployed bartender and an ex-con. His name is Ricky Tate."

CHAPTER 53

SARAH

I WAS GLAD THAT DADDY HAD TOLD ME WHERE CURTIS WAS. IT MADE me feel so much better. Since I had not been able to reach him by telephone or catch him at home, I thought he was trying to avoid me. And I knew that even if I went to the store, he wouldn't be able to talk to me. I didn't know what was going on with him until now.

I had to call several airlines before I found the one he had booked his return flight on. He was scheduled to arrive around 6:00 p.m., but I gave him enough time to collect his luggage and get home. I called him up at eight.

I was so glad his mean mother didn't answer the phone!

"Curtis, I've been worried to death about you. I've been trying to get in touch with you for almost a whole week. I didn't know what had happened until Daddy told me today about your uncle."

"Baby, things happened so fast. When my aunt Nettie called and told us that my uncle Marvin had died, me and Mama had to hop on a plane that same night. I didn't get a chance to get a message to you about me going to Detroit before we left. And I didn't have your phone number with me or I would have called you before now. I had called up your daddy at the store and I told him what was going on. I'm surprised he didn't tell you right away."

"And why would he have done that? I have a feeling he suspects we're fooling around and if that's the case, he wouldn't be telling me your business," I said.

"He's wrong," Curtis said in a low voice.

"He's wrong about what?"

"About us fooling around."

"Oh? Are you telling me you don't want to see me again after all?" I had been dumped by other men before and I had promptly recovered. But now that I was older and *risking my marriage* for a man, this was one time I knew I would not recover so quickly.

"Sarah, I'd see you every day of the week if I could. But the thing is, I've been thinking about us a lot lately. It bothers me that we have to sneak around. I'm not used to that. I've told you that already. I swear to God, girl, having a relationship with you is stressful."

"I thought you cared about me!" I wailed.

"I do care about you and I'd love to see you again. But you're married. I . . . I've never been involved with a married woman before."

"So? You knew I was married that day we had lunch when you lured me to your apartment and fucked my brains out!"

"I was caught up in the moment—"

"You were caught up in my *ass*! And I was caught up in your ass! Is it . . . Are you seeing another woman? Is that the real reason you don't want to see me now? I'm not buying this shit about me being married making you have second thoughts."

"Sarah, I love you," Curtis choked. "I knew you were married, but I didn't care. I wanted to be with you that bad."

We remained silent for almost a full minute. I was breathing through my mouth and from the loud snorting noises coming from Curtis's end, it sounded like he was breathing through his mouth and his nose.

"I'm not involved with another woman at the moment. And I want to see you, too, baby. But while I was gone, I had a lot of time to think about some things. Things that I need to change in my life."

"Some things? And one of those 'things' include me and you?"

"Sarah, if you were not already married, I'd ask you to marry me."

His last statement hit me like a ton of bricks. I didn't think a man who worked a dead-end job and lived with his mother thought about marriage that much. "You would?"

"Honest to God I would. I've been looking for a woman like you all my life. And now that I've found you, I don't like sneaking around to be together and not being able to show you off to my friends."

"Well, you know I don't like sneaking around either. But what else can we do?"

"That's up to you. You have to decide if you want to be with me or your husband!"

"Are you asking me to choose?" I gasped.

"Yes, I guess I am. I'm telling you, you need to choose who you want to be with. It's either him or me. When you do that, let me know."

"Uh, that might be real soon. I . . . I think Bo's thinking about getting back with his ex."

"You've told me that before. If you think that, why are you still with the dude? Why don't you have it out with him and move on?"

"It's not as easy as you think it is, baby. I'd be hurting my daddy as much as I'd be hurting Bo. I try to do things to make the people in my life happy."

"Well, all this pressure and sneaking around is not making me happy and I'm sure it's beginning to take a toll on you too." Curtis paused. I was just about to speak again, but he cut me off. "Sarah, let me make myself real clear. Baby, you have to decide if you want to be Bo's wife, your daddy's little girl, or my woman. Do you hear me?"

"I hear you. I hear you loud and clear," I pouted. "You know, it's been quite a while since I saw you and I'd rather finish this conversation in person. Are you going to be home for a while? Is your mama there?"

"Yes, I'm going to be home for a while and no, my mama is not here. She didn't even have time to unpack because she had to go back to work tonight. And she's got to work a double shift to make up some of the time she took off. Do you want to come over here?"

"I'd like to do that, Curtis."

"I have a hard time controlling myself when I'm alone with you, girl. You know what's going to happen if you come over here. . . ."

"I know. Whatever happens, happens. Well, you know . . . and we'll do whatever, " I said with a submissive sigh. "I've missed the hell out of you. I want to . . . *I need you.*"

"Oh shit! What the hell—I need you, too, baby."

I was in Curtis's arms for three hours that night.

Bo barely crossed my mind when I was with Curtis. Lately, he barely crossed my mind even when I wasn't with Curtis. And I wondered if Bo spent much time thinking about me and my feelings. Other than to have me scratch his back one night after he got out of the shower, Bo and I had barely touched each other since he'd returned from his trip to L.A. a month ago. From the way he avoided me when he was in the house and the short conversations we had when we did talk, I had a feeling something, or somebody else, was on his mind. And it was not hard for me to figure out who that somebody was: Gladys. It didn't matter to me if he had made love to her in L.A. or not. Just knowing that he'd agreed to see her made him guilty as hell in my book. I didn't want to stay with a man who wanted to be with another woman and I wasn't going to! I had decided that I was going to take birth control pills again and I would stay on them until I left Bo. When I produced a grandchild for Daddy, it would be by Curtis.

Before I left Curtis's place, I promised him I would tell Bo I wanted a divorce.

"Are you sure this is what you want, Sarah? You're going to divorce Bo for me?" Curtis asked, his arm around my shoulder as he escorted me to my car.

"I'm sure," I told him. "I can't go on like this."

When I got home, Daddy was in the living room sitting on the couch. And he was alone. The television was not on and he didn't have a drink in his hand. This was very peculiar behavior for him. I had no idea what was going on.

Before I could speak, he cleared his throat and spoke first. "Where have you been, honey?" he asked, looking at his watch. "This time of night."

"I went to the movies with a friend," I said, standing in the doorway with my car keys still in my hand.

"Is that right? Which one?"

"Rhonda Porter."

"I meant which movie?"

"Huh? Uh, Tyler Perry's latest." I looked around the room. "Why are you sitting down here by yourself?" I asked, diverting the attention away from me.

"I just wanted to be alone for a few minutes so I could think about a few things," he mumbled. From the weary look on his face, I was afraid to hear what those few things were, so I decided not to ask.

"Oh. Where is everybody?"

"Everybody's retired to their bedrooms. After all, it is after midnight. . . ."

"Yeah. And that's where I'm going. If you don't leave for work before I get up in the morning, I'll see you at the breakfast table."

"Yeah." Daddy's voice sounded almost like a growl.

I turned around when I got to the stairs. He was still looking at me, and with the oddest look on his face. But I wasn't going to worry about that for now. I had other issues to attend to.

When I entered my bedroom, Bo was sitting on the side of the bed with a puppy-dog expression on his face. Well, there was no telling what kind of expression he was going to have on his face in a few minutes.

"I need to talk to you," I told him as soon as I closed the door. Not only was I going to tell him that I knew his ex had met up with him in L.A., but I was also going to ask him for a divorce.

"I need to talk to you, too," he told me, perking up. There was an amused look on his face now. He patted his lap and motioned for me to sit on it. But I didn't. I plopped down onto a spot at the other end of the bed. "I'm not going to bite you," he chuckled. I was glad to hear him laugh because after he heard what I had to say, it was going to be a long time before he laughed again.

"You might bite me when you hear what I have to say," I warned.

"Oh? And why do you think that?" He no longer looked amused. Now he looked alarmed.

"I'd rather hear what you have to say first."

Bo blew out some air and released words that irritated my ears like a torch. "I saw Gladys when I was in L.A.," he confessed.

"I know. I've known all along."

His mouth flew open, his eyes widened, and he looked thoroughly surprised. "You do? You knew all this time—a whole month—and you didn't say anything? Who told you? That blabbermouth Cash?"

"Cash didn't tell me. I, uh, I saw that letter she sent to you that you left in your jacket pocket. I called the hotel and they told me she had checked in."

"I see." Bo stared at the wall for a few moments.

"I bet you couldn't wait to get to L.A. to fuck that bitch!" I accused. I was not just angry; I was also relieved. Bo's infidelity was all I needed to justify mine.

"No, I didn't!" He held up his hands and shook his head. "I swear to God I didn't! We just talked! That's all she wanted to do!"

"Then how come you didn't tell me she sent that letter and that she came to L.A. just to 'talk' to you?"

"I was going to—"

"Oh yeah? When? You've had a whole month! Look, I know she's been trying to get back with you! If you don't care about her and don't want to be bothered with her, why did you agree to meet up with her in L.A.?"

"I told you! She just wanted to talk!"

"Oh really? She just wanted to talk? She flew all the way from Houston to L.A. just to *talk*? Well, I've got news for you, brother. You are not that hot! And I am not that gullible. I don't believe that bitch traveled that far just to talk, goddammit! I know you fucked her!"

"No, I didn't! I did have a real long talk with Gladys. I made it clear to her that I have no desire to be with her again. And I begged—no, I *ordered*—her not to ever attempt to contact me again. I told her that if she called, I wouldn't talk to her. And I told her if she sent any more letters, I'd return them to her unread. I swear to God I'm telling the truth!"

"You can sit here and swear all you want to. I don't believe you."

"Look, baby, I'll call her right now and let her tell you herself!" Bo leaped up off the bed and shot across the floor to the dresser where he had left his cell phone. He grabbed it and turned it on. "She'll tell you!"

"I don't want to talk to that damn woman!" I hollered. I ran over to him and snatched the cell phone out of his hand and turned it off. "I don't care at this point. All I care about is the fact that you lied to me!"

"I didn't lie to you!"

"Well, since you didn't tell me you were going to talk to her in person, that's as good as lying." I dropped his cell phone back onto the dresser and turned to walk away. Bo grabbed my hand and pulled me into his arms. Before I knew what was going on, his lips were on mine.

As soon as he reared his head back, he said, "Sarah, I do love you. I don't want to lose you and that's all that really matters to me." His embrace was so tight I could barely breathe. No matter how hard I tried to get loose, it did no good. He even tightened his grip to a point where I felt like we were part of the same body. "I'm not going to let Gladys *or anybody else* come between you and me!"

"It's too late," I managed. Those three words must have really had an impact on Bo because he released me so abruptly I almost fell to the floor.

"What the hell is that supposed to mean?" The look he gave me was enough to frighten the Devil. He narrowed his eyes, and his nostrils and jaws twitched. A purple vein stood out on the side of his neck like a snake. I would have been a fool to tell him I wanted a divorce while he was looking so scary.

"I, uh, we just have to work on a few things," I said with a hollow grin. "That's all."

I was glad that I had taken a shower before I left Curtis's apartment. When Bo pulled me to the bed and climbed on top of me, he couldn't stop talking about how fresh I smelled.

Curtis and I had used condoms. And I had not had time to get my prescription for birth control pills refilled yet, so I was worried about getting pregnant by Bo tonight. I needed to put having a baby on the back burner for a while. Even if I did get pregnant by Bo now, I had made up my mind. I didn't know if he had told me the truth about his meeting with his ex. But it didn't matter if he had or not. I was still going to leave him. I realized now that I didn't want to stay married to him no matter what. Had he been the right man for me in the first place, I would not have gotten involved with Curtis. I didn't feel comfortable in Bo's arms now. But until I left, I had to endure his "affection" and make the best of it. . . .

To my surprise, Bo's lovemaking tonight was better than it had been in months. But it was still too late.

I didn't sleep much that night. When he made love to me again the next morning, I thought I would scream. For one thing, Curtis had made love to me with so much vigor the night before I was sore between my thighs and I winced every time I urinated. Bo was just as rough as Curtis, so by the time he finished with me, I was walking like I had a stick up my ass. But being in pain didn't slow me down. I visited Curtis again that same night. When I got home, Bo made love to me again and he did so for the next four nights. By then I didn't know if I was coming or going.

Ironically, I was enjoying all the attention and it must have shown because a few days later on a rainy Monday morning, Daddy cornered me in the kitchen. He was still seated at the breakfast table, finishing up his coffee. Bo and Cash had already left to go to work. That meddlesome Collette was still in her room putting on her face (or I should say her "two" faces). Vera had an early morning session with her trainer, so she had left the house before any of us got up.

"Good morning, Daddy," I said as I pranced into the kitchen, still in my bathrobe.

Daddy stared at me for a few seconds. He had been giving me a lot of exasperated looks lately, especially this time. Once I gathered up enough courage to tell everybody I was going to divorce Bo, they would all give me exasperated looks. He set his coffee cup onto the table and folded his arms. "Sarah Louise, what's going on with you? I've noticed how you've been walking around all week beaming like you just won the lottery. What are you up to, girl?"

"Nothing, Daddy," I said with a shrug. "I'm just a happy woman."

"I wish I had some of whatever it is that's making you such a happy woman so I could be one too," Collette clucked, entering the room with an impish expression on her face. "You haven't walked around with such a glazed look in your eyes since you were pregnant."

Daddy's eyes got big and his lips curled up into a smile that reached from one side of his face to the other. "Baby! Are you—"

"No, I'm not pregnant again. I'm just happy, that's all."

The exasperated look returned to Daddy's face. Collette tilted her head and looked at me out of the corner of her eye. "Like I just said, whatever it is making you so happy, I wish I had some."

CHAPTER 54

VERA

"BABY, I'M SO GLAD YOU CAME OVER. LAST NIGHT I DREAMED I WAS making love to you." Ricky waved me into his posh apartment in the exclusive Nob Hill district that I had paid for and furnished with my money. He immediately gave me one of the longest, deepest French kisses I'd ever received. I could taste the toothpaste still on his teeth and gums. "You are the sexiest woman alive and I can't get enough of you!" he rasped. Then he lifted me into his arms and just stood in the middle of his living room floor looking into my eyes.

This boy was too good to be true. Not only was he a damn good lover, he was too gorgeous for his own good. He wasn't as tall as I liked my boys, but he had a fantastic body, muscles in places where some men don't even have places. He had deep dark brown skin that was so smooth and flawless it looked like his complexion had been spray-painted on. His mother was Ethiopian, but he had no idea who or even what ethnicity his father was. He had bone-straight black hair, worn in a buzz cut, and high cheekbones, so he could have been mixed with just about anything.

"Don't tell me, show me, dammit, you pretty motherfucker you!" I ordered.

"Oh, I am going to show you all right. By the time I get through busting you down, you won't know what hit you," Ricky threatened. He walked toward his bedroom and kicked open the door with his bare foot. Then he strode across the floor and gently placed me on his bed.

"I'm sorry to be coming over here at eight o'clock in the morning, but I wanted to see you so badly I couldn't help myself," I apologized. "And I'm sorry I didn't call first like I usually do."

"Vera, you can come over here whatever time of day or night you want to. And you know you don't need to call before you come," he replied, unzipping his pants. He stepped out of them and removed his underwear in record time.

"You're right about that. I just needed to hear you say it." I didn't like to remind Ricky that I was his sugar mama, but just to keep things in perspective, I did every now and then.

I didn't want to waste any more time talking. There were much more important things that I wanted to do with my mouth. With his eyes still on my face, he removed a package of condoms from his nightstand drawer and slid one on. I was still dressed, but I knew I wouldn't be for long. As soon as he eased down on top of me, I wrapped my legs around his waist and started taking care of business so fast I got light-headed.

After I had given him a thorough workout and a blow job, he swooned like a Baptist preacher. Then he scrambled out of bed and danced a jig. "Baby, that was the best head I've had in years. My dick felt like it was being sucked by a vacuum cleaner. Oomph!"

"I've had plenty of practice," I said proudly as I rolled over onto my side.

"I need a drink after that!" Ricky exclaimed, giving me one of the most satisfied looks I'd ever seen on a man's face. "You want me to fix you one too?" he asked, trotting to the dresser where he had set a bottle of rum and a bottle of Coke.

"Not this early in the morning. I don't know if that fool husband of mine will still be in the house when I get back home. All I need is for him to smell liquor on my breath when I'm supposed to be at the gym working out."

"Speaking of working out, take off them clothes so I can finish my job."

Ricky didn't give me time to undress myself. He did it, all the while whispering filth into my burning ears. The last thing he said before he tied my wrists and ankles to the bedposts with my stockings and two of his neckties was, "Show Big Dick Ricky whose whore you are."

After a fuck-fest that made me squeal like a pig, Ricky untied me and got up to fix himself another drink. The telephone on the nightstand next to his bed rang, but he ignored it. I was glad he had turned off his answering machine because if I had heard a woman leaving a message for him, he would have had some explaining to do. Each of my boy toys was mine exclusively for the duration of our affair. If they even so much as *looked* at another woman (or man) without my approval and I found out about it, I "fired" them. I'd only dismissed two for that reason so far.

"Baby, I don't know how you can still stand that old Geritol-guzzling geezer!" Ricky blasted, shooting me a hot look as he returned to the bed.

It was on the tip of my tongue to tell him that I guzzled just as much Geritol as Kenneth. I usually kept my mouth shut when it came to subjects that were offensive to me. And age was at the top of my shit list. But this sweet young thing was so incredible I'd almost let him get away with murder.

"Vera, you are too beautiful and delicious to be with a gargoyle like Kenneth. I seen him up close when I was in his store one day and he looked right beastly to me!"

"Tell me about it! And it's really beginning to get on my last nerve. I hate the man and I don't know how much longer I can put up with him. Eeyow! Just the thought of making love to him turns my stomach. When he kissed me last night with his sloppy wet rubbery lips, it was like kissing a toilet plunger. I made sure I got up before he did this morning, just so I wouldn't have to kiss him again."

"Baby, I'm so sorry you have to put up with some shit like that." Ricky took a long drink and let out a mighty belch. "I know you signed one of them prenup things that state you won't get much if you divorce him, which was a bum deal if you ask me. Sister, what was you thinking when you done that? You must have been out of your mind at the time." Ricky paused and gave me a look that made me feel about two feet tall. He was right. I must have been out of my mind to sign that prenup.

"If I hadn't signed, he probably would have thought I was marrying him for his money," I whimpered.

"That is why you married him! You told me that to my face right after we first met!"

"Yeah, I know. But it's over and done with now and there is nothing I can do to change it."

"Humph! And you black women think you all are so smart! Ha! You sisters get the shortest end of the stick of all the women on this planet! I bet them white bitches don't be signing no prenups like the one you signed! I used to do this teeny-weeny Japanese chick before I met you. She's married to a fucking *billionaire.* The prenup she signed is banging! She'll get half of whatever he's worth if they divorce, and *everything* if he dies before her."

"Maybe you should get yourself a white woman or another teeny-weeny Japanese woman," I said with a smirk. I gave Ricky a scowl, so he changed his tune when he saw how pissed off he was making me.

"Oh, baby, I'm just blowing off steam," he said in a much lower voice and a more sensitive manner. "You're all the woman I need. I really do care about you, Vera." He was doing okay until his last sentence. "You remind me so much of my grandmother—"

"Hey! Shut up! You hold on there right now!" I hollered, my blood boiling like water for chocolate. "I'd stop while I was ahead if I were you!" I warned, shaking a finger in his face.

"Oh, well, you know what I mean. My granny is a real cool woman and when it comes to looks, she's sharper than a serpent's tooth. And she looks way younger than she really is. Just like you."

"That's better," I sniffed.

"Anyway, I don't like to see you fretting over what you're going to get from Kenneth. I feel that as long as you've been married to old dude and as good as you've been treating his sickly black ass, that rich bastard would *probably* make it worth your while if you left him now. I mean, at his age, what do he need with all them millions? Shit. If he's any kind of man, he'll break you off a couple million just for the hell of it. Shit."

"Be patient, sweetie. I am not about to just up and leave a gold mine like Kenneth—unless it's for somebody with more money than him. But I've put up with him this long, I can hold on a little longer. He's got one foot and a big toe in the grave already. However, if I do decide to leave him, I know he'd probably be fairly generous to me. Especially after all the years I've tolerated his gas and foul breath and sweat. But I deserve more than just a couple million. I'll come out a whole lot better if he dies while I'm still with him. I want it all."

"I'd want it all, too, if I was in your shoes. And you'll get it because you're a real pro when it comes to getting paid. I bet there ain't a man alive who could short-change you. Oomph! It's a good thing his daughter is retarded. After he's out of the way, you won't have no trouble with her."

"Retarded? Sarah's not retarded. What made you say that?"

"You did. You said she was a slow-wit that didn't know her asshole from a hole in the ground."

"Oh." I laughed. "I was just talking out the side of my mouth when I told you that. As a matter of fact, Sarah is pretty smart for an idiot," I laughed again, this time louder and longer. Then I got serious. "I'm not really worried about her. Once her daddy's out of the picture, I'm sure I can keep her under control. With me and Bo working together, she'll be like putty in our hands."

"That's true. But Kenneth will probably leave her a bigger cut than you."

"Like I said, once Kenneth is out of the way, Bo and I can handle that ninny daughter of his. Shit!"

"Uh-huh. Well, I just hope you get everything you got coming, baby."

"Don't worry. I have a feeling I will."

CHAPTER 55

KENNETH

VERA WAS GOING TO GET EVERYTHING SHE HAD COMING. I WAS GOING to make sure of that.

I met Tim in his office two days after our last telephone conversation. He greeted me with a long face and promptly waved me to a seat. My legs were too stiff for me to cross them, but I shifted around in the soft leather seat and made myself as comfortable as I could.

It was a gloomy day that had started out with rain, dark clouds, and thunder and lightning. I had encountered a traffic accident on my way to Tim's office, and I had almost run over a dog in the crosswalk. And if all of that had not been enough to get me off to a bad start, Vera had entered the bathroom while I was taking a shower and insisted on giving me a blow job, which I had not enjoyed. I couldn't figure out why she was being so affectionate. She had not gotten that intimate with me in the shower all week. She was up to something and I would have bet my bottom dollar that it had something to do with her and her lover. Maybe she was feeling sorry for me and the blow job was a gesture of mercy. Or a display of guilt, which was even worse. It didn't matter which one it was because that bitch was toast!

Tim sat with his arms folded. He remained silent while I looked through a stack of photographs he'd just handed to me of Vera and her young lover. After I'd flipped through the first few pictures, I had to stop. I paused, loosened my tie, and took several deep breaths. Tim handed me a glass of mineral water and I looked at the rest of the pictures.

I was so visibly upset by the time I'd seen them all, Tim handed me a shot glass filled to the brim with scotch. I swallowed it all in one gulp.

"That woman is a straight-up whore!" I roared. I was so angry I could barely talk. I wanted to beat the shit out of Vera, but I had never struck a woman before in my life and I was not about to start now. I had a better punishment in mind for her. I'd "hit" her where it would cause her the most pain: in her wallet. That woman worshipped the almighty dollar. I was going to teach her a lesson she would never forget. By the time I got through with her, she'd be so broke even her cash would bounce! "I'm fit to be tied!"

"I know exactly how you feel."

"My wife is cheating on me with this sleazeball?" I hollered, fanning the air with a picture of Vera sitting on her punk's lap on a bench in Golden Gate Park—a place she had once told me she only enjoyed when she was there with me. "Lord have mercy!" This Ricky character looked like a typical thug to me with his beady black eyes and sharp, weasel-like features. In almost every picture, he wore jeans and either a T-shirt or some plaid mess with the sleeves missing and the buttons undone, revealing his smooth chest that had the kind of ripped muscles I could have only in my dreams. I stared from one picture to another with my mouth hanging open and my head pounding and throbbing like somebody was going at it with a drill. "I'm meeting with my lawyer first thing tomorrow morning to modify my will again!"

"I'm sorry things turned out the way they did, my man." Tim gave me a pitiful look. "I mean, your daughter is having an affair—that's enough bad news for you to hear. But your wife . . . man, it doesn't get any worse than that. After what Sherry did to me, I'm almost afraid to get involved with another woman."

"Tell me about it." I had to stop talking so I could catch my breath. I closed my eyes for a few moments and wheezed so hard I got light-headed.

"Dude, are you all right? You want another shot of scotch?" Tim asked, looking worried. He was already reaching for the empty shot glass I had set on his desk.

"I'm fine, Tim. I don't need anything else to drink right now." I cleared my throat and looked through the pictures again. There were twelve in all, glossy eight by tens suitable for framing. In one picture, Vera and Ricky were strolling out of Neiman Marcus grinning from ear to ear. He was holding more shopping bags than she was. I remembered that day well. It was last Saturday. I knew that because Vera wore a lime-green dress that she had just purchased two days before and she never wore anything twice. She had left the house in that dress to go "shopping" and had come home six hours later with just one bag. So all of the other bags must have contained merchandise that she'd purchased with my money for that sucker she was fucking. That low-down funky black bitch! Other photos showed her and Ricky coming out of a movie theater, a massage parlor, and La Scala, one of the most expensive restaurants in the Bay Area. And in the detailed report Tim showed me, Vera's lover had just quit his job as a bartender in the nightclub where Vera had met him. His finances had been as raggedy as a bowl of sauerkraut, and his credit as spotty as a leopard when Vera first met him. But she had changed that. She had been covering his car note and other expenses from day one, even his rent. That was another thing: his residence. She had previously moved him from a flophouse on Sixteenth Street to an apartment in *Nob Hill.* A retired TV star I knew and one of my most expensive attorneys lived in this neighborhood! She'd bought him furniture and thousands of dollars' worth of new clothes on a credit card she'd opened in her name. Three days ago she took him to the bank and opened a checking and savings account for him with a ten-thousand-dollar initial deposit. Oh! I couldn't wait to confront her, but I didn't want to do it right away. I wanted to give her just enough rope to hang herself and when she did that, I wanted that bitch to hang until that noose around her cheating neck rotted!

Tim continued in a firmer tone of voice, which told me this mess was having almost as much of an impact on him as it was me. "I have some lovely shots of your daughter and her friend too. And boy are they juicy. But maybe you should wait and look at them another time. You don't look well, dude."

"Tim, I'm fine. Let me see the other pictures too. I may as well get all of this shit dumped into my lap at the same time."

He removed another stack of photographs from his desk drawer and handed them to me. I could only stand to look at the first few on top. I was horrified by what I saw. The way Curtis was holding on to my daughter as they strolled along Fisherman's Wharf like newlyweds, I knew her marriage to Bo was as dead in the water as mine was to Vera.

I wobbled up out of my seat. "I've seen enough, Tim. You can put this one to bed. How much do I owe you?" I wheezed some more as I rubbed my chest, which had tightened up even more since I'd entered Tim's office.

"I'll send you the bill," Tim said, waving me back to my seat. "I'm really concerned about how bad you look right now. Did you drive over here?"

I sat back down. I was dizzy and my mouth was so dry it tasted like I'd been chewing on a sheet of old newspaper. "I drove over here," I managed, blinking rapidly. My vision had become blurred and my left arm was throbbing and tingling. "I'm fine," I insisted, rising again.

"You're not fine, my brother. And I'm not letting you leave here alone. I'll drive you home and I'll have one of my assistants follow us in your car."

"Yes, please do that for me, Tim. I really appreciate having a friend like you," I told him, shaking his hand. "Thank you for all you've done for me." I let out an eerie laugh. "You can scratch Vera's name off your next Christmas party guest list."

"It's already done." Tim gave me a sharp nod.

I was glad that Tim had insisted on taking me home. I knew my body well enough to know that it was finally going to shut down for a while, maybe even permanently. I just had to hold on until I got all my affairs in order.

I had a heart attack in Tim's car, just three blocks from my house. He made a U-turn and rushed me to San Francisco General. I passed out as soon as they loaded me onto a gurney. When I opened my eyes, the first person I saw was Vera, hovering over me like a vulture. Seeing her was so ironic I wanted to laugh because *she* was the reason I was knocking on death's door. Had I been able, I would have sprung up out of that bed and choked her.

"Baby, you're going to be just fine," she told me, looking at me with her lying eyes blinking and her eyeballs rolling from side to side. As usual, her makeup was impeccable, which told me she had not shed a single tear. She was also dressed like she was on her way to a party at the White House. She even had on white gloves and some of her best jewelry. "The doctor will be back in a few minutes, so you just lie there and rest."

That heifer had a white silk scarf wrapped around her neck. But when she leaned down to kiss me, it slipped. She quickly adjusted it, but I had already seen the purple sucker bite on her neck. It looked like a goddamn tattoo! I couldn't get the images of her and her lover out of my mind.

"Where's Sarah?" I whispered.

"She's on her way," Vera replied. "Bo and Cash were here a few minutes ago, but they had to get back to the store to meet with those vendors from Sacramento. They'll be back in a little while. Collette called to say she was praying for you. So did all the rest of your staff in all five stores. Your friend Tim brought you in." I noticed how the worried look on Vera's face intensified when she mentioned Tim's name. She knew he had done a lot of investigative work for people we socialized with, so she was probably wondering *why* I had been with him.

"Tim said you got sick while he was having lunch with you," she told me, giving me a guarded look. "And he also told me he had come to the store to get a birthday gift for one of his grandsons and invited you to have lunch with him."

"That's right." I went along with Tim's version of events. It sounded reasonable. Had he told Vera the truth, that I'd been in his office on business, she would have figured out what I had really been up to.

"Oh. What restaurant did he take you to?"

"Uh . . . some hole-in-the-wall I can't remember the name of. Those places all look the same to me. You know how cheap Tim is."

"Yeah, I know. I'll never forget that time he took us to Wendy's for lunch and paid for our burgers with coupons!" Vera laughed. I didn't. Then she got real serious. "Uh, he told me that he and Sherry are going through a divorce."

"She was cheating on him."

"What? Why, that's a damn shame! Tim was so good to Sherry!"

"Yeah, he was good to her," I agreed with a sneer. "But to some women being good to them is not enough."

"Uh, is he still doing private investigative work?" Vera rotated her neck a couple of times and tied the scarf around it even tighter.

"Uh-huh. And he's got more business than ever." I blinked at Vera a few times. That must have made her nervous because she started to shift her weight from one foot to the other. She smoothed down the sides of her dress and clutched the handle on her purse like she was afraid somebody was going to run up behind her and snatch it. I couldn't remember the last time she'd looked this nervous.

"Well, like I just told you, you're going to be fine. And I can't wait to get you home!" she squealed, forcing a smile. She lowered her voice to a whisper. "I have a big surprise in store for you."

Another surprise was the one thing I didn't need. "I have one in store for you, too, Vera." That slipped out, but it was very effective. She looked like she had just seen Caesar's ghost.

"That's nice, Kenneth. I can't wait to see what it is." I saw tears in her eyes for the first time since she had entered my room.

"I need to see my daughter," I said, attempting to sit up.

"Honey, be still and please don't try to talk or stir around too much." Vera gently pushed me back down on the bed.

"I need to see my daughter!" I said again in a much harsher tone of voice. "And I want to see her *alone.*"

CHAPTER 56

SARAH

As soon as I entered Daddy's hospital room, I could feel the tension. He lay on his back looking up at the ceiling. Vera stood by the side of the bed with her hands on her hips.

"Hi, Daddy," I said meekly, still standing in the doorway.

Daddy turned sharply and looked at me. Then he looked at Vera and snapped his fingers in her face. "Vera, leave this room so I can talk to my child," he ordered.

"What the f—" she began, but Daddy cut her off.

"Get out before I have them throw you out!" Daddy boomed, pointing toward the door.

With a horrified look on her face, Vera scurried out like a scared rabbit.

"Sarah Louise, you get your tail in here and shut that door! I need to talk to you!" he bellowed.

I didn't like the tone of his voice and the angry look on his face. He had never spoken to me or looked at me this way before. I knew that whatever he needed to talk to me about, it was serious—especially since he'd ordered Vera to leave the room in such a brutal manner.

I closed the door and walked slowly toward the bed, dragging my feet like I was on my way to my own execution. I swallowed hard and clutched the strap of my purse. "What's wrong, Daddy? Are you mad at me?" I asked, hoping I didn't look as dumb as I sounded.

"I know you've been seeing Curtis!" he barked. "I know you've been rolling around in bed with that man! That's what's wrong, *Jezebel*!"

"Now, Daddy, just let me explain—"

"Explain what? Don't even bother lying or trying to make up excuses!"

"Daddy, don't holler like that. I don't want other people to know my business." I glanced toward the door, wondering if Vera was outside with her ear pressed against it.

"You didn't care about other people knowing your business before now! I've got pictures of you out in public with Curtis all hugged up with strangers looking at you from every angle! Shame on you, Sarah Louise!"

I almost choked on some air before I could speak again. "You had somebody following me around?" My voice sounded shrill and frightened.

"Yes, I had somebody following you around!"

"Oh," I mumbled. I sighed and offered Daddy a weak smile, hoping it would defuse the situation a little. My smile didn't even faze him. The angry look was still on his face. "Well, I'm not going to lie about it. I'm tired of keeping it to myself. I love him, Daddy. I have never loved a man as much as I love Curtis. Not even Bo."

Daddy looked at me like I was speaking Gaelic. He shook his head and clucked like a rooster. "Why in the world do you want to hurt me and your husband like this?"

"I don't think I love Bo anymore."

"What? What do you mean you don't 'think' you love Bo anymore? When did you realize that?"

I looked away because I didn't want to see the pain in Daddy's eyes when he heard what I said next. I stared at the wall and said, "I know Bo was with his ex when he went to L.A. with you." When I turned to face Daddy again, he looked like a pillar of salt.

"Say what?" As weak as he was, he managed to sit bolt upright with his back as straight as a broom handle. "Who told you Bo was with his ex in L.A.?"

"I found a letter in his pocket that she had sent to him in care of Cash asking him to meet up with her when he got to L.A."

"Did he tell you he met with her? Bo was with me most of the time, so I don't know how he could have spent any time with her without me knowing about it."

"Did you and Bo sleep in the same room?"

"Hell no! What's wrong with you, girl? You know I don't hang like that!"

"Then how would you know what he did when he wasn't with you? I called the hotel and she'd checked in."

Daddy's jaw dropped and the pupils in his eyes got so dark, they looked like ink spots. "What are you telling me? Is Bo thinking about going back to that wench?"

"He claims he only agreed to talk to her so he could tell her to her face that he didn't want to be with her again."

"Did you believe him?"

"It doesn't matter now, Daddy. I'm going to divorce him no matter what."

"Lord have mercy!"

"He can still work for you and he can still live in the house if you want him to. I'm going to move in with Curtis anyway."

"Have you lost your mind, Sarah Louise?"

"No, I have not lost my mind. I want to be happy like everybody else. I want to have a long, strong relationship with somebody I love. Just like you and Vera."

Daddy started to laugh so hard he choked. I slapped him on the back, but that didn't help. He was gasping for air so hard I had to summon his doctor back into the room. Dr. Mason came right away, with Vera trotting along right behind him with a scared look on her face.

"What's the matter?" she yelled as the doctor waved her out of his way.

"I'm fine, I'm fine," Daddy groaned, pushing the doctor's hand away.

"Mr. Lomax, I think you've had enough company for today,"

Dr. Mason said gently, adjusting his stethoscope and then feeling Daddy's pulse.

"What did you say to him, Sarah? He was doing fine until you got here!" Vera snapped, wiping her nose with one of her dozens of monogrammed silk handkerchiefs.

"I just told Daddy that I'm leaving Bo so I can move in with Curtis," I told her, speaking in a firm, proud manner. I didn't feel scared anymore. As a matter of fact, I'd never felt bolder and more determined in my life. My words must have really slammed into them. I couldn't tell which one groaned louder, Vera or Daddy. Neither one said a word. They just stared at me and blinked, shook their heads, and groaned some more.

Dr. Mason cleared his throat and looked from me to Vera, shaking his head. "Okay, that's enough! You two are upsetting my patient," he barked, snapping his fingers. "I insist that you both leave this room at once." From the stern look on his face, I knew this doctor meant business. The last thing Daddy needed to see was Vera and me being escorted out by hospital security.

"Daddy, I'll come back as soon as the doctor says it's okay," I sputtered. I gave him a quick peck on the forehead and then I left. I had made it halfway down the hall when I heard the heels of Vera's Jimmy Choos clip-clopping on the marble floor behind me.

"You wait a minute!" she snarled, grabbing me by the arm as soon as she caught up to me. "What the hell has gotten into you—besides Curtis's slimy dick? What about all the dealers and gangsters and whatnot he told us about who want him dead for being such a snitch and a busybody? I'm surprised he hasn't already been snuffed out! Do you want to get caught up in his mess and get yourself hurt too?"

"Curtis can take care of himself—and me too—if he has to. He's no fraidy-cat punk!" I strongly declared. Curtis kept a baseball bat, a stun gun, and a can of mace for protection in his apartment and had only had to use them a few times. If he wasn't too worried about getting "snuffed out," I wasn't going to worry about it either.

Vera was so exasperated she was trembling. "What's wrong with you, girl? You can't leave Bo for that scumbag *security guard.*" She made "security guard" sound like the two most obscene words in the English language.

"I can't? Well, you just watch me!" I retorted, slapping and pinching her hand until she released my arm.

"Bo will *never* give you a divorce!" Vera yelled. "I'll see to that myself. He listens to me more than he listens to you!"

"Yes, he does. I noticed that a long time ago, Vera. Maybe that's why it was so easy for me to get involved with another man." I sniffed and narrowed my eyes. "If he had been more of a man, women like you and his ex couldn't have turned him into such a wimp, which is what he was by the time he got to me. Well, he can listen to you all he wants. Whether he agrees to a divorce or not, I'm leaving him anyway."

Vera noticed how people were looking at us, so she lowered her voice. "Haven't you caused everybody enough pain? And why now?"

"What do you mean, 'why now?' Now is as good a time as any for me to leave."

"Can't you wait until your daddy gets better? Can't you see what all this drama is doing to him? You are the most selfish bitch—"

"Look, Miss Prissy! I don't have to stand here and listen to that kind of talk coming from you. I've tried to put up with your snooty ways since I was a teenager, and I'm tired of trying to be nice to you. And you have some nerve calling me selfish. You are the most selfish bitch I've ever met! No wonder you don't have any friends."

"What? I . . . I have plenty of friends, little girl! You don't know what you're talking about!" Vera roared. Her eyes looked like two pieces of coal. Blood rushed up her face, settling mainly in her nose. It looked like a strawberry. It was a funny sight, but I was too angry to laugh.

"Then how come you asked *me* to take you to the hospital when you had to have that fibroid surgery?"

Vera looked so stunned and vulnerable at that moment I was surprised she was still able to stand on her own. I couldn't wait to hear her response. I braced myself. But nothing could have prepared me for what she said next. "I hate you, Sarah. I have always hated your ass," she told me with her lips trembling and her eyes pooled with tears.

It took a few seconds for my brain to register what she'd just admitted. I had always suspected that Vera didn't really like me. But hearing her say she *hated* me made me feel unbearably sad. "I don't hate you, Vera. But I hate what you say and do. I feel sorry for you."

"Oh my God!" She covered her mouth with her hand and shook her head. This time the color drained from her face. Now she looked almost like a ghost. I actually did feel sorry for her, but just for a few moments. "I'm sorry I said that!" she choked. "You know I didn't mean it! It's just that I'm so worried about your daddy and . . . and I'm so stressed and confused! Let's try to be more civil to one another, sweetie." Vera grabbed my arm again and smiled. I slapped and pinched her hand again. People were still looking at us. She began to fan her face with her hand, but that didn't stop the sweat from forming on her forehead. Her thick makeup began to slide down her face like mud sliding down the side of a hill. "We have to live under the same roof, so we need to try and get along."

"Didn't you hear what I just said? I'm going to leave Bo. There is nothing you, Daddy, or anybody else can say to make me change my mind." A couple of nurses and a few other visitors walked by, looking and listening to our heated conversation. I was embarrassed and I attempted to leave again, but Vera grabbed my arm and held me in place. "I'm moving in with Curtis today!" As soon as she heard that, she released my arm on her own this time.

"All right, BITCH! You go on to that motherfucking security guard. But I can tell you now, Bo is going to make you regret it! I'll make sure of that!"

"I know you will, Vera." I trotted on down the hall with her still following me, panting like a coyote. I bypassed the elevator and ducked into the stairwell. I had on my Nikes, so it was easy for me to run down three flights of steps. Somehow, Vera managed to run down the same steps, not even stumbling in her impossibly high heels. When I got to the ground floor, she was right behind me, holding her shoes in her hand.

"Sarah, we need to talk some more. Please let me talk some sense into your head. If you want to leave Bo, at least wait until your daddy is out of the hospital. Didn't you see how upset he was?"

"All right," I said. "I'll wait until Daddy gets well and comes home."

"And please don't even mention that security guard to Bo until then."

"Why? I think the sooner Bo knows what I'm planning to do, the better. He's not stupid. He *knows* I'm sleeping with Curtis and have been for a long time. And I know you know it too!"

Vera nodded her head hard. Then she swept her hair back with her hand so far I could see the faint scars behind her ears from her last face-lift. "I suspected you were. Don't you know that's a sin and a shame, girl? I'm sorry I had to stand here in public and hear you admit that you've been *cheating* on your husband."

"Don't be sorry. Be glad that it's finally out in the open now," I said sharply.

"Lord, what a mess you've created, child. I'm . . . I'm feeling sicker by the second," Vera whimpered, gulping for air. She sounded like a sick puppy now and looked like the hag she really was behind the mask she wore. Despite all of the surgeries that had been performed on her face, the vigorous workouts with her trainers, and the makeup, Vera looked every minute of her sixty-two years now. "Let me talk to Bo first so he won't take it so hard," she rasped. Even her voice now sounded like it belonged to an old woman.

"Woman, what's wrong with you? I don't need for you to talk to my husband! That's my job! You and Daddy have been running our marriage long enough. That's part of the problem."

"Yes, we did interfere more than we should have. We can't change that now. But I'd still like to prepare my poor cousin for the bombshell you're going to hit him with. He's still in pain from the breakup of his first marriage." I enjoyed watching Vera squirm, but I was anxious to end this conversation. "Sarah, I helped raise Bo. I'm like a second mama to him. I know him a lot better than you do. Please let me talk to him before you do—for everybody's sake. I won't ever ask you for anything else as long as I live."

"All right, Vera! If it means that much to you, you talk to him, then. But you better do it real soon. Because as soon as my daddy is back on his feet, I'm hauling ass."

CHAPTER 57

VERA

I KNEW THAT RICKY WAS SLIGHTLY THUGGISH FROM THE DAY I MET him. He had spent most of his life in the ghetto, just like Sarah. Even though he lived in a much better neighborhood now and had classy neighbors, he was still just as ghetto as ever, just like Sarah. But in his case, it didn't matter. I didn't have to live with him or take him around any of the sophisticated people I associated with. But other than that long tongue in his mouth that he was so proud of and that big stick between his legs, he had other things I could use to my advantage, like criminal connections.

Right after my run-in at the hospital with Sarah, I called Ricky up from my cell phone before I left the hospital parking lot.

"Can you get me an untraceable gun from one of your homeboys?" I asked him.

"An untraceable gun?" he asked with a loud gasp. "Why you need something like that?"

"Don't ask any questions. Just tell me if you can get me one or not."

"Yeah, I can get you one. It'll cost you a pretty penny, though."

"I don't care about that. You just get me a gun and make sure it's loaded. And if you can, get me one with a silencer."

"Look, baby. This ain't *CSI* or one of them other cop shows where a dude can get his hands on shit like silencers and whatnot at the drop of a hat. Now listen up; my cellmate was this Vietnamese dude and he had a bag full of tricks. He might be able to put together a homemade silencer. But he won't get out of the joint for another couple of weeks."

"I can't wait that long! I need it right away."

"Vera, I don't know what kind of mess you done got yourself into. But take some advice from somebody who's spent time in lockdown—prison ain't no place that a dainty lady like you want to be. You wouldn't last a week behind bars! If you didn't die from eating the prison slop, them husky bull dykes would *eat* you to death—literally."

"I'm not going to prison. I'm not stupid enough to get caught!" I hollered.

"That's the same thing I said, and the same thing every convict done said at one time or another. With DNA and forensics and all the shit they got now, there ain't no such thing as a perfect crime. They're catching folks for crimes they committed *thirty* years ago. Like I just told you, take some advice from somebody who's been in prison. When you commit a crime, there are dozens of ways you can fuck up. I don't care how smart you are."

Ricky had just been released from Folsom two weeks before I met him. He had done time for car theft and a home invasion, crimes that he had committed when he was high on cocaine. He didn't tell me that until I had known him for a couple of months. By then I was so addicted to him I wouldn't have cared if he'd just been released from an insane asylum. A few more weeks into our affair, he told me about some of the other crimes he had committed that he'd never been arrested for. He'd broken into several houses and taken whatever he could carry. One night after too many drinks, he'd beaten one of his partners in crime to death because he'd stolen the loot from Ricky's apartment that they'd stolen a few days before. Even though he'd never even been suspected of that crime, he was worried that someday he would turn himself in. Not because he had found Jesus like so many other cons and ex-cons claimed, but because he had turned his life around.

As far as I knew, I was the only person that Ricky had told about him killing his accomplice. Since I had *that* on him, I was not concerned about him tattling on me for coming to him for a gun. But I thought it would be wise for me to mention it anyway. "Uh, on account of that thing you told me you did to your friend, I'm sure I don't have to worry about you telling anybody about this conversation."

"Hell no!" he hollered. "I ain't in no position to be ratting you out, or nobody else. Shit. My glass house is way too fragile for me to be that big of a fool."

"Good. Now you get me a gun as soon as you can. I'll come over and give you five thousand dollars today and another five when you get it. Use it to pay for the gun. I'm sure it won't cost ten grand—you keep the change. Do you hear me?"

"I hear you. Especially the part about the ten Gs!" Ricky yelled. "You know when money talks, I listen. But you'd better listen up, baby. I'm a little more experienced in certain areas than you. Do you want me to help you do whatever it is you planning to do with this gun? I might even know somebody who would do the deed real cheap as a favor to me. Is that something you might want to consider?"

Apparently Ricky had not "turned his life around" too well. The fact that he was so eager to backslide for me was touching. I appreciated his offer, but the problem I had to resolve was too personal and I didn't want to involve any more people than I had to.

"Didn't I tell you not to ask any questions? I don't want you to do anything but get me that gun. I'll see you later tonight if I can, or tomorrow morning for sure."

"That's fine, baby. I can't wait." Ricky made a loud kissing noise. "And don't forget to bring the money."

"I won't."

I was not ready to go home and deal with Sarah, so I drove to Fisherman's Wharf. I pulled into the first parking lot I saw. I wasn't hungry, but I went into a nearby café that I often visited and ordered a glass of merlot. I had a lot of thinking to do. I had to make sure I had all of my thoughts organized when I talked to Bo about what we had to do—kill Curtis Thompson.

After I'd drunk my second glass of wine, I called Bo's office. I was prepared to leave him a voice mail. He was not in a meeting or off somewhere else for a change. As a matter of fact, he answered his own phone. "Bo, what time are you coming home this evening?" I asked.

"I'm not sure," he told me in a cheerful tone of voice. Well, he wouldn't be cheerful for long. "Why? What's up? Oh! I was going to swing back by the hospital to see Kenneth on my way home. Are you at the hospital now?"

"I left there a little while ago."

"How is Kenneth doing?"

"Pffft! He looks like he could haunt a house."

"Hmmm. That bad, huh? I have a feeling dude is not going to be with us too much longer. The other day he passed out while sitting on the commode in his office bathroom. It was a good thing I found him before somebody else did."

"He didn't tell me about that."

"You don't have to tell him I told you. He was embarrassed about it and tried to play it off. Did his doctor give you any hopeful news?"

"That damn quack tells Sarah more than he tells me. All I know is this—Kenneth is worse off than ever before. One of the nurses took me aside today and suggested that when and if we do take him home, we should make him as comfortable as possible. To me that's as good as her telling me to start planning his funeral."

"It's that serious, huh? This must be pretty hard on Sarah."

"Humph! Well, I smell a rat, and it stinks to high heaven."

"You do? Why do you say that? Do you think Kenneth and Sarah are cooking up something? And you know what, you could be right. His estate lawyer called here a little while ago, and when I told him Kenneth was in the hospital, he told me he was going to go see him immediately."

"Well, the man has been a friend of Kenneth's for more than twenty years. And most of his other friends have already paid him a visit."

"Vera, I know that. But the lawyer also told me that Kenneth had made an appointment with him for this morning. When Kenneth didn't show up or call, his lawyer called the store."

"Hmmm. I wonder why Kenneth wanted to meet with Donald, you know—oh shit! I bet it's got something to do with his will!"

"That's my guess too. Did Kenneth say anything to Sarah about his appointment with his lawyer?"

"I don't know. He made me leave his room so he could talk to her in private."

"Oh?" Bo didn't sound the least bit cheerful now. "And what did he want to talk to her about in private?"

"How would I know that if he made me leave the room? I tried to snoop around and listen at the door from outside but too many people were walking by."

"This doesn't sound good for us. I'm worried. . . ."

"You think I'm not worried?"

"Well, did you ask Sarah why Kenneth wanted to have a private conversation with her?"

"Bo, if Kenneth wanted to talk to Sarah about something in private, what would be the point of either of them telling me what it was about?"

"You're right. Well, I just hope it's nothing too serious."

"Any time a man's estate lawyer comes to visit him while he's in a hospital at death's door, it's serious. Especially if Kenneth had made an appointment to see him."

"Listen, I think we need to sit down and talk when I get home. Just you and me, and maybe Cash. Afterward, I'll take Sarah aside and I'll try to get as much information out of her as I can."

"Uh . . . there's another thing you need to know. And this can't wait."

"Oh? What is it?"

"Sarah's going to drop one hell of a bombshell on you. Maybe even before the day is over. And you are not going to like what she tells you."

"What are you talking about?"

"You heard what I said."

"Well, what the hell kind of bombshell is Sarah going to drop on me? Did she tell you that?"

I sucked in some air and held it for a few seconds. Then I let it out with a whoosh. "Bo, your wife is fucking that security guard!"

"No, she's not!"

"Yes, she is! And that's not the half of it. *She's going to move in with him!* She told me so herself to my face before I left the hospital!"

I could hear my poor cousin breathing through his mouth.

"Bo, are you all right?"

"No . . . no . . . no . . . she can't do this to me," he cried. Nothing broke my heart quicker than a man in tears. "I'm firing that happy son of a bitch as soon as I get off this phone!" he boomed, choking on a sob.

"I don't know why you didn't do that back when we first found out she was getting too close to that fool!"

"Has she been seeing him since we confronted her?"

"It looks that way to me. You should have heard her going on and on about how she was in love with that skunk! I can't believe that damn girl!"

"I'll kill that motherfucker before I let him have my wife!"

"Uh-huh. And I don't blame you one bit, cuz. I'd do the same thing myself. We'll talk about that tonight."

CHAPTER 58

SARAH

I HAD NO IDEA WHERE VERA WAS, BUT I WONDERED IF SHE HAD RE-turned to the hospital to try and kiss up to Daddy. He was mad at her about something, and it was in her best interest to resolve whatever that was. I decided to call and check on him, but I was also calling to be nosy about Vera. Donald Baskerville, his estate lawyer, answered the telephone.

"Sarah, it's so nice to hear your voice. You had just turned twenty-one the last time I saw you," Mr. Baskerville said. "You were nothing but legs then."

"Well, I still have the same legs," I said, forcing myself to laugh. "Is my stepmother there?"

"No, she's not."

"Uh, is my daddy able to speak to me?"

"Hold on, sugar. I'll check with him."

I heard some muffled talk in the background and a lot of coughing. It was a couple of minutes before Mr. Baskerville came back on the line. "Your father will speak to you now. He's still fairly weak, so I advise you not to keep him on the line too long."

"I won't. I just wanted to check on him now before they give him a sedative or something. Um, I'm sure Daddy was glad to see you. . . ."

"I'm sure he was and I was glad to see him. He missed an ap-pointment with me this morning, so I decided to meet with him here. But I won't take up too much more of his time. You take care of yourself and don't spend too much time worrying about your daddy. He's going to be just fine."

I didn't believe a word of what Mr. Baskerville had just said about my daddy going to be just fine. Daddy was dying and I think everybody knew that. Why else would his *estate* lawyer be visiting him in the hospital instead of waiting for him to get out and come into this office? I answered my own question. Daddy was making more adjustments to his will, and I had a feeling *somebody* was not going to be happy with the new changes.

"Hello, sugar." Daddy's voice was so weak I could barely hear him.

"How are you feeling?"

"Tolerable, I guess. Are you at the house?"

"Yeah. I came straight home after I left the hospital. Do you know where Vera is?"

"HELL NO!" he boomed. His reaction stunned me. Daddy had never used such an angry tone of voice when Vera was the subject. "She's so mysterious these days, there's just no telling where she is or who she's with!"

Something was going on between Vera and Daddy. His last comment sounded pretty ominous to me. I had no idea what he was implying. But I silently agreed with him. There was just no telling where Vera was and who she was with. That woman had always been a "suspect" in some regard as far as I was concerned. After all these years, she *still* had not given me enough information about all the charities she allegedly spent so much time working with so I could help too. It was very suspicious, even more so now. That woman was up to something no good, but I had no idea *what.* But from the way Daddy was acting, I had a feeling that he had an idea what it was.

I didn't like that Vera had stuck her cosmetically enhanced nose into my marriage. And since I didn't want to cause Daddy any more emotional pain than he was already in, I decided to keep my nose out of their marriage. I was not going to encourage him to tell me why he was upset with her. Me being nosy and meddlesome might make matters worse. Besides, I needed to stay focused on my own problems.

"Daddy, I'm sorry I let you down. I tried to be the daughter you wanted me to be, but I couldn't. I have to be myself if I want to be happy." I had to blink real hard to hold back my tears, and knowing how emotional Daddy got, he was probably doing the same thing on his end. "I'm real sorry for all the trouble I'm causing you about Curtis. But . . . I can't undo anything now."

"Yeah, I know. Neither can I. All I can say now is that you do what you want to do. I can't stop you. At the end of the day, all I really want is for you to be happy. Even if it means you leaving Bo for Curtis. It's your life and I don't need to keep interfering. I realize that now."

"You're not interfering, Daddy. You're doing what every other daddy who cares about his child would do. And just so you'll know, Curtis is not interested in me for my money. When I go out with him, he always pays the check. I've already told him that I'd give up the generous allowance you give me every week and my inheritance if he wants me to. Vera can have it all!"

"'Vera can have it all? BAH!" Daddy roared. "We'll see about that!"

"Is that why Mr. Baskerville is with you now? You're changing your will again?"

"Don't you worry about my will!" Daddy said sharply in a very loud voice. When he spoke again a couple of seconds later, his voice was so weak and hollow I had to press the telephone closer to my ear so I could hear him. "Now, if you don't mind, let me finish up my business with Donald. I don't feel well and I need to get some rest."

"Good-bye, Daddy." It was so hard for me to hang up. I was tempted to go back to the hospital and spend as much time with him as they'd let me. I even thought about spending the night in his hospital room.

Since I had decided to delay my departure from the house and my marriage, I knew that it was going to be harder than ever for me to sleep under the same roof with Bo and Vera. Especially after the way she had exploded when I told her about Curtis and me at the hospital today.

If me ending my marriage was having this much of an impact on Daddy and Vera, I couldn't imagine how it was going to affect Bo. But I had made up my mind, and nothing was going to make me change it.

CHAPTER 59

SARAH

ABOUT TWO HOURS AFTER MY TELEPHONE CONVERSATION WITH Daddy, I heard Vera and Bo enter the house. A few minutes later, I heard Cash's voice. I happened to be standing at the top of the upstairs landing, so I couldn't really make out what they were saying until I eased down a few steps. Then I heard Vera say, "I'll check on her." I knew she meant me, so I scrambled back up the stairs and sprinted down the hall to my bedroom.

When Vera tapped lightly on my door a few minutes later, I was stretched out in my bed. "Come . . . in," I said, speaking in a voice that was as weak as I could make it sound.

The door swung open immediately. I couldn't understand why she even bothered to be nice enough to knock, especially after our heated conversation today. She usually just barged in.

"Oh. I just wanted to check and see how you're feeling," she said, giving me one of her fake smiles. She had had so many face-lifts and other procedures on her face, sometimes it looked like she was smiling even when she wasn't. But this time the ends of her lips curled up so high her mouth looked like a horseshoe. "I'm really sorry about what happened at the hospital. I was pretty mean to you and I'm so sorry. You know that wasn't the real me. I didn't mean any of those nasty things I said."

"I didn't either," I said, sitting up on the bed. "Uh, was that Bo downstairs I heard?"

Vera glanced at the door and nodded. "He and Cash were just pulling up as I arrived."

We looked at each other for a long time. "I'm sure he'll come up to see you in a few minutes. He swung by the hospital to visit Kenneth on his way home."

"Did Daddy tell him . . . ?"

"That you're leaving him?" Vera shook her head. "I am sure Kenneth feels the same way I do. You should be the one to tell Bo you're leaving him for that security guard."

"I thought you wanted to prepare Bo before I told him."

"Well, I can still do that. I won't tell him exactly why you're leaving, just that you are. He probably knows the rest anyway. And the more I thought about that part, he should hear it from you."

"Uh-huh. Well, I will tell him when the time is right. Right now I'm more concerned about not upsetting Daddy any more. If Bo does something crazy when I tell him I'm leaving him, like punch me in the nose and Daddy finds out, Daddy will be even more upset than he already is." Vera looked like she wanted to punch me in the nose herself.

"I doubt if it'll come to that. Bo's not a violent man."

"He told me he wanted to kill his ex. That sounds pretty violent to me."

"He's a changed man now. Listen, sugar, you look so tired. Why don't you just get some more rest and I'll keep Bo occupied for a while. He had a rough day, so the first thing he did when he got inside was make himself a stiff drink. Let him relax for a little while." Vera glanced at the door again and then back at me, trying her best to look casual.

"Thanks, Vera."

"Are you hungry? Do you want me to have Delia bring you something to nibble on?"

"Thanks, but I'm not hungry." I turned onto my side so that my back was to Vera. I hoped she would take the hint and get the hell out of my room. She did.

I waited ten minutes before I eased off the bed and padded down the hallway to my old bedroom. It had been a few days since

I'd eavesdropped through the air duct. As soon as my ear was in place, I heard the last thing in the world I expected to hear.

"He told us out of his own mouth that a lot of people want to see him dead. Nobody will suspect us." It was Bo talking. I couldn't make any sense out of what he'd just said. But when he spoke again, what he said chilled me to the bone. "I just hope it doesn't hurt Sarah too much. She told me that funerals have a bad effect on her."

What the fuck was he talking about? But the biggest question spinning around in my head was *whose* funeral was he talking about that would have a bad effect on me? And who was the person that a lot of people wanted to see dead? Curtis was the only person I knew of who had enemies who wanted to see him dead. . . . *OH NO!* The thought that my husband was planning to kill my lover was so overwhelming I couldn't believe it. I had to find out what was going on and I had to find out fast.

"I'm picking up the gun tomorrow," Vera said, speaking in such a hard voice I could just picture the sneer on her face.

"You sure it can't be traced?" Cash asked. "We can't afford no slipups."

"If you don't want to get involved, don't!" Bo yelled at him. "I can take care of this issue on my own anyway."

"No, you are not going by yourself. Cash is still going with you like we originally planned. If somebody sees you coming or going by yourself, they might get nosy. If you and Cash roll up into that place, jive-talking with each other, those lowlifes will think you're just another couple of middle-aged broken-down brothers like they are. I'll pick up some cheap outfits from Goodwill tomorrow for you both to wear."

"Why can't we dress like we always do?" Cash whined. "I told you years ago, right after Kenneth gave me such a good-paying job, that I'd never wear no used or hand-me-down clothes again."

"Don't be a fool, *fool*! You can't go to Curtis's neighborhood wearing one of your Armani suits and your custom-made shoes. For one thing, you'd probably get jumped and robbed as soon as you get out of the car. And speaking of cars, leave your SUV at the house, Bo. I'll rent a Toyota or some other piece of shit, cheap-ass car," Vera said. It sounded like she was the one in charge. But at this point I was not sure of just what she was in charge of. All I could determine so far was that it had something to do with Curtis! She didn't make me wait long to find out the rest. "I did some snooping around in his neighborhood. I went over there earlier and approached a few folks on the street near Curtis's building. I pretended to be a survey taker for Walmart. Those idiots are so dumb I could have claimed to be working for the CIA and they would have believed me. Anyway, I told them that Curtis and his mama had been randomly selected to receive a huge prize. I had a clipboard in my hand and pretended to be writing down everything they told me. I told them it's a surprise deal, so I needed to get some information about Curtis and his mama's schedules from the neighbors without them knowing. Those nosy idiots were hesitant at first. The questions they asked *me* made me feel like a bill collector or process server trying to track down somebody! I'm sure that's what some of them thought at first. But as soon as I passed out a few bucks and a few twenty-five-dollar gift certificates, those fools started singing like a Christmas choir."

"Vera! You went over there snooping around? Woman, are you crazy?" Bo hollered.

"No, I'm not crazy!"

"You must be! Those porch monkeys are ignorant as hell, but don't you think that at least one of them will remember a woman like you asking questions about their neighbors? All we need is for the cops to talk to the wrong one after . . . after we do what we have to do."

"Bo, I'm disappointed in you. Do you think I'm stupid enough to go over to that place asking questions about Curtis without a disguise?"

"I hope not. And I hope it was a damn good disguise. I know a lot of other black women are running around with blond hair like you, but you dress as fancy as Michelle Obama and Oprah put together. You'd stick out like an elephant in a spa."

"Ha!" Vera roared with laughter. "I wore a frizzy black wig, one of Sarah's old mammy-made dresses that she bought before I got her to stop shopping in discount stores, and some low-heeled pumps I picked up at Payless. And I wore some glasses that made me look like the kind of nerdy woman who'd be roaming around taking a survey. Anyway, the first old bat I approached told me that Curtis's mama leaves for work around six every evening except Saturday and Sunday. Another neighbor told me he's almost *always* home alone every Friday night watching *Sanford and Son* reruns. His mama works a split shift every Friday night and never gets off at the same time. He has to be available so he can pick her up when she calls. Can you imagine a man with such a dull life?"

"Why in the world would Sarah want to be with such a straight-up loser?" Cash wondered. "She ain't just licking the jar—she's scraping the bone! Bo, my man, this must make you feel like a used ass-wipe! I mean, having your woman choose a man as low on the food chain as Curtis Thompson over you must be hellish! I could understand if she was taking off with a banker or a rapper, or at least a gangster. But she's leaving you for a hood rat that ain't got a pot to piss in!"

"Don't worry about how I'm feeling. You worry about yourself and keep an eye on your own woman!" Bo boomed. "Vera, your plan better work and you better pray that nobody suspects us."

"Be serious! Only a fool would think anybody else but the thugs killed Curtis. Even a dumb bunny like Sarah! Remember how she told us about all the murdered friends' funerals she attended when she lived in that war zone?" Vera hollered. "Nobody in their right mind would suspect people like us of killing a hood rat. If anything, people will recall how this family tried to help Curtis improve his life by you and Kenneth giving him a job and making such a fuss over him in front of other employees. Now listen up. I think the sooner we get this done, the better. This coming Friday. I'm having my Botox treatment and a small blister removed from the back of my neck the following Monday, and I won't be in the mood to console Sarah. I'd like to do *that* on the weekend before and get it over with. If she's still grieving Curtis's death longer than she should, she can cry on your shoulder, Bo."

The Friday in question was two days from now.

"Shouldn't we wait until Kenneth leaves the hospital?" Bo asked. "It's bad enough we can't let the old goat in on our plan. But the least we can do is let him get his strength back. He'll need it when the time comes for him to placate Sarah after her loverboy gets what he's got coming."

"No, we can't wait. Kenneth might leave the hospital in a hearse. But if he's going to get well, when he hears the news that the gold-digging motherfucker that broke up his daughter's marriage got killed during a home invasion, it'll make him get well a lot quicker!"

"Besides, we need to complete this project before Sarah bolts," Cash threw in.

Project? These cold-blooded monsters had the nerve to call other people thugs and hood rats! And here they were plotting to kill an innocent man and referring to their crime as a project! My ears were burning from what I'd heard so far. My head felt like it wanted to disintegrate. I was so stunned and angry that *I* wanted to kill somebody and I was one of the good guys.

"If we don't, we'll have another mess on our hands, getting her back into this house after her boo has been killed. Hell, she might even suspect us of being behind it!" Bo guffawed.

"One more thing, Cash." Vera paused. "I just want to remind you again not to let Collette know anything about this. She's got a mouth on her like a fishnet!"

"I won't tell her nothing!" Cash said hotly. "For all I know, she could be messing around on me! I see the way she be eyeballing other dudes when we go out. If we pull this off with Curtis, then something might have to happen to the suckers Collette's probably fooling around with!"

"Let's stay on track now. We are not here to discuss Collette and her punks," Vera said calmly. "We need to stay focused on Sarah. Now, listen up. Shoot him in the head. That'll do the trick. In case Curtis's mama stays home from work Friday night and she's in the apartment, do her too. And a head shot for her too. That'd make it look even better. Competent thugs don't leave witnesses behind anyway. That's why only the incompetent thugs go to jail."

The silence that followed for about ten seconds was excruciating.

Cash broke it, speaking in a nervous voice. "His mama? Oh Lord! I don't know if I can kill an old woman. What if somebody else is there with him?"

"I don't care if the *Reverend Jesse Jackson* is in the neighborhood on one of his brown-nosing, publicity-seeking visits! If he gets in the way, blow his ass to Kingdom Come too. Don't leave behind any witnesses. Period!" Vera snarled. "If we're going to do this thing, we might as well do it right. Shit."

"Okay. Vera, you pick up that gun from your contact tomorrow and the Goodwill clothes and it's on," Bo said. "I can't wait to see that motherfucker's face when I blow his brains out!"

I didn't need to hear anything else. I wobbled up off the floor and padded back to my bedroom so I could organize my thoughts. I didn't know what to do next. I couldn't run downstairs and confront the people who were planning to kill the man I loved. And I certainly couldn't go to Daddy with this information, or anybody else.

I was back in bed when Bo entered our bedroom about twenty minutes later. He whistled as he undressed and got in bed. Still whistling, he nudged my shoulder and patted my butt, but I didn't respond. He stopped whistling. When he reached over and squeezed one of my breasts and then kissed me on the lips, I thought I'd vomit. It was pure torture even being in the same room with the man who was planning to ruin my life.

I didn't care how hard Bo tried to arouse me, I ignored him. He didn't try too hard or too long. He gave up and fifteen minutes later, he was snoring like a moose. I waited a few minutes more and then eased out of bed and went into the bathroom and had myself a good cry.

I was up against a brick wall: Cash, Vera, and Bo were on one side and Curtis and I were on the other.

What was I supposed to do now? I couldn't prove what I had

just heard, so I couldn't go to the cops. I knew enough about them to know that they wouldn't do anything until a crime had been committed anyway.

Warning Curtis by telling him everything I'd heard was out of the question. So was begging him to leave town. For one thing, he was not a coward. If the thugs who had been taunting him had not scared him off, he wouldn't leave town to avoid a confrontation with Bo and Cash. Knowing Curtis, he would be prepared for their attack with a gun of his own. As an ex–gang banger, he'd grown up fighting battles with men a lot more vicious than Bo and Cash. If Curtis did get a gun to protect himself, there was no telling how this mess would turn out. If he killed Bo and Cash, even if they broke into his apartment, his life would never be the same. And mine wouldn't be either. I couldn't imagine how something like that would affect Daddy.

My mind was spinning with all kinds of outrageous thoughts about how I could save Curtis. I even considered telling him I was pregnant with his baby and that we needed to run off somewhere together. That way I wouldn't have to tell him about his pending murder. But no matter where we went, we'd never be happy if he knew what I knew. He would keep in touch with his clingy mama, and sooner or later, he'd tell her too much and she'd blow the whistle on us.

There was only one thing left for me to do. I'd be in Curtis's apartment when Bo and Curtis busted in to kill him. And since they couldn't leave any witnesses, they'd have to kill me too. In death, Curtis and I could be together.

I couldn't think of any other way to end this mess.

CHAPTER 60

VERA

When I called up Ricky the next morning, I didn't even have to tell him why I was calling. He answered the question I was going to ask him right away.

"Vera, I got you a gun like you asked me to. A Glock. It's real easy to use and nobody can trace it. It, uh, my contact told me it fell off a truck in Oakland, so it's never been registered."

"Good work! You will get a major bonus for this!"

"There's only one thing about this gun—I couldn't get my hands on no silencer like you wanted."

"Oh well. That's really not a big deal." I wasn't going to worry about a little thing like not having a silencer. The sound of gunfire wouldn't even faze those idiots in Curtis's neighborhood. Last Saturday the news reported that three people on his block had died from gunshot wounds in three separate incidents on the same day! Several people had "witnessed" the shootings but so far nobody had come forward and probably wouldn't. For once I was glad that the people in the ghetto didn't like to talk to the cops. There was a strong possibility that even if somebody saw Bo and Cash lurking around Curtis's place—before and after the shooting—they still would not blab to the cops. Now that we had the gun, it was going to be smooth sailing from this point on. However, I still couldn't afford to get too sloppy by telling Ricky too much.

"Baby, I know you told me not to ask no questions, but in case you want to tell me more, I'm listening."

"You can stop listening. This does not concern you."

"You trusted me enough to ask me to get you a gun. Why can't you trust me enough to tell me what's going on?"

Even though I had convinced myself that killing Curtis and getting away with it was going to be as easy and simple as a walk in Golden Gate Park, I knew it was in my best interest to be careful who I discussed it with. Other than Bo and Cash, nobody else needed to know. Ricky certainly didn't. For all I knew, he could get into more trouble and cut a deal with the authorities by ratting me out! "Don't ask any more questions," I said firmly. "I'll see you in a bit."

I hung up fast. I still had things to do to make sure this project went well. I had never committed a crime before, and I prayed that our getting rid of Curtis would be the first and last one. This involved more work than I had expected.

I drove to Mission Street, one of the roughest, seediest areas in San Francisco. Hopeless-looking people in this predominately Hispanic neighborhood meandered about like lost sheep, babbling in machine-gun Spanish and broken English. The smell of urine, vomit, stale rice, greasy tacos, and fried bananas seemed to be everywhere. I could smell it all even though every window in my car was closed. I parked on the street and checked my purse to make sure my can of mace was easy to reach. It was a good thing I was paying attention or I would have stepped into a pile of shit on the ground as soon as I stepped out of my car.

I strolled down the street, walking with caution. Like I was afraid I'd step on a crack or stumble upon another pile of shit. This part of town was just as filthy, primitive, and gloomy as the one that Curtis lived in, so I knew I wouldn't run into anybody I knew.

I headed to a Goodwill store two blocks from where I'd parked. I had to step over two bums lying on the ground near the entrance. I shook my head. I couldn't believe that Sarah was willing to give up a life of luxury to move into a neighborhood with the same crap as this one!

The people inside the Goodwill looked and smelled just as gruesome as the ones outside. I didn't want to spend any more time in a hole like this than I had to. I quickly picked out some tattered jeans, plaid shirts with patches on each elbow, and some black hooded sweatshirts for Bo and Cash. I couldn't find any beaten up old tennis shoes for them to wear at Goodwill, but I found some at another nearby thrift store. I had never purchased ski masks before in my life and wasn't sure where to find them. I checked in three different stores and didn't find any. Just as I was about to give up and have Bo and Cash wear a pair of my old stockings on their faces, I came across a sporting goods store that sold ski masks. I had no idea that planning a crime could be so complicated! That damn Sarah had caused me so much trouble I was going to enjoy watching her mourn the death of her lover.

About an hour after I'd left the Mission District, I called the hospital to check on Kenneth. His nurse was giving him a bath, so I told her to let him know that I'd be coming to see him within the hour.

When I arrived at the hospital, Kenneth was sitting up in bed. Boy did he look bad! I had just seen him the day before and he'd looked bad then, but now he looked like he had aged ten years! I was surprised that he was still alive.

"Hi, baby," I said, leaning over his bed. He didn't react when I kissed his forehead. He smelled like sweat and liniment, so kissing him was not a pleasant experience for me—not that it ever was anyway. He also looked like he'd lost about ten pounds in the past week. His face looked drawn and emaciated and as dry and tough as old leather. His eyes looked like two black holes that somebody had poked into his face. He hadn't shaved since he'd been admitted. His brittle whiskers irritated my face and smudged my makeup when I kissed him. "I'm glad to see you looking so good, honey."

"Hello, Vera," he mumbled, looking at me like he was seeing me for the first time.

"I couldn't wait to get back here, baby. I'm so lonely," I lied, giving him one of my biggest smiles.

"Humph! I bet!" Kenneth reared his head back on his pillow and gave me a look that made me nervous. I was confident that he didn't know about me and Ricky or any of the other dozen or more boy toys I'd spent time with over the years. I had always been discreet. Whenever I even thought that somebody was getting suspicious of my activities, I slowed down until the heat was off. That little issue with the fibroids and my outpatient surgery had been a blessing in disguise. Had that not happened, I may have gotten careless. Ricky had been pushing my buttons and licking my pussy so well, I had been acting like a love-starved teenager and I'd done a few stupid things. One night when I thought I was in the house alone, that nosy-ass bitch Collette almost caught me giving Ricky some phone sex. And then there was the time that Bo noticed bite marks on my thigh when he and I both happened to show up at the gym at the same time. I was a lot more careful now. I had never been busted before in my life because I was too slick and I knew when to slow down. And anyway, if Bo, Cash, or Collette had proof of my affairs, I was not worried about them exposing me. They wouldn't dare. I was the one who had made it possible for them to live the lifestyle of the rich and famous. That's why I couldn't imagine why Kenneth had given *me* such a guarded look.

"What do you mean by that, honey?" I asked. My heart was racing and my blood pressure was rising like a tide. Since I'd found out about Kenneth and his affair with Sarah's mother, he'd been too afraid to approach another woman. He knew how much he had hurt me and had promised that he would spend the rest of his life making up for that. He didn't want to do, say, or even think about anything else that would hurt me again and jeopardize our marriage. With all of that in mind, I couldn't imagine him even *thinking* that I was cheating!

However, I was still nervous.

"Don't worry about it, Vera," he responded, his eyes on mine. He had replaced the guarded look with a scowl. That made me even more nervous. Was he mad at me about something? I wondered. If so, *what*?

"Uh, everything and everybody is well," I told him, trying to sound upbeat, hoping it would cheer him up a bit. "Bo's got everything under control at the store."

Kenneth let out a loud rattle of a breath and blinked. "How is my daughter?" I was disappointed that he had not asked me how I was doing, but I managed to give him a smile anyway. I had never known a man who got so giddy when it came to his daughter. You would have thought that heifer was the Queen of Sheba.

"Sarah? Oh, she's fine. Bo told me he was going to take her out to dinner this evening. But first he's going to bring her to see you."

"I pray to God she doesn't leave Bo! She broke down and told me she's in love with Curtis and is going to move in with him. I don't know if I believe her, though. The girl is going through a phase. She's depressed and confused. But I suspect she's got just a mild crush on Curtis because he came to her assistance in the parking lot the day she lost the baby." Kenneth began to talk so fast he had to slow down and catch his breath. "I wish I could talk some sense into her head." He paused and shook his head. In all the years that I'd known this man, I had never seen him look so hurt. I was glad that I was not the one who was causing him so much pain. "So she's still at the house?"

"Oh, yes! And to be honest with you, I don't believe she's going to do what she said. I had a little talk with her yesterday, and I think she's giving it a lot of thought. I don't believe she's stupid enough to move from a palace to that flophouse Curtis lives in!"

"What if she does? She sounded real serious to me," Kenneth said, coughing. The longer I stood over his bed, the worse he looked. Now his lips were so dry they looked like metal. Sweat and dead skin had formed a necklace around his neck.

"Well, even if she does, I don't think she'll be gone too long," I declared. Kenneth nodded, so what I'd just said must have been what he wanted to hear. "Once she sees just how bad off she'd be shacking up with that security guard, she'll come running back home so fast it will make your head spin."

Kenneth nodded again. "I hope you're right. As long as Sarah hasn't carried out her threat to leave, there's still some hope. We just might get lucky and Curtis will be removed from our lives somehow."

"You mean one of the people he ratted out to the cops might finally kill him?"

"Vera, that's not what I meant. I thought that maybe he'd meet another girl or move away to Detroit like he said his mama was talking about doing."

"Him moving away would be nice, but I don't think that's going to happen. At least not in time to keep Sarah from making a huge mistake. I honestly feel that Curtis's life is in danger. From what he told us at the dinner table, his name is on more than one hit list." I didn't think it would hurt to remind Kenneth about the danger Curtis faced every day. So when he got what he had coming, Kenneth wouldn't be surprised.

"Oh, I don't believe those guys are serious! The ones who threatened Curtis are probably just a bunch of teenagers trying to flex their muscles."

"Why do you think that? You know how dangerous that part of town is and the young gangsters nowadays are even more dangerous than the OGs were back in the day, Kenneth."

"That's the point. If a real gangster wanted to get rid of somebody, they wouldn't put it off. Curtis is not in hiding, so if somebody wanted him dead, they'd know where to find him and he would have been dead long before now." I was glad to hear Kenneth chuckle. "I just hope that Sarah will see how little Curtis has to offer her and what a potentially dangerous situation she'll be putting herself in." He paused and let out a great sigh. "However, despite what he's done, I wouldn't want anything bad to happen to the boy. After all, he's . . . he's only a man and his only crime was falling in love with Sarah."

"I hope nothing bad happens to him, either," I said, sounding like I meant it.

Kenneth closed his eyes. I took a deep breath, folded my arms, and remained silent. When he didn't open his eyes after several seconds had passed, I realized he had dozed off. I went to the window and looked out, wondering what things would be like if Sarah had not invaded our lives. One thing I knew for sure: I wouldn't be conspiring to have a man murdered.

Five minutes later, when I returned to the side of the bed, Kenneth was snoring like an ox. Had he not been snoring and his chest rising with each breath, I would have sworn that he was dead.

It was almost over.

I had a late lunch downtown at a popular Italian restaurant called Buca di Beppo on Howard Street. It was a cheap establishment with outlandish Italian décor and black and white poster-size pictures of every Italian entertainer from Frank Sinatra to Sophia Loren on the walls. But the food was delicious and so were some of the male servers. This was where I'd met my first boy toy many years ago, an Italian stallion name Mario. His dick was not that long, but it was as thick as a baseball bat. I had to dump him a year later when I found out he was swinging his baseball bat at gay men on a regular basis.

After I'd gulped down three glasses of chardonnay, a salad, and a lunch-size pasta plate, I headed to the next stop on my itinerary—Bloomingdale's, a few blocks away.

The brisk walk helped me digest my lunch, and since I hadn't been to the gym all week, I needed the exercise.

The clerks in the women's department, the makeup and perfume counter, and the purse and shoe department knew me well. This was one of my favorite stores.

As soon as I entered the men's clothing department for the first time in my life, a grinning, slick-haired, hawk-nosed clerk who looked like somebody straight out of *The Sopranos* approached me.

"How can I help madam today?" the clerk asked, grinning so hard now his teeth looked like they were trying to escape.

"I need to purchase a dark suit for my husband," I told him.

"Armani will do if you have something in stock in my husband's size."

"Very good. Armani! And will this suit be for a special occasion?"

"Something like that. My husband is going to be buried in it," I said without hesitation.

CHAPTER 61

KENNETH

It amazed me how suddenly things could change. I had loved Vera with all my heart since the day I first laid eyes on her. I couldn't stand the sight of her now. It was hard to believe that she was the same woman I had loved so unconditionally for so many years! But the woman that I had loved had existed only in my eyes. The truth was, she was two different people. She had a dark side and that was her true personality.

One thing I knew for sure was that Ricky was not her first lover. I had no evidence, but just based on what Tim had told me, I knew that cheating was something she was comfortable doing. The thought of her attending movies and going out to eat with that Ricky punk in public made my skin crawl. How stupid can a woman be? She obviously wasn't afraid that somebody who knew us would see her! I'd always believed that if a person was going to be unfaithful, do it right. Don't be seen out in public with your lover, especially in the city you live in. Don't run off at the mouth about your affairs to your friends. Be a smart cheater. Unfortunately, even smart cheaters like me still slip up and get caught anyway.

Had I not gotten Sarah's mother pregnant, Vera would have never known about that affair. It pleased me to know that she wasn't aware of all the others. The main thing that had eased the burden of my guilt was the fact that since I told Vera about Sarah's mother and me, I had not even looked at another woman. Vera must have decided to cheat on me to get back at me.

It didn't matter now.

All that did matter was that my wife was in a full-blown relationship with another man at a time when I needed her full attention the most. I was probably on my deathbed and here she was going out to dinner and movies with a lover young enough to be her *grandson*! I had no idea how long she'd been with this Ricky person, or how much of my money she'd spent on him. And I didn't want to know. I knew all I needed to know. But there was much more. A few hours later, around five, Tim called me up.

"I know I've hit you with a lot lately and I know you told me you had the information you needed, but I found out something else that you *really* need to know about," Tim told me.

"Is it about my wife?"

"I'm afraid so. I'll come over in about an hour if you feel up to having a visitor."

"Not really, old man. I'm really tired and I need to get some sleep." The truth of the matter was, I was feeling so rotten it felt like any breath could be my last. I honestly didn't know if I'd still be alive an hour later. The only thing that kept me going was the fact that Sarah had just called me up and told me she'd be coming to see me in the morning. "You can tell me over the phone."

"Your wife recently visited the neighborhood where your daughter's lover lives. She posed as some kind of promotions individual."

"What the hell did she do that for?"

"I guess she figured it was the only way she could get the information on this Curtis Thompson for whatever reason she needs it for. Maybe she's putting together a dossier on the fellow. One that would help her convince your daughter that this man is nothing but a loser and that she'd have a shit future with him. Anyway, she passed out several Walmart gift certificates, and Curtis's neighbors told her everything she wanted to know. When she ran out of those inducements, she bought one lucky fellow a chicken dinner."

"Hmmm. That's interesting, Tim. But it doesn't matter why

Vera was gathering information on Curtis. Even if she succeeded in convincing Sarah to sever her relationship with him, that wouldn't help Vera. Her goose is already cooked! She's an even bigger whore than my daughter! I will deal with Vera when the time is right. In the meantime, I wonder why she would check up on Curtis and not tell me about it."

"I'm here to help you as much as I can, buddy. But I can't answer that question."

"I want you to keep an eye on Vera until I get up out of this hospital. The more dirt I have on her, the deeper the hole I can bury her in—and I'd like to throw a snake in behind her!"

"There's just one more thing."

"What?"

"At her request, her lover procured a gun for her."

That piece of information felt like a brick going upside my head. The throbbing was so painful I had to shake my head and rub it. "A gun? A real gun?" I didn't realize just how dumb my last question sounded until it had slid out of my mouth.

"As real and as deadly as they come—a Glock."

"Tim, you're damn good at what you do. How in the world did you find out about my wife getting a gun?"

Tim chuckled softly. "Because I am damn good at what I do. But a good investigator never reveals his sources. Even though you and I are friends, I still have to remain professional, right? I will tell you this much, though; one of my associates is an expert hacker. She can access anything—phone lines, computers, even bank accounts. I had her tap into Ricky's home phone and use a recording device that can't be detected or traced. Unfortunately, by then your wife had already initiated her request for a gun, so I don't have all the details."

"Why would Vera need a gun?"

"Now that I don't know. If you'd like to hear the recording, I'd be happy to oblige."

"No. I don't need to hear that right now. What else did they discuss?"

"It was a brief conversation. Neither one of them mentioned

names or what the gun will be used for. But something tells me we will find out soon enough. The device is still on Ricky's phone, so if they resume that particular conversation, I'll let you know. All I can tell you at this point is that your wife's lover has picked up a gun that your wife requested. She sounded very eager to get her hands on it, so she's probably picked it up by now."

"Vera hates guns! She's afraid of guns!"

"That may be true. But apparently none of that stopped her from requesting one."

"If she needs a gun for protection, she could have come to me about that. I have an extensive gun collection and she knows about it."

"Excuse me for saying this, but I doubt if she would want to use one of your guns for whatever it is she's planning."

"What makes you so sure of that?"

"Well, for one thing, the gun she got is unregistered."

"Unregistered? Why in the world . . ." I was so dumbfounded I couldn't even finish my sentence.

"There's only one reason in the world I can think of. If a crime is committed with this particular firearm, it won't be traceable."

I held the telephone in front of my face and looked at it like Tim's words had just scorched my ear. "A crime?" I started talking again before the phone was even back up to my ear. "Are you telling me that my wife is planning to commit a crime with a gun?"

"I don't know what she's planning to do. But that would be a good guess. I'm sorry to have to tell you this, buddy."

"Damn! She couldn't be thinking about . . ."

"Thinking about what?"

"I've got to hurry and get up out of this hospital. My life is falling apart all around me." Something I didn't want to think about stormed my mind. "Vera's been looking depressed lately. Real depressed. Lord I hope that woman's not thinking about ending it all."

"Suicide? You think she's depressed enough to consider something that extreme?" Tim snorted. "No way, my man. If your wife is considering taking her own life, she wouldn't care if the gun was registered or not. And from what I know about women, especially elegant, vain women like your bride, they like to take themselves out in style. Typically, they slip into their favorite negligee and overdose on sleeping pills or they loop nooses around their dainty necks. They wouldn't want to be remembered as a bloody, mangled mess. Not even in death. Therefore, they don't go for guns, knives, jumping in front of trains, or diving off the Golden Gate Bridge. But let's not jump to conclusions. For all we know, Vera could have requested that weapon for someone else to use."

I had not expected the disturbing news that Tim had just delivered. But I had a feeling that news even worse than this was in the making.

"Thanks, Tim. I've heard enough for now. You can expect a nice bonus from me for this one."

"I'm glad you want me to keep an eye on your wife. Especially now that we know about the gun."

"Tim, I know all I want to know."

"Are you sure you don't want to know what she's planning to do with that gun?"

"Well . . ."

"Tell me now. Can you think of anybody your wife would want to do harm?"

"Not really." I sucked on my teeth and gave Tim's question a little more consideration. "Now that you asked, she dislikes a few people, my daughter's lover especially. But as long as I've known Vera, she's never even hurt a fly. I don't think she hates Curtis enough to shoot him."

"Dude, there's a first time for everything."

"Yeah, I know there is. Tim, I'm feeling like hell right now, so I really need to get off this phone. Call me again tomorrow morning and I'll let you know what to do next."

I had no idea that this would be my last conversation with Tim.

CHAPTER 62

SARAH

THE NEXT MORNING I GOT UP EARLIER THAN USUAL. EVERYBODY ELSE was still in bed when I left the house.

Last night, after Bo had been asleep for a couple of hours, I tiptoed into the bathroom with my cell phone and dialed Curtis's number. He didn't answer so I left him a voice mail.

"Curtis, as soon as you get my message, call me on my cell phone. I'm going to leave it on all night. If it's not convenient for me to talk when you call me back, I'll pretend you've called a wrong number and then I'll call you back as soon as I can," I told him. "It's *really* important." I wanted to add, "It's a matter of life and death." But there was no need for me to tell him that. He'd find that out soon enough.

It was Thursday. He had one more day to live. And so did I.

Knowing that my time was running out, I was determined to do everything I needed to do. My "bucket list" was so short I had only one item on it. And that was I had to see my daddy one last time.

Before I went to the hospital, I cruised around the city, looking at some of my favorite spots. I drove to the graffiti-covered apartment building where I had lived with my mother until she got married and dumped me on Grandma Lilly. The building had not changed at all. Several generations of bitter-looking people still occupied the porches, the balconies, and the street in front of it. As usual, most of them were drinking beer and hard liquor straight out of cans, bottles, and mayonnaise jars. Discarded furniture, dog shit, and other litter covered various sections of the ground like an ugly, unfinished patchwork quilt. Next I drove to the building where I had lived with Grandma Lilly. I was pleasantly surprised to see that the owner had at least painted it from a dull shade of gray to a light blue. I didn't see any of my old friends and that saddened me. Had there been more time, I would have tracked down some of my former homegirls. I knew they would have appreciated inheriting my designer outfits, my top-of-the-line electronics, and my Jaguar. I would have even greased their palms with a few thousand dollars. But in a way it was a good thing I didn't have time to do any of that. People would have started asking me questions as to why I was giving my stuff away. And I wouldn't have been able to tell them. But there was another reason why I was glad I didn't have a lot of time left. I was afraid that if I really thought about what I was going to do, I'd change my mind. And I didn't want to back out now. With Curtis dead, my life would not be worth living.

I didn't realize how long I had been driving around until I glanced at my gas gauge and saw that I was almost empty. By the time I gassed up my car and stopped for a cup of coffee at a Starbucks across the street from the gas station, it was almost ten. Before I finished my coffee, I called Daddy's hospital room.

"I want to come see you this morning," I told him as soon as he answered. "Do you feel like having company?"

"I'd love to see you, honey. But I'm not doing too well right now. I had a really rough night."

"Oh?"

"They tell me I had a mild stroke a couple of hours ago. They hadn't even noticed something else was wrong until they had poked and prodded me for a while."

"You had a stroke? I'm definitely coming over there!"

"I'm fine now, sugar! If you do come today, wait at least a couple of hours. By then they'll have finished running a few tests and poking and prodding me some more. As a matter of fact, I doubt if they'll let you in if you come now anyway."

"Daddy, I'm family. I don't know much about hospital rules,

but I think you need to have a family member present in case . . . in case your situation gets worse. I don't want you to die alone!" I immediately regretted my last sentence. "I didn't mean that!" I said quickly. For a woman who had only one more day to live, I didn't understand why it was so important to me now what I said about death.

"Honey, I know you didn't mean that. And that's not going to happen." Daddy snorted. He suddenly sounded like he was as strong as a bull. "I told Vera the same thing a little while ago when she called."

"Oh. What else did she say?"

"Not much. I told her the same thing I told you—call me or come see me later in the day. Like around noon or so."

"All right, Daddy." I hung up and ordered another cup of coffee, this one to go. I was just about to leave when my cell phone rang. It was Curtis.

"I'm sorry I'm just getting back to you, honey. My mama and one of her friends went to one of those Indian casinos near Sacramento and had car trouble. I had to go pick them up. You know what a rattrap I drive. By the time I got up there, it had conked out and had to be towed. I had to call around to find somebody to come pick us up. I just got home a few minutes ago."

"I'm so glad you called. I was going crazy," I said in a shaky voice.

"I guess you know I got fired for coming in late too often. Had that been the real reason, everybody else would have been fired by now. Bo didn't say anything about you and me, but everybody at the store knows. You know how Cash and Collette like to spread gossip. Anyway, Bo gave me my pink slip and he had two other security guards escort me off the premises. They even checked my backpack to make sure I wasn't walking out of there with any unpaid for merchandise."

"I'm not surprised he fired you. But I'm surprised he hasn't done it before now. Besides, the way things have been going, you would have had to quit soon anyway." I sighed. "Things have been so tense in our house lately I can barely breathe. I didn't realize until now just how sick and tired I am of everybody I live with trying to control me. Including my daddy."

"Well, you won't have to put up with that too much longer. You know I won't try to control you. I'm going to treat you like an equal partner, not a child like everybody else has been doing. When will you be moving out?"

"Uh, real soon. I've already packed up some of my stuff."

"My buddy downstairs has a truck."

"Oh! I don't need a truck. I'm only bringing some of my clothes and I can fit them in my car. Besides, I don't think *you* should be coming over here with a truck to help me move. That would be pretty stupid."

"Well, we've done some pretty stupid shit already."

"I know that. Uh, I want to come see you tomorrow night."

"That's cool. What time are you coming?"

"I'll come after your mama leaves for work. She is going to work tomorrow night, right?"

"She is as far as I know. Listen, I've been meaning to talk to you about her. My mama knows everything about us. I know you think she's not the friendliest person in the world, but she is pretty cool. Once you get to know her, you'll see what I mean." Curtis laughed. "And by the way, the same buddy downstairs with the truck, he manages that body shop I've been doing piece work for now and then. He's going to let me work full-time, starting next week."

"That's nice, honey."

"And Mama said she could help you get on at that warehouse where she works. You don't have to work if you don't want to, though. But if we want to get our own place eventually, and in a much better neighborhood, we'll both have to be bringing in some money. Mama's got her a new man friend and I have a feeling she's anxious for me to leave so she can move into his place with him." Curtis laughed again.

"I'll come over around eight tomorrow night. Do you want me to bring something?"

"A six-pack of Miller Lite and some smothered chicken from that place on Harrison Street like you brought the last time. I hope you can stay more than a few hours this time."

"I will be staying a lot longer than a few hours," I said. I had to force myself not to cry.

CHAPTER 63

VERA

BO ENTERED MY BEDROOM WITHOUT KNOCKING, BUT I DIDN'T MIND. He only did that when he had something important to tell me or ask me.

"Well, it's official," he started. He paused and began to pound his fist repeatedly into the palm of his other hand. "Sarah just told me with a straight face that she's leaving me for Curtis." He then turned with his fist poised to pound the wall facing my bed, but he didn't. He had told me that when Gladys told him she was leaving him for another man, he punched a hole in their bedroom wall. I made Bo promise me that day that he'd never do something that childish in my house. "I'm sorry," he said in a small voice. "I almost forgot where I was." Then he *smiled*!

"How did you react when Sarah told you she was leaving you?"

"I called her a few choice names and I raised my hand to slap her, but I didn't. I took a few deep breaths and told her we'd talk about it tonight when I come home. I also told her I wouldn't be home until around ten or so."

"Curtis will be dead by then. Or he should be."

"Uh-huh. He will."

Before I left my bedroom, I called the hospital to see how Kenneth was doing.

"Vera, I'm doing just fine," he told me. He sounded tired and impatient and I didn't really want to prolong the call anyway.

"I'm praying for you every hour on the hour, baby," I said in my sweetest voice.

"You keep doing that." Kenneth hung up before I could say another word. I knew that he belonged in the hospital and that he was on all kinds of medication, but it had affected his behavior in the strangest way. His whole personality had changed. He had never talked to me the way he'd been talking to me lately. I told myself that it was nothing to worry about. After all, he was a confused and elderly man, so he didn't know any better. However, something in the back of my mind kept nagging at me: Tim Larkin, the private investigator. Had Kenneth hired him to check up on me? I wondered. I didn't want to believe that he had. I had been careful, so Kenneth had no reason to think I was doing anything inappropriate with another man. And with Kenneth being so close to death's door, what good would it do for him to find out about Ricky and me now? At the end of the day as long as I ended up with a few million dollars—and stayed out of jail—it was all good.

I took a quick shower, got dressed, and pranced downstairs to the kitchen for breakfast where everybody except Sarah was already at the table enjoying Delia's homemade pancakes. As soon as I approached the breakfast table, everybody stopped talking.

I knew that Bo and Cash had not told Collette anything about what we were planning to do, but I was still paranoid. Especially when she gave me one of her sly looks like she was doing now.

"What do you have planned for today, Vera?" she asked. I noticed how she nudged Cash with her elbow as she stared at me, blinking like a damn night creature.

I cleared my throat and gave her one of my most annoyed looks. "Other than a hair appointment this afternoon, I don't have anything else planned. Why do you ask?"

"You've been real jumpy these last few days," Collette noticed. I wanted to slap that smirk off her face.

"The woman's husband is in critical condition. If it was me in that hospital bed, you'd be jumpy too," Cash said. For him to be such a nitwit, he occasionally said something smart. Then he turned to me and said one of the stupidest things he ever said! "Cuz, did you rent that car?"

I stopped breathing for a few seconds. Out of the corner of my eye, I saw Bo give Cash a look that was so full of contempt I was surprised Cash didn't turn to stone. "What car?" Bo asked.

"Yeah, what car? With all of the vehicles here, why would Vera need to rent one?" Collette wanted to know.

"I thought I heard you telling Kenneth over the phone this morning that your car was acting up and you was going to rent one for the weekend," Cash replied, his tongue snapping clumsily over each word.

"You heard wrong," I said casually. I sat down in the chair directly across from Bo. "There's not a thing wrong with my car." I looked up at Bo and he must have read my mind.

"I think my fan belt needs to be tightened up. Can you give me a ride to the store after you eat, Vera?" Bo said, winking.

"Why can't you ride with Cash and me?" Collette asked, wiping bits of poached egg off her lips and chin at the same time. "We're all going to the same place. But we won't be leaving for at least an hour, though."

Bo looked at his watch and frowned. "I can't wait that long." Then he looked at me, still frowning. "Some buyers from a couple of high schools are coming by this morning. That's a whole lot of computer sales. I need to be there in case they show up early." He rose, not taking his eyes off me. I was glad the frown was no longer on his face. But now he looked nervous.

"Oh! Uh, yeah. Let me get my keys. I guess I'm not as hungry as I thought, so I'll nibble on something later."

As soon as I drove out of our garage with Bo in the passenger seat, I turned my head just enough to look at the side of his face. "I don't think it's a good idea for me to rent that car now."

"How are we supposed to get to Curtis's place and back tonight? On the bus? Or should we take a cab and have some sharp-ass cabbie finger us?!"

"Calm down, cuz," I replied, my eyes back on the road in front of me. "I'll have Cash tell Collette he has to work late so she'll have to get one of her coworkers to give her a ride home. Drive his SUV and park it a few blocks away from Curtis's place or I'll think of something else. If I have to drive you guys over there, I will. I can't rent a car now. I don't trust Collette. She doesn't miss much. If she even thought we were involved, she'll remember a detail like me renting a car on the same day of the crime. And as dumb as Cash is, I don't think we should trust him too much either now."

"I agree with you on that." Bo slapped the dashboard with the palm of his hand. "I wish we hadn't even involved him in our plans!"

"I wish we hadn't either. But up until that stupid comment he made at the table, he was pretty cool. He knows too much now and if we change our plans, things could fall apart and we might have to postpone our project for a while!" I stopped for a red light and turned to Bo again, this time with a pleading look on my face. "We can't put it off any longer. We have to get this thing done *tonight.*"

"Yeah, I know. Sarah's already packed some of her stuff," Bo snarled.

"If we don't do what we need to do before she moves out, there's no telling what she'll do if she's already moved out after Curtis and her daddy are dead. As long as she's still in the house, we can maintain some level of control. And, her daddy is our ace in the hole. If he gets well—heaven forbid—we'll put more pressure on him to talk some sense into her head. If he succeeds in turning her around, she'll behave the way a good wife should, the way she did before she got involved with Curtis."

"I don't think Kenneth is coming home this time. The thing is, we *need* to move before Sarah bolts and before Big Daddy goes to meet his maker," Bo said. "That little stroke he had last night pushed him a little bit closer. I hope you're getting yourself ready for the lavish funeral you'll have to throw for a prominent big shot like him."

"I am." I still hated funerals and I wanted to get Kenneth's over with as soon as possible so I could go on with my life. And at least

I was sending him away in style. The Armani suit that I had purchased for him to be buried in was on a hanger in one of my walk-in closets, hidden behind my evening wear. I planned to pick out his casket in a day or so. I had also begun to plan a three-week cruise to the Caribbean for myself and Ricky as part of his "payment" for helping me out with the gun. And as a way for me to celebrate Curtis's departure—not to mention Kenneth's. But I couldn't finalize my travel arrangements until Kenneth had taken his last breath.

I was still looking at Bo. I didn't realize the light had turned green until the motorist behind me blew his horn. I stepped on the gas and resumed the conversation at the same time. "Uh, what I will do is drop you and Cash off a couple of blocks from Curtis's place. Then I'll go back home. Sarah will be my alibi. I'll make sure of that."

"Vera, believe me, nobody will suspect us, so we don't really need any alibis," Bo insisted. "Especially a woman like you."

"I know. But we can't take anything for granted and get sloppy. So just in case somebody does suspect a woman like me, I want to be accounted for during the time that this, uh, incident takes place. When the cops can't find out who killed Curtis, Sarah just might get a notion in her head that you had something to do with it. She'll recall how mad you got when she told you about him and her and how soon Curtis got killed after that confrontation."

"Well, the cops won't be able to prove a damn thing!" Bo yelled, slapping the dashboard again. "I'm just worried about Cash."

"You don't need to be. I'm going to sit his ass down and have a real long talk with him. I will tell him in no uncertain terms that if he ever mentions this situation again, in any way, he's going to be out of a job and a place to live. And he just might end up in jail holding the bag by himself. Nobody would believe him if he tried to bring us down with him!" I was so excited, I didn't notice the next red light in time and I shot straight through it, thankful that no other cars were close enough to crash into mine. Bo and I panicked at the same time. Once again he slapped the dashboard.

"I'm sorry!" I hollered. "I'll be glad when this is over. I'm going crazy!"

"Just keep your cool," Bo said in a gentle voice. "Vera, I just want to thank you for looking out for me. I wouldn't be able to take care of this Curtis problem without you coaching me all the way—and getting me that gun. I am even more grateful to you and I just wanted you to know that. Thank you."

"No problem at all, honey. I've had your back since we were kids. I wasn't going to let you get hurt by another woman again," I told him. "After this is over, and Curtis is six feet under, we won't ever mention it again. I think the sooner we put this mess behind us, the faster you and Sarah can work things out and start your family. I still think that a baby will keep us in the loop forever. Especially if something happens to Sarah, too, one of these days. . . ."

We remained silent until I drove into the parking lot at the store. "I'll find an excuse to come by the office this afternoon. I'll drop off the clothes you and Cash need to wear tonight. The gun too," I told Bo.

"Thanks again." Bo gave me a quick smile and then he squeezed my hand. "Tomorrow everything will all be over. And I'll have my wife back to myself."

I nodded. "You sure will," I agreed.

CHAPTER 64

SARAH

IT WAS TEN MINUTES TO TWO THAT FRIDAY AFTERNOON WHEN I ARrived at the hospital. Normally the cold antiseptic smell associated with a hospital, the sight of sick people wandering in and out of the rooms, and a grim-faced priest clutching a Bible bothered me. It all reminded me of death. But none of that bothered me this time. I guess it was because this was going to be my last day on Earth.

I felt numb and detached as I entered Daddy's room. I ignored Vera, hovering over the bed, looking down at Daddy with a blank expression on her face. As soon as she saw me, she suddenly got as animated as a cartoon character.

"Oh, Sarah! I'm so glad you're here!" she sniffed. I couldn't believe she could stand here and say such a thing to me with a straight face.

I continued to ignore Vera. When she attempted to hug me, I brushed past her and went over to the bed and grabbed my father's clammy hand. "I love you, Daddy and I'm sorry about everything that's happened," I said, tears flooding my eyes.

"Everything is going to be all right, Kenneth," Vera cooed. I hated when she used that fake-ass tone of voice! She had become so shallow I could see through her with my eyes closed. She touched Daddy's shoulder. "When you come home, we'll take a nice long vacation. All of us, Cash and Collette included."

"Uh-huh," I managed. "We haven't been to the Caribbean in a while. Maybe we should go there." I had heard the bitch on the telephone yesterday talking to her travel agent. She had already made plans for a cruise for herself and a person she had only identified as a friend. Who the hell was this mysterious friend? I wondered. She had no reason to refer to my daddy as a friend. Now that I knew she was planning a murder, I figured she was capable of doing just about anything. But since I was not going to be around to deal with her after today, I didn't care what she was up to. If she was going to have Curtis killed, what would she do to Daddy?

As much as I loved my daddy, there was only so much I could do to protect him. It was too late anyway. I was not going to let Curtis die alone. But Daddy was not stupid and I didn't think that Vera was stupid enough to do anything to him. I could see her getting away with Curtis's murder, but I honestly didn't think she'd get away with killing my daddy. He had too much money and too many friends in high places for that to happen.

The telephone rang and I answered it. It was Daddy's friend, the private investigator Tim Larkin. "Hi, Tim. I'll tell my daddy to call you back when my stepmother and I leave," I said.

"Hmmm. I hope he's doing better."

"He's about the same. I'm sure he'll be happy to talk to you."

"That's fine. Just let him know I'll call him later so we can discuss that . . . uh . . . issue. He'll know what it's about," Tim said.

"I will, Tim."

Vera wasted no time getting nosy. Her face looked like it was about to crack. Her lips started to move even before she got the first word out. As soon as I placed the telephone back into its cradle, she said, "I don't mean to be nosy, but was that Tim *Larkin*?"

"Uh-huh. Daddy's investigator friend," I replied. I noticed how Vera flinched.

"I guess he wants to keep up with what's going on with Kenneth's condition." She was trying to smile, but it didn't hide the frightened look on her face now. "Is that why he called?"

I hunched my shoulders and shook my head. "He said something about an issue they had already discussed. Why?"

"I'm just curious, that's all."

The longer I stayed in the room with Vera, the sicker I felt. It didn't look like she was leaving any time soon. Since this was the last time I'd see my daddy, I didn't care. I wasn't going to leave until I was good and ready.

Vera kept glancing at her watch. About twenty minutes later, she suddenly remembered she had a hair appointment.

"I'll probably grab a bite to eat after I leave the beauty shop and then I'll swing back by here before I go home," she said. "Sarah, I'll see you at the house around seven or so."

"I don't think so. I was planning to go to the movies tonight," I told her.

"Oh?" She flinched again. "Maybe I'll go with you."

"Uh, I'm going with a girl I went to school with."

"Oh," she said again. "Well, I'll see you when I see you, I guess."

"I guess you will," I sneered. She gave me a funny look before she left.

"What was that all about?" Daddy asked.

"Nothing." I sniffed and then rearranged Daddy's pillows. "Daddy . . . I'll always be with you. Even when I'm not."

"You sure are talking out the side of your mouth today. Is there something you want to talk to me about?"

I shook my head. "No, Daddy." We discussed a few mundane subjects and every time he steered the conversation back to me, I steered it to another mundane subject.

It was after 4:00 p.m. when I gave Daddy one last hug and told him I loved him. I kissed his cheek and told him good-bye; then I cried all the way to the hospital parking lot.

As I was leaving, Vera was returning. She didn't notice me and I did nothing to get her attention.

When I got home, I went to my room and looked at some pictures of me as a toddler clinging to my mother's legs, me as a teenager with my grandmother, and me with a bunch of various friends. Then I looked at the pictures I'd taken with Daddy and Bo. I had come such a long way and I didn't have one single picture of myself with Curtis. But it didn't matter now. We'd spend eternity together and that would be worth more than a few pictures.

I picked up the beer at the first liquor store I came to and the smothered chicken. I arrived at Curtis's place a few minutes before eight.

A few minutes after nine, we heard heavy footsteps approaching. I froze, but Curtis didn't even react. He was used to people running up and down the hallway outside. When somebody banged on his door, he set his beer down on the scarred coffee table and looked at me with an annoyed look on his face.

"Who the hell could that be?" he chuckled. "I hope it ain't that Donaldson woman begging for another beer." He attempted to rise and I grabbed his arm. "What's the matter, baby?"

"Curtis, I love you," I whispered. "I'll always love you."

"I know."

His door didn't have a peephole, so Curtis couldn't see who was outside. "Who is it?" he shouted. Before he could say anything else, somebody kicked the door and it flew open. The two men who stormed into the apartment had on ski masks and dark clothes, but I knew who they were. And as soon as they saw me, it was nothing but chaos.

"SARAH!" Bo yelled. A gun was in his hand and his hand was shaking like a leaf. "OH GOD NO!"

"What the fuck is this?" Curtis boomed, looking from me to Bo and back. "What's going on, Sarah?"

I couldn't say a word and I couldn't take my eyes off that gun in Bo's hand.

"Oh shit!" Cash hollered. He lifted his mask and stared at me with his mouth open. "Girl, you in the wrong place!" Then he turned to Bo, who was just standing there looking at me. Bo's ski mask was still covering his face, but it didn't hide the tears rolling out of his eyes.

He raised the gun and aimed it at my head. "Sarah . . . I'm sorry," he croaked.

Curtis lunged at Bo. There was a lot of cussing and yelling and all four of us were swinging our arms. The gun went off and Curtis hit the ground. Then it went off again.

I didn't feel a thing. When I hit the ground, everything went black.

CHAPTER 65

VERA

I HAD TRIED TO REACH BO AND CASH ALL EVENING, BUT NEITHER ONE answered his office telephone or cell phone. I wanted them to know that Sarah had plans to go out so she wouldn't be my alibi. Under the circumstances, all I could do now was sit back and wait.

I glanced at my watch every few minutes for the next hour. Finally, at exactly 10:45 p.m., Collette flew into my bedroom like a bat out of hell. "Vera, you will not believe what I just heard on the news!" She sprinted over to the bed where I lay with my head propped up on three pillows, waving her arms like she was going crazy. "Somebody shot that Curtis! Shot him in the head!"

It was hard for me to remain calm. But I wanted to leap up off the bed and dance a jig. I was so happy to hear that Bo had done exactly what I told him to do! "Do they know who did it?" I asked, forcing myself to look concerned.

"The news said it looked like a botched home invasion. But I have a feeling it was probably some of those dudes that's been threatening Curtis!" Collette yelled, still waving her arms. "And the worst thing—"

I interrupted Collette. "The worst thing is crimes like that happen over there all the time. I'm surprised they'd have a TV newsbreak about it, though. Curtis is not anybody important. He is just another lowlife with a lot of enemies." I shook my head and began to fan my face with my hand. I was so excited my face felt like it was on fire.

"Vera, let me finish!" Collette moved closer to the bed. "There was a woman with him and they shot her too!"

"They shot some woman too? He lives with his mama, so it must have been her!"

"Yeah, they shot a woman, too, but it wasn't his mama. The news said something about it being the daughter of a prominent businessman. They couldn't give her name out until her family's been notified. Lord, I hope it wasn't Sarah! That girl got on my last nerve, but I wouldn't want anything bad to happen to her. Kenneth will never get over it!"

"Sarah told me she was going to the movies with one of her friends," I whimpered. My head felt like somebody had stuffed it with rocks. I knew it had to be Sarah that Bo had shot!

"Well, I hope that's where she went. But I've got a bad feeling that . . . that it's her!"

"I better try to find Bo," I muttered. I got up and started pacing back and forth like a caged lion.

"Yeah, and I guess I need to locate Cash. I don't know about you, but I need a highball," Collette said. She was talking so fast she almost lost her breath. "We both need to calm our nerves until we find out what's going on. You want me to fix you a drink, too, Vera?"

"God yes! And make mine a very strong double."

Just as Collette and I made it downstairs to the living room, Bo and Cash entered. I was glad to see that they had changed from their thug outfits back into their regular clothes. I was also glad to see that they looked as normal and calm as usual. "Oh, I'm so glad you both are here!" I yelled, running up to Bo, throwing my arms around his waist. "Collette just heard on the news that Curtis got shot!"

Bo and Cash looked at each other, then back to me. "No shit?" Cash said in a hoarse voice. "I guess those dudes over there meant business. Being a snitch will surely get you killed. Poor Curtis . . ."

"Oh, he's not dead!" Collette hollered from behind the bar.

"What? Didn't you tell me the news report said he was shot in the head?" I asked Collette.

"Yeah, I did tell you that. But you didn't give me time to tell you everything they said on the news. Curtis and the woman with him were shot, but they are both still alive." Collette trotted from behind the bar without the drinks. "Bo, Sarah's not home. She is supposed to be at the movies. But the news said the woman who got shot is the daughter of a prominent businessman. Do you think it was her?"

Bo and Cash looked at each other and then at me again. I had never seen either one of them look so frightened before. Now they looked like they had just seen their own ghost. But I was even more frightened than they were. If Bo shot Sarah and she was still alive, she would be able to identify him and Cash!

"Let's not jump to conclusions! Sarah may have gone to the movies with her friend and then decided to stay out a little later," I said hopefully. But the look on Bo's face said it all. He had shot Sarah too. "Uh, Bo, don't you get too upset. There is no need for us to assume anything until we hear from Sarah!"

"Cash, where have you been all evening? I've been trying to get in touch with you for hours," Collette said.

"We had some real important work to finish up at the store that Kenneth had started," Cash rasped. "Then me and Bo went by that little Irish pub downtown on Front Street and had a few drinks. Didn't we, Bo?"

"Yeah," Bo mumbled. He looked like he wanted to sink into the floor.

"What pub? Harrington's is the only Irish pub I know of on Front Street," Collette said.

"Yeah, that's the one," Cash said quickly.

A puzzled look appeared on Collette's face. "Since when did you two start going to a place full of white folks?"

"They make some mean Irish coffee," Cash said quickly. "The best in town."

I couldn't believe Cash could come up with such a flimsy alibi. If they claimed they were in a lily-white bar like Harrington's, everybody would remember them if they had really been there. Lord, I hoped we wouldn't need an alibi!

"Bo, will you go into the kitchen and get us all something cold to drink?" I gave him the sternest look I could manage. "I put a few bottles of beer in the refrigerator a few hours ago and they should be nice and cold by now."

Bo gave me a strange look. Since Collette's eyes were on Cash, I was able to give Bo the conspiratorial look that told him I needed to talk to him in private. "Yeah, um, I'd love a cold beer," he stammered with that strange look still on his face. He left the room immediately, headed toward the kitchen.

"Baby, I just told Vera that I never wanted anything bad to happen to Curtis. If he had left Sarah alone, that would have been enough for me," Collette said, pulling Cash to the couch. He moved like a robot. If she hadn't grabbed his hand and steered him, I think he would have continued to stand in the same spot with a blank expression on his face the rest of the night.

While Collette was busy paying attention to Cash, I eased out of the room and headed toward the kitchen. Bo was standing in front of the refrigerator with his hand on the door handle, looking like he was about to faint. "You shot Kenneth's daughter?" I asked in a whisper.

"You told me not to leave any witnesses behind, goddammit!"

"You stupid fool you!" I hissed. "I didn't tell you to kill my husband's only child!" I was so distraught I wanted to kill Bo with my bare hands. "What the hell have you gotten yourself into?"

"Correction!" Bo shook a finger in my face. "What the hell have *we* gotten ourselves into? Your ass is as deep into this mess as mine! Maybe even deeper because this was your idea."

I wrung my hands and gritted my teeth. "It's a good thing you wore that mask." Bo gave me a bug-eyed look and shook his head. "You *didn't* wear the mask?" He shook his head again. "Do you mean to tell me they saw your face?"

"My mask got knocked off during the scuffle. Cash got so confused when he realized Sarah was there, he took off his mask before everything got crazy."

"The news reported that they're still alive! Why didn't you check to make sure they were dead?"

I was sick of Bo shaking his head, but he did it again. "I could hear folks outside in the hallway, so I panicked. We didn't have time to check their pulses or listen to their hearts. But I aimed for their heads like you told me to. If they didn't die on the spot, they will die soon if they haven't croaked already."

"Shit, shit, shit! Did you make it look like a robbery? Did you take anything?"

"We didn't have time to look for something to steal. But like we said, with all the enemies after Curtis, the cops will think it was a retaliation thing."

I held my hand up and snapped my fingers. "We just have to stay cool. And we need to find out if they both died—and if one of them talked before they did."

"What if one or both of them lives long enough to tell what happened?"

"Don't say that! Don't even think it! I . . . I don't know what we'd do if one of them talks!"

"I feel like horseshit! Damn, damn, damn!" Bo shouted. "I . . . I . . . when I realized Sarah was there and I had to shoot her, too, my mind snapped. I couldn't even think straight at the time. All I knew was we had to get the hell up out of that place!"

"Oh, this is the worst mess!" I folded my arms and glared at Bo. "If . . . if you shot them in the head in the right spot, they *have* to be dead and—" Before I could finish my sentence, Collette burst into the kitchen with a wild-eyed look on her face.

"The cops are here!" she announced.

CHAPTER 66

SARAH

WHEN I OPENED MY EYES, A HEAVY-SET ASIAN DOCTOR WITH THICK white hair was looking down at me. Most of my body felt fine, but the left side of my head felt like somebody had bashed it in with a brick.

"Good morning. You look a lot better than you did when they brought you two nights ago. And I am happy to say that you're going to be all right."

"My head hurts," I mumbled, sitting up. I was so tired and weak I could barely move. It took me a few seconds to realize I was in a hospital bed and there was an IV tube attached to my right arm. "I can't hear out of my left ear," I reported. I touched my ear, which had a bandage on it, and it tingled.

"You were shot. The thick, stone-filled earrings you had on saved your life. The bullet ricocheted off of it and only pierced your earlobe. You were very lucky."

"I don't know about that. I sure don't feel so lucky," I muttered.

The doctor, whose name tag identified him as Dr. Louie Choy, nodded. "You may have some minor problems with hearing for a few days. But other than that, you're going to be as good as new."

"Did Curtis Thompson get shot too, Dr. Choy?" I asked.

He responded with a weak nod.

I looked Dr. Choy in the eyes and said, "My husband did this to me. Bohannon Harper. His cousin Cash Booker was with him when he did it. I remember them kicking in my boyfriend's front door and coming into the apartment with a gun. And . . . my stepmother was in on the whole thing. She was the ringleader. They planned to commit murder days ago. I overheard them with my own ears. Call the police so I can tell them everything I know."

Dr. Choy gave me a sympathetic look. "Ma'am, all three of the perpetrators are in custody and they've all confessed."

"What? Oh my God," I moaned. I wanted to cry but couldn't. I didn't know what to do now. "My life will never be the same again."

Just knowing that three people I had lived with for years and had some feelings for were willing to kill a man—and me and anybody else who'd been with him—was almost more than I could stand. That was bad enough. But the fact that I had known about the crime before it happened and chose to let them do it said a lot about me. Bo, Cash, and Vera not having any regard for human life, except their own, was one thing. They were heartless monsters! But with me not warning Curtis and then choosing to sacrifice my own life, was the same true of me? Had I lost my way so severely that *I* no longer had any regard for human life either? Had I died, my poor daddy would have been devastated!

"You're a healthy and strong young woman. Take life one day at a time. I'll refer you to a good therapist and after a few sessions, you'll be just fine."

"Yeah. I'll get over this, but it's going to kill my daddy. Bad news like this is going to be real hard on him," I muttered. I didn't like the sad look on the doctor's face. "He's been so sick lately he's in the hospital too. Does he know about what happened to me?"

"Uh, Mrs. Harper, I am so sorry."

"What? Tell me!"

Dr. Choy moaned like a sick man himself. He removed his horn-rimmed glasses and massaged his forehead. When he looked at me again, he shook his head and took a deep breath. I knew that whatever he had to tell me was bad, so I braced myself. I took a deep breath too.

"Ma'am, I hate to tell you this, but the sooner you know the better. You are Kenneth Lomax's daughter. Unfortunately, you no longer have a close relative available to tell you this, but . . . your father didn't make it." Dr. Choy gently patted my arm. "When he got the news about what had happened to you . . ." The doctor paused. For a second I thought he was going to cry. That's how sad he looked. "The news was too much for him. He immediately suffered a massive heart attack. We did all we could."

"My daddy's dead," I mumbled. *"My daddy's dead!"* I couldn't hold back my tears any longer. Dr. Choy handed me a tissue. Before I knew it, I was crying and shaking so hard, I wanted to die more than ever now. I was glad that I had visited Daddy before I went to Curtis's place to meet my fate. At least I got to say goodbye to him. But I never thought that *he'd* be the one to die.

I stopped crying and blew into the tissue. After taking a few deep breaths, I was able to speak again. "I was supposed to die with Curtis. I overheard them talking about how they were going to kill him and leave no witnesses. I loved him and I was going to leave my husband to be with him. I went to Curtis's place because I wanted to die with him. That was the only way we were going to be able to be together," I said, staring at the wall.

"With all due respect, ma'am, that part of this tragedy is none of my business. But whatever you and Mr. Thompson decide to do now, I wish you all the best."

I turned sharply to look at Dr. Choy. "Is Curtis really going to make it? Can we be together after all?"

"Yes, he is going to make it, but he's in critical condition."

"Can I see him?"

"Only relatives are allowed to see him."

"How is he doing? Is he going to be all right?"

"Mr. Thompson will live, but I predict that he will have some problems in the future. I'd rather not say any more about his condition at this time. Now you get some rest."

How in the world could I rest knowing that Curtis was in the same hospital in critical condition and my daddy was dead?

I rested for about an hour. After a nurse with cold hands gave me a sponge bath, I called the hospital operator to get Curtis's room number. I was pleased to hear that he was on the same floor I was on, just four rooms down on the opposite side of the hall.

I sat up and carefully removed the IV cord from my arm. I didn't know if I was causing myself any physical harm or not. But under the circumstances, I didn't care if I lived or died. I scrambled out of the bed and didn't bother to try locating my street clothes. It dawned on me that they were probably covered in blood anyway, so even if I had them in the room, I couldn't wear them. I snatched a hospital robe off the hook behind the door and put it on. I was light-headed and my legs were kind of wobbly, but I managed to make it to Curtis's room in a couple of minutes. As soon as I got inside, I regretted what I had done. First of all, he looked worse than I expected. They had shaved off all the hair on one side of his head and a bandage covered his left eye. His other eye was closed so I assumed he was either in a coma or asleep.

A scowling, middle-aged black woman with a frizzy wig sitting sideways on her head occupied a chair by the side of the bed. I had never met Curtis's mother before, but I knew that was who she was.

"I'm . . . I'm Sarah Harper," I stammered.

"I know who you is. You Kenneth Lomax's daughter," Mrs. Thompson snarled, folding her arms. "You the reason my boy got shot up!"

I remained by the door, in case she got so hostile I had to bolt from the room. She looked like she wanted to wring my neck. "Ma'am, I'm so sorry about what happened. But I love your son and he loves me. I wanted to spend my last moments on earth with him. That's why I was there that night."

Mrs. Thompson's jaw dropped and she gave me an incredulous look. "So you *knew* what was going to go down, huh?"

"Something like that. I had heard my stepmother and my husband plotting to kill Curtis. But there was nothing I could do to stop them. And I figured that if I told Curtis, it would make the situation worse."

"So you *let* them niggers shoot my child? You must not have 'loved' him that much! As far as I'm concerned, you just as guilty as the rest of them devils and your black ass ought to be up in that jailhouse right with their asses! If the police don't arrest you for something, I'm going to hire me a smart-ass Jew lawyer and sue the shit out of your rich ass!"

"What's done is done and I can't change it!" I didn't care if this woman was Curtis's mama or not. I was not going to let her bully me. "You can stop talking that shit right now!"

Right after I stopped talking, Curtis opened his right eye. It was severely bloodshot. A black shadow had formed a ring around it that looked like a bull's-eye. He looked at his mother first, then at me. From the grimace on his face, I could tell he was still in pain. But he managed a smile anyway.

"Hello, baby," Mrs. Thompson said. She stood up and leaned over the bed. "You look way better today than you did the other night when they brought you in." Mrs. Thompson had attractive features and without that scowl on her face now, she was almost pretty. But as soon as I got closer to the bed, she got ugly again. Her evil-looking black eyes glared at me. Her thick lips quivered as she balled up her fists. For a moment, I was afraid that she was going to punch me in the nose. "You ain't supposed to be in this room no how, Miss Girl! You ain't even no relative!" she yelled.

"Mama, please," Curtis managed with a weak cough. He shook for a few seconds like he was having a spasm. Then he looked at me with his eye fluttering and pooled with tears. "Sarah, you can let your husband know that when I get up out of this hospital, his butt is mine," he told me with a tortured laugh and another cough.

"Son, you ain't got to worry about that motherfucker! He'll be doing some hard time," Mrs. Thompson shouted with glee, glaring at me some more. "And I hope you don't be fool enough to waste any more of your time with *this* woman!"

"Mama, this is the woman I love," Curtis declared. I was surprised that he was able to speak in a much stronger voice this time. "If she still wants me, I'm going to be with her." He turned to me with such an endearing look on his face it made me feel more loved than I'd ever felt before in my life.

"I love you, too, baby. And everything is going to be all right for us now," I assured him.

"I know it is," he agreed.

CHAPTER 67

VERA

THE MINUTE THEY LOCKED THAT CELL DOOR BEHIND ME, I REGRETted every wrong thing that I had ever done in my life. Even little things like cheating on a test in high school and sneaking into the movies through a side door so I wouldn't have to pay when I was a teenager. My mother had frequently told me that "God don't like ugly," and every time I'd heard those words I had laughed. I had laughed because I had convinced myself that I was too slick to get caught doing anything wrong. Nothing could have prepared me for the mess I'd gotten myself into now. And there was no way out of it.

Everything had happened so fast that night, but it was a poorly laid out plan from the beginning. Cash had driven his SUV and parked six blocks from Curtis's building. He and Bo had walked the rest of the way. Wearing the shabby clothes I had picked up for them, they probably looked just as much like a couple of middle-aged punks as the real ones. I had checked out Curtis's unit the same day that I'd visited his neighborhood to gather information about him from his neighbors. His place was exactly what I had expected—dreary and at the end of a long, dark, musty-smelling hallway on the fourth floor. The door to the stairwell was right across the hall from the door to his apartment. I had told Bo and Cash to get off on the floor below Curtis's and then take the stairs up to his floor. I had made it clear to them that they were not to put on their masks until just before they bolted out of the stairwell. After they had accomplished their mission, they were supposed to leave by the stairwell.

I had briefed them one last time that afternoon when I made a quick stop at the store and ushered them into one of the storerooms. "As soon as you duck back into the stairwell, put the masks and the gun in a plastic bag. Take the stairs all the way to the ground floor. When you exit the building, don't do anything to attract attention. If somebody says something to one of you, ignore them," I said, looking from Bo to Cash. They looked like a couple of scared rabbits and for a brief moment I had second thoughts about going through with this crime. But I ignored that thought. We had come too far to back out now. "Do not run—walk back to the car. Bring the plastic bags with the gun and masks to me and I will dispose of them."

"I just hope none of them punks over there jump us before we can even get up in that place," Cash said.

"Or after we get back out of the building," Bo added, nervously raking his fingers through his hair.

I rolled my eyes in exasperation and gave them an impatient, dismissive wave. "Well, if that happens, use the gun on them too. And then run like hell!" I snapped. "But I wouldn't worry about any of that happening. This job should be as easy as a walk in the park. Curtis won't know what hit him."

But Curtis had not been an easy target.

After Bo and Cash had arrived at his place and kicked in his door, there was a fierce struggle, and Bo dropped his wallet. During the struggle, somebody had inadvertently kicked the wallet under the couch. Bo didn't know he'd dropped it until it was too late. The cops found it and that was why they had shown up at the house shortly after Bo and Cash had made it back home.

From that point on, things fell apart like a straw house in a hurricane. Bo still had the gun in his pocket and my fingerprints were on it too. The plastic bag with the ski masks, with Curtis's blood on them, had been found on the floor of Cash's SUV. To this day, I ask myself how I could have been stupid enough to initiate such a serious crime with two stooges like Bo and Cash.

And those stooges had left no stone unturned when they made their confessions. They threw my ass under the bus with both hands. I had admitted to the cops that I had been foolish to orchestrate such a heinous crime. But I'd tried desperately to minimize my involvement by falling back on the "I've been having senior moments lately" defense. "Women my age do a lot of irrational things!" I pointed out, waving my hands and shaking like a lunatic in front of law enforcement officials who had already made up their minds about me. I had even tried to claim that a hormonal imbalance had affected my actions. Unfortunately, that had only made me look even more foolish. The bottom line was, I was going to be held accountable for my actions no matter what. Bo and Cash had been easy to manipulate and it had been their downfall. But for me, plain old greed had destroyed me.

My lawyer, Monty Klein, advised me to plead no contest to avoid a nasty trial and possibly get more time if a jury found me guilty. I eagerly took his advice.

I was facing some serious jail time and that was bad enough, but my standing in the community and my reputation were dead in the water too. For the first time in my life, I regretted not having a support system of my own. I had avoided people who had attempted to cultivate friendships with me. Kenneth's friends had become my friends by default, but under the circumstances, I didn't expect a single one of them to offer me their support. And none of them did. Not even the few women I'd associated with who had probably had way more sinister tendencies than I! However, two days after my arrest, I got a brief visit from Shirley Biddle, the woman I'd given one of my former lovers to as a Christmas gift a few years ago. She had worn dark glasses and a hat pulled down over her head when she came to see me. All she'd had to say was, "I'm sorry you're in the mess you're in—but please don't tell anybody anything about me and that boy you gave to me, or any of my other romantic activities! I don't want to end up losing everything I've worked so hard for." Shirley's desertion didn't even faze me. I was already depressed beyond belief.

Despite the hot water I was in, I had at least one cushion to fall back onto. I had a substantial amount of money in my bank account to use until I got whatever Kenneth had left for me in his will. I thought that would make my grim situation a little easier to deal with. My bail was high, but I had enough in my account to cover that and a place to stay when I bailed myself out. I knew I couldn't return to the mansion, so I needed a place to stay until they sentenced me.

I had been behind bars for twelve days and that was twelve days too many. Just being let out of that dank cell to meet with my attorney in the visiting area was like a breath of fresh air. I was going to get myself out of this mess no matter what. If things looked too bad for me, after I'd bailed myself out, I'd bolt. I'd use the rest of my money to relocate to a country that didn't have an extradition treaty with the United States.

I was wrong. That plan wasn't even going to get off the ground.

Despite the fact that this was the most serious situation I had ever had to face, I was able to smile at Monty. He didn't smile back. Instead, he gave me a profound look of pity and didn't hesitate to tell me why. What he told me next made my head spin like a top. "I hate to tell you this, Vera, but Curtis Thompson has retained an attorney. He'll be filing a massive civil lawsuit against you. And you need to know now that his attorney is a very aggressive one who has never lost a case." Monty could barely look me in the eye as he spoke. "Your stepdaughter has canceled all of the credit cards and frozen all of her father's bank accounts. She's the only one who can access them. And I really hate to tell you this, but the personal bank account you opened in your name a few years ago, the court has frozen it pending the lawsuit."

"What do you mean 'frozen'? That's *my* money!" I yelled. "It's not in a joint account with Kenneth or connected to his business! How can the court do that?"

"For the record, it's not just the court. You never filed taxes to report the interest on this account. That interest is considered income. One thing I've learned is that you don't want your name to be added to Uncle Sam's shit list when it comes to money. Some folks get away with it, some don't. But your name is all over the news these days, and Uncle Sam has eyes and ears everywhere, especially in the banks. I have a client sitting in federal prison right now because he went for years without filing . . . just like you. Even if the court releases the freeze, which will only happen if Mr. Thompson stops the lawsuit, Uncle Sam will refreeze it until he gets his piece of the pie. And I'm sure you know how slowly their wheels turn. With penalties, fees for late payment, and possibly a charge against you for income tax evasion, it could take *years* before this issue is resolved. And let's pray that the state doesn't jump on the bandwagon too."

"The state?"

"You didn't report your interest income to the state either."

"So I'm getting fucked in the ass, huh?"

"Oh, I wouldn't use wording like that. However, you might—"

I didn't even let Monty finish his sentence. "SHIT!" After all the plotting and planning and scheming I had done to stash away a small fortune of Kenneth's money, it had backfired. "What about Kenneth's will? I *know* he left me something!"

Monty gave me a pitiful look. I knew what was coming next was bad by the way he shook his head and sighed. "Yes, he did. I'll get to the will momentarily. But, uh, I'm afraid you're not going to benefit much."

"Why the hell not? Kenneth was not the one that got shot! He died of natural causes and I'm still his wife and in this state what's his is half mine. I don't expect to get any of the money he had before he met me, but he made millions more after we got married and I want my share!" I was groping for words and trying not to scream my head off. I was too afraid to ask the one question that had almost burned a hole in my brain: Had Kenneth modified his will so that I would get less than I deserved? Well, as long as I got a comfortable amount of money, I'd be somewhat satisfied. "The prenup I signed states that I will receive limited funds IF Kenneth and I get divorced! And what about his life insurance policy?"

"Yes, Mr. Lomax had a sizeable insurance policy as well," Monty said with a gentle sigh. "Another three million dollars to go to his beneficiary."

"And I'm the beneficiary! That and the money he left me in his will—I want it! I need it!"

Monty shook his head again. "I'll get to the insurance in a minute. But let's discuss another item first." He paused and pulled a three-page document out of his briefcase. He gave me a sad look as he cleared his throat and looked at the document. "This is a copy of your prenuptial agreement with your signature. Did you read it before you signed?" he asked, waving it in my face.

"Well, most of it. After I read the part about me getting some money, I just skimmed the rest."

"But you signed it?"

"Yes, I signed it! Dammit! You have the damn thing in your hand and you can see that I signed it."

"You should have read the whole thing. Your signature confirms that you accepted the terms of this agreement as stated. Such as, despite this being a community property state, you gave up your rights to half of Kenneth's earnings by signing."

"Do you mean to tell me I'm getting screwed because I didn't read some damn fine print?"

"There was no fine print, Mrs. Lomax. Would you like to go over the prenup you signed?" Monty waved that damn prenup in my face again. By now it was as disgusting as used toilet paper.

I shook my head. "No," I replied in a very small voice. My heart was beating so hard, I was surprised I was still conscious. The only thing that kept me breathing was the fact that Monty had told me I would still get *some* money. I was going to need it whenever I got out of jail. If they sentenced me to only seven or eight years, I'd be in my seventies by then. And even if I still looked good, even I didn't think I'd be able to snag another rich husband.

"Now about the insurance . . ."

My heart was beating so hard I could hear it. I was on the edge of my seat, holding my breath waiting for Monty to continue.

"Vera, I hate to tell you this, but your husband had recently modified his insurance policy," Monty said. The look on his face told me he had something else to say that I wasn't going to like.

Maybe I was going to have to split the three million with that bitch-ass Sarah! All I wanted to know was how much I'd get. I didn't even have to ask him my next question. Monty answered it right away.

"Kenneth's daughter is the sole beneficiary."

"I won't get any of it?"

Monty shook his head.

"Shit!" I covered my face with my hands and sobbed for about a minute. Then I blinked back my tears, wiped my eyes with the back of my hand, and continued. "Okay," I said with a sigh of defeat. "I guess I'll have to be happy with just whatever he left me in his will. I put up with him for a lot of years, so I hope he took that under consideration. You said he left me something but that I won't benefit much? What did he leave me? Was it the mansion, the cabin, or the Davis Street condo . . . or just a couple million bucks?" I was frantic. I had never felt so alone and helpless in my life. "And please don't tell me the court is going to freeze that too!"

"Not . . . exactly." Monty paused. For an excruciatingly long moment I thought he was going to laugh because of the way his lips were quivering. He cleared his throat and scratched his neck. I couldn't imagine why he was squirming in his seat when I was the one getting screwed. "Your late husband left you *two* dollars. He clearly indicated, only enough to cover the bus fare for you to visit Ricky Tate, your current lover. It would have been more if there had been a fare increase at the time of Mr. Lomax's passing. But as of today, the bus fare on the local city bus is two dollars."

If somebody had cracked open my head with a sledgehammer, I wouldn't have felt more pain. My brain felt like it was trying to bust out of my skull. "What? He knew about my affair with Ricky. . . ."

"The investigator he had hired was very thorough. I'm so sorry."

"He had me followed. That son of a bitch!" I hissed. I let out a loud breath and looked at Monty.

"You orchestrated a very serious crime in which your late husband's only child was almost murdered. And you've admitted your guilt. Even if your husband had left you more than, uh, the two dollars, his daughter and his attorneys, and the court probably would have prevented you from profiting from that too."

"I can't believe what's happening to me. I . . . I feel so *alone.*" My own sisters had not even come to see me yet. Nor had any of my lovers. And I had a feeling none of them would. My head wasn't the only thing spinning now. It seemed like the whole room was. I was so dizzy I was seeing double. "Thank you for all your help, Monty," I mumbled, blinking hard at the two images of my lawyer sitting across from me.

"If it's any consolation, I won't be charging you for my services. Kenneth was a dear friend of mine, and it's the least I can do in his memory. Now, is there anything else you'd like to discuss today?" Monty asked. He slid the prenuptial agreement back into his briefcase and snapped it shut before I could even respond.

I shook my head.

"I'll be in touch," he said quickly, glancing at his watch. Then he waved to the husky female guard to escort me back to my cell.

I didn't even realize I was crying until I felt the salty tears sliding down the sides of my face and onto my lips.

EPILOGUE

SARAH

Six weeks later

CURTIS WAS RELEASED FROM THE HOSPITAL YESTERDAY, THE SAME DAY that Obama won the election for the second time. I was ecstatic about both.

My man was going to live as normal a life as possible for a person with one eye. His mother made a big fuss when he moved into the Davis Street condo I'd inherited, the same one that my daddy had moved me and my grandmother into when he started taking care of us. But after a few weeks when Mrs. Thompson realized that her ranting and raving was only causing more tension between her and Curtis, she gradually accepted me.

"I just hope you make my boy happy," she told me, eagerly lapping up the wine I had just handed her. "You being rich and all, you'll be able to help me out a little, too, I hope."

"Mrs. Thompson, you won't ever have to worry about money again," I assured her. "And neither will Curtis."

My daddy had left me everything, all of his millions, his business, and every piece of property he owned. I sold the mansion right away. It held too many bad memories for me and I knew that Curtis would not have been willing to live in it.

I didn't know the first thing about running a business, but Daddy had a lot of competent, trustworthy advisors on his payroll.

They had all assured me that they would keep things afloat. So with their help and Curtis doing the same job that Bo had done, I knew everything was going to be just fine.

Vera, the mastermind of this stupid crime that had affected so many people, had been sent to a women's facility near Vacaville. The press described it as a glorified dollhouse. A retired model who had fed her husband a fatal dose of Jell-O laced with antifreeze resided in the same prison. And from what I had seen on a TV report about that place, the inmates walked around smiling and all made up like they had just come from a beauty parlor. Vera would be right at home. And it was going to be "home" to her for a minimum of twelve years.

Daddy's faithful servants, Delia and her meek husband, Costa, worked for me now. Delia did the cooking and cleaning and Costa drove us around when we didn't feel like driving. Curtis's mother loved being chauffeured to her bingo games and her favorite thrift shops two or three times a week. She lived with her new boyfriend now, but she visited us several times a week. Once I got to know her, she didn't seem so mean.

I had purchased a two-bedroom unit for my servants in the same building, directly below the one Curtis and I occupied. Delia went to visit Vera yesterday and I didn't have a problem with that. She was the kind of person who would never turn her back on someone who had been as nice to her as Vera. The report Delia gave to me when she got back to the condo was very bleak.

"Senora Lomax, she is so very sad. Jesus must be weeping," Delia told me, wiping her tears with the tail of her apron. I had just joined her in the kitchen where she was preparing dinner—barbecued ribs and baked beans. "I must pray for her. She looks like strange woman, hair no longer pretty blond but with gray roots now and stringy like one of my mops. She don't do nothing to make herself look good no more. And other than me and Costa, nobody else visits her so far. Not the young boyfriend who tell police she make him get her the gun or even her family. She in a very deep hole now. *Ay caramba*!"

Yes, Vera was in a very deep hole now—one she'd dug herself. I was sorry that I couldn't cover her up in that hole with horse manure! And except for the two dollars my daddy left her in his will, she was broke too. Everything she owned of value, including her jewelry and wardrobe and the new Mercedes she'd purchased a week before the shooting, would be sold. The proceeds would be held in a special account until Curtis settled his lawsuit against her. There was no need for me to sue her, too, since Curtis's lawyer was going to pick her clean enough for me. All Bo and Cash had were a few thousand dollars in the bank, but Curtis decided to be a nice guy and not go after them too. But since Bo's SUV was in my daddy's name, I sold it and all of Bo's possessions and donated the money to the church I used to go to. Vera's possessions are in storage, pending the outcome of the civil lawsuit.

A lot of people said that Cash was the lucky one because he had received the lightest sentence. Because Bo had been the aggressor in the attack, the district attorney had only charged Cash with being an accessory and criminal conspiracy, one of the same charges Bo and Vera got hit with. He had a huge fine to pay, some community service to perform, and an eight-year sentence in a maximum-security facility a few miles west of Sacramento. I was sure that Cash didn't feel like "the lucky one."

In addition to the conspiracy charge, they charged Bo with attempted murder, aggravated assault, and home invasion. He received a sentence of twelve to sixteen years in Corcoran, the same prison that housed the mass murderer Charles Manson.

As far as I was able to determine, Collette had nothing to do with the conspiracy. And I was surprised that she didn't even call to check on me or visit me in the hospital. When I returned to the house after the hospital released me, she had packed up everything she owned and fled. I heard from the girl who used to braid her hair that she was somewhere in Mexico using an alias.

I will be using a different name myself in a few months. As soon as my divorce from Bo is finalized, I will become Mrs. Sarah Thompson. I hope to be Curtis's wife until the day I die—by natural causes, I hope.

Our first child will be born next year in August. If it's a boy, I'm going to name him after my daddy.

READING GROUP GUIDE

FAMILY OF LIES

Mary Monroe

ABOUT THIS GUIDE

The suggested questions that follow are included to enhance your group's reading of this book.

DISCUSSION QUESTIONS

1. Vera was a gold digger to the bone. Do you think women who set out to marry men for their money even know what true love is?
2. Kenneth was a wealthy man who used his money to buy his women's affections. Do you think he got what he deserved by marrying a woman like Vera?
3. A lot of older women get involved in relationships with much younger men. Is this something you would consider doing? Would you do it out in the open or only behind closed doors?
4. If you were wealthy, would you spend money on a young lover as freely as Vera did? If so, why?
5. Do you think that if Bo had spent more time with Sarah, she would not have fallen in love with Curtis?
6. Sarah's friends in the hood expected her to share her newfound wealth with them. She did just that for years until she realized they were using her. If you suddenly came into a lot of money, would you keep the same friends? If so, would you give them money every time they asked?
7. Vera spent Kenneth's money like it was going out of style. If you had a chance to marry a very wealthy man, would you be as extravagant?
8. Kenneth was a smart man, but he was rather naïve when it came to Vera. When he found out she was having an affair with a man young enough to be her grandson, he was devastated. But since he'd had numerous affairs, did you feel sorry for him?
9. Tony, Andre, Ricky, and all the rest of the young men Vera had affairs with used her for her money. But Vera didn't seem to mind. Would you get involved with a younger man knowing up front that he expected you to be his sugar mama?

10. Vera often warned Sarah that one of her "hood rat" friends might set her up to be kidnapped and held for ransom. Vera's young lovers were somewhat thuggish. Do you think she should have been concerned about one of them setting her up too?
11. Sarah was willing to die to be with Curtis. Have you ever loved a man so much that you'd consider making such an extreme sacrifice?
12. Vera goaded Bo and Cash to kill Curtis. Did you think that they were going to get away with murder?
13. After all the plotting and planning to get the bulk of Kenneth's money, Vera ended up with two dollars to her name and a twelve-year prison sentence. Do you think she got what she had coming or was her punishment too severe?